PRIAM'S DAUGHTER

PRIAM'S DAUGHTER

GEORGIA SALLASKA

NEW ENGLISH LIBRARY
TIMES MIRROR

For S.C.S., my aging friend,
who provided an excellent, if unwitting, model.

First published in the USA by Doubleday & Co, Inc in 1970
First published in Great Britain by New English Library in 1974

*

FIRST NEL PAPERBACK EDITION FEBRUARY 1978

*

NEL Books are published by
New English Library Limited from Barnard's Inn, Holborn, London EC1N 2JR.
Made and printed in Great Britain by Hunt Barnard Printing Ltd., Aylesbury, Bucks.

45003649 9

CONTENTS

Book One: TROY

Book Two: THE WAR

Book Three: MYCENÆ

CAST OF CHARACTERS

For the Trojans:

ÆNEAS – only Trojan champion to survive the war
ADRASTOS – Trojan ally from the Sea of Marmora
ALEXANDROS – nicknamed Paris, son of Hecabe and Priam
AMPHIOS – Trojan ally from the Sea of Marmora
ANCHISES – cousin of Priam, father of Æneas
ANDROMACHE – wife of Hector
ANTENOR – brother-in-law of Priam
ANTIPHUS – son of Hecabe and Priam
BASTOS – small servant of Artemis
CASSANDRA – daughter of Hecabe and Priam
CEBRIONES – son of Priam
CORONUS – physician of the Trojans
CREUSA – daughter of Hecabe and Priam
DEIPHOBUS – son of Hecabe and Priam, later Guardian of Troy
GLAUCUS – Trojan ally, Prince of Lycia
GORGYTHION – son of Priam
HECABE – Queen of Troy
HECTOR – son of Hecabe and Priam, Guardian of Troy, foremost Trojan champion
HELENUS – son of Hecabe and Priam
HESIONE – sister of Priam
IDAIOS – herald of Troy
ISOS – son of Priam
LAODICE – daughter of Hecabe and Priam
LAOCOÖN – priest of Apollo
LAOMEDON – father of Priam
MEMNON – Trojan ally, Prince of Æthiopia
ORTHIA – nurse of Cassandra

PAMMON – son of Hecabe and Priam
PANDAROS – Trojan ally from Æsepus Valley
PENTHESILEA – Trojan ally, Spearmaiden King
POLITES – son of Hecabe and Priam
POLYXENA – daughter of Hecabe and Priam
PRIAM – King of Troy
SARPEDON – Trojan ally, King of Lycia
SCAMANDER THE FIRST – ancestor of all the Trojans
SCAMANDER THE YOUNGER – nicknamed ASTYANAX, son of Hector

For the Achæans:

ACHILLES – greatest Achæan champion before Troy
AGAMEMNON – King of Mycenæ,' leader of the Achæan host
AJAX – called 'Great' or 'Big', Achæan champion
AJAX – called 'the Runner', 'Lesser', or 'Little', Achæan champion
ANTIPHOS – Achæan champion
CALCHAS – renegade Trojan priest of Apollo
DIOMEDES – Achæan champion, War Leader of Argos
HELEN – Queen of Sparta, self-styled cause of the war
MACHAON – physician of the Achæans
MENELAUS – Achæan champion, King of Sparta
NEOPTOLEMUS – formerly PYRRHUS, Achæan champion, son of Achilles
NESTOR – Achæan advisor, King of Pylos
ODYSSEUS – Achæan champion, King of Ithaca
PALAMEDES – Achæan champion
PATROCLUS – Achæn champion, loved by Achilles
PHILOCTETES – Achæan champion
TALTHYBIOS – herald of the Achæans
TEUCROS – Achæan champion, cousin of Big Ajax
TLEPOLEMUS – Achæan champion

Noncombatants:

ÆACUS – the Lelegian, architect of Troy

ÆGISTHUS – lover of Clytemnestra
ÆTHRA – servant of Helen, formerly Queen of Troezen
BRISEIS – captive of the Achæans, quarreled over by Agamemnon and Achilles
CHRYSEIS – captive of the Achæans, daughter of Chryses
CHRYSES – priest of Apollo
CHRYSOTHEMIS – daughter of Clytemnestra and Agamemnon
CLYTEMNESTRA – Queen of Mycenæ
ELECTRA – also named LAODICE, daughter of Clytemnestra and Agamemnon
HERMIONE – daughter of Helen and Menelaus
IPHIGENEIA – daughter of Clytemnestra and Agamemnon
NYSA – servant of Cassandra, nursemaid to her children
OENONE – tribal nymph
ORESTES – son of Clytemnestra and Agamemnon
ORPHEUS – bard, King of Thrace, Apollo's spokesman
PELOPS THE YOUNGER – son of Cassandra and Agamemnon
PLEISTHENES – son of Helen and Menelaus
PYLADES – friend of Orestes
PYTHIA – chief priestess of Apollo at Delphi
SHAHBA – Memniode, servant of Cassandra
TELEDAMUS – son of Cassandra and Agamemnon
THESADIË – servant of Helen

AUTHOR'S NOTE

The *Iliad*, always. Belonging as it does to the world, it is everyone's story, and it is the heart of mine. It has seemed to me that the tendency of scholarly thought over the years has been to put Homer's great war novel on the dissecting table, picking out this or that reference to customs, geography, dress, armor, and other such details. In the doing, and in such controversies as to whether one man or several wrote it, or whether the author of the *Iliad* could also have composed the *Odyssey*, we nearly lose sight of the fact that these were supposed to be flesh and blood people engaging in a very real conflict. By telling it again from the point of view of the other side, it has come alive for me in an entirely new and fresh way.

Some scholars have discredited Walter Leaf's theories concerning the Trojan War. He maintained that there were nine years or so of guerrilla raids along the coast of modern-day Turkey, culminating in one fighting-season of actual combat, and that the whole dispute was based upon a struggle for trade. Others maintain with equal zeal that it was Helen and Helen alone. Others, that it was the irksome power of a Trojan navy and its blockade of the Dardanelles. Whatever the real reason, and whoever was correct – something we probably will never know – Leaf's concept of the annual trading Fair made a sensible and very workable framework in which to set heroes and ladies who have lived far beyond their own lifetimes. If one test of a theory is how well it actually works, then Leaf's ideas are as sound as Trojan gold.

My thanks and gratitude go to the library of the University of Oklahoma and its staff. They graciously allowed me the run of the stacks and made no complaint at the mountain of books they had to sort out at the end of the day. It is staggering how many books, papers, and dissertations have been written about the finest details of the *Iliad*, or about Troy; and if the University of Oklahoma library doesn't have them all, there can't have been very many overlooked.

The excellent publications of the University of Cincinnati Expedition to Troy laid the groundwork for any feeling of authenticity I may have achieved in my descriptions of the city. These painstakingly illustrated and carefully detailed findings are in many ways more valuable than a visit to the site itself, with its many subtle layers and tangle of ruins.

To write about the Heroic Age, it is almost enough to simply open Robert Graves's *The Greek Myths* at random and begin. Between his comments on various theories proposed through the years as to the basis in fact for the fanciful story of the Trojan Horse and the Cincinnati Expedition's proof that the city fell to an earthquake, I drew a conclusion which at least has the virtues of simplicity and workability. I will not claim originality; others may have been there long before me. But if they have, I haven't discovered it.

From the opening paragraph – even the title – it will be crystal-clear that I am actually an expatriated Trojan at heart. It's an old axiom teetering on the verge of a cliché that in a war there are no victors, only survivors. Like most well-worn phrases, it carries truth; and I feel that in this terrible beginning to the miserable legacy to which we find ourselves heir today, the Trojans may have lost their battle but triumphed in the end by bringing their enemies down with them. The Dark Ages preceding the Classical Age trod upon the heels of the Trojan War; and the lesson of the too-costly victory is one that today's warriors are still learning.

In a Trojan's eyes, the only good Achaean was a dead one. Agamemnon was malevolence incarnate; Menelaus a Goering- or Khrushchev-like figure, a clumsy target of jeering laughter; Odysseus's prudent planning became snakelike cunning; and Achilles could only be regarded as a monster summoned up from the lowest depths of Hell. If even Grecophiles have a hard time explaining many of Achilles's actions, what sort of effect must they have had on his enemies?

As for departures from tradition and outright manufacture of romantic details, I have only exercised the right of the storyteller from time out of mind to put his own small mark upon the tale. The basic fabric of the stories remains unchanged – the quarrel between Achilles and Agamemnon, the funeral of Hector, the betrayal at Mycenae.

And always, the *Iliad*.

BOOK ONE

TROY

I

THE DREAM

The stillborn scream shatters my throat and my mouth fills with blood. I taste it, red, warm, and salty. Before me stands the Murderer, and his image splits and refracts, dividing itself until there are hundreds, thousands of Murderers. The sight strikes my eyes like a splintered rainbow.

'Why do you do this thing?' I wail, and my heaving chest finds no air to breathe. 'I cannot see and my father is old.'

A laughter comes booming around me but I do not hear. Under my fingers there is dust. I look; I have brushed against a tiny shrine, filled with minute, impotent gods. And even as I look it vanishes under the weight of my gaze, leaving an empty place where my heart used to be.

'This is not as man has ever been,' I plead past the blood that fills my mouth.

Now the Murderer answers with a thousand mouths in a thousand faces and a thousand voices surround me until I cover my ears. 'Nothing must remain, not a single seed from which a plant can once again flourish.'

I can see a little now, and I know that I am in my city and it is whole and beautiful beneath the flames. I put my arm into the fire and watch as it shrivels and burns and the flesh falls away from the bone without pain, without pain, and when I withdraw it I am sound and entire again except that my mouth is full of blood.

Now with my two arms I go to embrace the knees of the Murderer. 'Do not kill the City,' I beg. 'Kill the men and the women and even the children, for this is a conqueror's due, but leave the City.'

'It has been a reproach to me and I will not rest while it still stands,' replies the Murderer with his thousand voices. Now he grows away from me, shooting upwards taller than Giants, and I am less than child-size beside him. His head knocks a hole in the blue vault of the heavens and the darkness comes pouring down.

Now he lifts his Murderer's foot to bring it down upon me and upon the City as one would grind a worm underfoot. My nostrils are stopped with dust and the silver kernel that holds my soul explodes softly in my breast.

The heaviness of the black horror above me presses me down, down unbearably and I open my eyes to find my own shriek echoing in my ears and my blood pounding dizzily in my head so that my couch shakes with my own heartbeats. Cold and shivering, I grope my way back to wakefulness.

Orthia is at my side, and already her hands are mixing the infusion of mint which the Ægyptian physician prescribed for such times, as being very soothing and beneficial to the nerves.

'Oh, Orthia,' I say, leaning my head against her with a shuddering sigh. Her nearness, the familiar, welcome smell of the brewing mint all help to bring me from the shadows of the terrible nightmare that lies waiting beneath my trembling eyelids on nights such as this.

'Was it the same, little one?' asks Orthia gently. Her strong, straight figure and kindly face that is comforting rather than beautiful are outlined to me in the brazier's light, kept low so that we do not disturb the rest of the household. My nightmares are a secret between us, though she often pleads that I allow her to tell my mother, when they are coming thick and fast on me. But something within me says 'No' and 'Not yet.'

'Yes, Orthia,' I answer. And then, with the rim of the cup against my lips so that I can taste the scalding mint mixture and inhale the clean fragrance, 'Orthia, how is it that when I dream this one dream I am all grown up? There are only nine notches cut into my doorpost.'

Each summer a new notch was added, at the beginning of that year's Fair. It was an event almost as impatiently awaited as the Fair itself.

'I do not know, Cassandra,' Orthia answers. 'It is a sign of the gods favor, I think, although we do not know yet what it means.'

'Favor!' I scoff. 'You tell me my name means "entangler of men". It is a cruel joke. If Apollo really wanted to make me his favorite, he would give me a prettier face and would make all the other children like me, and not send a nightmare to torment me.'

'It is not for us to question what the god gives us,' Orthia replies firmly. 'We must accept, and await understanding.'

And then I am quiet, and attend to my cup of mint, for I do

not wish to discuss religious matters with my nurse. Though she is counted wise and knows almost as much about women's matters as any midwife or healing-woman and has taught me much, I am still not certain that she is qualified to speak on matters this weighty. Silently we sit on the rumpled couch, for we both know that there will be no more sleep for me this night, and she will not let me sit up alone. Outside, there is a lightening in the sky past the battlements of the walls. There is a stirring from somewhere, and here and there a palace servant has begun to go about his morning chores. Now we hear a bird's song begin in the cool darkness that still lingers in the trees and know that this once I have been lucky. Most of the night has already gone by before I found the nightmare upon me. Many times I have not been so fortunate, and have found it waiting for me as soon as I closed my eyes.

I lean against Orthia in the cool dawn, and to my surprise find that I have dozed a little after all in this security, when she gently shakes me awake to find a bowl of warm oat porridge waiting for me in the bright new morning.

In those days, I thought that Troy must surely be the most perfect city that had ever been made. I had heard tales of Colchis, of course; who had not? Others spoke highly of Knossos of Crete, and of Athens and Mycenae far away on the Western mainland, but nothing I heard could sway me from my conviction that Troy surpassed them all. If there were such a thing as perfection on this earth, then Troy with its jewellike excellence must be it.

Three great terraces it had, spacious and well-ordered, ringed round with sturdy walls that seemed to grow from roots in the stony ridge upon which it sat overlooking the Trojan Plain. At the summit, on the First Terrace, was Priam's palace, far above the rest of the City. When the sunlight hit it in a certain way, at dawn and then again just as the sun set over Lemnos, it seemed to shine with an unearthly light that overshadowed the shrines and sanctuaries that crowded its walls. Here was the abode of the Lady of the Waves, and of Apollo, and of Pallas Artemis, the Maiden whom we regard as his sister. There was no longer a shrine to Poseidon because of an old quarrel that dated clear back to the ancestor of all Trojans, Scamander the Brave; but nearby stood the altar of Zeus Rainbringer, who walks often on the topmost peak of Ida, that one which we call Gargarus. We could often see his lightning flashing on this slope, and hear the rumble of his life-giving thunder down on the Plain. In some far distant time, the First Folk had erected for him a mighty Seat, from which he could peer directly into the City if he wished; I know, for I once sat in it briefly when the god was absent, on a dare. It was far too big for me, of course, for it was made for a god and I was only a girl; however, I felt the shiver of power along my spine and knew with awe that the might of Zeus lingered even in these stones that now and again cradled his gigantic body.

The Second Terrace held the women's quarters. Wives and concubines unnumbered dwelt here in the crowded cluster of houses built so closely to each other that there was scarcely room for a narrow alley between one and another. My father ruled in the Eastern style of kingship, and his many wives came from every quarter of the lands that depended upon the outlet of the Troad for their market place. No one had ever counted the children of Priam, for only a scribe had such skill with numbers. It was said that his sons alone numbered fifty or more, and his daughters were more numerous still; but no one knew how many there actually were because daughters were constantly going from Troy to other Houses in marriage to further strengthen our ties with our allies.

On the third and largest terrace, the warriors and tradesmen dwelt. If the First Terrace with its palace and its shrines could be said to be the head of the City, and the Second Terrace might enclose its beating heart, then surely the Third Terrace would be the body and thighs, and the strong manly arms of Troy. Here, only a little less closely packed than the Second Terrace, were the nobles, the scribes, the granaries and oil-storage houses, the vast treasure house, with the barracks for the soldiers nearby, the King's stable where his chariot was kept on its stand, and his horses and the onagers from Mysia waited to pull chariot or cart, as the King desired. Here was where Priam's sons lived with their wives, if they were old enough to have them, for otherwise they stayed with their mothers on the Second Terrace unless they happened to be Hecabe's sons also.

Here also was the purple-factory which plied its mysterious trade behind closed doors, while nearby was housed the local guild of carders and weavers. Though every Trojan woman spun not only her own household goods but cloth for the Fair as well, there was no competition; for the guild made its living in fancy-work which few of the women had the time or talent to undertake. The wealth of Troy rested on two great pillars: woven goods, and horses. All over the world, Trojan horses, those of the breed called Tros, fetched the highest price.

In another quarter was the pleasure house for the travelers wherein priestesses of Aphrodite waited in perfumed and scented alcoves. Besides the House of Aphrodite, there were also other provisions for the comfort of travelers whose rank would entitle them to stay within the walls and not in the low Troy-town that nestled into the hillside behind the City. Close by the south gate, called the Dardanian, where one began to climb up the broad ramp that led to the Palace, was a house wherein food, drink, and water for washing might be had for a price, so that the visitor could approach the King refreshed and not come upon him dusty and ravenous as is the barbaric custom of the Western mainlanders. Nearby stood the house of my brother Hector, with its beautiful portico of pillars in the Lycian style, close by the main gate as befitted the Guardian of the City.

Enviously, I would watch as the evening crowds strolled along the avenues of the terraces, wishing for the day when I would be old enough to join them. Though, I felt, I would be poor competition for them. I was thin and shapeless, as plain as a turnip but with a disposition more resembling the tart radish. My eyes were too far apart, and had a foxy look from the pale brows and lashes. Not until I would be allowed to wear kohl would my eyes come to any real beauty, and now I was far too young for sophisticated cosmetics. My skin was the bane of all redheads, prone to freckles and chafing at wool. If only my freckles could have run together, I would have been a delicious, even color like Polyxena or Laodice who turned a quick, glowing brown in the summer. My mouth was that of an unformed child, and my nose fit only for breathing. But still I wished myself grown, even unbeautiful in the company of the gorgeous ladies of Troy.

How I longed to be one of them, freshly bathed and combed and perfumed, holding the hem of her skirt so that it did not become soiled by the feet of the slave close behind. Every lady was so accompanied, and her slave was burdened with sunshades, spicy pomanders, baskets of cool fruit to slake a sudden thirst, a cage of twittering birds, or sometimes a marmoset or Ægyptian cat on a leash. Sighing, I would watch them as they paused for a moment to chat with a friend or a rival. I could imagine them comparing jewels, gossiping about who was the current lover of whom, all the while casting speculative eyes on the handsome young men who sauntered past on errands of their own.

Oh, they were the glorious ones, the noble young men of Troy. Many were my older brothers, those who were sons of Hecabe and those from other women as well. Cebriones, Antiphus, Isos, Deiphobus, Gorgythion, Pammon – once I could have named them all. From the time I was an urchin playing in the dust and far beneath their notice, I enjoyed the spectacle of the young men giving themselves airs and parading self-consciously as they went along the avenues, preening for the eyes of the nobles' daughters. Here one might have a new leopard skin, there another showed off an armband with jeweled serpents' eyes. Looking at these ranks of young men, each as beautiful in his own way as a god, I rejoiced in the virility of our father, who was still able to breed children though he had been past his middle years when I was born. I could not have known then that some day too soon upon us, all the glorious sons would lie dead before me, and those unfortunate daughters who survived would, like me, be led away into slavery, the nature of which none of the delicately bred ladies of Troy could imagine.

But do not think that I spent all my time moping and yearning out the window at the passing throngs. I was old enough and more to attend the maids at the washing troughs that were fed by the spring a little way outside the walls of Troy, when it came my turn. In some bygone time, workmen had channeled the flow, turning it into three goodly streams that fed the troughs. It was said by the superstitious that the work had been done in the Three Names of the Goddess, so that the spring would never run dry. Be that as it may, there was never a lack of water in the stone-lined troughs; and afterward we would lay out the pattern for a maze-dance while waiting for the linen to dry. Oftentimes, I would catch a glimpse of bright male eyes and knew that someone's young man had crept close to watch his beloved at her private sport. Even the boys would sometimes pause to watch us younger girls, though there never seemed to be any eyes for me. I looked carefully at the others; many of them, even some younger than I, had already begun to grow plump and appealing, while my body was still a bundle of skinny little sticks. And so I danced harder, and turned faster, and jumped higher than anyone else, but still there were no admiring glances in my direction.

Sometimes I would run to my nurse, my eyes hot with furious, unshed tears. Then she would laugh, and give me a sweet to suck, and would put me on her comfortable lap. 'In time, little one, in time,' she would say. 'Yours is a slow beauty, but it will come when it is ready.' And then, loved and secure again, I would forget my pique for a while.

We were wealthy and idle, and careless, as all great cities are, but there was never any cruelty or malice in our gay and carefree kind of life as there can be when a people grow rich and fat. We heard rumors of how the new – speaking in comparisons; they had ruled more than three lifetimes of men – Hellene overlords thought themselves far above their Cretan subjects as they looked down on them from the palace at Knossos. And we, who were sprung of the same stock as Cretans, would be better than they and so we kept our allies our friends, man to man. We treated our slaves and servants well, and no one wanted for food no matter how poor he might be. We surged with laughter, and with good will, and our people were happy. Each morning brought love-gifts of fox and wolf skins to our door, and the hides of those great, shaggy, manlike beasts which take a brave man to track and kill. Once this happened spontaneously in the great Houses of the Western mainland as well; but when they forgot to be Hellene and began calling themselves Achaeans, the people grew cool.

The troubles our people bore were light for the most part, being those which life itself brings; for we were also free of the irksome weight of intrigue and base political maneuvering. The alliances that Priam entered into were straightforward, and his schemes and plots were those of the good-natured market place where sharp trading is a game understood to all and a skillful player is much to be admired. There were no cunning phrases worked into his agreements which could be twisted until they took whatsoever meaning that any glib scribe might wish to give them. We were traders, and princes of traders, and we had grown wealthy beyond description because of it.

2

SUMMER FAIR

Though the Troad is not a healthy place in which to live, I was seldom sick as a child. One of my earliest memories is when, at the age of four or thereabouts, my twin brother and I were taken down to the Hall to hear a singer.

The Royal House of Troy attracted singers and storytellers from all over the world, and it was rare indeed that the younger children would be allowed to stay up and listen. That this was an extraordinary one was plain even to me. And young as I was, I noticed that he was heavy with gold, though most men of his profession kept their gold hidden in hopes of receiving more of it from their hosts. This one, however, declined all gifts from all would-be givers. His pleasure, he said, was in his song, for he had little time left in which to sing.

'I return,' he said quietly, 'to meet my fate. I will run to meet it with outstretched arms, for that is the way of the hero. My queen waits to send me to the Goddess and my soul is eager to go. I am a singer of Apollo, but the Goddess has long held my death in trust and now it must be offered up. But while I have journeyed to many strange places and have seen many strange sights, I wished to look upon the wonders of Troy and the High City Ilium, before black death closes my eyes and mouth forever. I am Orpheus, King of Thrace.'

Through the murmur of astonishment and pity that rose at these words, I remember thinking with satisfaction that the singer must be a very learned man, for only the Royal Kin bothers to remember the grand-sounding name that our ancestor Scamander tried to give our city when he built it up from the rude and rustic rubble below. But the settlement had been known as 'Troy' from time out of mind, and Troy it remained. Still, the lofty name was not forgotten.

'I must tell you, King Priam,' the singer continued, 'that I was a member of the crew of the *Argo*, the one ship that slipped through the Hellespont and back again many years ago without paying the toll. I tell you this from honesty, so that you will not think that I am trying to hide anything from you. And though there is many a lusty song of that voyage to Colchis, I will not sing any of them because it would be an unforgivable insult where hospitality is freely given. Instead, I will sing of another adventure which has become no less famous since I have begun to spread it on my travels.'

And then he gave us a long and stirring story, full of battles and beautiful maidens, and a horse that flew up to heaven. But the song, enthralling as it had been, was nearly forgotten when my twin and I were brought to him so that he might lay his hand upon us.

I can still feel his strong, thin hand, a thing of bones and sinew as slender as his harp, upon my head. He stared at me for a long time with his keen and piercing eyes, until I felt that my inmost soul was bare to him. Then he turned to Helenus, but he merely brushed the hair back from his forehead and tugged my brother's ear absently, as one does to one of the house dogs that nudge up to one to be noticed. Then he returned to me.

'There is the god's touch upon you, little one,' he said thoughtfully, and I remember feeling a faint thrill because he had addressed me directly and had not spoken to Orthia or to my mother or father. It was as if I were his equal in years and experience. 'I can feel it, who have borne the same touch all of my years. It is a hard life, to be a god's beloved, but one that brings satisfaction at the end of it, even though happiness might not be your lot. Will you accept what has been given you, reaching out for it with both hands as freely as it is offered?'

Wordlessly, I nodded, unable to help myself. I could not have refused at that moment if a dagger were to enter my back the next. Then, turned suddenly shy, I buried my face in my nurse's lap.

'She is so small,' I heard my mother say.

'Yet she knows what I asked her,' replied the singer. 'Do not despise what it has pleased the god to give to you.'

A prophetic strain runs through Priam's family. Others of his children have been known for their clear sight. And so my mother and father found it easy to accept what the singer told them for the truth.

Later, when we were given to the House Snake so that he might cleanse our ears, I remembered this, and the other things the singer had said. But I am sure that Helenus forgot, for he endured the touch of the snake reluctantly and cried when it was all over so that he had to be given a honey cake to sooth him.

But god-touched or not, it was a pleasant thing to be a daughter of the ruling family in Troy. My mother, Hecabe, was the Queen and so her children were always ranked higher than those whose mothers lived in the women's quarters on the Second Terrace. There were always women to serve me, and Orthia looked after me. I saw my mother every day, and I still remember the scent she used, for it enveloped me in fragrant clouds when I went to her to be kissed and hugged. I always insisted upon sitting in her lap to relate to her the story of my daily activities though I rumpled her flounces and sometimes ripped a delicate ruffle with my energetic bouncing.

'Strong-natured,' smiled my mother.

'Willful,' muttered the maids.

I was not Hecabe's only child, of course. Besides my brother Helenus, there were Hector the eldest, who was the heir, and Alexandros who was by far the favorite of the family. Alexandros, whose nickname was Paris, was the handsomest of all Priam's sons. He was middling tall, with hair the color of wet sand shot through with gold. His eyes were large and gray, and creased at their corners with laughter, and his chin bore a deep dimple that invited the fascinated touch of many a Trojan maiden. Being his parents' favorite, this meant that he was somewhat spoiled, though his disposition was so engaging that one scarcely noticed it.

After Hector and Paris came Creusa, Laodice, Deiphobus, Pammon, Polites, Antiphus, Hipponous, Polydorus, and Polyxena, who was my favorite among my sisters. There was still another child to come from Hecabe's womb before her fertility dried away, and that was Troilus, who was born in the same season that the Achaeans began their raids on Trojan lands. But even with such a large brood, she found time for all.

I remember how we used to make a game of it when winter came blowing down from the north, cold and straight, numbing everyone from peasants to the King with his nobles as they huddled around their braziers and rubbed their fingers in the flickering, fragile warmth. Then it was a time for staying indoors, though the heaviest of leather curtains, the stoutest of wooden shutters were no proof against the cold wind from the north. I have seen the Queen, my mother, dressed in furs and woolens with many petticoats, her breath puffing white and frosty ahead of her when she ventured into the frigid corridors. This seemed a very remarkable thing for her to condescend to do, for this was what any maid or warrior did; but I consoled myself that she did it far better than any of them.

We wore high boots, usually of foxskin with the fur side turned inward, and mantles of heavy wool, and when we went outside we had mittens made like the boots. And still, our noses were forever cold, with a drop of moisture on the ends of them. Braziers were kept going in every corner of the Palace, and still they did little except to turn the worst edge of the chill from the air. The only truly warm place was the thalamos, the great Hall, where the enormous hearth in which one could roast a whole ox and the trimmings too, blazed high and bright in the evenings. On the Western mainland, they call this room the megaron. The chimney led through my father's bedchamber and warmed it, too, though not as well as my favorite spot, a seat by one of the pillars of the hearth.

Even in the summer, when the ever-present wind died down only to return hot and dry and dusty, we were not allowed to do away with our boots. Then we put on buskins of whitened doeskin, gold-trimmed and ornamented, because of the scorpions and the great hairy spiders whose bite is painful and sometimes fatal. So, we wore buskins lest we brush against a poisonous ground-dweller with a naked foot. One of the first things I was taught was to shake them before I put them on in the morning, and many a time a hairy crawler or a many-legged worm tumbled out of its place of concealment. To counter this restriction which necessity put upon fashion, the ladies of Troy wore long and graceful skirts that trailed upon the ground, so that their buskined feet might be hid. The flattery of these garments made up in some measure for the inability to show a dainty white foot beneath one's hem.

Because of the severity of the climate, visitors to the Troad were never comfortable for long. One must be born to it to endure it, much less love it, as I did. In the summer, the heat descends with an intensity frightening to an outsider. The two rivers dry away; the Simoïs vanishes utterly, and in the worst seasons all that is left of the larger Scamander is a string of bogs, weed-choked and ugly until the autumn rains bring flooding to the Plain, which has sometimes changed the beds of the rivers. Even the triple spring that still bubbles outside the truncated walls, where the maids once went to wash the clothes, diminishes in its flow, though it doesn't dry away entirely. Green and brown lizards pant in the shadow of every chance stone on the Plain, and people who are wise seek shelter from the merciless rays of the sun at midday.

All of the children of Priam, along with the children of the nobles, had a season in the shrine of Sminthian Apollo to be taught the things that those of the Royal Kin must know. They stayed as long as they liked, and learned what they would beyond the essentials which were mandatory. For my older brothers, a season or two at the most sufficed; then they were out in the courtyard with the wooden swords, or taking their turn with the herds on Mount Ida where the green leaves never fail, even in summer. In this herding, my brother Alexandros excelled, and it was from this that he got his nickname, Paris, from the wallet which all the herdsmen carried with their day's portion of bread, dried meat and cheese. Though he was frivolous enough in the City for two men, with the herds it was another matter. He could calm a sick lamb with a touch, and coax goats who butted everybody else to trot docilely at his heels, and there was never a better one to help a nervous, high-strung mare to foal.

He missed many a summer's Fair by being occupied in this way, but then he was never greatly interested in this yearly event the way the rest of us were. When he was in the City, he would go and make eyes at the traders' daughters; but they were careful of their girls and he never got close enough to them to sample their delectable sweetness. He found it a far simpler matter to coax a hill girl to accompany him for a day or so on some mountain's slope where the nights were cool enough to encourage closeness. For the other children of Priam, myself included, years were measured impatiently from Fair to Fair. When the cold winds began to abate, then we would venture out onto the Plain.

'Here is where the Levantine camps, with his jasper and indigo,' we would say. And, 'This is the place where the Scythians always stay, with their loads of gold-heavy fleeces and bales of strong, heavy wool.'

Already we could see the piles of raw linen and hemp, the dried fish, the strange green stone from beyond the Euxine, often as not carved into strange winged lizards with horned backs and frightening, fierce eyes. There would be cinnabar and henna, and fine timber for ships and furniture, grain and oil, camel's hair, cotton, leather, fragrant saffron, silk, wax, corn, Ismarian wine, white horses and wild mules, Hittite iron already worked into the precious hunting arrowheads, chalcedony for seals which the workman would carve on the spot. And there was the jewelry. Agate, sardonyx, amethyst, bits of Ægyptian porcelain, ivory, alabaster cosmetic boxes, amber beads and blue ones from Ægypt and trinkets of all sorts in precious gold and silver showered in profusion from the stalls of the dealers. Smiths would work late at their forges, making their best weapons and armor to sell to the traders, and the unguent-boilers would never rest at their kettles, while the scents of their perfumes overpowered even the stench of the sun-dried fish. Here would be a slave dealer, hopeful of turning a neat profit on his merchandise; there, a trader in spices with his jars of myrrh, his bales of cinnamon, his sacks of fragrant cloves. And now the women of Troy would bring out their bundles and bales of woven wool and linen over which we all worked, even the Queen and her women, during the cold winter, for Trojan woven goods were famous even on the Western mainland.

Sometimes, there would be a dealer with cages of bright birds, wide-eyed marmosets and charming monkeys on leashes, and sometimes Ægyptian cats in wicker baskets. That is where I got Bastos, though there were cats in plenty that roamed the palace; it was said by some that they were as helpful as Apollo Sminthos in keeping down the mice. But when I saw him, long-necked and proud though miserable in his cramped basket, I had to have him. I gave the trader a snake arm-ring which, though only gold-washed bronze, still had jewels for eyes. He must have thought me as mad as others did later, but for me, I felt myself ahead in the bargain. Besides, some of the songs have it that when the gods fought with Giants and were having the worst of it for a while, they ran away to Ægypt to rest and recover themselves from their many hurts. Hera became a cow to disguise herself, Hermes a hawk and so forth, and Pallas Artemis turned herself into a cat. As such, she is still worshiped beside the Nile as cat-headed Bast; and so I gave her outlander's name a masculine ending for my new pet. Many times I was to whisper into his soft fur and feel his cat's understanding reaching through me to the god from which he was sprung.

Along with the traders came those whose only wares were entertainment. Jugglers and acrobats, stripped and oiled so that their bodies gleamed in the sun, sweated through their skilled performances, hopeful for a bit of gold from a passing visitor, and they were seldom disappointed. All of the children loved to watch them, nobles' heirs and peasants' brats side by side, elbowing each other in the dust.

An ear-dizzying babble of tongues and dialects sounded from all sides, though most of the traders had some command of the common tongue, which was the speech of Achaea and Troy as well. There were some differences, of course. The Achaean language was sharp and angular in some of its words and pronunciations, while in the mouths of the Trojans it had become softer and more rounded. For example, we were apt to call ourselves Troyans, as the harsh 'j' sound sat awkwardly in our mouths. Likewise, the common name 'Aias' was 'Ajax' to them. But we bent generously and allowed ourselves to be called as they would, until even we began to adopt Achaean speech habits for ourselves.

Merchants and traders came from both sides of the Hellespont to meet in the summer on the Trojan Plain in this breath-taking mixture of sights, sounds, colors, smells. There were always strange children for us to meet and play with while we were young, and to regard with shyness when we grew older. It was here, at this one spot, that East and West met and exchanged goods – while a steady stream of gold poured into the treasuries of the City from the levies on each of the endless transactions.

Now the visitor nursing his discomfort in the chilly halls of the Palace could understand why Priam clung to this unpleasant spot, when just a little way to the south lay a far more comfortable site. Indeed, in some respects it was more impressive than the tag end of the hills on which Troy stood. We called it the Stronghold, and had built dwellings there for some of the more delicate and sickly of the wives and concubines to retire during the harsh winter. But here, only a morning's leisurely walk from the Scaian Gate, flow the dangerous waters of the Hellespont, the gateway to the Marmoran Sea which is the antechamber to the fabled Euxine. Through this portal is the only path to the lands around it, where riches lie piled upon the ground during the year, waiting the time for trading. And Troy was the lock upon this gate.

But we cared little for such things when we were small. Our eyes were only for the ships drawn stern-first on the shore and clustered in the shallow Sigeum Bay, for the gay tents of the merchants, for the piles of dyed goods heaped in careless profusion, for the hawkers of sweetmeats and trinkets. We watched in awe as a dealer recounted the virtues of the woman he tried to sell a crowd of interested onlookers. 'A Carian, versed in music and skilled in weaving as well!'

We never noticed the Achaean princes striding through the

market places, glaring about them at the expensive and profitable gathering over which they had not the least control. Or if we did, when we were brusquely pushed from some prince's path, we were unheeding. We were always in some noble's way, it seemed, one no more than another.

We were everywhere, fingering goods, sampling spices, getting underfoot. I remember touching a piece of cloth that had a softness I had never felt before. The dealer, a wrinkled old man with skin the color of amber, and raisin eyes nearly hidden by heavy lids, smiled when he perceived by the blue tunic and amulet which all the royal children wore, that I was of the House of Troy. 'For you,' he said, and handed me a piece of the stuff, dyed a soft, translucent rose.

I thanked him hurriedly, as graciously as I could, through our lack of language; and then I raced back to the Palace with my prize, unable to wait. His booth had held some of the green carved-stone goods, and I persuaded my father to buy from him a cup decorated with the familiar winged lizards of this ware, and a chain with a bit of rare peach-colored stone carved into a flower hanging from it. And so the old man was well repaid for his gift to a young girl.

The rose cloth was too fragile to wear except as a veil. I remember that I held it in place with a circlet of oak leaves worked in gold, and joined with thin links, though properly speaking I had no right to do so as I was not a member of the Oak Cult. I kept the veil for several years before it grew too shabby to wear; but the cup and chain I kept in my jewel box until the Citadel fell.

Too soon, the summer would end and the merchants would depart, having enriched not only themselves but the coffers of Troy as well. And then we must live through another winter until the whole glorious panoply would begin again.

Now, as I grew, my horizons began to expand beyond the nursery door, and farther ahead than one Fair to another. Orthia, who deserved her name because of her upright and straightforward nature, tried to keep the maids from chattering, but I soon found that even they considered me as something special and set apart from others of Hecabe's children. Though they were ignorant, and one must not put much stock in what they said, they were still a means of finding out what the rest of the Palace was saying.

It was through them that I found out the exciting and

mysterious circumstances of Helenus's and my birth. I had long ago discovered that by playing silently and alone in a corner I might be overlooked and others in the room might talk as they would. And the story, later confirmed by other and more reliable sources, was this.

My twin and I were born on a day when a shadow fell over the sun, threatening to blot it out entirely and forever. But when all was dark, and in the midst of the daytime it was black as the deepest night and the terrified, wailing maids had to run and light lamps so that they could see to tend the Queen, a single brilliant edge of light appeared on the terrible dim circle. It was the god's promise of hope to his children; and sure enough, he crept slowly back to us as quietly and awesomely as he had disappeared.

Though the Philistine astrologers had predicted this phenomenon which they called an 'eclipse', still it frightened Hecabe into labor three weeks before her time. And then when my twin and I were born, each with red hair, which though common among the Achaeans, was rare in the Troad, the Levantine midwives instantly made the sign against witchcraft even as they cleaned us and gave us to Hecabe.

But strangely enough, my twin showed no signs of the unnatural brightness that seemed to shine upon me. I attributed it to the fact that he was born while it was still dark, and I had made my appearance as the sun's warm rays once more began to light the earth.

Impatiently I waited the time when I could go into the schoolroom in the shrine of Apollo Sminthos and let Laocoön, the priest-teacher, begin to teach me those things which I thirsted to know. And, mindful also of my dream which now visited me one night in ten, I felt it needful to prepare myself; but if anybody had asked me against what, I would have had no reply. And sometimes I would talk to Helenus about the future that lay before us, as straight and plain as the patterns of stonework that decorated the high walls of Troy, if one did not count the dream.

'Do you not look forward to being the highborn servant of Apollo and being in the circle of his favorites?' I would ask him.

'It is what is expected of me,' he would reply with a shrug, 'and I do not think of it very much, one way or another.'

When he talked like this, I would always regard my twin with disfavor. 'I think about it a great deal,' I would say severely, 'and you ought to know that Apollo listens to you. You should not be so light about such an honor.'

'Perhaps it is an honor to you. But no one asked my opinion about it. I am only doing what I am told, for I am not like you.'

And then I would hold my hands over my ears so that I would not hear any more. But then his sullen mood would soon fall from him, and we would go on and play like other children. It was only in this one thing that a disagreement arose that was severe enough to disturb our friendship.

The second breach came when we began our schooling in the shrine of Apollo Sminthos.

As every visitor to the Troad knows, there are many shrines to Apollo in and around Troy. On the Plain, half-way between the gates and the shore, is the shrine of Thymbraean Apollo, the god in his pastoral mood. It was here that Laocoön held his classes during the months of the Fair for those who chose to come; but during the winter, the Mouse God's shrine was our schoolroom.

During a lull in the lessons, I loved to go and look at the white mice in their golden cages. It was said that they could give oracles, though only the initiated knew how this was done. I often brought morsels from my plate for them, and would whisper endearments to them as I pushed the crumbs through the bars. They were so different from the little gray beasts who were so terribly destructive that it took a god to stand before them and keep them from the City. Who could imagine the havoc they might wreak if Apollo turned his back on us? With the grain stores – not only of the City but of the traders as well – with the fruits, the oil, the many fragile and perishable stuffs that merchants constantly poured through our Plain, a real infestation of mice could ruin us.

Once, when there was no one else about, I brought Bastos to see them. I thought that, as one god-connected to another, they might greet each other with friendship. But no, it was the same as if Bastos had been confronted with any other mice; his eyes grew wide and mad with anticipation, and his jaw quivered as he sought a way past the golden cage. And the mice scurried here and there, seeking refuge from the terrible creature that moaned in his eagerness to get at them.

Now the days of my childhood were passing swiftly; I learned writing, and reading, and some of the scribe's art of counting. There were lessons in music, for that is one of the things most loved by the god. We learned the names of some of the stars, and it was here that I found traced in the heavens part of the story that the dead singer Orpheus had given us. There were daily lessons in manners and deportment; and when these were ended, the boys and the girls went their separate ways for further instruction in manly and womanly things. I learned weaving and embroidery and was soon as nimble as any other at the loom. Often Bastos amused himself with the loom weights on a quiet afternoon.

When I had first come to the schoolroom I had asked for instruction in the arts of healing, in the application of salves and simples, being ever mindful of my dream. But I said nothing about it yet to anyone but Orthia who continued to brew my mint and hold me against the terror. And for what Orthia could not teach me, I was sent to a healing-woman in the Thymbraean Shrine where I learned with a will. Some of the remedies seemed odd; a spear point's rust to heal a wound, spiders' webs for the stanching of blood and moldy bread for infections. But they worked, as many a living warrior could vouch.

To my disappointment, Helenus left immediately after the obligatory season had passed and nothing I could say would persuade him to return.

'I can read well enough, and I can sign my name and tune a lyre, and I do not disgrace myself or others in the Hall,' he said. 'What more is necessary?'

'Only what you feel called to learn,' I said sharply, a little disgusted with him and his thickheadedness, as I thought it at the time. 'But do not blame me when your ignorance makes you a laughingstock before the people later on!'

'I promise you that I won't,' he retorted impudently, and went away whistling. I thought him a fool and said so to his retreating back. As for me, I would drain Laocoön dry of knowledge and the women instructors too, and then go on elsewhere if necessary.

I was in love with learning, and I scarcely noticed when my mother gave birth to Troilus, and news began to come into the City about the Archaeans's terrible land raids on Trojan territory. Relations grew strained between East and West, so that for some years the annual Fair was not the success it had always been heretofore. My father grew more worried daily; his hair turned white as the snows that lay perpetually on Mount Ida. But my nose was buried in my lessons, and I scarcely looked up.

Among the things we received of the priest was the history of our House; it goes straight back to its roots in the noble civilization that fostered Crete. And we can trace our own beginnings straight to the beautiful city that now lay beneath our feet, that our ancestor Scamander himself built. We learned both the fanciful tales that sufficed for the people, and the plainer story that was only for the nobles, as well. And this was the story, as it was told us in the classroom by Laocoön, our teacher.

Many lifetimes ago, before men had learned to keep time except by this event or that, a magnificent people came into being in a land that is now vanished from the earth. Atlantis, some called it, and the tops of the drowned mountains the Westerners call the Cyclades are all that is left sticking up out of the Ocean Sea when the waters came to swallow it up.

Having foreknowledge of such things, part of the people went to Crete, that long island safely south of the coming disaster. But others, under the first Scamander, came to the Troad, bringing with them the culture of the Lady of the Waves, the Triple Goddess whose three gracious faces everyone knows as Hera the Woman, Aphrodite the Nymph and Artemis the Maiden.

The inhabitants of the Troad, mainly isolated tribes and clusters of rustics, worshiped a strange variety of gods and goddesses, and here and there a savage remnant of the foreign rites of the south could be seen. Here Poseidon was strong, and Apollo Lawbringer whom the newcomers recognized in their familiar sun god. Scamander and his followers were quite willing to accept these new gods in order to keep the peace; the only reservation they made was that Aphrodite was to reign supreme. As the Pelasgians, or First Folk, had always known the Goddess under other guises, this was agreeable to them. And so the peoples of the Troad welcomed the joyous rites of Aphrodite and new shrines sprang up everywhere, all dedicated to her.

But though the people might accept the newcomers and their new gods, the priesthoods of Apollo and Poseidon became jealous of the rising power of Aphrodite, knowing that their own hold over the people was thereby diminished. Then, so the songs go, they conspired with each other to plot against Scamander and throw him down so that they might resume the power they had enjoyed before he had come. But Scamander was Atlantis-born; he had wisely set spies everywhere and he now moved quickly to stop them before they had fairly begun. As punishment, he forced them to build and fortify the walls of the new city he had begun to construct on the ruins of the rude village below. The chief priest of Apollo took it with as good a grace as he could muster under the circumstances, but the chief priest of Poseidon grumbled aloud, all during the time of the building and thereafter as well. But grumble as he might, he and Apollo's servant had to resign themselves to Scamander's rule. It was plain that either they did this, or they would die and be replaced with Goddess-worshipers from Scamander's own picked band of Companions. Apollo and his servant reconciled themselves to things as they were; but Poseidon has never smiled upon the Troad to this day.

Scamander named his new city Ilium, 'the Strong', but the common people continued to call it Troy because it stood at a vital spot on the Troad and because it was the name the settlement had had since man knew how to speak. And soon, the peoples of the Troad came flocking to Scamander's Strong City, to ally themselves with the noble House that had come to dwell among them. There were the Pelasgians, of course; after them came the Dardanians from the south, and Thracians and Phrygians and wild, nameless tribes from across the swift-flowing Hellespont. Soon word had spread to the ends of the Euxine about the new House that inhabited the Troad, and embassies began to trickle south and west, some bearing goods for trade. For their part, the Thracians had spread the story to other tribes on the Western mainland and other embassies likewise burdened journeyed their way eastward.

This was the start of what would become the great annual East-West Fair. Now the islands that guarded the mouth of the Hellespont, Samothrace, and Imbros, Chios, Lemnos, and even the more southerly Lesbos, began to be used as points of debarkation in the nearly harborless area of the Hellespont. Scamander instituted the levy of a toll on each ship that passed through these waters, and soon set vast sums to flowing into the City's coffers. Even the pack-beasts jingled with gold, so the songs say.

Other songs, not so reliable, say that Scamander was the one who brought the Palladium to the Troad, and placed it in the shrine of the Goddess. From time out of mind it has been there, this huge boulder from the sky, strangely streaked and melted in its passage, but whether King Scamander brought it to us or not is a matter for dispute among the poets. Then, as later, it held the place of honor in the shrine, directly beneath an opening in the roof so that it could be exposed to the sky from which it came, though it was generally veiled from the sight of the common folk.

But whether he brought the Palladium with him or not, Scamander was a good king, and a brave one, too. For when the rain-making dances failed to bring the storm clouds gathering and the dancers twirled their bull-roarers until their arms dropped like stones from exhaustion in spite of the urgings of the drum beats day after unceasing day, he fearlessly leaped into the Xanthian River for the good of his people. That night, the rains began and the river was known by the King's name from that day forward.

3

SEASON OF WILDNESS

Laocoön, our teacher, was a man of middle age, though I thought him quite old then and beyond any feeling for a woman. Besides, he and his fellows were sworn to chastity. Despite this, there had been mention of his name in some of the whispers that ran like river currents through the Palace. I had pieced together the scandal long since, and had forgotten the most part of it because it made no sense to my youth and inexperience. However, having heard his name mentioned by the gossips was enough to make me daring when I grew bored with the slowness of the lessons which had to be paced so that the halting could keep up. Now when I was restless, I grew fractious when it pleased me, and often presumed to dispute openly with him. It seemed to me that his eyes rested on me more often than on others of the royal children; and when this happened, the younger ones would cringe nervously in their places, for they were sure to bear the brunt of the displeasure that he would not dare vent on me.

And then, one day, as I left the schoolroom, he caught my sleeve and drew me back so that he could speak with me in private.

Even today, a certain scent of the classroom, an odor of overworked wax, the smell of a freshly sharpened wood stylus, the air of many children in a close place, will bring it back to me when I thought I had had done with it long since.

I waited patiently and respectfully, for he was my teacher after all, and a person of some importance and authority. If he did not hold the place of, say, an uncle in my esteem, then surely he might have been some far-distant cousin entitled to the courtesy and dignity his bearing and station in life called for.

Now he fidgeted at his table, fiddling with a stylus, shuffling the tablets of wax and clay. He began to dig at one with the stylus, marking meaningless scribbles and smoothing them out again.

'It is nearly time for you to leave the sanctuary,' he said at length, his brows drawn together in a thoughtful frown. 'Have you given any attention to what you will do now?'

'Why, I will stay and serve Apollo, even as Helenus will,' I replied innocently. Surely he must have heard of the singer, and about my dedication. It was even on the tip of my tongue to tell him about my dream which urged me to prepare for calamity when none was looked for, but a god's finger must have touched my lips and told me to be silent. I was glad, when I heard his next words.

'I had heard that you harbored that childish error,' he said now, 'for your father reminded me of it less than a moon ago. And that is why I have asked you to wait so that I might speak to you. How can you believe that a woman can serve Apollo? It is a thing unheard-of, and Apollo is sure to be insulted.'

'It was Apollo himself who chose me,' I replied, puzzled at this opposition from an unexpected quarter. 'He chose me through his singer, and through the dedication that my parents subsequently made. Even the Goddess blessed me with her snake. It is Apollo's will that I serve him, and it is at his urging that I seek out instruction past the time I would be expected to serve as a learner; I am preparing myself to sit among the wise, in the life that awaits me. Would a simple priest bar the way so that I may not pass through where a god beckons?'

'It is no ill will of this simple priest that prevents you, my princess. I only ask you to consider; though women and womanish men serve the Goddess, men only may serve Apollo, and so it has always been. For though a man may offer up his manhood for the privilege of serving Hera, is there a like sacrifice a woman can make? Even if she burns away her bosom as the Amazons are said to do, does that stop her monthly course and make her not a woman? No, since you and Helenus are those of the royal children chosen to tread the paths of priesthood, let Helenus go into Apollo's sanctuary and you, Cassandra, do your prophesying from one of Aphrodite's couches. It is not unpleasant, I am told.'

'There would be little call for the learning I have set myself to, on Aphrodite's couch. And besides, other women have made my way smooth before me. In Ægypt there was a queen who strapped a false beard upon her chin when she would be Pharaoh. I once heard Ægyptian traders speak of it, when they wished to mock some folk behind the Euxine who would give themselves airs.'

Evidently Laocoön had not heard this rumor, for he raised his hands in horror. 'An abomination!' he exclaimed. He paced back and forth across the deserted classroom several times. From his knotted brow, I could tell that there was something weighty passing there; though what it might be I did not know. Then he stopped and looked at me keenly. His eyes seemed to recede in his head as the flesh around them swelled and grew hot.

Suddenly, between one breath and another, I was aware of myself. There were now twelve notches in my doorframe, and my breasts were already beginning to sprout and show themselves in the soft folds of my gown. Soon my monthly courses would start; in some parts of the world I would be nearly ripe for marriage.

'I will strike a bargain with you,' said the priest, and something in his tone made the hairs on the back of my neck stir as if someone had come along and brushed them with a feather. 'Come and lie with me. Then, you may stay in the shrine of Apollo, and through me, prophesy in his name, for I will see to it. It is a small thing to ask, Cassandra, in return for the fulfillment of your ambitions.'

Now I knew why he had urged me to Aphrodite's couch before, and a bitterness welled up into my mouth. I felt utterly betrayed, for this had been someone who had held my trust. And with my betrayal came fear and anger and a rising panic it was hard to swallow down.

'Through me, you will live in love with Apollo himself,' he continued and he held out his arms and came toward me so that he blocked me from the door. I backed away from him, not knowing what to do, and found myself caught in a corner with no escape. His words continued to pour over me in the soft and soothing tones one would use to a snared rabbit one meant to tame and make into a pet. 'Believe me, Cassandra, this is the only way you can do what you seem to have set your heart on doing. Though you may not serve the god directly, you will serve his priest. This is a thing that is not unheard-of in our profession.'

And then my panic was stilled in the coolness of that kind of fear that sharpens every wit and sense and makes it possible for one to fight again. I wondered how long he had rehearsed his little set speech, for it to come tumbling out so smoothly now. With my new-found cold anger, the gossip came rushing back to me, now full of the meaning it had not held before. This priest, this same Laocoön who stood over me this very moment, mouthing my name so that the sibilants hissed in my ear like the Mother's snake, already had a woman he kept in the shrine of

Thymbraean Apollo that lay outside the walls, and it was said that he had bred sons from her. In fact, I thought I had glimpsed her on occasion, when I went to the healing-woman. Thin she had looked, and ashamed and frightened as she ducked through the corridors trying to avoid contact with everyone who came there. How many other would-be servants of Apollo had he debauched in this manner, to be reviled by the decent and pious townspeople? Did he want one for every shrine? And which was to be my home?

And even as he spoke now, he smoothly made it seem that Priam would not even object, for this was the one way I could serve the god for whom I longed. Though what he was proposing was forbidden to him and the woman was obliged to keep herself thereafter within the walls of the sanctuaries for fear of harm from the people, still it was said that Apollo winked his eye at this behavior. 'After all, Apollo himself has loved many earthly maidens. Could his priests do less?' droned the insinuating voice.

More than ever I felt like the rabbit in the snare when the hunter comes. Then I remembered a trick of battle I had once heard the young men arguing; it was designed to draw your enemy off, and give you time for a telling blow when he thought the victory was his.

I lowered my head and pretended to be thinking deeply. I let my eyes slide back and forth under their lids so that he might think me flustered, timidly approaching what might be my first passion. 'You swear that you will listen to the words that the god speaks through my mouth, and send them out truly to the people?' I asked as guilelessly as I could, looking up at him sideways. I watched a bead of sweat trickle down his forehead. 'You swear that my prophecies will be truly acknowledged as having come from the god himself?'

'I swear,' he replied fervently. Laocoön had come so close now that I could smell the sweat on him. He laid his hand on my breast, but I didn't even feel it, so caught up was I in the dangerous game I was playing. 'I swear by Upright Apollo, as he comes to me now!' And then, before my unbelieving eyes, he pulled aside his garments to show me what awaited me.

Now, there was no false modesty in me, as there was in other girls who peeked through their fingers at the athletes when they stripped for a game, and pretended that they were too nice to look. From my earliest days, when Helenus and I were bathed in the same tub, I was aware of the differences in the male and female bodies. But I was completely unprepared for this thrusting of a man's private member, swollen to bursting, virtually under my nose.

Instinctively I recoiled from this assault on my maidenhood. I turned blindly and struck the wall behind me; and flailing out in an attempt to keep my balance, I accidentally delivered a sharp blow to the priest's groin, where the cause of my confusion dwelt. To my mixed pleasure and consternation, he gasped aloud and the turgid blood drained from his face as he clutched himself and bent double, grunting with pain.

An older and more experienced girl would have fled then, but I was torn with curiosity and fear, and the awesome knowledge that I had caused pain to somebody who had been placed in a position of authority over me.

Still bent over, catching his breath to hold against the pain, Laocoön hobbled to his table where he sat down as if gratefully. I heard the rustle of cloth, and knew that he was putting his clothing to rights. I was still in my corner, not daring to move, yet longing to be away from this intolerable situation. Everything had changed abruptly for me, in this most familiar of surroundings and I wished someone would come along and put it all back the way it had been before.

At length, Laocoön looked up, and his eyes were cold and hostile. 'Know now that you will never enter Apollo's sacred precinct, Cassandra.'

'But you swore,' I whispered, clinging to this fresh betrayal in the midst of the confusion that clangored through me.

'You would not fulfill your part of the bargain.'

'But you swore to me that I would be allowed to prophesy in Apollo's name before I knew what waited for me in return.'

'That does not alter the fact that Apollo's door is closed to you.'

'In that case, the price of opening it is too high. I will enter the service of Pallas Artemis instead. And even though you may think that Apollo's gifts are for the likes of you to barter, you cannot take back your promise, or the other pledges made to me, no matter how much you may want to!'

'You have learned better than I thought. You will make a worthy priestess some day, for you have a mind for details, and such is the stuff of judgment. Yes, it is true that I cannot take back the gift of Apollo that I swore you would have, but I can at least soothe his pride – and my own.' And then he came at me suddenly and caught me by the shoulders. My mouth dropped open in surprise that he would dare touch me again. But there was no lechery in his grasp this time, I found. Quickly, he bent down and spat lightly into my mouth. 'There. Now, though you may prophesy, no one will believe. You will be a seer without vision, a speaker without listeners. It would have been far better for you if you had never been called upon to bear the confidence of a god.'

Even as his hands loosened their grip on my shoulders, I tore free of him to run sobbing out of the schoolroom, hawking and spitting, and wiping my tongue and mouth with the hem of my garment.

I never went back, and I refused to tell Hecabe and Priam why. I dared not confide even in Orthia, she who held with me the awesome secret of my returning dream; and as for Helenus, my twin had grown even farther apart from me because he was of the same tribe that had bred Laocoön, the man. I was only able to ease my heart by pouring out the whole sorry story to Bastos while I wept into his thyme-scented fur. Since I was now to go to Artemis, it was appropriate that I confide my inmost thoughts to one of her own; I dared not relate what had happened to human ears for I thought in my confusion and terror that the curse might not come true if nobody knew of it. I had never had anybody wish me ill before, and I did not know what to do with it.

And there was that something else gnawing at me that I could not speak of, that had had its start then. From that day in the schoolroom, there was something twisted within me. I found myself trembling whenever I thought a young man might be looking at me, where I had been impatient for masculine glances before. I avoided the company of even my own brothers and was glad that Helenus had found other things with which to occupy himself. It would be a long and weary time before I would be comfortable with one of the man-tribe again. I longed for the safety of the Pallae, the Maidens of the Maiden, for to touch one of them was death for any man, even a king. But now I could not even bear to remain behind the same city walls with my once-trusted teacher.

I began living outside the walls, staying with this one and that one in the low Troy-town. Bastos went with me for a while, but he did not like my restlessness and returned to his ordered life in the Palace. I ran wild, going dirty when it pleased me and washing only when I felt like it, which was seldom. I quickly drew a following of youngsters from the town, and even from the houses of the nobles in Ilium, who were fascinated with my daring and defiance. They were mostly girls, and the only boys I allowed in my pack of young outlaws were much younger and very childish children. We roamed where we would, even making the dangerous journey through the Scamander Valley and climbing Mount Ida, where the shepherds kept their flocks close to the warm and cool springs. Neaera had dared me to sit in the Seat of Zeus, and I was bound to do it.

It delighted me to come upon the herdsmen unawares, to watch the rude rustics flee in terror when I was still far off, certain that I was one of the Immortals with her band of attendant nymphs and young satyrs. One only held his ground, and flung a handful of harmless pebbles at us.

'Go home, children,' he called. 'Do not go where you are not wanted, and where it might be dangerous besides. I recognize most of you, even through your dirt, and I know that your parents must be despairing of you. Now, go by yourselves or I shall abandon the flocks and take you back to Troy by force.'

The other children turned and began to run away, but I stared long and hard at the young man before I, too, turned away, even though I did not want to risk having him come closer to me. It was Æneas, one of my kinsmen, and the heir of one of Ilium's noblest families, though he was not above taking his turn with the herds. And even if he was one of the hated man-breed, he had been able to shame me where everyone else had failed up to now.

We made our way back to the City – not, however, before I made good the dare – only to find that we had not been missed as sorely as we had fancied, because of the furor of the new building that had just begun. Only Orthia lifted up her face with closed eyes when she knew that I had not been eaten by beasts, but I would not let her see how this touched and affected me.

Now the children and I found mischief to our liking close to home. As the seasons passed, we deviled the masons and the architect, who lived in constant fear that one of us would be crushed by a falling stone. We scaled the walls, we raced along the battlements that reared a good five cubits past the inward batter of the stonework, we pulled thatching off the pitched roofing over the plaster. No matter where a workman stepped, we were underfoot, impeding the work, even though servants from the Palace were sent hourly to take us away.

And then, one day, digging in the earth, I found an earring. The others, giving the workmen a rare interval of rest, had begun to hack away at the ground near where a new section of wall had been marked out. This was where a new flagstone terrace had been planned, and they would have some trouble to fill in the hole again, but we cared nothing for that. The children had dug at one place remarkably deep, so that the smallest of them could barely see over the rim of the hole and had uncovered a line of curiously angled stones, set one against the other.

'Come and dig, Cassandra!' cried Phaedrus. 'We shall find gold and make ourselves rich!'

'I do not care to dig, but I will watch while you do it,' I replied, getting into the hole and leaning against one side of it. As I did so, a clod of earth loosened itself and showered down on me, and even as it fell I saw the gleam of gold in the dirt. I bent and retrieved the object, spitting on my finger and rubbing to get some of the accumulated grime of years off it.

The other children clustered around me, with excited coos of pleasure at the pretty bauble. The smell of their unwashed bodies smote me, reminiscent of the house dogs when they had been out for a run in the rain; and suddenly and unreasonably I felt that it would be a profanation for any eyes but mine to look upon it until it had been properly cleaned. I clasped it tightly in my hand and climbed up out of the hole.

I stood looking down at them, and suddenly a wave of revulsion swept over me at our foolishness and our shabby behavior.

'Go home,' I said, unconsciously echoing Æneas's words on Mount Ida. 'We have played long enough. It is time for us to cease this aimless and meaningless life of roaming and mischief, and to pay attention to what our parents desire of us.'

The faces below me, dirty and streaked, gaped up as openly as those of the rustics at the summer Fair. I was their leader, and I had urged them into this folly; why now was I abandoning them in their game?

'But why, Cassandra?' one of them ventured.

All the feelings that I had held so long so tightly within me burst their bonds at that moment. The fears, the dismay, the bitter ashes of betrayal, the awareness of what lustful manhood was about before I was ready for it – all this filled me to the brim so that I thought I should laugh, or cry before them. But the children would not have understood even if I had told them that the earring clutched tightly in my hand, riding the crest of the dammed-up flow, had suddenly brought me all too sharply to the realization of myself. Someday I, too, would be dead, and my jewels would be lying beneath the earth for some impious urchin to dig up. And what was I doing that would be worthy of the dead?

'Because I said so!' I snapped, and turning on my heel I left them staring behind me as I entered the Dardanian Gate and made my way up the broad avenue to the Citadel. There, I allowed my maids to wash and comb me for the first time in too long, and, arrayed in fresh linen dyed with seaweed to a delicate green, joined my surprised family that evening in the Hall for dinner.

4

SERVANT OF ARTEMIS

It was not a bad life, serving Artemis, though I never ceased to envy Helenus who had access to the inner shrine of Apollo. But I was now the leader of the Pallae, the Maidens of the Maiden, as my rank entitled me to be, and it was my duty to sit, the living representation of virgin Artemis, watching as the young mystics turned and wove their patterns in the rain-bringing dances.

In their hands they held the hollow bull-roarers to coax the reluctant thunder down from the mountaintop and kept them swinging at the end of the string in an eternal double-loop around their heads. To one side, the maidens danced their own measures, holding lighted torches that described the same double-loop. To keep the time, an old man tirelessly beat upon an ancient bull-hide shield with a double-ended hammer. One side, then another he struck, his hand steady at the slim waist of the shield and the knotted tendons of his wrist flexing as he struck now one end, then the other, of the archaic, echoing hide. Sometimes, when the rain was slow in coming, the dance would go on and on until the beat and the inflexible rhythm entered my very blood and pulsed against my temples in time with the throb that lived there until I longed to scream to relieve the tension but dared not lest the spell be shattered.

On feast days my brother and I walked in the processions, three times around the city walls as had been the custom time out of mind to where the sacrifice waited. Many a strong ox, many a young heifer or ewe without blemish went from our hands to the gods.

The two of us were dressed in identical white tunics on these days, and we bore the symbols of the gods we served. Helenus's bow was of ivory, decorated in gold leaf as befitted the sun god with his yellow rays; but mine was coated with the far more precious silver, and my sheaf of arrows had silver crescent-shaped points. On my head I wore a disk of silver, bound in place by a ribbon, so that wherever I turned my head, I shed moonlight upon the worshipers. Our faces were painted and we held them still because on these days the god entered our bodies and was there for the people to see. Only my mother, representing Hera the Crone, and Chryse, the wife of Anchises who led the more seemly portion of the cult of Aphrodite the Nymph, Lady of the Waves, walked before me.

Now my father, in accordance with a promise he had made to the dead singer, built a hero's shrine for Orpheus and installed me therein. There I sat, dressed in white and heavy with silver ornaments, working at a loom as did all the ladies of Troy, and waiting for the supplicants and listening to the heartbeat of the great City that went on just beyond my door. On days when there was little shrine business, I liked to let even my loom lie idle for a little while, as Bastos drowsed at my feet and from somewhere far off I could catch the faint, sweet echo of a harp and a girl's answering laughter.

It was during this time that I became aware of the opening stages of the war in which we were just beginning to realize we were involved. I heard, and this time I listened to, the accounts of the Achaean raids along our coasts; of fields burned, of towns sacked. They descended out of nowhere, wreaked their destruction, and vanished. Nobody could be sure whether they were simple pirates, or whether this was part of some well-thought-out plan, though the latter possibility presented itself more strongly to me. A name began to be mentioned more and more frequently: Achilles. It meant 'the lipless one', and I wondered how he had come to be so called.

Now was the reason for the workmen at the walls made clear to me. My father was willing to take no chances on these raids being the work of isolated bands of disgruntled marauders, unconnected except for their origins. And so he had engaged Æacus the Lelegian to come and strengthen and rebuild the walls of Troy.

In contrast to my former indifference, I now began to take a passionate interest in the building, and learned the names and uses for each section of the defenses that rose before my eyes.

The patterned walls, stout and massive, were nearly as high as the level of the First Terrace, and now, under Æacus's watchful eye, new battlements reared fully the height of the main walls themselves. In places he patched the mud-brick structure with worked stones; and so cleverly did he match the stonework with the former brickwork, it took an equally clever eye to pick the one from the other. Below, the great walls presented an inward slope sufficient for a determined warrior to scale; however, the new additions to the tall parapets surmounting them kept the city secure from that avenue of attack. Under the overhanging thatched roof there was a crenelated passageway for soldiers to go. The sun shone through these crenelations at some hours of the day, and one could see the shadows of the sentries who paced without ceasing along each section of the Trojan wall.

Besides the Dardanian Gate, there were two more large ones and a small, little-used sally port to the east. The Scaian Gate, newly opened with its Great Tower to guard it, fronted on the west, and the labyrinthine East Gate with its cutbacks that put a man's unshielded side to the walls served the road up the Simois Valley. The little sally port lay to one side of the Water Tower. It was seldom used, except by the townspeople who came to the Tower for water during the summer. But the main gate of Troy remained the Dardanian Gate on the south. It was also protected by a tower, erected by Æacus after the wall had been rebuilt, both to strengthen the gate and for aesthetic reasons, to balance the Great Tower on the west. Here, at the Dardanian Gate, one could enter the city and go directly up the ramp to the Palace. Outward from the gate, three roads led. One wound its way east, one southward to Dardania, and one west, to the sea where the traders came and went. These three roads converged into an open plaza outside the gate, and it was here that we set up a line of standing stones in honor of whatever strange gods our visitors might worship. Here beggars waited, and children from the low town who hoped for a handful of sweetmeats or copper beads tossed by a wealthy merchant; here was where the lifeblood of Troy flowed, in and out.

Steadily now, as evenly as a heartbeat, the Lelegian led his builders around the circuit of the walls, starting where he covered over an old gate, abandoned for the new Scaian Gate, and proceeding around westward to the Dardanian Gate and so around the City. When he was through with his enormous work, only the part of the wall that directly faced the Hellespont remained untouched.

As if it were yesterday, I can still hear my father the King, railing at him when he found the architect had not planned to reinforce that section.

'It is from that direction that an enemy could be expected to come!' he shouted. 'Are you in the pay of my enemies, that you would leave it as it is when the rest of the walls are sturdier by far? Would you abandon me to whatever fate some god who hates me might decide? No, I say. Take your gold my enemy has given you and depart, for I'll not pay you further for my own betrayal!'

But the Lelegian had his answer ready for the angry King. 'It is true, my lord Priam, that at this one point the walls seem to be weak. But this is only by comparison. Observe; though they may seem thin when judged by the rest, still they were strong enough in their day to withstand Heracles himself. Further, my leaving this portion of the wall untouched was from design, rather than oversight or neglect for the safety of the Trojans or their mighty king, let alone an unthinkable treason. Even Heracles, the strongest man living, could never have breached these walls for all his strength, if it had not been for the earthquake sent by Poseidon of the Blue Hair. That was what shook the fortifications down around the defenders, not Heracles' futile battering against them. Only this one stretch endured untouched; therefore some magical property that is proof against the earthquake must dwell within it. I fear to cover it over with mortar and plaster and stone, lest its magic be smothered and die. Rather, I hope that it may transmit some of its virtue to the other, newer wall, so that this Troy may endure for all time to come.'

My father could not hold his anger in the face of the Lelegian's good sense and sound reasoning. However, he stubbornly insisted that some sort of additional strengthening be done. So, at last, they reached a compromise wherein the new gateway that was planned to occur near the point that marked the place where the new wall ended and the old began, that being the Scaian Gate, might be strengthened by the erection of the Great Tower of which I spoke. And then the Lelegian volunteered the construction of a small tower flanking the East Gate, which further molified my father.

That evening, he called for the Song of Heracles, so that he might freshen his memory of the events of which the architect had spoken.

Though Heracles was his name, you must not think that he is the same Heracles that one hears so much about in these days. I have seen this latest one myself, when he came seeking a divine counsel, and I must say that he wears the name much better than any before him.

But there is always some strong man who is ready to call himself 'Heracles' springing up here and there in the country, for it has been prophesied that there will be a hero of this name whose fame would never die. In fact, 'Heracles' and 'hero' mean much the same, that being 'dedicated to, or glory of, Hera'. This prophecy is a common one, occurring in every people who pretend to civilization, so common in fact that refined sophisticates often dismiss it as just a folk tale.

But this early Heracles, as the song goes, was the immensely strong, if nearly witless fellow who had accompanied Jason the Iolcian, by rumor the most handsome man in the world, on his illegal voyage through the Hellespont. Jason's venture was thinly disguised piracy, and he chose to pay no toll, either entering or leaving. Heracles had gone foolish about a boy named Hylus, and when the lad finally escaped his clutches during the trip through the Hellespont, this Heracles jumped ship and came looking for him. He brandished his club threateningly at everyone he met, knocking heads to pieces right and left, not realizing that the boy had fallen into the hands of a tribe of Dryopian nymphs who had sacrificed him in their sacred pool.

He got it into his thick head that Hylus was being held captive in Troy, for he could not believe that the boy did not excite lust in everyone who beheld him. He had some small justification, at that, because everyone knows about the Ganymedes, the order of sodomitic priesthood that Scamander himself had had to put down. They still flourished in the south, at places like Joppa, and Tyre, and Uru-Salem, but it was Troy that had had the scandal, and which still hadn't been entirely lived down.

Heracles laid siege to the City, which was ruled at that time by my father's father, Laomedon. Laomedon was inclined to laugh at the spectacle of one fellow conducting a siege, no matter how huge and bulking he might be; but the priests of Apollo and Poseidon seized this opportunity to revenge themselves upon the King. Ever since the time of Scamander, they had sued regularly, once a year, at the festival of Poseidon, for wages they claimed were owed their respective shrines for the building of the walls of the first Troy so many years before, and which was the subject of another song. Like his predecessors, Laomedon had always brushed them aside with the same answer Scamander had given, namely, that no debt was owed them, and their claim was a false one. Now, however, he was astonished to find them going over to ally themselves with Heracles.

This put an entirely different complexion on the matter, for between them, the priesthoods of Apollo and Poseidon constituted no small number of men, each grimly determined to right what they thought an old injustice. During the siege, Poseidon clearly showed his partisanship in the matter by sending a mighty earthquake. It breached the walls, and before the last stone had fallen, Heracles and his priestly army had fallen upon the helpless inhabitants of the devastated city.

When Laomedon and most of his sons lay dead, then Heracles's few wits returned belatedly to him, and he mourned bitterly and shivered with fear because he had shed kingly blood. Contritely, he placed young Podarces, one of Laomedon's few living children, on the throne, and turned the priests back into their shrines; then he volunteered to stay long enough to mend what damage he had done.

Now, Podarces was the son of Laomedon and a Dardanian concubine. He had never dared raise his eyes as far as the throne. Indeed, he had already married, though he was still a very young man, and had a son named Æsacus by her; he had named her First Wife, because he had never thought to have another. The girl was one of the common people, and in no wise fit to sit beside a king. Therefore, when he was placed on the throne by Heracles, Podarces changed his name to Priam, or the 'redeemed one', which was a far better name for a king than the other, which meant merely 'bear-foot'. As Priam, he had no wife; so he gave the girl to Hyrtacus, one of his nobles, who was immensely flattered to bind his House to the royal one. Æsacus was sent away to a shrine close by the river Cebrene where he gained a good name for prophecy by his interpretations of dreams. He was soon chosen as the yearly sacrifice to the Goddess, and so he gained an easy Paradise.

Priam's way was now clear to make the young Xanthian heiress Hecabe, who had been promised to his older brother, his queen; and this he lost no time in doing.

Though he had no real grudge against Heracles, for he had brought Priam a kingdom where he had not hoped for one, still he prudently set spies to watch the madman, lest he lose his sanity again. While the rebuilding was going on, Jason took the opportunity to slip safely back through the Hellespont, his ship bearing its load of gold-soaked fleeces from Colchis. Heracles would have rejoined his ship, but he was prevented by Priam's guards and made to fulfill his promise.

He stayed at Troy only until Priam loosened his precautions, being taken up with the new wives and concubines he had fallen heir to. That the ascending son took over his father's women, excepting his own mother, of course, was a custom so old that its origins were forgotten. This has lately begun to fall into disfavor on the Western mainland; they have a song about it in which the boy takes the mother, too, and never finds an end to his ill luck thereafter. I think the Achaeans have hit two targets with one stone, as the saying goes; for not only do they disdain the Eastern style of kingship, they also look with a sour eye upon the Pelasgian king-sacrifice wherein his young replacement is called his son until he kills the king and inherits the queen's bed. But that is another song entirely, and does not belong in the tale of Heracles.

As soon as he was able, the giant crept away as silently as he could into the night. There was a low ridge to the west of the Citadel, along the shore close by Sigeum Bay. Here was where the Westerners customarily camped when they came to the Troad for the Fair, and it was not difficult for Heracles to force an early comer to take him back to Achaea. The price was no doubt right, that being that the captive seamen were permitted to continue living. Thereafter the ridge was given the derisive nickname of 'The Wall of Heracles', the joke being that he had flung it up as a breastworks, being mistakenly of the opinion that he could batter in the walls of Troy with rocks hurled from that distance.

Priam never saw him again, though tales of various stout fellows calling themselves by that name continued to circulate through all of the civilized world.

After he had heard the song, my father spent a day or two in contemplative thought. Then, having reached a further agreement with the Lelegian that he would reface the old wall with a layer of stone on the outer side only in the same offset pattern that made the otherwise huge and beetling fortifications attractive to the eye, my father planted a fig tree, sacred to the Goddess. It was a shoot from his holy orchards, and he planted it with his own hands where its shadow might fall on the weak portion of the walls and put them under her divine protection.

It was well that he did so, for in the season following the first flowering of the fig tree, the Achaeans came to the Troad.

They were not unannounced, of course. I remember well the deputation that arrived, for it was a memorable one of itself, beyond the personal meaning this event would have for me.

It was Menelaus himself who strode into Priam's council chamber; Menelaus of Sparta, the brother and right hand of Agamemnon who styled himself High King of all the Western mainland from the Isthmus to the Peloponnese. His beard was black, and his garments of snowy new wool, and on the hand resting on the fold of his cloak dyed with sea-purple were rings set with amethyst and massive with gold. His beard had been plaited and combed with oil so that it rippled in the light like a living thing, and his eyes, never still as they took in all the wonders and strengths and weaknesses of Priam's city, were cold and reflected no friendly gleam from the fire. He scorned the high, warm boots that were still being worn though it was early spring, and his feet were white and strange-looking in their Western sandals.

But he conducted himself with the easy grace of a man of integrity, as he acknowledged himself subject to my father during his stay in Troy, and accepted the place of honor by the fireside. The children of the royal family, those of us who were old enough to conduct ourselves properly before the people, stared at him covertly, under pretense of applying ourselves to our platters as the joint was carved and served. My brother Paris, as bronzed and gleaming in the firelight as a young god, served as page to Menelaus, giving him the first slice of the joint, keeping his and my father's cups filled with the delicate wine from the south that took a careful hand to press, and an equally cautious hand to dilute so that none of the fragrant bouquet was lost. It was always the custom of the royal Houses of the East for the sons of the host to serve in this manner; it did the guests of honor of the most subtle kind, and maintained in the young men the proper degree of humility so that they would never lose sight of the fact that they above all stood before the people and accepted the will of the gods. And though the same customs had prevailed time out of mind on the Western mainland, in recent years they had been allowed to fall into disuse. I saw clearly the look of thinly disguised contempt in Menelaus's eyes as he accepted his food and drink from a smiling, carelessly graceful Paris, and knew the reason for it. And then, as the evening progressed, I saw the contempt fade, to be replaced with a secret, speculative look that expressed itself in a narrowing about his dark and crafty eyes that returned no gleam of light. Now I was uneasy, because I did not yet know the reason for that look.

At length, having feasted and observed the circuitous amenities of a visit from one king to another, Menelaus got to the reason for this unexpected and difficult journey to Troy.

'There is a plague now raging in Sparta,' he said in his heavy voice. 'Old and young alike are perishing, and their faces darken and they choke on their own spittle. The doctors can do nothing. And no sacrifice there would calm the angry god who sent it. I sought advice at Delphi, and was told that the only sacrifice that would satisfy Apollo's wrath must be made at the shrine of Prometheus's son Lycus. And so I have come with many bullocks and bright horses from the herds that roam the mountains, to try to mollify Apollo's anger. It has been a toilsome journey, for the sailing season is yet early, and I have been a long time on my way.'

'The shrine of which the oracle speaks lies two days' journey north and west,' replied Priam, 'by the shores of the Marmoran Sea. I will send my son Paris with you to be your guide, for he knows the countryside well.'

Now there was a light in the Spartan king's eye, quickly damped, and I knew that he had achieved one of his objectives. 'Not all the horses I brought are destined for sacrifice,' the Spartan said. 'Troy is famous the world over for its horses, and it would do me honor if you would accept a few of the best of my beasts, which look insignificant beside those of Trojan breed. In addition, you would put me deeply into your debt if you would allow a few Tros stallions to cover a dozen of my best breeding mares, so that I may improve my own stock.'

This was immediately and generously agreed upon, as his speech and gifts had pleased my father; and the two kings parted soon afterward with many declarations of good will on either side.

But I was not easy within myself. That the Spartan's mission to Troy had nothing to do with any plague, real or otherwise, or the breeding of horses, I had no doubt. But what could his purpose be, and what could it have to do with my brother Paris?

Long after the rest of the household had gone to their beds, I remained in the shrine of the Maiden, praying before the Palladium which was her sacred image that she had been pleased to send down to us in the form of the gigantic thunder-stone. But for all of my pleadings and prayers, I got nothing but an empty voice repeating within me, 'Wait,' and again, 'Wait.'

And as if to seal my foreboding, my dream came upon me as soon as I had closed my eyes, when it had begun to seem that the torment had begun to go away and leave me free of it for weeks at a time. There was no sleep for either Orthia or me that night.

When they departed for the shrine, Paris and Menelaus seemed to be on the best of terms. Gone now was the older man's contempt, replaced with a smooth and oily solicitousness. Paris, who had never noticed the difference, was gay and confident in his youth and beauty of form. One might have thought them lovers, like those of the Sacred Band of Thebes, except that Paris stood winking at every girl whose eye he could catch. He was well known for his fondness for the lovely limbs and soft breasts of the girls in the Troy-town and shepherds' daughters in the hills.

But the sight of them, standing close together in a cart drawn by two of the horses destined for the useless sacrifice at Lycus's shrine, turned my mouth bitter so that I left the porch of the Palace before they had reached the bottom of the ramp.

When my mother Hecabe came after me to chide me for my poor manners, I refused the rebuke. The dream was still heavy upon me, and I felt my eyes dry and hot, sunken in my head. 'Let us all beware of Menelaus,' I said ominously, and quoted a saying of the market place. 'Trust an Achaean with one side of your mouth and whistle for a wind with the other. Either way, you're apt to get more than you bargained for.'

'It does not become you to be common, Cassandra,' admonished my father, who had come up by this time. 'It is well that the Western mainland opens negotiations with us in this way, for they have been the aggressors in this unfortunate business of the past several years. In fact, I am so cheered by this, I plan to send Paris with King Menelaus back to Sparta on the pretext of purifying him of that unhappy accident in the practice yard.'

Over a year ago, Antenor's young son Antheus had died from a fall. Antheus had playfully challenged Paris, who was much older of course, and Paris had good-humoredly indulged him with the wooden swords. Caught up in their game, Antheus failed to see a curb behind him that rimmed a fountain built there for the refreshment of the youths who came to perfect their skills in the yard. Down he went and his head broke where it hit the fountain's edge. As it was an accident of the purest sort, no guilt had been laid on Paris, though he had grieved as much as his lighthearted nature would allow.

'And what is to be his real mission, Father,' I asked now, 'since you have learned this trick from the Spartans?'

'What has gotten into you, daughter? You are rude and common this morning, and you look as if you have not slept for a week. But though you are ill-tempered, I see no harm in telling you. Paris is to further cement good relations between Troy and the mainland, of course. Do not think your father entirely the fool, Cassandra. I fully realize that there was another reason for Menelaus making the dangerous voyage to Troy.'

'Then send another in Paris's place!' I pleaded from the dim ache that blurred my eyes and set my tongue free to wag as it would. 'There is danger in this, and you should know it well! I can see that nothing but fire, and terror, and death will result! All night I prayed to Artemis to send a favorable sign, but she was silent.'

'That does not give you the right to dispute with your father,' my mother said sternly.

'Let her be,' said my father in his calm and gentle way. 'She was touched by the god at an early age, remember, wife, and bears the mark of it. One cannot expect the same restraint from one such as this, as from another. She is only mistaken, that is all.'

He turned to me. 'It is apparent that Menelaus has come to make amends for the Achaean raids with which we have been plagued for the past several years. That is the plague he meant, I am sure, and not any that is currently in Sparta. It is just an opening step, Cassandra, and must not be confused with darker motives. You have often seen merchants haggle with one another. This is just another form of haggling, but on a higher plane because it is between kings.'

I stared at him, my mouth open and my dignity forgotten. Could it be that he had not sensed the malice that lay behind every easy phrase, every glance from those dark, bottomless eyes? For a fleeting instant, when he spoke, I thought he might acknowledge a further motive than the question of the raids; now I knew better. Could he not realize that there was a dangerous game being played here, one that must be analyzed carefully, lest the wrong move cast game, board, and all into the Spartan's lap? But no; a single look at my father's aging, peaceful face, told me that he had no such apprehensions. Skilled though he might be in the benign manipulations of the market place, he was helpless as a babe in the deeper waters of political intrigue into which Menelaus was irresistibly drawing him.

And then, all at once across my eyes that were gritty from lack of sleep, there swept a waking echo of the terrible dream I had known just the night before. It seemed that Hecabe and Priam stood in the fire, and that their garments and flesh were consumed without their knowledge as they went their placid ways. A coldness hit me in my belly, like the griping of sickness, and spread until I thought my heart would surely freeze and stop within me. And then I knew – I *knew*! The god had touched me, and as clearly and coldly as I knew the chill that clutched at me, I knew which was the fatal piece on the game board.

Scarcely aware of what I was doing as the piercing numbness threatened to lock my very breath prisoner within me and the terror of my waking dream mingled with the reality around me, I pulled the pins from my hair, unable to bear the pull against my scalp, and let its living warmth spill in profusions about me. 'At least send another back to Sparta,' I gasped, falling down on my knees so that my hair covered Priam's feet. 'Not Paris! Please, not Paris!'

'Paris and Menelaus have formed a friendship which will be invaluable and this should not be overlooked when one king deals with another,' my father said soothingly, taking my elbows and coaxing me to my feet. Even in my frenzy I did not fail to catch the little significant glance that passed between my father and my mother, and how she turned at once and hurried through the doorway. It seemed only a heartbeat later when servants came hurrying in. 'But I will send Æneas with him, to please you.'

But this was like trying to fool a god who sees everything; Paris should not go at all, and no companion, no matter how level-headed, would change things. I heard myself wail aloud from my prison of ice and fire as I was led away. In that moment of coldness, as I saw the flames lick the wrinkled cheek of my father, I had seen foolish Paris enmeshed in whatever it pleased Menelaus to entangle him and then the flames had shot higher until it seemed the very roof of the Palace was engulfed.

All that night I wept in an agony of apprehension, and the dream never left me. When the chill left my body it was only to be replaced by a fever. I did not see the triumphant re-entry of Menelaus and Paris into Troy and I missed seeing my brother with Æneas set sail in the company of Menelaus of Sparta in the fine new ship that my father gave to his favored son. It bore the customary figurehead of the Lady of the Waves without which no Trojan ship was complete. But even this, had I known it, carried its burden of ominous portent. For, departing from custom, the artisan had portrayed the Lady with the infant Love-Spite in her arms, and everybody knows the blithe irresponsibility with which that one shoots here and there with his love-arrows.

'Why?' I found myself saying over and over, as I tossed restlessly on my bed, made lightheaded with the fever. 'Why could not my father have kept Paris at home where he belonged, and sent another in his place?' Hector, or Deiphobus, or even Helenus in his youth would have been better off in a strange land, at the mercy of a cunning king. But no, it was featherheaded Paris who went, leaving better men behind, and now I had no doubt that I had spoken with god's voice for the first time. Menelaus had deliberately selected Paris as his companion, and whether for good or for ill, the thing had been done.

Paris and Æneas were not the only deputation sent from Troy, as I learned after I arose from my sickbed. At last, despairing of me, Orthia had gone to the Palace physician and had obtained from him poppy leaves. Mingled in the mint which was all I would accept, even from her trusted hands, they brought me at last to a healing and dream-free sleep.

Some years before, Telamon the Æacid had stolen my aunt Hesione and carried her away with him, back to the Western mainland. There had never been a bride price paid, nor any mention of restitution for her, though she was my father's youngest sister and the last living child of Laomedon and Strymo, his queen. She had been but an infant during the time of Heracles's siege, and Priam had sheltered her with his own body when the earthquake came. Now, since Menelaus had opened negotiations between West and East, Priam felt that the time might be good to correct this old wrong. And so he sent Antenor, his brother-in-law, and his cousin Anchises, the ranking nobles of Troy, to Telamon's court virtually on the same tide.

But though they left only a little later, they were the soonest returned. In scorn, they had been summarily turned away from Telamon's court, being barely allowed to state their errand before they had been driven out by dogs and by Telamon's hangers-on who pelted them with bones and offal. Anchises still limped as a result of a dog's bite on the tender portion of his heel.

'Now,' Antenor said bitterly, 'I repent of my urging you to moderation and avoidance of the use of power where these Achaeans are concerned. That is the only thing they understand. We should arm and destroy them all within the moon!'

'Patience, brother-in-law,' counciled my father gravely. 'Let us not judge all Achaeans from the actions of one haughty household. Let us wait, instead, until we have the results of Paris's trip to Sparta.'

In this way he was able to still the rumblings of discontent and resentment at the treatment handed Troy's noblemen, but only for the moment. As the summer wore on and still no word came from Paris, the whispers began again in the City, though the Fair's splendors offered diversion enough for any civil disturbance of a lesser nature. Now I often saw one or the other, Anchises or Antenor, and others of my father's Council of Nobles, in brief and private conversations with him, and I noted the lines of worry and concern that daily etched themselves deeper into his aging face. It was apparent to me that he was holding his nobles in check only by his personal strength of will; unless Paris returned swiftly, he would be able to restrain them no longer.

Even little Troilus, my brother who was then eight or nine summers of age, sensed the disturbance. He took to spending much time with me, and I was glad of his company for he was still sweet and innocent, far removed from the man he would become too soon. I walked with him daily through the strange and exciting streets formed by the rows of pitched tents of the traders out on the Plain.

'Why does our father look so strange, Cassandra?' he would often ask, even as I tried to divert him with the spectacle of jugglers and tumblers performing for the crowds.

'He has a great and powerful City to look after,' I would answer lightly. 'I dare say you would have a wrinkle or two even at your young age if you had to endure this yearly bustle.'

But Troilus was a bright lad, far too sharp-witted to be put off for long. He allowed himself to be amused and entertained only so long, and then he would not be turned away.

'But really, Sister,' he persisted one day as we walked back on the dusty Plain toward the Citadel. 'Since Uncle Antenor and Great-Cousin Anchises returned, there has been a strangeness in the Palace. It makes me uncomfortable. And you know everything, Sister, since you are a prophetess. Please tell me.'

'Just because I sit in the shrine of Orpheus does not make me a prophetess, little one.'

'Everyone knows you are. Everyone knows the story of how you spurned Apollo's own love.'

'Oh?' I said carefully.

'Yes. They say that though you bear the touch of the god, your gift has been made worthless. Some even say that you are mad, because of your season of wandering, but I do not believe that. And I believe that you speak truly, even though Apollo himself spat in your mouth to make sure you would not be believed, when you would not go and live with him in his sun-palace of gold and jasper in return for his great gifts. I think my father is wrong when he doesn't believe you.'

How could such a story come from such innocent, untroubled lips? Where does this brightness of childhood go, I wondered, thinking of Paris, who had been just such a youngster once. But boys of this age know everything and I would do well to listen. Somehow, I was able to keep my face grave and still while Troilus happily poured out all the stories that were circulating through Troy about me. There was no meanness in the boy; he thought I knew them all beforehand, and I would not tell him otherwise for fear of stopping up the flow. But it was painfully apparent to me that I must know. I felt a premonitory icy thrill and knew that Apollo had had a hand in Troilus's artless outpourings.

Hoping that the image of fire would not also come to me, I drew the boy out with a comment here, a question there, trying to keep him from realizing the unquieting effect his story was having on me.

This, then, was the legacy of that wretched encounter with the false priest, Laocoön! Placed as he was, where all the high-born families of Troy sent their children to him to be educated, he was in a perfect position to provide the slanders against me with a fertile ground in which to flourish. How easy it must have been! A hint here, an innuendo there, a skillfully worded remark dropped as if by accident before some of the gossip-loving nobles' wives who had never understood the differences between me and other women anyway, and he could sit back and watch the infection grow. How he must have hated me, and feared me too. I grew dizzy with the thought.

At length, pleading a headache which was not all excuse, I sent Troilus back to the nursery, happily unaware that he had broken my world for me as surely as the potter smashes a spoiled jug. But I could not deny that he had done me a great service, for with this information, many puzzling things fell quickly and neatly into their places. Now I could understand the sideways glances of the Trojan matrons; the awe mixed with fear from the children of the nobles; the curiosity from the men who wondered at a girl who refused the embraces of a very god, and who could not help wondering if they would be so summarily rejected if Pallas had not stood in their way. I even remembered the look that had passed between my father and my mother that day I had seen the flames at them, and knew the reason for it.

So neat was Laocoön's trap that even my own dear parents had tumbled into it.

Now I sat down on my rug beside my bed, and pulled Bastos's warmth against my aching forehead. Tears began to roll from my eyes, and I let them come as they would, knowing Bastos the only living creature I could now dare weep before.

Some years before, there had been a scandal on the Second Terrace. Some concubine had lost her head over a captain of Priam's soldiers despite the fact that she belonged to the King. When it came to light, she was already with child by the man and so they forced her to take the medicine to disgorge it before its time. They executed the soldier, of course, and when the concubine saw her lover and her infant both lying dead she went out of her mind. It was a temporary thing, but when she would have come back to the world of the sane and whole, she was not permitted. If she visited the midden heap, the whispers ran that she was exhibiting herself shamelessly. If she stayed in her chamber and used the jar, the whispers had it that she was ashamed to have herself seen. There was nothing the poor creature might do that would place her on the side of the healthy, and either way she turned, she was wrong.

Now I wiped my eyes and got up from the floor, to go to my dressing table. I brought Bastos with me, and set him among the jars and bottles. I took my silver mirror and stared into it somberly. The reflection it gave back to me was that of a young woman whose facial bones showed too sharply, whose red hair escaped the coil the maid had wound it into, and which the ever-present wind had teased loose. My nose was too thin and still given to freckles. My wide, sea-blue eyes, now touched up with kohl, held my main beauty but they were pained and troubled. How could such a person, I thought, be the center of so much unrest, the object of such a malignant revenge? I had not even come into the beauty my nurse had promised me, and I felt myself very insignificant-looking indeed, far from the entangler of men my name promised. Could it really be as the stories said? Should I have submitted to Laocoön's embraces, so that through him Apollo himself might have come to me?

But no, I thought. Apollo had claimed me long before Laocoön had pushed forward his own base demand. Now Apollo, for his own reasons, allowed my world to work against me and stopped up the ears of those who should listen to me even as he had sent the tormenting dream and the frigid grip on my belly to remind me that a god's finger was upon me. In his own time, he would put things aright. That hope I must cling to, or I might go as mad as Troy now thought me.

'Well, Bastos, what do we do now?' I said aloud. Bastos closed his eyes and settled himself, paws tucked inward, among the mess of the dressing table. 'It is a sure thing that any protests I might put forward concerning my own sanity would be taken as sure proof of my madness. So how can we catch them in their own game?'

Impulsively, I dragged my jewel box toward me, rummaging through it until I had found what I sought. It was the single gold earring I had found in a shower of dirt and had kept hidden from all eyes but mine. For a while, I had anointed it with oil whenever I uncovered it from the bit of rag in which I kept it wrapped, and then I had nearly forgotten about it entirely.

Now I held the golden thing up so that it swung freely. It was a splendid, barbaric piece of work, though hopelessly outdated according to current fashions. It was nearly as long as one of my fingers and bore designs of serpents and fig leaves delicately incised with other symbols that had no meaning for me. On an impulse, I fastened it into one of my ears, and the uneven weight was strangely satisfying to me.

'There, now,' I said aloud, holding the mirror up and disarranging my hair further. 'That is how a mad seer should look, for no one in her right mind would wear such an old, unfashionable thing, and a single one of them at that.'

I stripped off all my other ornaments and dumped all such rubbish into a scarf and tied it securely into knots. I kept only the greenstone cup and the chain with the carved peach-colored flower, for they had come from far away and they had no connection with Troy. But everything else, the bracelets, the oak-leaf chain, the necklace of amber beads, I poured from the jewel chest into the scarf. I tucked it into a corner of a clothespress used only for little-worn garments. If the maids found them, they could have them. I no longer cared.

Putting away my jewels had, in a curious way, lightened me and liberated me from a burden that had weighed down my shoulders. I began to get caught up in the new game I was playing. I wiped all the paint from my face, the reddening on the lips, the flush on the cheeks, but left the blue on my eyelids. Then I took a bit of charcoal from the brazier and rubbed it along my lower lashes, knowing it would smudge softer than the kohl. I critically surveyed the results in my mirror. A touch more, and my face was magically transformed.

My skin, always the color of milk, now took on an unnatural pallor when compared to the reddening that was always given the faces of the Royal Kin; it would not do that any of us should look sickly or weak in front of the people. With the blue on my eyelids and the charcoal smudging beneath, my eyes seemed to burn from deep shadows. I touched the charcoal with a little of the blue, and the effect was complete. In a few moments I had transformed myself into a haggard wraith; and when I stared unblinkingly at myself, I could almost believe that I was as mad as rumor would have it that I was. The single barbaric earring swung insanely against my neck, and I smiled a pale-lipped and frightening smile.

I put my hand on Bastos's head. His eyes came open; they were a shade half-way between green and blue. He nibbled affectionately on my finger and then licked it.

'Let them say what they will, Bastos,' I told him, pleased because his loving lick had seemed like a message straight from Pallas Artemis, whom we both served. I stared again at my reflection, and knew that I had chosen the right path for myself. By making myself into what half of Troy thought me to be, I would free myself from Laocoön's baleful influence.

Now, if I liked, I could even approach Apollo openly, and could speak the god's truth as I felt it without fear of rebuke. The madman is protected by the same universal laws that keep harm from heralds, and supplicants, and bards. If it would open my father's ears to me, then let him think my mind had cracked beneath the weight of the god's hand. It was all one, if it would bring the day closer when I could strike back against Troy's enemies, and my own.

You see, I was still as big a fool as any in that cynical drama that was being enacted, and I thought that I could yet prove helpful.

5
HELEN

To my secret amusement, my new appearance brought about little outward reaction. A startled look, quickly wiped away, a gasp stifled in its inhalation were all that I received. That, and a grieving look from Orthia, who kept her own counsel. Only little Troilus was openly astonished, and he was drawn quickly into my conspiracy when I explained to him that it was a game I was playing.

Behind my back, I knew tongues were wagging, of course; and I could imagine the false commiseration with which some of the ladies of Troy discussed my open fall into madness.

But it was true that I was freer than ever before. It seems that once one has begun to have a name for madness, it never leaves. What I had now done seemed to have been long awaited by those around me, and now they accepted it with a kind of relief that they no longer had to be careful in my presence.

My timing had been fortunate, for scarcely had the talk begun to die down when lookouts ran into the City with the news that Paris's ship had been sighted off the isle of Lemnos.

My father could scarcely contain his relief and joy, and he bade the entire household wait formally for Paris on the Third Terrace and in the outer court when he should enter the City and begin the climb up the ramp to the Palace.

And then, when he appeared, a buzz of speculation arose, as quickly hushed as that which I had aroused, when it was seen that he had with him a woman. For a brief moment the thought came to me that it might be Hesione; but this woman had not the modest bearing and cloud-soft brown hair of my aunt. This one walked proudly, haughtily, and she moved her body restlessly even when standing still, as though an inner fire that could not be quenched burned within her. And when she moved, dimples winked from everywhere; her knees, her hands, her cheeks. Even her back was dimpled, as I discovered later. There were no angles and planes on her body, as there were on mine.

Everything was firmed and rounded and polished and seemed to invite the touch of a man, any man. The sun glinted on her hard gold hair and as she approached I could see the sharp curve of her lip which could so easily turn to a scornful curl, and the flash of her proud eyes as she looked about her at her new home.

Good manners forbade anything but a warm and courteous greeting for Paris, Æneas, and any companions they might have brought with them; any explanations would be called for and given later, in privacy. But even the thick door of my father's room could not hold back all the shouts and accusations. Hecabe ran out crying once, only to return a little later grim-mouthed. Paris had always been her favorite, and she was prepared to stand up for him, even in this latest folly. As for me, though the woman's name had not been given, I could guess.

All afternoon the frightful row continued, and servants crept white-faced and soft-footed past the door, not daring to stop and listen for fear someone would come precipitously out and catch them at it. Nobles came and left and still I lingered nearby, wanting to know if my guess had been accurate.

But I was not invited in; my opinion remained unasked for. I had to restrain my curiosity until that evening in the Hall, when the song my brother gave us answered forever what questions might have been asked, and sealed our fate as surely as if the City had fallen that night. I have often wondered if Paris knew at the time the full consequences of his acts. I do not believe that he did, nor did he know the road upon which he was setting our feet. But if he had been an intriguer from the most subtle court, he could not have done it any more surely.

But though its effects were ultimately those that I had foreseen all along, I must admit that at the time it was a wonderfully funny and ribald song, and that it made all of us laugh – even those of us who could see beyond the laughter – and won for Paris the approval of the lesser nobles and the wildly enthusiastic support of the people, among whom the story ran like a brush fire. They loved a good joke as well as any, and they felt that the Achaeans were long overdue a daring touch of the sort that Paris had made.

And this is the song that he sang.

One day, while he was minding his cattle and his own business on Mount Gargarus, the highest point of Ida, and thinking to himself about Oenone, the nymph who had recently admitted him to being her year-lover, three beauties appeared to Paris out of nowhere. From their shining appearance, unnatural height, and overwhelming loveliness, he knew himself to be in the presence of the Goddess in her three radiant forms, Mother, Nymph, and Maiden. With them, as he was now able to discern with his dazzled eyes, was a youth bearing a herald's wand; and so he knew the Ladies to be accompanied by Hermes Herald.

He abased himself in the dust, wondering whatever fate awaited him that four of the Immortals should visit him. Hermes came forward, his feet dancing lightly in his winged sandals and with a touch brought Paris upright and placed and apple made all of gold in his hand.

'There has been an argument in Heaven,' the Herald said, 'because of a piece of mischief some naughty Sprite has worked. As you can see, this bauble is inscribed "To the Fairest"; and so naturally, all three of these goddesses want it for their own. Since no one in Heaven could settle the dispute, it was decided that you should award it as you saw fit.'

'I?' exclaimed Paris. 'I am only a mortal, and somewhat stupid into the bargain. I am sure to make a botch of it and then I will have everyone angry with me. Award the thing yourself, for I want nothing to do with it!'

But the goddesses all came clamoring about him, promising that they would not be vexed in the least even if they should lose. Their perfumes made his head whirl, already dizzy from the proximity of so much divine beauty, and his will was not equal to the task of refusal.

And so, dazed with the honor, Paris found himself agreeing to be the judge of the most unusual contest of beauty and loveliness ever to be held.

'If I must do this thing,' he said now, brisk after he had made his decision, 'it must be done correctly or not at all. You must come to me one at a time, and unclothed; for it is well known among us mortals that a becoming dress may disguise some flaw in the body beneath.'

At this, there was some pouting and squabbling amongst the Three, for each of them wanted to keep some small thing on her person that might be to her advantage. But Paris was firm, and so they had to agree, for they wanted the golden apple even more. Then Hera laid aside her wand of power, Aphrodite took off her famous magic girdle that made everyone fall in love with the wearer, and Athene removed her helmet, self-consciously ruffling her close-cropped curls that were appropriate for a warrior but not becoming on a woman.

Hera approached Paris first, for she had insisted on this right because she was the Queen of Heaven.

'Turn around slowly, if you please,' directed Paris, his voice full of admiration. 'My Lady, if you will forgive my saying so, those who term you Crone are either blind or ignorant, or possibly both.'

'The title does not displease me,' replied Hera serenely, 'for I can appear as I wish, being young maiden or old hag if it suits me, for I am the most powerful of all the goddesses. Power is mine to give, as well. If you judge me fairest, I will make you overlord of all the Eastern lands, and the richest man who ever lived.'

'Please do not attempt to bribe me, my Lady!' exclaimed Paris virtuously. 'Thank you, and please ask Hermes to send along the next goddess.'

Then came Athene, with her athletic, buoyant stride.

'You are not familiar to me, my Lady,' said Paris. 'Would you please tell me who you are?'

'I am the Maiden of the Achaeans, and Zeus's own daughter. Athene Spearmaiden, I am called. Here in the East, you know me as Artemis, but we are not the same.'

'Of course, I think I understand. Though maidens do not usually interest me, Zeus-born or not, except for bringing to bed. Would you please hold your hands away? I cannot see, which I am bound to do though it distresses your virgin modesty. That is why I usually prefer a girl whose field has already been plowed; she is not reluctant to add another furrow.'

'If I had stripped for a race or other games, it would all be as one. By the way, if you select me, I will make you the greatest warrior and the wisest man who ever lived, because these things are mine to give.'

'I am a herdsman, not a soldier, and am generally thought spoiled and foolish, so that I would have no use for wisdom. My father, King Priam, rules wisely enough for me, and my ambitions do not go very high, as I am not the heir an any case. But I promise you that I will consider your claim to the apple fairly. Now, may I see the last?'

Aphrodite was already near, and now she came so close that her breasts brushed across his bare chest and she giggled, so that he smelled her lily-scented breath.

'Surely you recognize me, don't you, Paris? I am Aphrodite of the Waves, the Lady of Troy, and you have loved me since infancy. I am the same, East or West, and I am everywhere, for my sole function is to make love. Do you know, I said to myself as soon as I saw you that you are possibly the most handsome man I have ever seen. But what a waste, to spend your time herding cattle and mooning over some trivial tribal nymph! You should marry a woman as beautiful as you are handsome. Now let me see – of course! Helen of Sparta! She is as beautiful as I am, and nearly as passionate, and she of all women would make you a suitable wife! Besides being beautiful, she is of noble lineage. Zeus himself would not be ashamed to call her daughter. And to think that she is wasted on that dull Menelaus. She married him only because his brother is High King in Mycenae, for all the nobles in Achaea were after her. But that makes no difference at all, for you can have her if you want her.'

'I am half in love with her already!' cried Paris. 'And it happens that I am to return to the West with Menelaus himself, who has been a visitor in our city.'

'Well, what could be easier, then?' cooed Aphrodite. 'When Helen sees you, she is bound to fall in love with you; and even if she should have some strange idea about faithfulness to her stupid husband, I will see to it that she soon thinks otherwise, for it is my divine business to arrange matters of this sort. You have my oath on it, if you wish.'

Without a second thought, Paris handed her the apple and went away whistling happily.

And now, true to Aphrodite's promise, here he stood, and with him stood Helen of Sparta who had thrown aside her home, her family, her children, her position as Queen of Sparta to come with him, a younger son of Priam who had not many prospects, but who could offer her all the love she could desire.

With a flourish, Paris finished his song, happy in the flood of laughter and applause that greeted it. Even I smiled and clapped my hands, for it had been very funny and audacious.

I could not help looking around my father's Hall, curious about the reactions of others to Paris's song. There sat Hector, wiping tears of laughter from his eyes with the hem of his wife's himation. Deiphobus applauded heartily, but through the smiling mask of his face I thought I could detect some reflection of the desire that shone plainly in Paris's eyes whenever he looked at the Spartan. Helenus, Pammon, Antiphus – even little Troilus who had been allowed to stay up to hear the song – all showed indulgent good humor toward the singer.

Then I looked at my father, the King. There was relief in his eyes even as he held out his hands in formal welcome, and I knew that the uproar that afternoon had resulted in this staking of everything on one throw of the dice. If the nobles and the people had not accepted Helen, it would have been a grim business indeed. But as it was, they saw it as a joke; the return of stroke for stroke. After all, hadn't the Achaeans done as much when they stole Hesione? Paris had but evened the score, and the fact that the lovely Helen had been his mainland host's wife only added spice to the gibe.

I knew, of course, the meaning of the Apple of Destiny, even if many of the listeners did not and thought it only a pretty conceit. This was the device the Achaeans used to keep themselves reminded of the pledge of the Royal Kin everywhere; once it had been a noble thing indeed, with a ritual involving a king's death being given twice, but the Achaeans scorned it nowadays as being so much religious rubbish. So low had it come in their estimation that it could be used as a bauble to be squabbled over.

I knew, also, that the goddesses Paris had slighted were both Achaean in their origins, for the Hera of the song had little in common with the Hera we knew. They would not quickly forget that they had been insultingly passed over for the sake of a woman from Sparta, and at the behest of Trojan Aphrodite at that! There was more at work here than an amusing song might indicate on the surface.

Now, of course, was Paris's tardy return explained. He had been in no hurry to resume any kind of life of responsibility, when a long voyage home offered so many delights to explore. He had not even stopped to wonder at the fact that Menelaus had offered no pursuit. If he had, Paris would not have arrived home at all.

I looked at Æneas, who had witnessed Paris's blatant thievery, and his eyes were somber though his lips smiled. Yes, there was more, far more to the story than Paris's lighthearted song would indicate; and then with that chill in my belly that was becoming increasingly familiar, I knew that Paris had not been the one responsible for the making of his song. Why had I thought for a moment that he was clever enough for that?

Of course not. There was far too much knowledge and deep understanding of Achaean customs displayed in the mockery of it for Paris, who barely understood the Trojan forms on religious days. One had only to look at Helen, where she sat holding a cat on her lap in the firelight, and to see the identical creamy smile on her face to know from whose quick brain the measures had come. It had probably not been difficult, during the long and active nights, to convince Paris that he had called it into being himself. She had judged well. The people now accepted her because of it.

And then, though I tried to hold it back, the fire blazed up out of my icy bowels and seemed to envelop Helen where she sat.

I had thought myself so well lately, I remember thinking fleetingly before the horror overtook me.

'The fire!' I screamed, and all the laughter stopped as though a lid had been clamped over it. 'Destruction and death are the bride gifts from Helen of Sparta! Send her back, my father, send her back before she brings the fire upon us!'

There were hands on me. The stewards had come up and caught my arms on either side.

'Forgive us,' I heard my father say in the shocked hush that lay over the room. 'She is not well. A god lives in her and her wits are sometimes disorganized and she speaks of nothing but death and fire at those times. She meant no unhospitality, I am sure. She will be better tomorrow.'

I shook off the unwelcome stewards and darted across the room to where Æneas sat. 'You know, don't you? I saw your face. You saw through the song!' But he shrank away from me, and I saw fear in his eyes.

'Are you all fools?' I shrieked. 'Will you leave off soothing the Spartan woman long enough to know that this whole thing is a Western intrigue? It is an excuse, nothing more, and it will have the Achaeans at our doorstep before we know it!'

'Cassandra, calm yourself,' said my father sternly. He came to me and took me by the hand. Over his shoulder, I saw Helen. The cat had leaped from her lap, frightened by the commotion I had made, but her pointed little rosy fingers continued to stroke her thighs, as if they were in love with the flesh under them. Strange she looked, and outlandish, in her Western clothes. She never adopted Trojan dress for herself, and she remained the exotic beauty from across the waters all the time she was in Troy.

'You bitch!' I shouted at her. 'You whore! No, worse than that, for the whore at least gives value received for payment given. You give nothing. You only take. What payment have you received, that you and Menelaus and probably Agamemnon as well connived at fooling Paris and tricking him into taking you away with him?'

'Cassandra!' cried my father sharply.

'Father, for nine long years we have suffered the Achaeans' raids along our coastline,' I said, tears beginning to run down my face. 'It made you strengthen the City's walls. But they are not strong enough to turn back an invader's tide, if he is determined enough. Can you not see that the forces are gathering even now? They will not see it as a lighthearted joke. It will not matter to them that it is payment in kind for Aunt Hesione. It is their great excuse! And even as they sail, you listen to a song that the Spartan probably made up herself to further bemuse you. Please, Father! Send her back! Send her back! Ai! Ai! The flames!'

The phantom fire that only my eyes could see now seemed to consume the hair from his head and the flesh from his face so that I pleaded with a grinning death's head. I could no longer bear it. Yanking my arm from his grasp, I ran crying through the Hall, screaming and shrieking as I ran without thought through the echoing corridors, seeking to outdistance the flames that paced me and consumed everything behind me.

When my throat tore and I tasted my own blood, I fell; and then the fire came up and burned me away to nothing.

BOOK TWO
THE WAR

6

WARRIORS BEFORE TROY

They came, of course; how could they not? One day the Plain was empty of all save the rubbish of the departed Fair, and the next the sea was black with their ships and the bay of our landing began to be scarred by the drawing of pitch-darkened hulls up onto it.

With others of our royal household, I stood in the shadows of the north porch of the shrine of Thymbraean Apollo on the Plain half-way to the shore. With a kind of drained wonder, my brothers and sisters stared outward at the gathering forces, so awesome in their numbers that it would take a clever scribe to count them all. For myself, I watched Helen's face and attended closely to the tones of her voice instead; there would be time enough to look at our enemies, later on.

Now Helen, breathing clouds of perfume, came close to my father so that she might read for him the sail emblems of his opponents with her farsighted eyes.

'Yonder are Boeotians, from across the Isthmus,' she said, pointing. 'And Locrians, led by Ajax the Runner! There must be forty ships of them! And there is the serpent-emblem of the other Ajax, who fights behind a towering ceremonial shield it would exhaust another man to lift. I see the emblems of the Euboeans, who wear their hair clipped short before and grown long behind in a bushy mane. And there are men from the Argolid. The royal sign of Tiryns is not among them, so the king must have stayed behind, and noble Diomedes would be their leader. Now I see Spartans, and Menelaus must be there. With them are Mycenaeans; do you see that ship with the golden lion figurehead gleaming so brightly? That is Agamemnon, the High King, and he commands all the leaders of all these hosts of men. There are formidable opponents facing you, King Priam.'

Her voice prattled on, never ending, telling of Odysseus and Nestor, of Antiphos and Tlepolemos, and most of all of Achilles with his mighty band of Myrmidons. But I no longer listened to the content of her words. I had heard enough when she declined to number herself with those threatened by the massing army before us. Instead, I watched her face, seeing the proud gleam of her eye, hearing the boastful undertones in her voice.

Calchas, the high priest of Apollo, appeared in the doorway behind us.

'There is a deputation of Achaeans gathering,' he reported respectfully to Priam. 'Let us send for them, rather than let them stride arrogantly into Troy unannounced.'

'We must not be caught goggling at them like rustics,' my father agreed. 'Take a herald's wand and go to them, and conduct them to me in a seemly manner.' And so saying, he led his household to where the mule wagon waited to carry us swiftly back into the City. Then he sent the women to their quarters and took his warrior sons with him into his council chamber so that they might wait and receive the Achaeans with dignity.

For myself, I would rather have jumped from the Great Tower than go meekly off to my room as did Helen and my mother and sisters. And while I waited quietly, unnoticed in a corner, I let myself dwell upon the character of Helen.

Helen's loyalty is as false as glass beads when the gilt has worn away, I thought.

I had made it a point to get to know as much of her as I could during the weeks before the Achaeans arrived on our shores. As I had hoped, she paid little attention to me, thinking that my wits were too scrambled for her to bother. And soon, she no longer troubled herself to keep up any sort of pretense before me. She would bathe, or pare her nails, or attend to any of a thousand and one intimate tasks in my presence as if I were as stupid as the doorpost. If this had not been my design, I might have been angry.

However, this much I had to give her; she was truly beautiful. Everywhere there was flawless perfection; the delectable turn of her cheek, the short, straight beauty of her nose that made hardly an indentation as it met her brow. The sharply chiseled lips that often wore a scornful curl were none the less beautiful for it and her great eyes were covered by smooth and glossy lids under which she peered out from time to time, in response to the ardent glances that came her way from every side. Even her little ears, half-concealed by ringlets which were artfully allowed to escape the hair that had been piled into a rich and lustrous mound atop her head, seemed to invite a lover's whisper.

But through some joke on the part of the god who made her,

what lay within fell far short of what covered the outside.

I had early a glimpse of her brazen turn of character in the goods and chattel she chose to bring with her to Troy. Though she had abandoned her daughter, Hermione, a child of nine summers, she had brought her six-year-old son Pleisthenes with her, presumably because Menelaus might have caused harm to befall the boy because of her unfaithfulness. The boy could only have been a handicap, for she was never able to say no to love-making, and getting rid of the child must have been a burden at times. In addition, she had looted whatever the Spartan palace treasures as suited her, and had gold to the value of three talents. The bars had the mark of Apollo inscribed on them, and so I could only believe that she had caused them to be stolen from the shrine. The closest I could come to unraveling her motives was that the boy was to demonstrate her fertility and the gold was for her comfort, in case Paris proved stingy-handed.

And there was the further matter of the comb. I had one, of course, for I was modern in those days and such a useful novelty appealed to me. My mother, Hecabe, being conservative in her ways, declined to use one, preferring to comb her hair with her fingers as she had always done. I still remember how her twinkling hands untangled the least snarl and wove the lustrous braids, one over each ear, more quickly and neatly than any maid could have managed. My comb, bought at one of the stands at the Fair, was of ivory with a slim band of silver along the back. Helen's, by contrast, was of that rare clear wood that smells eternally sweet. Well-loved and indulged is the woman whose husband gives her a fragment of such wood to encase in a filigree and hide between her breasts. She wheedled Paris to commission it from an Assyrian trader, who seemed shocked at the request. It had a spine of gold, with doves along it and lilies at either end, both signs of Aphrodite. Later, Paris had the Palace smith make her a mirror of gold-washed bronze to match it.

But it was among her serving-women that I found the most damning evidence of Helen's being merely an empty, vain, shallow bit of bait held out to an equally shallow Paris to provide the excuse for the war that had now come knocking on our very gates. There was one in particular, a tall and slender woman whose proud bearing bespoke of a life not spent in servitude. Quietly, when an opportunity presented itself, I questioned her.

'I was not born a slave,' she replied, gazing at me calmly with dry and expressionless eyes. 'Nor would I now be where I am if my son were still living. I am Æthra of Troezen, the mother of

Theseus, lately King of Athens. While my son lived, Troezen enjoyed immunity from Agamemnon and Menelaus; when he was dead they came against us, having nothing further to fear from Athens. In revenge, Menelaus kept me alive and gave me to Helen. And so, now I apply her paint and comb her hair and dry her body after her bath, where I used to have women of my own to tend me. Nor was I the only recipient of the revenge the brothers took against the Athenian king who had kept them from overrunning all of Hellas. Here is Thesadië, her only crime was that she happened to be the sister of Theseus's great friend, Perithous.' And she pointed to a younger woman whose bearing was also out of the ordinary. This one had not learned the dignified resignation of the former Queen of Troezen and quick tears of humiliation welled in her eyes.

'I cannot correct this wrong,' I said. 'Not yet. The people think me mad and perhaps in some ways I am. But I have not gone so far into the world of the unsound mind that I cannot be indignant on your behalf. This one thing I can promise you. No one, whether horse or ox or slave or servant, is mistreated in Troy. If ever your mistress breaches this rule, you have only to tell me, and mad or not, I'll plead your case to the King himself.'

'Thank you,' said Æthra gravely, and in spite of her slave's garment and the worn beauty of her once-lovely face, she seemed to address me as one daughter of the Royal Kindred to another. And I knew that we were of the same Kindred, though descended from different families of men; further, I somehow knew that the former queen was aware of how much of my 'madness' was pretense, and perhaps had even divined the reason for it.

Impulsively, I reached out and grasped her hand, placing my forehead on it for a moment; and when I straightened up, I saw the tears in her deep eyes that had not been there before.

I was rudely jolted out of my reverie by the stamp of men's feet in the corridor. In another second they had burst through the door, and I recognized Menelaus with two other nobles and a small armed following.

'We meet again, Priam of Troy!' exclaimed Menelaus harshly. 'It is a far different meeting from that first one, when no member of your family had offered a contemptible crime against mine.'

'Do not speak about crimes against your household, while my sister Hesione is still held captive in the house of Telamon,' my father responded mildly.

'Captive?' echoed Menelaus, his eyebrows rising elaborately. 'I had only heard that she is there of her own will, through lust for the body of her Æacid host. Surely, if she wishes to return to your hearth, all you would have to do would be to send an embassy to Telamon, for an unwilling woman in his bed would be of no joy to him.'

Now my father's brows met in the middle and a single deep line marked the center of his scowl. 'As to that, King of Sparta, we will speak no further, but will discuss the errand that has brought your own embassy to me.'

'With me stand Odysseus and Palamedes, stout Achaean champions both. We are sent by our overlord, Agamemnon of Mycenae, to ask for the return of the body and goods of my wife Helen, whom your son Paris has seduced away from the side of her rightful husband. We have come with men and ships in plenty to reinforce our claim, should you prove obstinate. What is your reply?'

Around my father, his sons and certain of his Council of Nobles stood, their faces black and clouded with their rage. Paris was absent, and I found myself wondering what his reaction to the studied insults of the Achaeans would have been. But there was no question as to the responses of the men who faced the deputation; there was murder in nearly every eye.

'I say you should take your ships and your men and return to whatever kennel bred you,' growled a deep voice.

'Who spoke?' demanded Odysseus, glaring about him.

'I did,' said my oldest brother, bringing his vast bulk into view. 'I am Hector, the Guardian of the City. On the Western mainland, that would make me War Leader. And I say to you that you have no honorable claim, until such outstanding charges against you should be cleared away. Go, and tell your craven brother that Helen remains in Troy.'

'I mark you well, Hector. I only hope that we should meet some day on the battlefield.'

'There will be no question of that. I am not one to hang back like an Achaean, and have to be prodded along to the fight with the sharp end of a spear.'

Both Odysseus and Palamedes took a step forward, their hands on the hilts of the swords that swung from tooled neck straps. Menelaus held them back, however, for even with their guard, the Achaeans were greatly outnumbered.

'Pay no attention to these Trojan brayings,' he said. 'They are as empty of intelligence as the outcry of any other ass and are meant only to tempt you into losing your heads so that they may fall upon you and kill you here and now, without waiting for the honor of the battlefield.'

'There are some of us who would preach moderation,' said Antenor's calm voice. 'Even though we were ill repaid for it when we made the tedious journey to Telamon's palace which you suggested, only to be pelted with garbage and have the dogs set at our heels. Is this typical of Western hospitality?'

Now Menelaus's face was the image of concern and solicitousness, overdone just that fraction that makes it into a mockery. 'Can this be true, my friend?' he inquired tenderly. 'Perhaps Telamon was not aware of who you were. Yes, that must be it.'

'Do not demean yourself with jesting,' replied Antenor grimly. 'And do not try my patience further, for I think that I am the only one here who would be against killing you out of hand, and that only because the good manners that should be known all through the world would forbid such a thing.'

'Yours is not the voice I wish to hear in any case,' said Menelaus, abandoning his mask of considerateness. 'What say you, Priam? Yours is the only vote that means anything in the long run, though you have been conspicuous in keeping quiet while others of your pack of jackals have taken their turns at worrying us. But we have taken as little note of their yelping and yapping as the lion does. We are under the protection of the Lion of Mycenae. Come, Priam! You have kept silent long enough!'

'I say,' said my father, and then he coughed and reached for the slim pitcher of wine that was always kept handy in the council room. 'I say,' he repeated when he had washed out his throat, 'that Helen stays.'

Menelaus and his men stared long and blackly at the King, and then without another word turned on their heels and stalked out the way they had come. Calchas turned and went with them, and it was plain to see that he had cast his lot with what seemed to be the stronger side. The men let him go without a murmur.

But I could not stay in my dark corner any longer. 'Why did you not give her to them?' I cried, rushing toward my father and falling at his feet. 'It is what she wants anyway. They are bound to fight us, you know that, so why not at least force them to state their purpose baldly and not hide behind a woman's skirts? If you sent Helen to them, they would have to own before the world that they have come to conquer, and to steal, and burn, and kill – not to rescue an errant wife!'

Tears ran from my eyes, and with all my being I tried to hold back the vision of flames that had come upon me at other such times. Then my father looked down at me where I crouched beside his chair. An absent smile played around his aging lips, and he put out his hand and stroked my hair.

'It is always fire and death, is it not, Cassandra?' he said musingly. 'Ah, well, it comes from the god, though to what purpose I do not know. I have seen nothing to indicate that Helen is not happy with us. And in any case, do you not think that I know the fighting is inevitable? For nine long years I have lived in dread of this day, which Achilles and his men coursed along our shores, even threatening some of our best men on Ida in his daring. And now that it is here, all that is left to us is our pride. And for our pride, Helen must stay, whether she will or nill. We can delay the fighting no longer, and even that appeasement would not make the ships go away back home meekly, like lambs into the pen. Our pride you see, is all that we have left. And so we will keep it.'

My father was no longer looking at me, and I do not think that he was conscious that he was speaking his mind to a daughter whom most of the nobles thought incapable of understanding. I doubt that he even remembered that he still stroked my head. I might have been his favorite dog, or a house cat come with a freshly-killed mouse and looking for praise; I might even have been the arm of the chair under his hand for all the notice he took of me, or of anybody else in the room.

And then he straightened up, a king once more. 'Send for runners,' he directed. 'Let us begin at once to summon our allies to our aid.'

7

CITY IN SIEGE

Time out of mind it has been the custom in the Troad to sacrifice and pray that Zeus send us a mild winter, if it pleased him. An entire day in the autumn festivals is set aside for this sole purpose, and bullocks are led three times around the City walls and then burnt whole with no portion reserved for men. Now, for the first time, Trojans prayed for a hard and severe winter. And Zeus, astonished at the inconsistency in the nature of mortal men, sent one as mild as any that I could recall.

We watched all through that unseasonably gentle winter, waiting for the cold, wet, biting winds that refused to come, while the Achaeans settled themselves into the section of the Plain that was to be their home until the warm winds should return, bringing with them the season for fighting. From behind our walls, and occasionally from the safety of the Pastoral Shrine, we could mark them as they found such anchorage and beaching for their ships as they might. There is precious little in the way of sheltered bays and inlets where it is safe to cast the anchor stone; with grim pleasure we watched as a number of black-hulled ships attempted to put into the attractive and inviting bay directly across the Hellespont. We knew, of course, that beneath the smiling water there were spears of rock like sharp and hungry teeth waiting to rip out the bottom of any vessel whose captain did not know the few safe places to go. We would have cheered if all the pitch-darkened ships with their red eyes painted on the bows had tried to make Death Bay at the same time and had gone down together. But no, when one ship had fed the waiting rocks, the rest turned and ran. They built the dead captain and his crew a hero's shrine on the tallest headland overlooking Death Bay. I do not know what his name was, for they renamed him Protesilaus because he had 'gone before' the people to become the first man to fall in the siege of Troy.

Most of the ships lay empty, drawn up on the shores of Imbros and Lemnos and even as far away as Samothrace, though it has no harbor worth mentioning. There, it was said, Agamemnon held reserves waiting to descend upon us in the name of Poseidon. He is strong there, and has an old shrine on the highest part of the mountain. Later, many would say that he sat there, overlooking the battles even as Zeus sat on Gargarus.

Those ships which had served as ferries to bring the Achaeans to their camp on the shore were drawn up on it now, sullying and scarring it with their presence. It was odd, how the most rapacious trader had been welcomed, and even the ones who came from tribes that customarily had their only baths from the midwife's hands seemed to have defiled it less.

A distance inland, between the beds of the Simois and the Scamander, they built their own wall, fortifying it as strongly as they were able to make it, with breastworks and ditches. The songs one hears nowadays would have it that the wall was a hastily built thing, thrown up in a single day when Achilles deserted the field; but I saw it in its building, all through the winter.

It was a sorry thing, to be sure, beside the splendor of the great walls of Troy. In its time, though, it was strong enough in its way to discourage any who would come upon them unawares. It is true that the gods of Troy did not consent to its building, for the Achaeans disdained to consult them; it is gone now, demolished even before Troy fell, but it did its work beforehand. It was a palisade structure, of rough-hewn trunks of trees set like stakes into the ground. We were careful to avoid thinking highly of ourselves for our superior fortifications; we still remembered the Song the Heracles. The strongest wall a man can build, even if it be crafted of Hittite iron, will crumble beneath a god's touch, while one built of the down from a nightingale's breast will endure if a god shields it with his hands.

You must not suppose that the Trojans were sitting idle and smug behind their walls while the Achaeans were making their camp as snug and secure as they might against the coming winter and the war to follow with the spring. Indeed, I had seldom seen the City so bustling except at Fair time.

First, there was a horse caravan to be organized and the women with their belongings to be packed up and moved out of the City. Priam had wisely decided to send the most part of the women from the Second Terrace and such others of the City and the Troy-town who wished to wait out the war in comparative safety, down to the Stronghold that lay deep in a fold of the Scamander Valley a goodly distance to the south. All over the City, one could hear the wails from the women's quarters; but I noticed that most of them were spry and agile enough in scrambling onto their piles of goods and bales of clothing heaped into the carts. These were the ones who could contribute nothing to the welfare and defense of the City, but who must be kept safe so that the allies from their homelands could be persuaded to come to their defense. And in clearing out these useless women who would only be mouths to feed, Priam made room for those same allies whose arrival we waited daily.

The royal family stayed, of course. It would have been scandalous for the Queen and her children to have deserted their King. For that matter, none of us would hear of it, not even Polyxena who was of a delicate and timid nature.

Now the only other people in the City besides Priam's sons and Hecabe's daughters were the craftsmen, the smiths and armorers and slaves enough to cook and attend the warriors who would live where the wives and concubines had lately stayed. These we put to digging up the flooring in houses and setting pithoi, those enormous jars that could hold a standing man, into the floors so that the mouths of the jars came to floor-level. Then, when the dirt was packed into the spaces and the flagstones replaced, all that one needed to do was pry up the lids and dip into the contents. There was some talk of sinking another cistern under the flagstone plaza just inside the wall near the Water Tower, but the one near the East Gate seemed adequate when counted with the enormous, ever-flowing well in the Tower itself.

There were two more small cisterns once used by the purple-factory, when the guild used to ply their mysterious trade of rendering the murex into the lustrous purple dye for which rich men were willing to pay much gold; and these were cleaned of their accumulations of leavings so that they could be used by men. The purple-makers had fled with the rest, of course, and now there were no longer any crowds of children to play among the fascinating piles of discarded shells that they allowed to collect on the avenue until Priam forced them to clear the way. He was disinclined to disturb them, lest they take their profitable trade elsewhere, and would wait until the piles interfered with foot traffic and the people began to complain. A heap of shells lay there now, dead and colorless in the sun, and the factory itself lay open for the curious to go and look for the secrets of the purple dye in the empty rooms. We turned the entire factory into a storehouse, with pithoi piled upon pithoi. There would be no more carts and wagons bringing the murex to be unloaded into the East Gate.

Nor would many of us ever taste again those succulent shellfish murex-hunters would bring along with their more precious cargo, and upon which we had made many a meal in other, brighter days. Now it was corn, and wheat and barley when we could get it, and wine and oil siphoned into jars and hidden away under the floors of our homes. Nearly every house held its hoard of precious foodstuffs snugly packed underfoot.

Now, while we waited, the sound of spades in earth and the tap-tap as slaves refitted the flagstones were all that one could hear in the echoing avenues of the deserted City.

How glad I was that I was my father's daughter, and had not been sent away to the Stronghold that was perched atop a steep and unassailable hillside, along the foot of which ran the Scamander in its deep and sheltering stream. I could not have borne being away from the heart of the conflict. My overactive imagination would have driven me mad indeed with its workings in the paucity of news. But most of all, I was a Trojan; this was my city, and I would have never left it willingly, even though it might be tumbling down around my ears.

And then the allies began to arrive, first a few and then many so that within a matter of days the City was more crowded with war than it had ever been in the days of peace.

In the van was Æneas with his Dardanians. In the first days following the Achaean deputation's visit, he had hastened along the road to where his and Priam's kinsmen lived. They came willingly, those whose business was soldiering first, with others to follow soon after. Then came Adrastos and Amphios, leading a band of men from the western shore of the Marmoran Sea, and marching them briskly under the very shadow of the Achaeans' wall, to make us all cheer at his audacity. Pandaros was next, from the Æsepus Valley, the upper basin of the Scamander. His men had met the refugees on the way, and had lingered to escort them to the Stronghold and see that they were safely established therein. Then, after having provisioned them well with game, they resumed their march into Troy.

Now came Pelasgians from Larissa in the southern Troad, famous for its olives. Others came from Lyrnessos, Pedasos, Chryse, Cilla, those remnants of the places Achilles had raided during previous years, thirsting for their chance at revenge.

We kept the highest-born of them inside the City, to do them honor; but the rest, with the common soldiers, had to find their lodgings in the Troy-town outside the walls. And here, they took an arrow from the Achaeans' quiver and built their own stockade wall. They made one gate in it, so situated that it communicated with the Water Tower and the East Gate of the City, along the well-marked road that led toward the Simois Valley.

The burden of feeding and maintaining them fell upon Priam, of course, in addition to the gold and goods and trade considerations he had already promised in return for their aid. There were some who came only for the gold; but there were more who realized that with the Achaeans in control of Troy, their trade might not be as open as it had always been under the just and generous Priam. But whatever their motives, they were not lazy parasites, to be fed at their leisure. Many of them were skillful hunters, and they were able to add a goodly quantity of dried meat to the stores, as well as provide food for the garrison to eat daily. Still, my father daily grew more worn-looking, so that one's heart was touched with pity when one looked at him.

For myself, I had long since ceased to depend upon cosmetics for my haggard look. I seemed to grow thinner by the hour, not caring to eat when there might be want in the City later. I abandoned my pose of the mad seer and put my ancient earring back into my jewel box. Now I wrapped a plain blue chiton around my sharpening bones and covered it with an unadorned himation of washed wool.

But even as I spurned ornament for the spare comfort of austerity, Helen grew more luxurious. She waxed sleeker, it seemed, the more men there were to admire her. She took to leaving the boy in charge of a nurse and walked about the City, lightly veiled so that all could see the living, scent-breathing cause of the warfare that waited only for warm weather to begin.

If I have given the impression that she was stupid beneath her beauty, it was an error. Her wits were quick enough; it was only that there seemed to be no substance to her. A man who cared about such things would be bored in her company after an hour had passed.

And then, latecoming but joyfully welcomed, came the men from the south, from faraway Caria and Lycia; and with them came one such whose glances were not for Helen, but for me alone. And for myself, it seemed that I had lived and breathed all my weary years only so that I might survive long enough to behold him. The bitterness of my hatred for the rough-handed breed of men parted to admit him and him alone. Then my appetite returned, and I ate bean broth with scraps of meat in it so that my scant beauty would not desert me entirely. He didn't know who I was until we had fallen in love, but I do not think it would have mattered even if he had; and that story is one that my heart folds closely inside me, even today when all are dead and the cold ashes of Troy have long ceased to be blown by the never-ending wind.

Now rumors began flying thick and fast in the City. There were giants among the Achaeans, it was said, fell creatures sprung from those who had dared battle with the immortal gods. They heeded no dart or arrow, and could only be killed with a poison distilled from a virgin's blood. Their greatest champion, Achilles, it was said, bore a charm that made him invincible in battle and while he took the field the Achaeans would prevail. It was said that Calchas, the renegade priest, had taken with him the secret for the invocation of Poseidon and would flood the Plain if the Trojans dared venture from behind their walls. This last was patent nonsense, of course, because Calchas had been Apollo's servant, not Poseidon's. But that did not stop the stories. And I began to have an uneasy feeling inside of me, recalling that Poseidon had been turned out of Troy by my grandfather and that no altar had been raised to him in all that time. He is a powerful god, and we didn't need any more enemies than we already had.

Every hour brought new rumors, each one more terrifying than the last. And I knew I had to do what I could to sift the truth from the immense clouds of wild speculation that seized upon every movement from behind the wooden palisade and enlarged upon it so that the tales grew as they spread.

I walked through the City and the town, marking this one and that one, slaves and craftsmen I had known all my life and whose good judgment I trusted and from whom I was safe because of my station. With warriors, it might not have been the same. And I did not stop at men, either, but enrolled women and a few bright, monkeylike children of the people who had escaped the exodus to the south, maintaining that they were old enough to fight, or would be by spring. To each of them, I quietly promised gold in return for reliable information.

'No lies,' I told each of them sternly. 'Because you will not carry weapons, you are more free to go where you will. You can talk with the servants of the Achaeans and learn much in that way. Develop your own ways of gathering knowledge. Bring it to me only, and you will be well paid for any danger you might undergo.'

And to my surprise, there were no sidelong looks from any of them, as I had come to expect of the nobles and their families to whom I was just mad Cassandra who prophesied only death and fire, fire and death. There was a respect in their eyes, and loyalty and a quickness to obey that had nothing to do with our comparative stations in life. And I must own that it was pleasant, after so many months of condescension and tolerance.

So, one by one, my people began to work into their own ways of spying out the enemy. Here, a woman in the clothing of a rustic from the fields behind Canakkale might chat briefly with the captured concubine of one of the Achaean lords; there, a man grubbing for edible roots or gathering firewood might overhear two sentries talking. But by far the best of them were the children, the boys on the verge of manhood who could slip quietly into places an adult could never manage, and who were so quick that none might catch them. On their own, the boys thought up and executed an audacious stunt that cheered the city of Troy for days with its grim humor.

It has always been the practice for Trojans to burn their dead with great respect, and inter the ashes in special jars along ridges of the hills around the City. But contrariwise, it had become well known that the Achaeans had adopted the barbaric practice of burying their dead whole in elaborate tombs, there to go into stinking corruption. There could be nothing of this sort that would take place on Trojan soil, of course; there was hardly the time to spare for the making of their elaborate burial chambers even if we had been willing to grant them the ground for it.

Will or nill, they would do as the Trojans did, when it came to disposing of their dead. And so, the boys gathered an enormous supply of Trojan burial jars, and loading them on the backs of donkeys, carried them stealthily across the Plain, and stacked them at the Achaeans' gate where they would be discovered with the morning's light.

When this joke was made known in Troy, all the warriors whooped and guffawed so loudly they must have heard them out at the camp, and even Andromache, Hector's doleful wife, forgot her woes for her own safety and smiled.

Slowly, as the truth began to trickle in, I began to winnow it from the surrounding exaggerations and outright lies. In a short time, I knew the names and pedigrees of every warrior of note among the Achaeans; but by far the most chilling stories were about Achilles, and I could understand why the rumors flew.

It was the same Achilles of whom we had heard so much during the years of the Achaeans' land raids. And with the years he had grown, if anything, even more savage and cruel and intemperate in his character. He was, according to some of the captured women, one of those strangely twisted men whose only joy lay in killing. Even love was, with him, an appetite of the body only; and man or woman served to satisfy his indifferent lust. He had with him his cousin Patroclus, his current bed-mate and the only one for whom he had any of the human feelings of love. Patroclus was of a far nobler turn of mind and by many reckoned the better man; but Achilles outranked him by his birth. It was said that Patroclus did not dare refuse him though he was by nature a man for girls. But he, like everyone else, was deathly afraid of Achilles for he had been known to run amok for no discernible reason and destroy friend and enemy alike in his blind and raging hatred.

Achilles had his name, the 'lipless one', because of the way his mouth drew back in a perpetual snarl when he fought, like the mouth-hole of some mask designed to frighten. And even in times of peace, between the battles, he went about with his mouth compressed into a thin line, and his mad eyes darting back and forth with the white parts so reddened that people stepped, shivering, out of his path as quickly and quietly as they could.

He was rated the Achaeans' best warrior, because he knew no fear on the battlefield. Indeed, it was said that he courted death, and that he was destined to find it here at Troy. But instead of approaching his end piously, as any other man would, this same madness carried him onward into new atrocities like a ravening wolf who stops only when the javelin has penetrated its brain.

Even his supposed overlord, Agamemnon, approached him warily and through Patroclus whenever he could; for Patroclus was the only one who seemed able to reach past the blood-madness and reach the pitiful, feeble spark of sane manhood that lay within.

It was the Achaeans' boast that even Hector declined to take the field whenever Achilles was abroad; and in that one boast of many they are correct. But it was not because of any cowardice or fear on my brother's part; indeed, he faced him without trembling when the time came. But Hector had taken Achilles's measure the first time they met, when the war was still young, and had discovered that the training and rules of combat learned in the practice yard were useless against him. Not for Achilles was the discipline of the measured war dance, and his insane battlefield joy led him to ways of fighting that were against all the rules of war. It is one thing to fight bravely for your homeland and City, and it is quite another to throw your life away uselessly, to be spitted on a madman's spear in the same way that anyone else would shoot at a rabbit.

Now, during this winter preceding the time of the great battles, Achilles made his presence known to us in a variety of annoying ways. He was even so bold and impious as to raid my father's fig orchard, cutting down the tender trunks right and left as though they had been armed enemies he was dispatching. He seemed to care nothing for the fact that the fig is sacred to the Lady. After all, he was expecting death anyway with the coming summer; what punishment could she invoke that would mean anything to one such as he?

But except for incidents such as this that scandalized conservative religious thought, a few desultory raids northward, and amusing himself by keeping the maids from the three-troughed fountain just a few paces from the City walls, Achilles was able to do us no real harm that winter.

I put the time to better use. I strengthened and enlarged my band of spies as knowledge of the craft came to me with its practice. Payment was easy; I still had the scarf full of useless trash tucked away in the clothespress when I had emptied my jewel box, and even if that had run out there were trinkets and chains in plenty whose owners had forgotten them or lost them or abandoned them when the women had left the Citadel. But I had to be nimble in gathering them, for Helen was there before me and I had to be content with her leavings.

Still, it was sufficient. A single chain might last a long time, as I broke off a few links now and again to pay the men and women and daring boys who had thus come to possess more gold than they had ever dreamed of in a lifetime spent in service to the nobles of Troy. The shrine of Orpheus became the center of the web, wherein dwelt I, the spider, who touched this strand and that, and shook drops of knowledge like dew into my waiting lap.

8

SARPEDON

Now, as preparations for the war continued at an increasingly feverish pace, I became aware for the first time in many years of Helenus as a person apart. Up to now, he had simply been my twin, an extension of myself, and someone with whom to walk in the processions. He had not been invited to join me when I had roamed in the hills, seeking to purge myself of a childish inner agony. He had been male, after all, and I had thought him dull and priggish, and had never bothered to admit him into my friendship from then on. The strongest feeling I had for him was jealousy because he had access to where my soul still longed to go; and all told, I had regarded him in an absent-minded sort of way, much as one would think of a toe on one's foot. Less important than a finger, it is still a part of one, and one would miss it if it were absent.

Since the traitor Calchas had abandoned Troy, Laocoön had stepped into his place as high priest. In happier times, Helenus would have inherited the post of teacher in the Sminthian schoolroom. Now, however, he discarded his gold-girt bow for a real one, of Scythian make. It was well-faced with horn strips along its inner surface and fitted with dried sinew outside, still stinking of the tanner's. When I first saw it unstrung, bent backward with its firm ends and handgrip and springing shaft, I could not believe that it could ever be coaxed into a proper shape. But Helenus, smiling at a sister's ignorance of the mechanisms of war, cleverly braced it with his leg and strung it with a twinkling skill that made me know this was not the first time he had handled such a weapon. Then, without pausing, he plucked an arrow from his quiver, nocked it to the string and pulled until the straining cord grazed his cheek, all in the same smooth motion, and let fly at the marksman's wicker that was never removed in these days until practicing warriors had shot it into pieces.

'There,' he said in satisfaction, as the arrow lodged close

enough to the center so that had the wicker target been an approaching enemy the man would have fallen mortally wounded. 'Let no man say that my bow is an ornament and Apollo's toy only.'

'Can it be,' I wondered aloud, 'that you welcome this war?'

'I am pulled two ways, Cassandra,' he answered. 'Nothing could make me glad that we stand facing an armed enemy. These Achaeans, with their trumped-up excuses, will have us all down with our faces in the dust if they have their way about it, I know very well. But even so, I cannot help the fact that my heart lightens when the time comes closer when I can show everyone that I am more than one of those painted dolls that the women used to make of cornstalks and dandle for a season, to bury and make the fields fertile. I can do more than walk with the rest of the priests, behind the priestesses, carrying a mock bow with mock arrows. I will be a warrior with the best of them!'

'Then I wish you good fortune and hope that you may gain what joy there is to have of it,' I responded dryly.

And then a messenger came and told me that new companies of men were approaching the Dardanian Gate, the long-awaited allies from Caria and Lycia. And with them had come their king, Sarpedon, and his brother Glaucus who had been given the captaincy of the Carians out of respect, though they had their own Carian lieutenant.

I had taken it upon myself to see to the quartering of the nobles in the Second Terrace, and since I was more seemly in my behavior these days, this was a task gladly relinquished to me in all the bustle and confusion. And so, when I had seen that the men of Lycia and Caria had been turned toward the Troy-town and that the amenities of greeting had been observed, I approached the leaders where they stood in the plaza inside the gate to play my part in making them welcome.

Even if he had not had the leopard skin slung round his shoulders, I would have known him for their leader. He was radiant with that power that is bred in the bones of a favored few, and one of his greatest charms was that he didn't know it. He thought that love and obedience were his by right, the natural accompaniments to kingship; and if anyone had told him that there were those who ruled through fear, he would have found it hard to believe.

He was, perhaps, less handsome in a physical way than Paris, though I would have never admitted it then. His chin was a trifle less perfectly turned and lacked the deep dimple, and his eyes were not as lustrous, though they were set farther apart. His brow was flawless, however, wide and deep, and his hair flowed back from his temples like clean, washed gold. There was the stamp of greatness upon him, though he was not destined to find its fulfillment.

Now that I had come close to him, I stopped and my mouth hung open in spite of myself. I had been prepared to lodge incoming nobles, more soldiers among a city of soldiers, and not to find my heart flying from my breast to go and meet his as we exchanged our first glance.

He recovered sooner than I, and came toward me, taking my hands courteously. From another, I would not have tolerated the contact, avoiding it smoothly as had become my habit. 'Are you the daughter of the ruling House who is to tell us where we should live?' he asked, and a shiver went through me as much for his touch as for the deep and manly timbre of his voice.

'There are many daughters of Priam,' I said, suddenly unwilling that he should know that he addressed the one thought mad. 'I have that honor, though my station in this House may not be of the highest. If you like, I will go and bring another, so that you may be escorted as becomes your rank.'

'No, stay,' he said gallantly. 'You suit me very well. Your dress is plain, and your countenance grave and you do not go trailing perfumes and dripping with gold. I would not be comfortable to find myself shown the way by one such as that. You are a fit girl for a soldier, daughter of Priam.' And he looked at me steadily, so that I felt my cheeks go warm and I could not meet his gaze.

'Perhaps you will not think so later,' I could not stop myself from saying.

He laughed, a clear and delighted laugh in sharp contrast to my somberness. 'Highborn or bastard, it matters not to me! Lead on, Priam's daughter, for you will not find Glaucus or myself ones to give ourselves airs.'

Beside him, his brother smiled warmly at me, and I knew that they both thought me the child of a concubine and touchy because of it; and I was content to have it so for now.

Then I turned and led them to one of the wives' houses, close to the ramp that led to the First Terrace.

'You are bidden to the Palace to eat with Priam and his kin this evening,' I told them, 'for you are princes of the Royal Kin, even as he. When dusk begins to fall, all will gather in his Hall.'

'Will you be among them, daughter of Priam?' he asked.

I only smiled and walked away, taking a different route back to the Palace, so that they would not know where I went.

When I asked Orthia to bring my dinner to me in my room, it did not surprise my family, for I often did this, or neglected to eat entirely. But this evening, I ate everything on my platter, even the rusks of bread, for I had looked well into my mirror and did not like the thin wraith that had peered back at me.

As I ate, she came and began to comb my hair, putting her hand into scented oil and smoothing it in.

'Don't, Orthia,' I said, a little cross at her interruption of my thoughts. 'You will make my head ache.'

'Continue with your eating,' Orthia replied serenely. 'There is a tangle here that is causing the ache. And when you are finished with your food, I will put a light touch of paint on your face so that you will be beautiful in the moonlight.'

I stared at her, astonished and resentful. 'What makes you think I would wish to be beautiful in the sunlight, much less in the moon's paleness?' I retorted.

'Do not think that yours is the only head in Troy with any sense in it,' she replied, unruffled. 'I saw the look on your face when you came back this afternoon from taking the princes to their house. Which one is it, the Lycian king or the Carian prince?'

'The Lycian,' I admitted. 'Oh, Orthia, what shall I do? Everyone thinks me mad, and he will not look at me when he finds out who I am. I should be happy, but I find that I am more miserable now than I have ever been before!'

'I am only a nurse, and too old and worn out for much of anything else, but I can tell the little princess I sheltered in my arms against the terrors of the night that not everyone thinks you mad. Only those whose eyes and ears have been stopped by your enemy hold this opinion, and the worse for them.'

I clutched her hand and she dropped the comb. 'What else is known about me?' I demanded tensely.

'Enough. You think to hide everything, locking it away safely inside that too-keen mind of yours, but someone who loves you as I do can learn everything worth knowing. And also, I know that you have the love of the people, if you care about such things. Those who come to your shrine go away with new wisdom under their caps and their mouths are not stopped up. But mine will be, if you like, and I will hold what I know as close as you do.'

I let go her hand and she picked up the comb and continued

dressing my hair as though she had not been interrupted. 'But the love of the people is nothing, if everyone else thinks me half-witted,' I said sadly.

'It is more than you think now. But you are still young. And even though your father and his nobles will not listen to you now, the day will come when you will be sought for your wisdom.'

'Now you are speaking of things beyond you, Orthia. It is enough to have these secrets already spoken aloud, and for you to have seen how my heart has opened to a man who may turn his back on me when he finds out that I am just mad Cassandra, after all. Hold your peace.'

But truthfully, my heart had been eased by her words perhaps more than if I had whispered my heart's fullness into Bastos's soft fur. I would still tell him everything, of course, for though I served Pallas Artemis, whose servant he was also, I felt in some way that he stood closer to her than I did, with my soul already given away to Apollo. But with him as a go-between, I could come closer to her whom I served.

Silently, Orthia finished her combing, though she was not resentful of my rebuke; indeed, her face was close to smiling. And when she had put a bit of color on my cheeks, and arranged my shining hair, and had laid out a fresh chiton for me to put on, her smile was plain.

'Princess or rustic, it is all the same,' she said into the pile of soiled garments she gathered into her arms to be taken for washing. And then she was gone before I could rebuke her again.

Though she had given me much to ponder and I still had my story to pour out into Bastos's ear, I laid it all aside as I stole down the stairway so that I could watch from the shadows while he ate and drank in the company of my father and his nobles.

When I reached my place of concealment, far enough away from the doorway so that I could not be seen, and yet close enough for me to get a good view of most of the room, I wished myself away again. But I could not make my feet move; it was as if they had taken root when I glimpsed him through the smoke in the flickering gleam of the lamps.

There sat Helen, of course, the living cause of this great gathering of warriors, and when I saw her my heart sank within me, for it seemed that after he had once beheld her great beauty, he would never have eyes for me again. I hated the paint on my cheeks, the fragrance of the oil, the sweet rustle of my clean garments; it seemed a mockery of my plainness and angular thinness that had nothing of the Spartan's opulent and luxuriant body.

She was likewise dressed in blue, but of a lighter shade; and her robe was embroidered with gold in many glittering designs that winked at one as she moved. It was girdled in tightly at the waist, displaying curve of hip and bosom in a sleekness that made any man's hand itch to stroke along it. She sat in her accustomed place, where the hearth's light could show her to best advantage; and though Paris was beside her it seemed to me that her eyes rested ever lingeringly upon Sarpedon and that he returned her glances no less ardently.

Now I turned to go, and I had overstayed for my own safety. Absorbed in my melancholy observation, I had failed to notice that the banquet was finished, and before I reached the steps leading down into the outer courtyard I was surrounded by the outrushing of people from the Hall. And then, unhoped for, there was the touch of a hand on my arm.

'I did not see you in your father's Hall, daughter of Priam,' said a newly familiar voice behind me, and even as I turned my heart leaped up at the thought that he had searched for me past Helen's beauty. 'Will you not walk with me for an hour or so? It is dark, but you can show me the things that you will show to me again tomorrow.'

He smiled at me, and slow and unaccustomed, an answering smile came to my lips that had known sadness for too long.

The first time of many, that night we found a perfect place for lovers to go in a crowded, war-torn city. It was accidental, for I had already led him past the storehouses, and my brother Hector's house, and had shown him the gates and the towers.

'Let us go up there!' he proposed, indicating the Great Tower by the Scaian Gate.

'In the daytime, you can see past Samothrace,' I replied. 'But at night, all that is visible are the campfires of our enemies.'

'Then let me see that. I have journeyed a long way in order to behold just such a sight.'

And so up we went, to the wide platform that had been erected for Priam and his family to come and watch the activities on the Plain.

Out beyond us, glittering like so many fireflies, were the lights of the Achaeans's camp. It seemed that one could reach out and scoop them into the palm of one's hand, pouring them out to enjoy their harmless shine in a child's game.

Beside me, he said nothing, staring outward; and I knew that his thoughts were not of fireflies or games. Somehow, our hands clasped and clung as we stood there while the cold spring night's breeze swept through our hair. We must move or freeze where we stood and so, hand in hand we walked along the crenelated passageway the Lelegian had built atop the patterned walls of Troy. There was no one to bother us, save an occasional sentry. Later, they would be easy to avoid, but now we stepped aside, to allow them to pass. Surprised, they touched their foreheads at the two royal visitors in such an unlikely place. And as we walked, we talked to each other and opened our hearts as we never had before.

'Mine is a life that the song makers and storytellers have made a scramble of,' he said with cheerful wryness. 'Everywhere you will hear that I am a son of Zeus, if you please, and that Glaucus is Bellerophon's son. But all of us are Bellerophon's children. Laodamia, our older sister, reared my two brothers and myself. We left Isander home, to keep a watch over the kingdom, even though he wanted to come along and try his luck in the fighting. But even if we had said yes, Laodamia would have said no. She is very fond of him.'

'How have the storytellers mixed up your life?' I asked, thinking about what they must have done to mine.

'Well, they have it that I am Laodamia's son, by no less than Zeus himself. Did I say before that Glaucus was Bellerophon's son? Well, then, I have mixed myself up, in the confounded tangles they have made of it! Laodamia was his daughter; Glaucus was the son of Hippolochus. But this was our father's name before he changed it to avoid a curse. Isander is Laodamia's brother in the tales, though it would have been more reasonable to suppose him her son than me as he is the baby of the family. Isander and Hippolochus were supposed to have been striving, one against the other, for the kingdom. And the victor was to be the one to first shoot an arrow through a gold ring on a child's chest. That was the way they actually chose the king, in the old days before my grandfather came to rule in Lycia. The child's death sanctified the king.'

'Because he accepted the king's death for him,' I said. 'I have heard of the custom.'

'There was a fuss about who was to supply the child, Isander or Hippolochus, who had Glaucus, if you will remember,' he continued. 'And then Laodamia was supposed to have come forward and offered my heart for the arrow's lodging. Though if you ask the storytellers why Zeus would have allowed it if I had been his son, you will get no answer. At any rate, both Isander and Hippolochus were so astonished at the whole business that they resigned their claims and little Sarpedon became king, with Glaucus as his War Leader. No mention is made of Isander's "son" – probably because he doesn't have one yet!' He laughed, delighted with the tale he was telling me. 'That is the way of the Lycians. They love the old stories, and the more involved the better. They will sit around the hearth evening after evening, disputing upon some remote point in a story few have heard of and fewer still care about. And the new stories must fit the mold of the old ones, or they will have none of them.'

I laughed with him, hearing it come up rusty and creaking from long disuse. I could see the Lycian elders conjured up by his words, hotly disputing minor details across the fire; so had Trojan gentlemen, grown old in service, passed their time before the war had come.

'And what about you, daughter of Priam? Do you realize that I do not even know your name, though I have spilled out my life's story when not even my wife knows the straight of it?'

'Your wife?' I asked through lips suddenly grown stiff and wooden.

'It was not suitable that the new King of Lycia be unwed. So I took a noble's daughter and she has given me a son, though I have not named her First Wife nor made the boy my heir.' He turned to me, frowning thoughtfully. Then he took my shoulders and turned me into the moonlight so that he could see my face more clearly. I was grateful for the trace of paint on my cheeks, for I was afraid that I would have looked like a death's-head without it. 'It seems that I am seeing you for the first time, Priam's daughter,' he said with wonder in his voice. 'It must be that the Love-Spite has kept his arrows from my heart until now.' And then his voice grew teasing. 'But why he should have saved me for a thin little girl-thing with great eyes and a mop of red hair that everybody knows must cover a demon's temper, I do not know. But there is something unusual within you, that much is plain to me. I did not feel it when I talked with Helen, though her outer beauty is so much greater than yours that I do not wonder that you did not want to sit in its shadow in the Hall. Still, there is that something in you that makes me think you might be far better suited to sit on a throne than the Spartan woman for all her beauty. She will go to fat some day, while your bones will only grow more noble. Daughter of Priam, it does not matter to me if you are the child of some bath-maid who received your father's passing favor; you are the one I want for my queen.'

'I would rather I were a bath-maid's child,' I said bitterly. Whether I wanted to or not, I would have to tell him everything, for his unlooked-for declaration made it the only honorable thing for me to do. Let him turn away from me if he would; I could not go on with my pretense now.

I drew a long breath. 'You have picked a poor daughter of the Trojan House for you to declare yourself to,' I said now, determined to have the thing uttered and done with. 'I am the mad one, Cassandra.'

'I have heard of you,' he said gravely, and I did not dare look at him for fear I would see the shadow of distaste etching its way around his nostrils. 'But now that I have seen you, I cannot believe that you are what the stories make you.'

'You have not seen me when the fire comes up before my eyes and I can see only death,' I said, trying to make my voice light and feeling that I had failed.

'Tell me about the fire,' he suggested. And that was all it needed for me. As though he had drawn the stopper from a jar, the story came tumbling out. I found myself telling him about the tormenting recurring dream, and how it came upon me awake of late, about the day in the classroom and its consequences, how the nobles and their families looked sideways at me, and the children screamed and hid – or worse, laughed – when they saw me.

'And that,' I said when the telling was finished, 'is something which only one other person knows beside you, and then not all of it. You see, now I have matched you, tale for tale.' And I tried to laugh again, but it came out as a croak perilously close to a sob.

Beside me, he shook his head. 'That does not sound to me like madness, though I have not seen much of it. But there are prophets who abound in the wilderness, and sometimes they come to the citadel of Lycia. They are often overcome by the truth that lives in them, and fall to the ground to roll about and froth at the mouth and shout what seems nonsense at the time. Afterward, when they have recovered themselves and gone away again, when it all begins to come true and the people can see what was meant by the strangely turned warnings spewed up by a prophet in the grip of his god, they realize that it was not nonsense after all. I think that it is very possible that you may be such a one.'

'My nurse has told me, ever since I was a little girl, that this torment was the sign of Apollo's favor. But I could not see how it could be so.'

'Who is to understand the ways of the ever-living gods? This much I do know, however. If you were truly crazed, if it went all through you so that you were muddled in all your senses, I would have felt it long before now, and would never have declared for you as I did before I even knew your name. No, I think that your theory is correct; the priest Laocoön is responsible for your having the name for this kind of madness even while he seemed to be mouthing in sympathy for you. Well, it does not matter to me. Once you are in Lycia with me, they will forget all this nonsense about your mind being unsound.'

Now I dared look at him. And he was smiling at me, a world of steadfast love in his eyes. He held out his arms to me and I almost walked into them.

'There is one thing more I must tell you,' I said. 'I am the servant of Pallas Artemis here in Troy.' His face fell with dismay, and I rushed to reassure him. 'But I am not given to her heart and soul, like another might be. I was Apollo's before I was hers, and Pallas but offered me a shelter against the storms raised against me. In fact' – and I smiled bitterly again – 'my father has gone so far as to betroth me in return for a new ally with a sharp spear.'

'This is a fine thing!' he exclaimed, and his voice was light again. 'You are betrothed, and I am married. And while the law allows me more than one wife, you surely can't have two husbands!'

'Oh, that is nothing. Just a trick he has learned from the Achaeans. I would not hang up my girdle for the likes of Othryoneus of Cabesos.'

'Do you still hold that custom in Troy?'

'Yes. When it comes time for me to leave Artemis's service, I must go to the fig grove and wait for the first comer. The money he gives me goes to the treasury of Aphrodite.'

'Would that I had not already spoken for you, then, so that I might be eligible to initiate you into the ways of love.'

'Would that you had not. And would that I had left her shrine already, for I am still one of her own and forbidden to men.'

'Forbidden to a lustful touch,' he corrected. 'She will not mind a chaste kiss exchanged between newly found lovers. Let us seal our pledging. Passion can wait until the war is ended and your father is free to give you to me.'

And then he kissed me with heartbreaking gentleness. It was not his fault that my heart leaped upward in response. Yes, there would be a great deal to whisper into Bastos's ear this night when I finally came back to my room in the Palace.

When I let myself in the door quietly, I was surprised to see Orthia, who had been keeping a brazier going against my return. I was grateful for the warmth, for without realizing it I had been chilled through. She knelt down and took my boots off, massaging my cold feet with a rough, fire-warmed towel.

'He loves me,' I told Orthia with numb pleasure, entranced with the wonder of it. 'Even though he knows who I am, he loves me. He will ask for me when the war is over.'

'Poor princess,' said Orthia. 'You have lived too long with the cloud of madness hanging over your undeserving head. You could not believe that a stranger, coming to you fresh and untainted by the stories and gossip that has circulated for years, would be able to see past it to where your real beauty lies.'

'Where is it, Orthia?' I asked, a wondering child again. 'My real beauty. Where is it?'

'I will say what you stopped me from saying earlier,' she answered. 'The people love you, and know you better than your own family does. They know that you are not mad, not really mad, though the god in you drives you to do strange things. They believe, as do I, that when this thing is purged of you that the god requires, the wisdom that you seek will grow within you until kings will come and listen to your words. Hear the people, Cassandra, for sometimes their voice is clearer than the utterings of a priest or priestess fingering the entrails of a sacrifice for the omen.'

Suddenly I stifled a deep yawn, though I would not have done Orthia a discourtesy for anything, for these words she brought me from the people. 'I seem to have had so much love this day that I cannot hold any more,' I said with a smile that turned into another yawn. I was tired all at once, so heavy with sleep and warmth that I could hardly sit upright. 'It is a heady dose coming after years of distrust and hate.'

'I think that you will sleep, Cassandra, and I do not believe that your dream will disturb you this one night at least.'

And sleep I did, as though I had never slept before. But not until I had drowsily whispered it all into the delicate brown ear of Bastos who lay waiting on my couch to comfort me with his warmth through the chilly spring night.

9

THE WAR BEGINS

The first fighting, when it came, was short, brutal and ugly. But perhaps that was because I had to stay and watch it from the Great Tower. Perhaps if I had been a warrior on the field I might have found it as great and glorious as the songs have it. And perhaps, too, my mouth was still turned sick and bitter at the thing that had happened outside the city walls, in the very courtyard of the Pastoral Shrine which the fighting men had tried to take as just another passage of war. Still, I had seen many of them go pale and had marked many mouths in the unmistakable set of repressed nausea when the pitiful little bundle had been brought back into Troy.

It had been a long and tedious time that winter for anyone to be cooped up within the city walls, and especially so for little Troilus. The preceding autumn, he had been given his first colt for his very own, from my father's herds of Tros horses, and he was impatience itself to take it somewhere where he could behave like anybody with his first horse.

At any other time, his decision to shelter himself in the shadow of Thymbraean Apollo's sanctuary would have been a sound one, for this was an area of neutral territory half-way between the opposing camps. But he reckoned without Achilles, whose madness made mine grow pale by comparison, even in my wildest moments.

It is a hideous story, quickly told. Achilles came upon him there, as he exercised the colt, and killed him in the midst of one of those unnatural embraces for which he had become notorious. It had been Laocoön who had found him and brought him back, wrapped in a heavy cover. For a moment I almost forgot my hatred of my old enemy as he carried the still little bundle through the Dardanian Gate. Even wrapped as it was, one could see that there was something wrong about the chest, and the neck was at a painful angle. Laocoön's face was set and grim, for he had beheld the entire horror-filled scene, and had covered

Troilus's crushed body with his own cloak when Achilles had left.

Though he kept Hecabe and Priam from the sight, he allowed Hector and a picked group of his warriors to see Troilus's body uncovered, to give them fresh hatred and strengthened resolve that the Achaeans would never set foot in Troy. Then, still wrapped, the body was burnt with grief and great tenderness, and buried beside the ramp instead of in one of the many cemeteries along the ridge, so that it would remind those who passed by it daily what sort of foeman they faced.

Nothing would have kept the Trojans and their allies inside their walls after that. They sallied out on the first good day, calling the Achaeans to the field, and the Achaeans answered.

My heart was in my mouth, as I stood atop the Great Tower, for Sarpedon had been among them. Beside me, Andromache wept with fear, and I hushed her irritably.

'You don't understand!' she cried accusingly. 'You haven't got anybody out there. Nobody would care if the Trojans were defeated and you were carried off! But I have Hector's heir to worry about!' She turned to the little boy, held by his nurse. 'There, darling, don't worry.'

But the child, so far from fretting, seemed to be enjoying the show down on the Plain, and dodged his mother's solicitous arm in order to see.

There was a sharp answer ready in my mouth; but then I bit it back. Her father Eëtion had been the chieftain of the Cilicians, and he and his brother Podes had fallen to Achilles when he had raided Thebes. Seven of her brothers died also that day, and Achilles in a rare act of respect for the dead, had burnt them all fully armored. And so I supposed that she had even more to fear than the rest of us, and should be forgiven a certain amount of her weakness.

Soon, the Trojans came streaming back toward the City. The battle had been a draw, which they counted almost a victory. But even better than that, my brother Helenus was laughingly borne ahead of the rest, and he was counted to have won the day. He was flushed and proud, and by the time the dinner was ready in the Hall, had already made it into a song.

When the armies had come together, Achilles had sought out Hector, even as Hector searched for Achilles. They had gone at it with a will, and it seemed that Hector had taken on more than he could manage handily, because of Achilles's erratic fighting style. Sometimes, when a pair is well-matched, their combat becomes as beautiful to watch as a dance. I saw many such that summer, from the Tower's roof. They move together, and back, and circle each other while they feel out their opponents' strengths and weaknesses; and only when the final measures are trod does it become ugly.

But just when it seemed that Achilles might prevail with one of his wild rushes, Helenus, watchful of his opportunity, had let fly with his bow. It was a minor hit, in the hand, but it had been the one Achilles held his spear in, and so he had been forced to drop it and retire behind the stockade wall. A tumultuous cheer went up from the Trojans, for they had seen proof before their very eyes that Achilles's reputation for invulnerability was just another Achaean tall tale. When he was cut, he bled like any other man; and Helenus became that day's champion for having demonstrated this to them. Their spirits were lightened even more than they had been with the boys' joke of the burial jars; and though the skirmish had ended indecisively, the Trojans had thought themselves ahead with some justification.

And as he told his story, I marked well the look in my brother's eye and the set of his head. He had had a taste of something that day, and he was bound to have more of it, at any cost.

The next day was rain, and the day after that the priest of Apollo came. In between, I helped to care for the wounded. We had turned the House of Aphrodite into a hospital, as no warrior would live in it; and now the small rooms housed men who slept alone if they slept, and who groaned not with love but with the pains of war.

While the work went on, I helped bandage and splint, and apply simples and salves, and ease bruises and dislocations with hot water, without much thought of what I was doing. But after it was all over, and the last patient had limped out of the house, I came near to fainting and had to vomit into one of the copper bowls the surgeon had used to cleanse his instruments.

'Go and rest,' he told me kindly, 'and do not think poorly of yourself. I have done as much, when I was new at my trade.'

I gave him a smile for his understanding and left, weary in every bone. Tonight, Sarpedon and I would surely meet to wander along the crenelated passageway, so secure in our privacy that only a few suspected that a romance had sprung up. I wanted to lie down and rest, so that I would not look worn and tired. Some measure of my former looks had begun to come back to me, as I slept well and ate well; even my dream had not visited me since the night Sarpedon had declared for me. To my satisfaction, my bones did not now loom so fearsomely sharp through my clothes. I often wondered what I would say if Hecabe or Priam asked me about this inexplicable change for the better in me, but they were beyond noticing the vagaries of a daughter generally thought harmlessly mad, in the more urgent business of war.

But rest was put off for me when word came that the priest had begged an audience with my father, pleading great cause and promising a new weapon to use against the Achaeans. Then I got up and went down to my father's Hall, for curiosity would not let me sleep when there were Achaeans to be harmed.

'I have already petitioned Lord Agamemnon to return Chryseis,' he was saying as I slipped through the door. 'But he drove me away with curses and a kick on my backside which fortunately harmed only my dignity. She is my only child, Lord Priam, and a pious, good girl. When my wife died, I turned to Apollo for solace and entered his priesthood. My daughter followed me into the religious life; and as I became Chryses, "the golden", in the god's honor, she changed her name from Astynome to Chryseis. It did me no good to send her to Lyrnessos for protection when the Achaeans came. They took her with the rest of the women and goods, and Agamemnon chose her for his couch.'

'What is this weapon of which you spoke, Chryses?' asked my father, and everyone in the Hall leaned forward to hear.

'It came to me in a dream, Lord Priam,' the priest replied. 'Apollo is no less offended than I am because he loves me. And so he has given me the power to punish the Achaeans, if you will do as I say.'

'We are no less anxious to bring discomfort to our enemies than Apollo,' replied my father. 'Tell us, and it will be done.'

'You must begin to gather your slops and your night soil, and instead of throwing them onto the midden heap, you must empty them into the river Scamander,' said the priest serenely, and around him a shocked protest arose.

'The Scamander is a sacred stream to us,' said my father, his snowy brows pulled together. 'It received the sacrifice of the first Trojan king. Would you ask us to defile the same stream that received him with filth, as you suggest?'

'I would, and I am aware of the gravity of my request. But listen; the holy river will not be contaminated in all of its stream.

Only that part that runs from here down to the Hellespont will receive the castings.'

'But how will this bring disaster down upon the heads of the Achaeans?'

'That was not revealed to me in my dream, Lord Priam. But I trust in Apollo's truth, and think that he would soothe the angry stream if it came to that.'

'Let me think on it, Chryses. I have directed a steward to find you a lodging, and I will give you my decision in a day or so.'

'There is one lodging that I would desire above all others.'

'Name it.'

'If what I propose brings success, then give me the shrine of Thymbraean Apollo.'

My father frowned again. 'This is not as safe a place as you might think, priest. There has been murder done there, when sanctuary had been sought.'

'I am aware of these things,' the priest returned in his placid, tranquil voice. 'Still I would have it, to restore such order as I may. I do not fear any danger.'

'Then if I decide in favor of your proposal, and if it brings success with it, it is yours.'

'I could ask for no greater generosity.' And then he bowed, and was gone.

Instantly there was a buzz of voices raised, some opposed and some in favor of the priest's proposition, but Priam hushed them with his raised hand. 'Enough. It is my decision, though I will listen to any who comes to me privately and alone. I will not be shouted into it or against it. Now leave me, all of you. I have thinking to do.'

Ultimately, of course, he decided to do as the priest requested. And as soon as the maids began surreptitiously emptying the chamber pots into the stream, which we had first propitiated with a calf sacrifice, the Achaeans began mysteriously to fall ill.

The rumors came back to me, through my spy network, that they thought Apollo's arrows were falling on them for Agamemnon's highhanded treatment of one of Apollo's own priests. And there was a rising tide of pressure directed against him to give the daughter back. Even Calchas, the renegade priest, concurred. It was a sign from the god, he said, because the mysterious plague afflicted only the soldiers, while the kings and princes went free.

For ten days we did as Chryses directed, and for ten days the arrows of Apollo fell among the Achaeans. And on the tenth day, which was the last day his dream had said these measures would be effective, a deputation arrived from the Achaeans's camp, bringing Chryseis with it.

I could not help wondering if the fact that the kings and princes of the Achaeans commonly made their drink wine, while the common soldiers dipped out of the river, might not have had somewhat to do with the plague; but I never found out, because Chryses forbade us to use this trick again, saying that Apollo would be angered anew and would turn his arrows against us the next time. We didn't dare after that, of course, but still I wondered.

My spies brought back another story, concerning Odysseus and his cunning turn of mind. He was so proud of this, that he had connived at the death of Palamedes the Cretan who was the only one among the Achaeans who might be his rival.

It seems that Palamedes had managed to irk Odysseus beyond measure while the armies were still gathering at Aulis on the Western mainland. He could not forbear to boast about the many accomplishments of his people. There, claimed Palamedes, had the art of writing been invented. There had the idea of balancing scales been conceived, and the concept of equal measures. Cretans, he maintained, were the first to post sentries, though this claim was open to dispute from any people who ever had the wit to go to war. But no one could dispute that the Cretans were the first to have the idea of kindling bonfires near dangerous shoals and reefs, to warn terrified sailors caught on the water at night. Trojans knew better than any, for these things had come to Trojans and Cretans alike from our common ancestors in Atlantis, the cradle of all human knowledge.

Odysseus brooded about his fancied slight; and then he drew his abject henchmen, Diomedes of Argos, and Agamemnon himself into his plan for revenge. He got Agamemnon to send him off on a foraging expedition, from which he returned deliberately empty-handed, in grain-rich Boeotia, of all places. As he had expected, Palamedes took him to task for his failure.

'Go yourself,' Odysseus retorted. 'You'll not have any better luck than I did.'

Quick to take up the challenge, Palamedes departed the same way Odysseus had gone and within a day or two brought back all the carts groaning with their load of corn.

Now Odysseus had a real slight to add to the imagined ones, and one that would sooner or later call for an overt act of revenge on his part in the view of everyone. And now, the result of this unsavory dispute was many days of unfavorable winds. At last, Agamemnon called for a sacrifice, and pulled his own daughter Iphigeneia to the altar, charging that she had raised the contrary winds through witchcraft. What he actually meant was that his wife, Clytemnestra, had done so; but even he would not dare kill the Queen. It was enough that he defied the custom that has been with us time out of mind, that women, whether priestesses or Royal Kin, were always exempt from sacrifice.

But the last act of Odysseus's vicious little drama was still to be played on the beaches of the Trojan Plain. He waited for an auspicious moment, which happened to fall just before the first skirmish; then he hid a sack of gold nuggets in Palamedes's tent. Being well versed in the Cretan art of writing which he had pretended to despise, he forged a letter supposedly from Priam to Palamedes to the effect that the gold was Palamedes's price for betraying the Achaean camp to the Trojan. He told a slave captured in one of the many land-raids of previous years that delivery of this letter to Agamemnon was the price of his freedom. Needless to say, when the army stoned Palamedes for his supposed 'treachery', the slave died as well; and Odysseus was left with his reputation for cunning intact.

To our delight, there was a second, unexpected result from the stratagem which Chryses had worked against the Achaeans. When Agamemnon had been forced to relinquish the girl Chryseis, he had seized another captive, Briseis, from Achilles, to whom she had fallen by lot. Some god who favored the Trojans must have put that into his head, for it was folly of the very worst sort.

Achilles was not the kind of man to endure lightly being despoiled of his property even if he had not been suffering from that oppression of the mind that made him so very dangerous. But instead of descending upon Agamemnon's hut and killing all who would withstand him and bringing his girl back, he fell instead into a black sulk and refused to help the Achaeans by fighting for them. It was a good day for the Trojans that had made Achilles twisted in his personal drives; for if he had been goaded onward by desire of the girl, he would have had it out then and there, and gone back to the fighting with his honor satisfied.

But instead, now he sat day after day, gloomily reviewing his injustices which grew ever larger in his mind with the recounting He sent back deputation after deputation, even when

Agamemnon offered to restore Briseis to him untouched. Little he cared about that. It was Patroclus's embraces alone that charmed him, and he would not have cared if the entire Achaean army had enjoyed her in turn. And while he remained sullenly behind the stockade fence, the Trojans had the field to themselves until the Achaeans began to doubt that they would ever prevail.

Now there were skirmishes repeatedly on either side, not amounting to much though they kept the House of Aphrodite well stocked with convalescents. And then one day there came a call for a truce, and our herald Idaios went to meet their herald Talthybios, both holding herald's staffs, but both secretly bearing swords as well in case of treachery.

'My lord Agamemnon proposes that a duel be fought for the outcome of this war between the two chief figures in it, Menelaus of Sparta and Paris of Troy. The victor will be clearly shown in the right by the gracious will of the gods, and so there will be an end to the bloodshed.'

'What a fine little speechmaker you are, Talthybios,' said Idaios with a sneer. 'But it is not my duty to judge the content of your message, only to fetch and carry back the answer. In this case, however, I come with my answer ready beforehand. Priam of Troy takes note of the fact that when their greatest champion retires from the field, the Achaeans are ready to talk. Would they be this willing if Achilles still fought among them, I wonder? But this thought is my own, and not my lord's. Take this message back with you: Say to your Lord Agamemnon that Priam of Troy sends him his greetings as one king to another and that his son Paris will gladly meet whomsoever it pleases Agamemnon to send against him. He will be close to the Pastoral Shrine when the sun rises tomorrow.'

'Done, Trojan,' said Talthybios. 'You'll find Menelaus no less anxious to be at the mark at first light.'

When dawn came, it found everyone who could find a place crowded onto the Great Tower platform. The servants and workmen, and those nobles and warriors who would not be needed for the honor guard, crowded even onto the passageway atop the walls and hung from the crenelations in their eagerness to see.

How fine they looked as they marched out through the Scaian Gate! They were shined and polished and combed and brushed and oiled as though they were going to a festival where there would be girls to see them. One could number the companies, and the gods under whom they fought, by the standards which

Trojans have carried into battle from time out of mind. Made of wood and painted with the god's symbol, these plaques were fitted onto a long, sturdy, spearshaft so that they could be seen above the battle. We could see the standards of Aphrodite, of Hera, of Apollo, of Artemis.

In imitation, the Achaeans had done likewise, and we could count among them the hastily daubed symbols of a younger and more robust Hera, of Athene their strange Maiden, of Poseidon, and others whose names and titles we did not know. Now the lines of standards came closer, one to the other, until they met and halted, a respectable distance apart, close by the rise topped by the Pastoral Shrine. Two figures stepped forward in the space between the lines, and we could tell which one was Paris by the glint of gold from his corselet. He always liked to go well-dressed, and the flashier the better; and beside me I heard an indrawn gasp.

Unwilling as I was to look away from the scene before me, I turned, only half-expecting to see Helen. There she was, at the other end of the platform, leaning on Deiphobus so hard that she might as well have been naked. Her Western dress had an unpinned slit in the skirt that came nearly to her waist, though it was modest enough under ordinary circumstances owing to the fullness of the garment. But now, as her pointed little hands with the dimples on the backs stroked down her leg this way and that, her dress somehow fell back of its own accord and exposed a white thigh. She hastened to rearrange her clothing, but I saw the sudden flush of my brother's face and the satisfied smile on Helen's as she modestly made herself decorous again. I looked at the young woman by my side and saw that she had seen the brief passage, too.

'It is Oenone, is it not?' I asked.

'It is,' replied the young woman with that clear directness that comes from living always out of doors and never having had to exist in a palace with its intrigues and deceptions. 'He was mine before *she* came,' she added jerking her head in Helen's direction. 'Now he's apt to get himself killed and all for nothing. I was prepared to take him for husband, beyond being a year-lover, and forsake my tribe. But here *she* comes, with her airs and her dimples and her switching her skirts about, and Paris runs after her like a dog after a bitch in heat and no thought for me.'

I looked into the level gray eyes that met mine without flinching and knew that behind the hard words, she truly loved my brother. Well, the more fool he, I thought, because he was unworthy of her even if she did come from an obscure hill-tribe with strange and outlandish customs.

'Stay,' I said now, 'and watch with me. I will make room for you beside me.'

'The mad one and the rejected one,' she replied, her mouth twisted. 'Well, then I thank you, Cassandra Storm-crow. I'll watch until he falls, and then the wolves will eat me before I set foot inside Troy again.'

There was a sharp smell from her, and her hand where she laid it next to mine on the parapet was none too clean; but I felt more comfortable with her than I ever did with any of the noble ladies of Troy. And even though the duel did not turn out as we expected, she remained true to her word and never entered Troy again, though she left me a legacy when she departed. People standing nearby caught her words, and I became Storm-crow in everybody's mouth. I could think of worse nicknames to bear.

Though we both expected it, Paris was not fated to die that day, though if all else had been equal, Menelaus would have taken him. The Spartan king was by far the better warrior, being older and more experienced and sterner of character by far. Indeed, when one contrasted the two of them as they circled each other out on the Plain, looking for the first chink in the other's defense, Menelaus resembled one of those fierce, shambling manlike beasts from beyond the Euxine while Paris reminded one of nothing so much as a primped-up lap dog. Indeed, Menelaus had him down and would have made short work of him if Aphrodite's standard-bearer had not run forward, and holding the Goddess's symbol over the fallen Paris, put him under her divine protection.

Enraged, Menelaus would have knocked the plaque aside and the standard-bearer with it except that Pandaros, who had led his men from the Æsepus Valley in hopes of this day, pulled his bow quicker than any man could have sprung to the defense of either Paris or the standard-bearer. It was a goodly shot, even as hastily aimed as it was, and pierced through Menelaus's buckle and corselet. It was stopped by his loin guard, however, or it would have put an end to him then and there, though the blood ran down, making the Trojans cheer and the Achaeans suck in their breath.

The duel was now forgotten. Already the men were pounding down the stairs and ladders, rushing for their armor, and the grooms ran to the chariots to fly to the aid of the men on foot out there on the Plain.

Little time did Pandaros have to enjoy his victory; for even as Menelaus was carried groaning behind the stockade walls, Diomedes of Argos had taken the field and the first man he sought was Pandaros. The archer aimed at him as he had at Menelaus, but this time his shot was not so fortunate. The arrow was stopped by one of the plates on Diomedes's corselet, though it skidded and brought blood with a shallow cut. It was a showy wound, but not serious; and when Diomedes's companion had plucked out the arrow from the leather where it was lodged, he came straight for him, cursing all bowmen who fight from a distance.

'Come within the length of my spear and let us see your bravery then!' cried Diomedes.

'What, is there no killing you?' called Pandaros. 'Few men can boast of what I have done this day, in shooting both the King of Sparta and the War Leader of Argos. But if you still live after being hit by my keen arrow, then come ahead and we will see if my spear cannot make an end to you.'

At this, Diomedes laid aside his long spear and took up a sharp thrower because he had seen that Pandaros was likewise armed and he would not give or take an advantage. This much you can give the Achaeans; some of them were in love with honor on the battlefield and there, if nowhere else, the rules of life and death were strictly kept.

Pandaros cast first, and Diomedes took it on his shield. The spear's blade came straight through and struck his corselet. This time, however, no blood was drawn though it looked as though Diomedes had surely received his death wound. And even while Pandaros cried aloud his paean of triumph, Diomedes made his cast. It went high, and Pandaros had lifted his head to cry his victory to the skies, so that it took him in the face. I saw his body myself, and the bizarre death wound puzzled the surgeon until he had heard the story.

Æneas hurried forward to save Pandaros's body from being despoiled, and Diomedes hit him with a well-aimed rock from his sling. Down Æneas went, as he had taken his hit at the hip's pivot, and that would have been all for him had not the same brave standard-bearer of Aphrodite shielded him until his chariot could come up and bear him out of the battle with Pandaros's body. The man came out of it with an arm wound, but he was lucky at that, because Diomedes had become blind with his battle fury and could not see that the standard-bearers had no weapons, and were thus as inviolate as the persons of the heralds.

He even struck the standard-bearer of one of the uplands tribes, who followed the cult of Ares; the Achaeans term him Enyalios, and call him war incarnate. But his standard-bearer bore the brunt of the attack Diomedes would have made against the god himself, in his current mood. Straight at the man's belly his long spear went, and only when the man turned sideways did he save himself. As it was, the spearhead sliced open his skin and let out quantities of his blood; you would have thought he had been disemboweled when we treated him later in the House of Aphrodite.

After this, the Trojans were glad enough to retire from the field, and let Diomedes have it. Enough Trojans and Achaeans had fallen on either side to satisfy ten war gods, and there were sons of Priam among them. We had to burn our dead without delay, the same day they were fallen, if possible; only the King or his heir were mourned beforehand. And so the long afternoon's rays were streaming through the crenelations in the walls of Troy when the army came limping back into the City, a sorry parody of the jubilant, laughing men who had gone light-footed to see a duel put an end to the fighting.

10

HECTOR AND AJAX

When I did not walk with Sarpedon on the parapets, we would meet in the deserted purple-factory, which had become a storehouse. Nobody went there except at regular times during the day, and we had the place to ourselves. But at night, the parapets were ours.

If there was no fighting that day because of foul weather or bad omens, we would amuse ourselves playing the new game he had brought with him from Lycia. It had come, he explained, from a land far to the east and south, a fabulous place where great cats marked with stripes on their backs instead of spots roamed the forests and fought with elephants, enormous gray beasts the size of walls. There had been some influence from the countries beyond the Euxine for I recognized the queer winged lizards they were so fond of representing in their trade goods. Sarpedon called them dragons.

It was a great improvement over the game of Squares, for here one had opposing forces which had different capabilities of movement. Played on the same kind of board, alternating dark and light squares, the Elephants lined up at one side, and the Dragons faced them. Each side had its Captain and a line of foot soldiers before each Dragon and each Elephant. The Footmen moved one square at a time and always forward, while the Captains moved in any direction they pleased, one square at a time. Elephants moved on the straight of the squares, Dragons went on the diagonals.

Always I liked to be the Dragons, for the novelty of the diagonal move never lost its freshness for me. Sarpedon good-naturedly took the Elephants time and again without murmur.

Ours was not the only board in Troy, of course. The game spread through the warriors like water through oil, and always eager to find ways of amusing themselves between the battles, the most part of them took the game up eagerly. The dull-witted among them dropped it nearly as quickly, for it took agile wits to play well. Before long, I was winning as often as Sarpedon.

Nowadays, Cretans take all the credit for the game of Elephant and Dragon, for they brought it away with them with the sack of Troy; and I must admit that they have made it better. With the addition of a Citadel Tower at each corner of the board, they have made the protection of the Captains a chore easier and more difficult at once. The warlike nature of the game is emphasized these days, and it was a fitting pastime for those of us who were engaged in the mightiest war the world had ever seen.

Now, as we played on a day gray with rain and noisy with thunder, Sarpedon related to me the battlefield stories in which all warriors rejoice when the fighting is ended.

He told me how, after the wounding of Æneas by Diomedes, he had rallied Hector to Æneas's defense. ' "Come, Hector," I said. "Where is your courage that you are so proud of? Your boast has been that you could hold the City with just your brothers at your back, but it seems that the Lycians are bearing the brunt of the dirty work! We have come out of friendship and sympathy, but you do not even rally your own men to help us." '

'You said that to Hector?' I said, aghast. 'And he let you live to tell about it?'

Sarpedon laughed as he moved an Elephant to capture one of my Footmen. 'It is the way of the battlefield, Cassandra. It's a rough sort of fellowship out there and a man may say, bluntly or laughingly, things that would cost him some blood behind the walls.'

'Take care that you do not overstep these bounds, Sarpedon, even though you are named in the same breath with Hector and Deiphobus and Æneas when the men are talking about capable fighters. It is enough that I worry myself into an early old age when you are out there. I do not want to be further tormented with the fear that my brother might put his spear in you in a moment of anger.'

But he merely laughed. 'Don't meddle in men's business, sweet heart. How many times have you women warned us men away from something that was yours alone? Well, then, give us as much. Besides, you didn't even ask me how Hector took it.'

'How, then?'

'Why, he was properly ashamed of himself and went and did his duty in rallying the men, as he should have! But don't despair, my love. The only women who really understand the battlefield are Amazons, and they have been bred for it from the cradle.'

'I have heard that there is a tribe of Amazons who may come to help us later this summer.'

'I think that I would like that, as I have never fought beside one and I am curious as to how skilled they really are in war.'

'It is said that they are all dedicated to the Goddess I serve, and they call themselves Spearmaidens of Artemis. They believe that if they remain virgin through all their lives, they will go immediately to join Artemis's band of followers upon their deaths. But having a child is no real disgrace, so long as it is a girl. In fact, some tribes take so much pleasure in the couch that they take male prisoners for that sole purpose.'

'Yes,' he said. 'And they mutilate their captives most horribly, as they are said to mutilate themselves. They believe that if one bodily member is destroyed or defaced, its strength will flow into the one closest to it.'

'It will be good to have a few women's faces in Troy that are not all for the soldiers.'

'What is the matter, little Storm-crow?' From his lips the derisive nickname became gentle, affectionate teasing. 'Are Helen's flauntings and twitchings becoming annoying to you? Believe me, every man in my Lycians at least, knows her sort and what she is about, and she does not disturb any but the most susceptible among them.'

'If it were just Helen, I would not be troubled,' I said gloomily. 'But now she has persuaded my own sister Laodice who already has a healthy husband to embrace her as she wishes, to go about imitating her. Now Laodice goes dressed in gauze and gold, wearing Helen's perfumes, and she walks among the warriors. And those who would hesitate to touch Helen, no matter how seductively she might reveal her feet and knees, have no hesitation about Laodice who is, after all, one of us. It is said that she goes nightly to the Troy-town to amuse herself there, and that poor Helicon thinks she visits a shrine to pray for victory, and so he calls her pious and self-sacrificing.'

'It was a bad day that brought war to the Trojan Plain,' said Sarpedon, shaking his head.

'Worse still the day that saw Helen set foot on it.'

'If it had not been Helen, it would have been another,' he said. 'Pity her for what she is, rather than hate her.' He stared at the board between us, from which I had removed the Elephant that had captured my Footman. 'We are all of us no more important than these pieces on the gameboard. The gods move us here and there at their will. But also, little Storm-crow, do not forget that we are no less important than the least of them.' And with that, he moved one of the insignificant Footmen, pinning my Captain so that he could not move away from inevitable capture. The game was ended.

When Æneas had been cured of the injury caused by the flung stone, and those on the Achaean side were likewise healed, the heralds ran out onto the Plain and set the day for another fight. But Diomedes did not have the field all to himself this day, as he had before. He had to share his honors with Great Ajax and Little Ajax the Runner, and with Odysseus. But our men were no less valiant, with Æneas doing the work of three men.

Hector needed no urging on to the fight this day, and he strode out under the plaque of Ares. If he had not been my brother, I would have said that he was Ares himself. He went after Diomedes straightaway, but he called his Achaeans to him so that Hector would have hard work in getting through to him.

For me, that day's fighting brought with it a time of fright and panic so grave that my heart was in my throat. There was worse waiting for me later, but I thought that it had reached me then.

Sarpedon found himself facing Tlepolemos, who called himself the son of Heracles. Then, as warriors will, they whipped each other up to battle fury, standing and exchanging insults before they fought.

'So this is the renowned Sarpedon!' sneered the Achaean. 'They say you are well thought of by your own people, but I had to come looking for you to make you fight!'

'Since you seem to have such a high opinion of yourself, why don't you knock down the walls of Troy with a few well-placed stones?' inquired Sarpedon. 'Your father was supposed to have done so in another time – if, indeed, he was your father. Or was that just the story your mother told?'

That stung Tlepolemos. He lifted his spear to cast. Sarpedon had expected this, and they both let fly at the same moment. Sarpedon's spear took his man in the neck, where it is unprotected by the cheekpieces of the helmet; but Tlepolemos's cast was almost as good. Right through his left thigh it went, grazing the bone.

When a warrior goes down, there is always a greater fight over who should get his arms. And when, as in this instance, both are down but one still lives, there is always a scramble to finish off the wounded and take both sets of armor.

Now the Achaeans claimed Tlepolemos's body, but Sarpedon's Lycians were already dragging him back to safety. This was the only thing that saved him, because greedy Odysseus came riding up at that time and leaped from his chariot, ready to hang a king's head from his tent pole. But the Lycians came at him, and he was forced to fight then and there, and leave Sarpedon to his friends. Many of the brave Lycians fell to the crafty Achaean – Coiranos, Alastor, Chromios, Alcandros – Sarpedon named them all grievingly when their bodies were brought back.

As for him, when his comrade Pelagon had taken him to the shelter of an oak tree, the man wrenched out the spear from his thigh, where it had been lodged all this time. Sarpedon fainted away, and they brought him, still unconscious, back to the Citadel.

When I saw him lying among the wounded I thought him dead for a moment, and the world turned slowly around for me. But when we found that the spearhead had missed the great veins, though they were exposed in the gaping wound, and discovered that he would live after all, I felt relief so great that I must leave then and there and go to give thanks before the Palladium.

On my way to my room, I looked into the Palace shrine where it stood, and found a curious rite going on. Hector had returned briefly to the City, bearing word from Helenus who had seen some sort of omen in the birds overhead. Now my mother, surrounded by her daughters and daughters-in-law – excepting Helen and Laodice, who undoubtedly had pressing business elsewhere – was holding a fine robe from her own clothespresses, preparatory to draping it around the great thunder-stone.

'And in addition we will give you twelve yearling heifers that have never felt the goad, if only you will come now to our aid, and stay the hands of the Achaean champions against us. Spare the City, Maiden Goddess, we implore you!' she intoned.

I slipped out the way I had come, wanting to put my thanks before the goddess when my mother's sacrifice was done, and not wishing to disturb her. And as I waited, I caught sight of Hector and Paris coming from the direction of Paris's and Helen's apartment. There was a sleepy look in Paris's eyes, and I could guess what he had been doing, to delay him from the fighting, so that his brother had gone to fetch him when he had delivered his message to Hecabe.

'Helen again!' I muttered. 'And me they call Storm-crow!

What kind of name would she have with her shameless behavior if she didn't have that beautiful face to hide behind?'

I caught a few words of their conversation as they departed, enough to know that Helenus had also advised Hector to issue a general challenge to whichever Achaean champion would come and fight him; and this I would not dare fail to witness from the Great Tower. And so when I had found Bastos and knelt with him before the Palladium, telling him my thanks for the sparing of Sarpedon's life so that he could give the message to the Maiden, I let him go to return to my room if he wanted to, while I went back to the Great Tower to watch the duel.

On my way, I checked on Sarpedon's condition in the House of Aphrodite; he was sleeping quietly, the doctor having given him poppy to drink. To my surprise and pleasure, I discovered Orthia sitting by him keeping the flies away from his wound with patient brushings of her hand. She nodded to me and smiled, her finger on her lips and so I knew that all was well with him.

He would be interested in hearing about the duel when he awoke, so I climbed up to the platform, shading my eyes against the sun that was beginning to lengthen into afternoon. Below me, Hector waited while the Achaeans drew lots to see who would face the mighty Trojan.

Even as I took my place, I could hear my brother laughing out on the Plain below me.

'Let us have a champion!' he called. 'He will have fame indeed if it can be said of him that he fought face to face with Hector and fell at his hands!'

Menelaus would have come forward from the huddle of Achaeans to grapple with my laughing brother, though he knew he was far outmatched; but others pulled him back, more's the pity.

'You are too eager, Achaeans!' jeered Hector. 'Or are you jostling among yourselves for the pleasure of feeling my sharp bronze?' He turned and tossed a grin at us over his shoulder; I saw his teeth gleam very white against the blackness of his beard and knew that he was enjoying himself thoroughly.

'Where is Æneas, do you know?' asked my sister Creusa at my side. She stared anxiously out over the Plain, and I was surprised to see her come to the platform at all. She had married Æneas a year before and was now pregnant by him; when he had sustained his hip injury she had been watching from the

Tower and had nearly miscarried as a result.

'Have no fears for his safety, Creusa,' I said to her now. 'He is sitting at his ease with others of our Trojans at the far edge of the space marked out for the duel.'

Below us, there was fresh commotion from the Achaeans. Old Nestor, whom Agamemnon had insisted upon bringing along to Troy though he was long past fighting age and had turned into a droning old bore besides, now threatened to go and fight my brother himself if no champion would step forward. And then, abashed, a number of warriors came and offered themselves to a lottery, so that the gods might pick their own chosen one.

Hector strode back and forth on the scarp beneath the Great Tower, exchanging railleries with this one and that one atop the walls and a discussion arose, pitched so that it would carry to the Achaeans' ears, as to whether one of them would ever be persuaded to fight or not.

Then, from the pack, a large man disengaged himself. 'All the names in the lot are Ajax,' he commanded gruffly. 'I will go and fight the Trojan and teach him what it is to face a real warrior.'

His companions sprang forward to arm him for the duel with an alacrity that suggested they were thankful it was he and not they who were meeting Hector. They gave him two throwing spears and placed his sword about his neck. The long spear was never used in personal combats like these, but only in the press of battle.

Seeing his opponent come forward at last, Hector sprang with a glad cry down the scarp to where a fighting-ground had been cleared. It was good and level, reasonably dried from the unaccustomed rains with which we had been afflicted in this most unusual of years, and had no bushes growing there to catch an unwary foot and cause a man to stumble.

'Then it is Great Ajax who is to tread the measures of the war dance with Hector this day!' exclaimed my brother. 'Good! I would not want it said that I must needs face an unworthy enemy.'

'Perhaps I will teach you a new step,' responded Ajax from behind his great shield. 'But let us not do as lesser men and waste our breath in insults. I do not think that either of us has to be pricked along to fight.'

'Almost I like you, Achaean. But not enough to give you the first cast!' And with that, he sent his sharp thrower along its way. But Ajax was nearly as quick, and the spears crossed in the air. Both made fair hits, on the shield, and then Ajax was running toward Hector with his second thrower, in an unexpected maneuver.

As if it had been a long spear, he thrust at my brother and only at the last minute did he deflect the blow with his shield, from which the first shaft still projected. It was close enough; it kissed him on the neck with its edge as it went past, and let out enough blood to make him know that all was not sport. His own thrower, braced instinctively to parry, bent with its blade useless from the large boss on Ajax's shield, and so the warriors must move apart a little until they could wrench the shields free of the ruined spears.

Quickly, Hector bent down and picked up one of the stones with which the Trojan Plain is littered and heaved it at Ajax, who followed it with one just a little larger which knocked Hector down. He was back on his feet before he had fairly touched, however, and then the two champions began to go at it with swords.

And now the beauty of the war dance began; for it seemed that the two of them were so evenly matched there was scarcely a hair's difference between them. Back and forth they went, warily circling, two sets of teeth gleaming over the edges of two shields, and their feet reached out and gripped the ground as delicately as a dancer's would. One could not make a move without an answering counter from the other. Now Hector would rush to an attack, and Ajax would give ground pace by pace; then it would be his turn to come forward while my brother stepped backward so deliberately that it would seem he trod measures laid out beforehand.

Now and again they rested while the heralds clapped their hands ten times, and they grinned at one another as they puffed and panted. Now and again, a point would touch flesh and a few drops of scarlet would come out to show clearly against the sweat-drenched leather. But on and on they went, until it began to be as one of the rain-bringing dances, when the participants went beyond their own exhaustion into another state entirely and they could not rest even when they would. The watchers on the wall and on the Plain seemed equally caught up in it, and it came as a shock when the heralds Talthybios and Idaios ran out onto the contest-ground and held their wands between the combatants.

'The sun has touched the horizon, and no winner has been decided,' said Talthybios.

'Therefore, it may be that the gods love you both equally,' said Idaios.

And true enough, we now noticed that the sun had made its passage through the sky and lay along the western rim of the world. If Apollo had stayed to watch in his sun-chariot, he would have lingered like the rest of us, and given us one of those days the length of three one hears about in the old stories.

'It is not for me to call off the combat,' panted Ajax to the heralds as he leaned on his shield. 'He's the one who challenged all comers. Speak, Hector, and I will do as you say, whether we part now or continue to fight by starlight.'

'You have given me great sport and great joy this day,' replied my brother. 'We will perhaps fight again, for I will not avoid you in the press. Let us part now for a while, for nobody can say that we have not given our best efforts this afternoon. But before you go back to the Achaean camp and I return to my wife in my comfortable city, let us each give the other a gift. Let the whole world say that we fought bitterly, one with the other, but that we parted in friendship.'

'Why, that is a noble idea, Trojan,' exclaimed Ajax. 'Come! Your sword, from which I have endured much this day. And in return, I will give you my sword belt, which is made rich with sea-purple and with studs of gold.'

And so, full of respect for each other, they made their exchange in the deepening twilight. And if Ajax was welcomed back into the camp of the Achaeans where it was feared he might never return after meeting the courageous Trojan champion, what far greater rejoicing awaited Hector, the Guardian of the City, when he came once again inside the sturdy cedar gates of Troy!

11

DIOMEDES AND GLAUCUS

Though the Achaeans professed to despise the archer, they did not disdain to utilize that method of fighting themselves. One of their number got his main fame in that manner, though it was a ludicrous spectacle to Trojan eyes.

His name was Teucros, and he was half-brother to Great Ajax who had fought so nobly with Hector. Rumor had it that he had been fathered on Priam's sister Hesione by the same Telamon who begot Ajax on his lawful wife. It was an added insult of the most studied kind that sent the bastard son of Priam's own sister into battle against him.

This Teucros did not even use the horn-faced bow, like the one my brother Helenus carried, but used the Western one that had little range and could only be drawn to the chest for fear of fracturing the staves. And so, he went into battle behind the giant shield of his half-brother Ajax. Then he would dart out, let fly one of his ineffectual shots, and scuttle back, as a child runs behind its mother's skirts. How the Trojans laughed when they beheld this ridiculous sight! Teucros's shafts were easy to dodge, for outside the range of his bow they lost most of their force and clattered to earth harmlessly. But if a man looked the other way, he might have something to fear from the little scorpion Ajax kept hid like the daggers some warriors tucked into the wicker cushioning on the shield's inner face.

Now, after the stirring duel between my brother and the Achaean champion, the fighting settled into a dreary time of sorties and raids, and occasional skirmishes which produced no real result and only served to keep tempers fired to that indifferent level where they were in no danger of going out, but would scarcely blaze up either. For myself, I was glad enough of the respite, so that I could tend Sarpedon, who was insisting on getting out of bed and walking on his wounded leg though it threatened to open again with the exertion.

'You would keep me tied to the couch and forgo all the fighting!' he complained with a grin.

'Don't talk nonsense,' I retorted, binding a compress around the angry-looking place that had not yet developed strong white scar tissue. 'When you go to fight I die a little, but I would never hold you back. Not only do those who selfishly clasp what is theirs make themselves ridiculous and an object of derision to others, but the gods themselves often come and teach them the true meaning of ownership. We are taught to renounce personal possessions, because nothing can be taken from someone who has given it all away beforehand. Unfortunately, many of us do not quite live up to that ideal.'

Sarpedon looked at me fondly as I massaged a healing salve with a base of serpent fat onto the wound. 'Do you know, Cassandra, that in some places you would be thought a witch, if it weren't for your noble blood? And even with it, by some of the desert tribes back of Lebanon. Tell me; do you ever speak with the dead?'

'Do not jest with me in that manner, Sarpedon. Who knows what I see, or to whom I speak, when my dream is upon me?

'It was no jest. More and more I become convinced that you carry great gifts that will come to light when you are with me in Lycia.'

As always, when he referred to that unimaginable, longed-for time, I grew shy and diffident and my blood pounded in my throat. I stared at my fingers as they massaged the ointment into the wound on his strong and shapely thigh and the healer's impersonality fell away from me. 'I will bring you a cup of broth,' I said now, 'for there are other patients with other hurts to tend.'

'I have offended you.'

'No. But when you speak about the time that waits for us, I chafe against my ties to Pallas Artemis, and your resolution to honor them. I might find myself pleading with you for love, as some of the old queens were said to do when marriage to the Hellene newcomers became irksome. And then we both might offend the Maiden Goddess, who has a long memory.'

He smiled. 'My own father Bellerophon had cause to know the very situation of which you spoke. But have no fear. I will not be like Meleager the Argonaut, who took advantage of the long and illegal voyage to persuade the maiden huntress Atalanta to forsake her vows. She had come along to see that the Goddess was represented in that incidental pious errand that provided the excuse for the trip. Often they sat together, their heads close, while Meleager poured his arguments into her ever more willing ears. But she still refused him until the *Argo* had completed its voyage, lest she conceive to everyone's embarrassment. The very day the *Argo* was beached again at Iolcus, she gave herself in love to him, some say under the very prow of the vessel which bore a curse ever after. She was confident of marriage with her lover; but Meleager had somehow forgotten to tell her in all his nights of wooing that he was already wed under Western laws. When she learned how disastrously she had been deceived, all her former love turned to bitter hate. Though Artemis might still have listened to a plea of vengeance from her, she was too proud to approach the Maiden, no longer being one herself. Instead, she married another Argonaut who had loved her silently and chastely, being unable to do anything about the sorry situation developing with Meleager. But Artemis divined what was in the heart of her former servant and undertook her vengeance herself. Some say she borrowed the thunderbolt from Zeus, and others say she persuaded him to use it himself. Personally, I believe she stole a single streak of lightning from the Thunderer, fitted it to her bow, and struck Meleager dead as he made his way back to Caledon.'

'I have not heard this story, but I find it a strangely pleasing one to have come both from our Western enemies and the *Argo*, neither of which the Trojans have cause to love.'

'There were pious Westerners in those days, along with the renegades who bred the pack that faces us today. Men are men, a mixture of good and bad, no matter which side they fight on.'

'You have a strangely deep view of war.'

'Not so much deep as clear. I find that I fight better when I do not have to bear the burden of hate.'

'In that we differ. To me, it is no burden to hate those who have come against Troy. Though,' I added honestly, 'I daresay that if I had to take up a spear and fight I might come to your way of thinking. In that, as in other matters, a cool head is a better servant than a hot one.'

Once more a healer in command of myself, I bandaged the wound that kept Sarpedon fretting behind the walls of Troy, and went on with my self-appointed duties of assisting Coronus, our physician. I had come to be nearly as skillful as he with our never-ending procession of wounded warriors that the war kept pouring through the doors of the House of Aphrodite.

One day the warriors brought back a tale of a new duel which was so amusing that I hurried to Sarpedon with it, confident that it would make him laugh.

It seems that Prince Glaucus, Sarpedon's brother, had gone out onto the Plain in search of a morning's exercise and had come face to face with Diomedes of Argos, the one who had made such a rout of things earlier in the summer.

Cooler now, Diomedes had prudently inquired as to the identity of the stout Lycian he now faced. Glaucus had one of those rare gifts of the battlefield, a high and ringing voice that could be clearly heard across the din of battle. Often he entertained us in the evenings with a harp in his hand, and it seemed that the sweet and brilliant strains must surely float past the Achaeans's ears as well. Now he threw back his hand and laughed delightedly, for he knew that Diomedes was perfectly aware of who he was from his voice if nothing else.

Good-naturedly, he stuck his spear in the earth point-down, and leaned on it while he spun for the Achaean much the same story that Sarpedon had told me the night we had first walked together. Diomedes, his spear likewise grounded, listened intently, and at the end of it spread his arms wide.

'Why, then, we are family friends!' he exclaimed. 'It was the boast of my grandfather Oineus that he once entertained your grandfather Bellerophon for twenty days, though he was on his way in one of his great errands and impatient of delay! When they parted they gave each other rich gifts and swore friendship. Let us do the same, for there are Trojans enough for my spear without seeking you among the press, and you can try for plenty of Achaeans without adding me to their number. What say you, Glaucus, son of Hippolochus, son of Bellerophon?'

It was on Glaucus's tongue to revile Diomedes as a bare-faced liar for swallowing whole the mess the Lycians had made of his lineage, and then trying to belch it up again to convince Glaucus of his friendship. But then he noticed that during the telling, Diomedes's soldiers had crept up beside and behind him, ostensibly to listen to the conversation between the two champions, but effectively cutting him off from his own men at the same time.

Then it was Glaucus's turn to swallow his own story and agree to the exchange of arms that Diomedes insisted upon. Diomedes came well out of that encounter, for not only did he avoid fighting an opponent who could have very well laid him in the dust, but he got gold-studded Lycian armor worth fivescore oxen in return for everyday bronze and leather from Argos which was worth nine oxen at the most.

Glaucus came back into Troy sour-mouthed and chagrined at having his own elaborate hoax turned upon him and swore to take the difference in the worth of the armor from Diomedes's hide the next time he met him in battle. The Lycians had already made up a bawdy song and bawled it out as they came through the gates about how Zeus had sent Glaucus clean out of his wits so that he bargained gold for bronze in an even trade. And because the Lycians are traders second only to the Trojans, the jest was quickly taken up from one end of the City to the other. When Glaucus had downed a little neat wine, he showed that he could take a joke as well as hand one out. It was just that sort of thing that made him universally loved; for soon he was singing as lustily as anyone in that clear high voice of his that soared above all the rest.

When I told Sarpedon the story, he howled with laughter until the tears ran down his face. 'Let that teach my younger brother a lesson!' he cried gleefully. 'The field is no place for cleverness of tongue. He should have told the Achaean he was Ares' own get upon old Medusa herself, and then invited him to dispute the claim! But I am sorry that he lost the armor.'

Apparently the Achaeans's joke had not lightened their own spirits as well as it had those of the Trojans who had been the butt of it. Daily my spies filtered word in to me at the shrine of Orpheus or the House of Aphrodite that the enemies' morale ebbed ever lower. Achilles threatened constantly to leave, taking his Myrmidons with him, though he had not as yet actually begun to launch his ships. And the longer the war went on in this bored and desultory series of minor skirmishes, which was all the Achaeans would risk without their great champion, the more Achaeans began to align themselves with Achilles in his quarrel with King Agamemnon.

Now the Trojans had their Plain very much to themselves and became so careless in their newly regained mastery that they began to scorn to come within their walls at night, but camped out on the Plain where it suited them and built their fires for all to see. They felt that the Achaeans were too dispirited to do anything but stay behind their stockade, and hoped to further encourage them to depart with this show of fearlessness.

Not all the Achaeans were of the mind of Achilles, however; and behind their stockade some of them were planning a counter-move. They waited until a fresh company of Thracians, led by Rhesos their chieftain, had come and camped on the Plain, picketing their fine horses to their chariot rails. Then Diomedes and Odysseus, from who he had learned well, came soft-footed in the night and crept into the place where Rhesos and his bodyguard slept apart. They slaughtered all twelve of them, and Rhesos made the thirteenth, slitting their throats as they slept, and took away the chieftain's own horses as their prize. When morning came, it was discovered that they had killed the Trojan sentry as well, so that the religious insult which was no doubt one of Odysseus's little touches, was spoiled.

Aphrodite is the Lady of Troy, and her year has thirteen months, measured by the moon's coursing. There has been a movement in the Western lands for years to drop the thirteenth month as being unlucky, as that was when the king was given to the Goddess in the old days, and count the year by the sun instead. But there is a limit, even to religious reform, and I do not think that will ever happen.

Still, the insult was plain, spoiled though it was by poor Dolon's corpse. And this night raid, an unprecedented maneuver, served to bring the war back up out of the slogging boredom in which it had been wallowing. Both sides sharpened their wits and their weapons, and made ready to begin to fight in earnest again.

12

DAY OF FURY

Out they came in the early morning, from behind the stockade wall, the champions in their chariots rushing forward and the men on foot close behind. And no less eagerly the Trojans and their allies poured out of the city and the town, and the drivers whipped up the horses to make them fly.

We who were left behind made everything neat and clean in the House of Aphrodite, for we were soberly aware that much work would come to us from the exuberant outpouring of men from either side. The stocks of medicines were dropping, and I wished I had had the foresight to have sent for jars and sacks that lay in the healing-woman's cubby in the Pastoral Shrine. When we were ready for the melancholy tasks that lay ahead of us, I made my way to my accustomed place atop the Great Tower, for Sarpedon had been among those who had ridden out. He was not entirely healed of his terrible wound, but he would not remain behind any longer when it looked as if there would be satisfying battle-sport again.

It had been Agamemnon's fight up to the time I arrived, and he had ravaged among the Trojans like a wolf in the sheepfold; we could recognize him by his gold-crusted helmet with the towering red plumes. With a gasp, I recognized one chariot that now stood empty, while one of Agamemnon's minions came up to take it away. It had held two of Priam's sons, one from a wife and one from a concubine. They were the best of friends, having been born in the same season of the same year, and always fought together. The concubine's son was as clever with the horses as his brother was with arms, and they had made a joyous team. Now they were both dead, apparently by Agamemnon's hand, and their armor and horses and chariot were his prize. Now, as I watched, two of noble Antenor's sons came running up to try to avenge their kinsmen.

They were close enough to the walls so that we had no trouble in seeing the details of the battle. One of the young men dodged

Agamemnon's throwing-spear and ran against him with his own. But Agamemnon stepped aside calmly and, catching the spear by the shaft, allowed the young man to wrench it from his own hands as he rushed past; then the Achaean turned his own weapon upon him and stabbed him through the throat.

But while he was engaged in this bloody work, the other son of Antenor circled him; stabbing out at random, he put his spearhead through the Achaean king's arm. But Agamemnon had another stroke left in him before he left the fight. As the Trojan began to drag his dead brother away, Agamemnon leaped upon him and killed him then and there. But he could not stay to collect the armor, for his wound was very painful, and it would hamper him in any further fighting. He ran to his chariot, and the driver touched up the horses with a will, to take the injured king back to the Achaean camp.

This was what Hector had been waiting for. While Agamemnon had raged in his battle-fury, my brother prudently kept out of his way for it was clear that a god inspired him. Now, however, he rallied the eager Trojans onward, plainly intending that the day should be his now that Agamemnon was no longer in the field.

'It is our turn now!' he shouted, as he tossed his spear up and caught it again. 'Let us put them on the run and destroy their camp for them!'

And behind him a ferocious, jubilant howl arose at his audacity and like lean hounds of war they streamed out behind him, hungry for victory in their turn. Beside me, Andromache turned pale and left the Tower, but I took no notice of her. My eyes were straining, trying to pick Sarpedon out of the pack. I caught a single glimpse of him in the midst of his Lycians, who were easy to spot because of the loose-fitting quilted tunics they wore. He was waving them on as he ran to climb into his chariot. I remember noticing that he still limped though he tried not to show it.

I had brought him his corselet, shield, and sword this morning with my own hands since he had made it clear that he would not be left behind. With untutored fingers I buckled buckles and tightened straps, and laid the shoulder belts from which hung the shield and the sword neatly across his chest, one from each shoulder. The smith had been cunning in their design; where the straps crossed there was an inlaid boss, and a pattern of silver leaves was worked stemming from this central point.

'You wear a solemn face, little Storm-crow,' he had said with a smile.

'It is a solemn business, making a man ready for war,' I had replied. 'There. Now I am done, and can give you a happier face to look at.'

'Neatly done, too. One would think that you had sent lovers off to the field every day of your life.'

'Only you. And now that you are ready, I will not spoil it by begging you to take care of yourself in the press. You are far too proud for that, and for that matter, so am I. I will only ask that you take no rash chances, nor risk yourself without good cause or reason in your eagerness for battle.'

He grinned. 'Have no fear, little Storm-crow. I am coolheaded in a fight, as I told you before. It is the one who loses control of himself who will fall to me, and not me to him.'

'Go, then, and I will give you a smile to take with you instead of the tears with which too many women send their men off to war,' I said, for I could see that he was eager to be gone. And so I held my head up proudly and let my love for him shine through my eyes. He returned my wave with a parting salute gay and confident, and I was glad that I had not laid the burden of weeping upon him.

But alone on the top of the Great Tower it was another matter, and I was not so assured. Below me, as the Trojans rallied and raised a loud shout, the Achaeans facing them began to look at each other and their weapons drooped in their hands. Then, as we watched, they turned and began to run away. With an even louder cry, the Trojans hurried along in pursuit, cutting down stragglers as they ran. Atop the Tower, the women hugged each other in jubilation. I watched until there was no more to see, as the dust came up and hid all from our eyes. But I knew that the stories would begin to come in soon.

Of all the Achaeans, only Odysseus and his eternal companion Diomedes dared stand and make a fight of it in the rout. The rest of the Achaeans, dismayed already by Agamemnon's wounding in mid-career, were ready to believe that Zeus had tipped his scales in the Trojans' favor and thought of nothing but shelter behind the stockade wall.

Their stand did not long escape the attention of Hector, of course; and he came against both of them. Diomedes had wounded a man and was waiting for him to die so that he could strip him. He stood and cast, and the spear hit Hector's helmet. It did not go through, being deflected by the horns set there and the strengthening metal, but it dazed my brother so that he had to retire temporarily to regain his wits.

For once, Paris was in the field instead of enjoying himself in Helen's scented bedchamber. He picked his time carefully, and waited until Diomedes was kneeling to take his prize; then he let fly with his bow, and the shaft pinned Diomedes through the right foot and ran deep into the ground so that he could not get loose without considerable pain.

'What a pity!' exclaimed Paris. 'I aimed for the belly, but some god who loves you deflected the shot. Still, the god must not love you too well, or you would have been spared the pain you are enduring now.'

'Boast if you will,' replied Diomedes, who seemed resolved to bear his hurt without flinching. 'Leave it to a Trojan to botch his shot from where he lies hidden and then make a brag of it anyway. If you were man enough to face me, there would be another tune from your lips, pretty boy!'

As he spoke, Odysseus placed himself boldly before him so that Diomedes could cut himself loose, leaving the arrowhead still in the ground, and pull the shaft through his foot. Perhaps Odysseus thought Diomedes would come and back him in his turn, for he stayed where he was; but Diomedes had no such intention. He limped away to his car and his driver was glad enough to take him back to the ships. And that left Odysseus all by himself, for the Achaean footmen had long since run away.

It was well for him that Hector had found work along the banks of the Scamander. But the foot soldiers had grown courageous and began to harry Odysseus in his solitude. As a rule soldiers fought soldiers, and champions sought only other champions; but enough of the common horde will bring one down if they are given the opportunity. Even as he lay about him with his long spear, Odysseus raised a shout for help, and louder when a man ran a blade along his flank, tearing a showy wound. It was not mortal and touched no vital spot, but the sight of the blood made the Trojans redouble their efforts. If Menelaus and Great Ajax had not heard and been moved to come to the aid of their comrade, that would have been the end of wily Odysseus with his boar-tusk helmet!

For a little while, it seemed that they might be able to regroup the Achaeans, and indeed, they held the Trojans for a few minutes. But as quickly as their line held, more Trojans began to swarm to that point, and Hector was among them. Paris kept up a steady hail of arrows, wounding many, including one of the Achaeans's physicians. Normally, no member of the Sons of Asclepius took the field except as a noncombatant, and were in much the same class as the heralds and the standard-bearers whose persons were equally sacred. But the one named Machaon thought nothing of taking a sword and fighting alongside the footmen, though his colleague had the good sense to stay behind in the camp.

Now, slowly and surely, Hector and his forces were marching the Achaeans across the Plain to their stockade walls. Even Great Ajax could not withstand my brother and grudgingly threw his shield over his back and trudged along. Stubbornly, he refused to hide himself, evidently preferring to have it thought that he walked back toward the Hellespont because that was where he wanted to go, rather than join the sheeplike retreat of the Achaeans before the encircling Trojans.

When they came to the moat, they paused, and the Achaeans triumphantly slammed the central gate behind them. But if they thought they were safe from my brother in his current mood, they were mistaken. Hector paused only long enough to get his fighters dismounted from their cars and group them into attacking parties, for he knew as well as any that they could not get the chariots across the moat with its stakes set on both sides ready to tear the bottoms out of the cars and the life out of the animals with their wickedly sharpened points.

Hector himself led the first party, of course; and with him went Polydamas and Cebriones. Next came Paris, with Alcathoös and Agenor; Helenus and Deiphobus led the third, Æneas with two more of Antenor's sons the fourth, and Sarpedon led the fifth party, which consisted mainly of southern allies. With him were Glaucus and the Carian lieutenant. But while they were making their hasty plans for an assault upon the Achaeans's walls, Asios, the son of Hyrtacus, took matters upon himself to begin the attack.

Scorning to leave his chariot behind, he drove it straight at the left side of the camp, where the Achaeans themselves drove in and out. The gates there were wide open, in case stragglers might still make it inside the walls. Asios, gone wild with the excitement of battle, ignored Hector's prudent planning and with a loud cheer led his company straight at this tempting opening. It proved to be a trap. The gates were not unguarded, of course; and out sallied Achaeans to throw them back. They were Lapiths, and everyone knows they are among the best fighters in the world. Poor Asios never had a chance in his rash sprint toward victory; but while this diversion was going on, Hector began his own attack across the moat.

When many hands are pulling, even a well-rooted tree will come down; and the Achaeans only had tree trunks set into the ground. They pulled away the stones, and with the buttress beams they levered out still more trunks so that the wall was sagging in several places. But they would not have come across the breached walls, because behind them the Achaeans were fighting like wild men, if it had not been for Sarpedon and his followers.

He had been waiting impatiently; and when it seemed that the Achaeans were well occupied in trying to keep the Trojans out, he called his men to a part of the wall still standing, abandoned for the defense of the breach. Up they swarmed, those below giving a boost to the others and they dropped over lightly, looking about eagerly for a foeman. For the first time in the war, there were Trojans behind the Achaean walls.

They hadn't long to wait, for when it was seen what was happening, the Achaeans sent Great Ajax to them. There were plenty of the stones he loved to throw lying about in case of just such an emergency, and he began to heave them with a will. But it was not a stone from Ajax's hand that put Glaucus out of the fight; as he was scaling the wall, Teucros the archer who always liked to fight from behind Great Ajax's shield, sent an arrow into his shoulder. Glaucus dropped back behind the wall and went to the rear as quietly as possible so that no one could boast about his defeat. Sarpedon noticed, however, and he now came as close to anger as he ever did on the battlefield, for Glaucus was his own brother after all.

He went after Great Ajax and Teucros simultaneously, and though they both tried together, they could not bring him down. Teucros's arrow hit the boss where the two straps crossed, where I had laid them with my own hands, and was deflected. Ajax went for him with a spear, but Sarpedon took it on his shield.

Hector was already inside, and now his great voice could be heard crying for fire.

'Burn the ships!' he was shouting, and behind him a mighty crash answered. His men had battered down the large central gate of the Achaeans's wall, hinges, crossbar and all; and now those who had boosted their comrades over the walls came rushing through the ruined gates, ready to slaughter every Achaean who lived in the trap that their camp had become.

Elsewhere, Helenus found himself face to face with Menelaus. He tried for him with his bow, but the arrow bounced off. Menelaus sent his spear through Helenus's bow hand, and Helenus looked around for Deiphobus. But Deiphobus was having troubles of his own with Idomeneus the Cretan. He came out of it with an arm wound as well, though Idomeneus did not deliver it. And then my brother Polites took both Helenus and Deiphobus into his car to bring them back to Troy.

Flames began to crackle and a cloud of smoke brought realization to the hearts of Trojans and Achaeans alike that Hector was making good his threat and had set fire to at least some of the ships. Drenched with pitch, they would burn well after having dried for nearly a year.

If the fighting had been desperate before, it was nothing compared to what now arose. The Trojans met volleys of rocks from the slings of Locrians, and arrows from the bows of the archers the Achaeans pretended to despise began to rain down upon them. It was almost impossible to rally the men, and turn the confusion into some sort of ordered battle plan. But still Hector tried. He allowed his men to fall back, so that he could bring his champions to the front and advance upon the Achaeans again. With them being occupied with putting out the fires and fighting at the same time, he might be reasonably confident of victory. And once again he found himself facing Great Ajax in a personal contest.

'This is not agreeable playtime this day, Achaean!' he shouted, and hurled a sharp thrower at his opponent. But his aim had been too good; it hit at the cross straps and didn't go through, though it staggered Ajax. And then Ajax, with one of those stones that were never far from his hand, threw at Hector. My brother misjudged a trifle; it skimmed the edge of his shield and struck him in the chest, near the neck, and knocked all the breath out of him. If it had not been for Sarpedon, that would have been the end of him then and there, and Glaucus unexpectedly appeared at his side, a hastily applied bandage on his shoulder. With the help of their men, they were able to carry my stunned brother out of the fray, to the ford of the Scamander where they could revive him with its holy water. And without Hector, the Trojans allowed themselves to be pushed out of the Achaean enclosure and across the moat, where they sank down exhausted. Behind their ruined walls, the Achaeans were glad enough of the respite, though they were not allowed to rest as long as the ships still blazed.

As they squatted, still panting from their exertions, beside the Scamander ford, the weary Trojans were astonished to find that the sun was only a little past midday. So much had happened in not much more than a morning's work.

None of them was unscathed; Sarpedon's leg wound had opened again, and he daubed it with water even as Æneas and Glaucus poured water on Hector to revive him. Presently he sat up and vomited a little blood whereupon he felt better. And if any remarked upon the absence of Helenus and Deiphobus, who were less seriously hurt than many who flung themselves down beside Hector, they kept their counsel to themselves.

Some sharp-eyed observer on the Plain had noted the pause in the fighting; now a cart came up with barley bread and cheese, and on this Hector and his men made a light and strengthening meal. And while they ate, a cloud began to rise from behind the hills on which Troy stood, and a faint rumble of thunder rolled across the Plain.

'Now,' said my brother, straightening his shoulders with a deep breath. 'It is too bad that we allowed the Achaeans to push us back before we had properly completed the task that we set ourselves.'

Around him the warriors were gape-mouthed with astonishment at his unquenchable war spirit.

'Do you mean, Hector,' asked Æneas incredulously, 'that you would renew the attack, even though we have all been wounded and beaten back, and a storm is even now brewing?'

'I think that the rain will not come upon us before nightfall. And perhaps the thunder is a sign from Zeus that he favors us this day, since it comes from behind us to urge us on. And there was no retreat until I stumbled. Yes, I say that we should take up our spears again and return to the battle.'

'It will be unexpected, to say the least,' mused Sarpedon. 'They will be thinking that we will go limping back into Troy, and would be most disagreeably surprised to see us sticking our heads over their little fence again.'

'I wish Helenus and Deiphobus were here,' said Paris, wiping his face. 'But Polites took them away in his car.'

'Polites is here,' he said, shouldering his way through to where the council of war now sat. 'Who do you suppose brought you your little noonday snack? Nobody would think of reproaching your own brothers for taking their hurts back to be tended – nobody but you, Paris, who has to be pried out of Helen's arms in order to fight for an hour or so.'

Paris jumped up, a hot reply on his lips, and there would have been bad blood between the brothers except that Hector stopped them.

'Save your quarrels for the Achaeans,' he said severely. 'And listen to me while I speak. This time, let us not scatter our forces when we attack. That was well enough when we had to get the wall down, but now we can go through the center gate with no one to stop us. Let us go straight for the ships, and let no man stop to strip his opponent. If I see any do so, I will strike him down on the spot myself, and not many get up from one of Hector's blows! Seeing the ships on fire is what we want, not spoils, if any complains because of a rich prize missed, I will make it up to the whiner out of my own winnings. Now. Who will carry the word and order the men?'

'I will,' said Glaucus promptly, and soon his clear, high voice could be heard calling all Trojans and allies into marching order. No one appeared at the sagging stockade wall, and so they hoped that the Achaeans thought the Trojans were preparing to go back to Troy in as dignified a manner as they could.

From their surprise when Hector rushed through the gaping gateway, this was exactly what the Achaeans had been lulled into thinking. More than one of them had to drop a water bucket and take up a spear, and no few fell before they could find a weapon. Behind the Trojans, Zeus sent a mighty roll of thunder and a sweep of dust-filled wind into the Achaeans's eyes, and the Trojans raised an answering triumphant cry, certain that the victory was theirs.

One of the Achaeans kept his head, though he cried aloud. 'It is Hector!' he shouted. 'Is there no killing him? Let us form a square, with spears all around. No one will be rash enough to come against that, and perhaps Great Ajax can finish the job we all thought he had done this morning!'

And even as he spoke, the square began to take shape, double-rowed with bristling spears as one rank knelt behind their shields and the second rank filled up the gaps between them like brick-work. Over it all the thunder continued to roll, and from somewhere came a standard-bearer with the sign of Apollo rushing bravely alongside the fierce Trojan warriors.

But the square was demolished before it could consolidate; and the Achaeans were forced into another reluctant retreat. Back between the ships they were herded by the relentless Trojans, and they began to hold up their hands and call upon

Father Zeus. The thunder answered, but the Trojans knew it sounded for them.

Once more Hector found himself facing Great Ajax. But now Teucros unexpectedly bobbed out from behind his brother's great shield and his arrow was leveled straight at Hector's heart. Desperately, he pulled the bow, stretching nearly to the cheek as the Trojan archers did, and then a miracle happened.

Warriors, in telling of it later, swore that they saw Apollo touch the bowstring, but others were just as positive that Zeus's finger sent a spark of lightning at it; but however it happened, Teucros's bowstring snapped at the instant of greatest pull, and the arrow went spinning harmlessly away.

'It was newly put in just this morning!' cried Teucros in frustrated bewilderment. 'How can we prevail against a man whom Zeus covers with his own hands?'

'With long spear and shield,' growled Ajax. 'Go and find them, and call others to the fight if you do not care to join yourself now that your favorite weapon is spoiled.'

But the Achaeans had already seen how the Trojans were favored, and they began to fall back in fear. Then the ships, many of which were still smoldering from the first encounter, began to blaze up again.

It seemed now that there was nothing in the way of an all-out Trojan victory, and they were actually beginning to raise the paean when fresh shouts rose from the side. Here came more Achaeans, and now many a Trojan began to tremble because they wore the Ant-badge of the Myrmidons who had not fought at all in weeks and had their full strength. And when they saw the sturdy figure striding out before them in the awful armor they had come to know and fear, many of them with their senses overstretched from the day's terrible exertions gave in to terror and began to run away.

'Ai! Ai! We are lost!' they wailed. 'He has returned, and taken the field again! It is Achilles! Achilles! Achilles!'

13

THE DEATH OF SARPEDON

The turmoil in the City was almost as great as that on the Plain. We were overrun, swamped, buried in the House of Aphrodite, and everyone who had the least skill was pressed into service. No one knew what had happened. One minute, the smoke from the burning ships stained the skies and made the Trojans cheer from the battlements; and the next, the soldiers were running pell-mell, wildly as if for their very lives. These were brave men, we knew, for that had been proved long since. But here they came terror-stricken, and we were besieged by the wounded before we could begin to find out what prodigy had prompted such a wholesale rout.

There was water to be heated, arrowheads to be cut out, spear wounds to be bound up, bruises, broken bones, wrenched joints – in short, all the miserable work man can wreak against his fellows paraded before us as the skies steadily darkened. We kept only the most desperate cases in the House of Aphrodite, those who might die before morning, and it was crowded to the utmost. My himation soon went to cover a poor wretch who shivered in all his limbs though it was hot and sticky with the approaching storm, and I worked in my shift. In that first terrible hour I held many a hand and eased its owner into a poppy-lulled sleep, or gave a staunch clasp to aid a soul along into the deepest sleep of all. And I, who had shunned the hand's touch of friendship, did not shrink from this far more emotional and urgent grasping.

I do not know how long I worked in this fashion among the men whose grateful glances brought pity from my hardened heart; but after a while I had to go out into the courtyard to catch my breath before plunging into it again. To my surprise, I found Glaucus sitting wearily, a stained and dirty bandage on his shoulder and other untended cuts unheeded as he held his head in hands that seemed unequal to the burden.

'Glaucus, my friend!' I exclaimed, hurrying to him, for I had admitted him into my regard for his brother's sake. 'Let me bring you some wine! Why have you not come inside, for you need attention! And where is Sarpedon? Surely he has need of me too!'

He lifted his head, and the look of numbed hopelessness on his face stopped me in mid-step. 'Have you not heard?' he said dully. 'Sarpedon is dead.'

The moans of the wounded, the darkening courtyard, the City itself drifted away from me as I stood. My head whirled, but it was not the weakness that precedes fainting. Everything that had been alive in me drained away so that I was left a hollow husk, shriveled and dead in all the ways that mattered. A drop of rain touched my cheek and I looked upward as the first great drops began to fall.

'It is fitting for you to weep for him,' I told the heavens, scarcely aware that I was speaking, 'for I cannot. I have become a stone, and stones do not shed tears.'

Glaucus had begun to speak, and now he must tell it all for his own easing. I could not leave him, though I wanted to crawl away into a dark corner like a death-wounded animal. He was as a man in a dream, mumbling his terrible story in a dull monotone.

When they had begun to run away from the new terror that gripped them at the sight of fresh and unwearied troops coming upon them, led by what seemed to be Achilles himself, Hector knew that the battle had turned. He was no fool, and he was already aware that the outcome was like a blade poised on edge; a slight push from one side or another would send it irrevocably toward Trojans or Achaeans. And now the push had come.

'All together now, my champions!' he called. 'Cover the retreat, for we cannot stand against these new forces against us now that Achilles himself has decided to lay aside his grudge.'

But Æneas, who had keen sight, had been observing the awesome figure that was even now shortening the distance between them. 'But is it Achilles?' he said now, shading his eyes. 'It is his armor, true enough, but it seems to me that the fellow wearing it does not move exactly right.'

'I believe that you have seen what the rest of us have missed,' said Paris, pausing now in his turn.

'Of course!' exclaimed Hector. 'It is someone else, wearing Achilles's trappings, and we have been taken in by the ruse! But who? My guess would be Patroclus, for that is the only man I can conceive of Achilles's allowing to touch anything that belonged to him.'

Disgusted now at being taken in and duped, the Trojan champions fell back, though they scorned the headlong flight that was spreading across the Plain. For a moment, it seemed as though Patroclus would come straight for Hector, but then he chose a chariot instead and raced ahead, intent on cutting off the retreat and penning in the Trojans even as the Achaeans had been trapped within their walls. By chance, he fell among the Lycians and began to make a shambles of them.

The Trojan drivers came up quickly with the cars, and Sarpedon was first among them to leap in. 'I'll stop the fellow!' he cried. 'I'm not one to be afraid of armor! It's the man inside that counts, and that one is killing my own countrymen!' And then his driver slashed the reins across the horses and sped them along the Plain in pursuit.

While they were still a little way off, Patroclus saw them and cast a throwing-spear. It missed Sarpedon, but caught his driver Thrasymelos and killed him. Sarpedon's answering spear brought down one of Patroclus's horses, thus stopping him from flight. And then the two champions jumped out of their cars to face each other. They still had a throwing-spear each, and Sarpedon got his away first. Nimbly, Patroclus jumped out of the way and launched his spear in return. But Sarpedon's side step was on the wounded leg which he had quite forgotten; it gave under him, unable to do its work, and he fell with the sharp thrower protruding from his midriff.

'Glaucus, defend me!' he cried, but then Patroclus came up to him and, setting a foot on him, dragged out the spear. Sarpedon tried to say something else, but the blood spurted up in a fountain and cut it off.

From his chariot, Glaucus bit back bitter tears and breathed a prayer to Apollo. And then in his clear and ringing voice, he called the Trojans to avenge their greatest ally.

'He was your mainstay, Hector!' he cried. 'Let us forget our hurts and save his body! Though he is dead, let him not be despoiled by that pretender yonder!'

But Myrmidons were already nimbly unbuckling Sarpedon's handsome armor and had run away with it before the Trojans got to them, though they were forced to leave the corpse where it lay. It was Hector who got to Patroclus first, though he did not give him the first wound; a Dardanian struck him from behind. At any other time, it would have been thought a coward's wounding; but now no one cared for the nicer points of honor in their burning desire to bring down the man who had stretched Sarpedon lifeless on the Plain.

Dazed by the Dardanian's blow Patroclus seemed to stand quietly waiting for Hector. Even his driver turned away from him and ran for the Achaean camp.

In an act of supreme contempt, Hector disdained to drag away Patroclus's body but left it there after he had stripped it of Achilles's armor. But the body of Sarpedon he carried tenderly in his arms back through the gates of Troy for the honorable burial that was the due of a noble and brave king.

Glaucus's words came slower and slower, in disjointed phrases and half-sentences. He spoke of their childhood back in Lycia, of a dog they had once hunted with who seemed equally devoted to both of them, and then all at once he was asleep. Some of the Lycians came then and carried him in to the House of Aphrodite for Coronus to dress his hurts.

I remained outside, unheeding of the rain, and walked all night through the avenues of Troy. From some messenger whom I do not remember I received the news that Othryoneus of Cabesos was dead. He had been lured to fight at Troy with the promise of my hand, and now he had fallen to Idomeneus the Cretan. I gave the messenger nothing but a blank stare in return for his news. What did I care about that? It was Sarpedon who had held my heart, and now my only concern was that his funeral pyre should be as magnificent as the dwindling resources of Troy could make it.

But when Glaucus learned of these plans, he humbly came before Hector and Priam with a petition.

'Let him not be burnt,' he said, 'for he was the reigning king in Lycia, being the eldest male grandchild of Iobates who left only two daughters, Anteia and Philonoë. Let his body be sent back to the people he loved, and who loved him, so that they might look upon him once more before the earth covers him forever.'

'It is a long way to Lycia,' said my father gently. 'It may be that he will fall into corruption before he gets there and all his nobility will be forgotten in the ruin.'

'Still I would have it so.'

'Would you go with him?' asked Hector gravely. 'Though you may have forgotten it in your grief, his death now makes you king in his stead.'

Glaucus shook his head. 'We thought of that before we ever left Lycia. If I ever have a throne, it will be in Caria. Isander waits at home. Sarpedon and I chose to come to the aid of Troy, and now that Sarpedon is gone, I will not desert the errand we both set ourselves to accomplish.'

'Then do as you will with your brother's body.'

It fell to the physician Coronus to prepare Sarpedon as well as he could against the long and unprecedented journey, and silently I came to help. Coronus would have turned me from this grim task, but he looked long into my dry, hot eyes, and stepped aside without a murmur. Together we washed him clean of the blood and the dust and combed his hair neatly. We stuffed his nostrils full of herbs, and put myrrh in his mouth. Coronus pulled the gaping edges of his wounds together and sealed them with wax, and we crossed his arms over the one that had taken his life.

Coronus had heard something of how the Ægyptians prepared their dead by wrapping them tightly head to foot in swaths of bandages, and so I contributed the length of fine linen that had long stood uncompleted on my own loom. We soaked half the linen in salt, and the other half in honey diluted with wine before we began to wrap him, and in every fold we laid rosemary and cloves, and such other sweet spices as we could find.

Custom forbade that I be allowed to scratch my cheeks and pull out my hair, for our betrothal was a private thing known only to a very few. But I secretly clipped off a lock of my hair, in the back where it would not show, and coiled it into his lifeless hand before Coronus began to wrap him. It was very red against his bloodless flesh. And before his dear head was covered up I gave him three kisses, sealing his eyelids and his mouth. Then I left, trusting Coronus to finish without me.

Sometime, I would have to come to the Palladium, but for what purpose I did not know. The only feeling that had come back to me so far was a dull regret that we had hewed so strictly to Artemis's demands. I still had my useless virginity and all that Sarpedon and I had ever shared had been a few light embraces and kisses as chaste as the one I had pressed on his cold lips.

Now I sat in my room, waiting for I knew not what. I did not even come out to watch as a small picked troop of Lycians carried Sarpedon's body out of the sorrowing City on their long and melancholy journey back to their homeland. When the bandages had covered up his face, he was gone for me as surely as if he had been transported back there instantaneously, by magic.

Orthia brought me food; sometimes I ate it, sometimes I didn't. Even Bastos was unable to coax more out of me than an absent-minded stroke along his side. How long I stayed awake in my deep and silent grief I do not know; finally I slept, and came screaming out of it with the nightmare more vivid before me than it had ever been, fresh and deadly from its long rest.

Then I went down to where the Palladium stood in the house-shrine. I knelt, and then lay full length on my face before it, feeling the floor hard and cool and strangely soothing on my forehead.

'Whoever hears me,' I thought numbly, 'whether it be Artemis who prizes my maidenhood more than I, or Apollo whose finger has been on me from my childhood, or thundering Zeus in whose chair I once sat, or Aphrodite who brought love to my deadened heart, or even Hera the Crone to whom I feel equal in years. Give me only a little help now, for now is when I need it most. It seems that everything is soon to end for us all, and I fear that my feet will stumble from weariness and despair before it is all over.'

I had learned well and truly that there are some kinds of grief too deep to be washed away in quick tears. And now, as I lay there, it came to me how I had once told Sarpedon about the way we had been taught to give all. It seemed that I had violated this by trying to keep something for myself, and had had to be beaten down for the transgression. Prostrate and humbled, I offered myself for what was handed me; and with the acceptance, came the small and weary strength to bear it.

14
MIDSUMMER DAY

I went back to my duties in the House of Aphrodite with my tears still unshed. It seemed now that I had no need of them, but the physician was wiser; he put me to work with the worst cases. And when one of them died, clutching my hand, I found my face wet for a man who meant nothing to me, and many a foot soldier went down the Road of Death marveling that a princess of Troy would weep for him. Little by little, the tight bands of sorrow loosened and eased until I could almost live normally with it, all but a hard lump that rose now and then in my chest and blocked my breathing so that I had to go by myself for a while to master it.

There would be no fighting for some time now, for the Day of Fury, as we had come to call it, had left much recuperating to be done on either side. It was now drawing on to midsummer, and there were sacrifices to make that would call for both Helenus and me.

Out at the Achaean camp, they tried to repair their stockade wall; but the efforts were dispirited and the results indifferent. I sent for the stock of medicines in the Pastoral Shrine, and discovered that Chryses had departed, taking his 'good and pious' Chryseis with him. She had been discovered to be pregnant, and so far from being grateful for her rescue, begged repeatedly that she be returned to Agamemnon. She insisted that she had been well treated, and only those of Agamemnon's closest friends had lain with her. It was obvious that she was a trollop at heart, and when the old priest had caught her trying to slip out of the shrine to rejoin her Achaean admirers, he forcefully took her back to his homeland with him. And so Laocoön returned to the shrine, where, it was said, his woman and two sons still lived. Now nothing prevented me from conducting the midsummer sacrifices myself; it was mainly Apollo's festival, and Helenus was indifferent and willing to leave it all in my hands.

The old habit of spying was still with me; and reports began to come in from the Achaean camp about the results of the Day of Fury. Though they had had to bear with their own dead and wounded as well as they could, nobody wanted to approach Achilles with the news of the death of his beloved Patroclus. Finally Odysseus came up with a story with his clever mind that might turn Achilles's anger, at least to the point that he would not go raging through the camp, spreading further death and destruction on top of that which they had already suffered.

After he had killed the noble Sarpedon, the story went, Patroclus followed up his advantage against the dismayed Trojans. Singlehandedly he had chased them clear back to Troy, whereupon he had leaped from his chariot and gone straight for the great walls. Three times he climbed up the slope of the lower wall, but the great god Apollo had stationed himself above, and three times the god had pushed him down again.

'It is Achilles to whom this honor belongs!' the god had boomed, and Patroclus obediently turned away to kill more Trojans.

So mightily was he cutting his way through their ranks that Apollo became enraged at the thought of all his favorites being stretched here and there in the dust by noble Patroclus. And there is none who can withstand the wrath of a god.

Forgetting all the rules of fair combat, Apollo came up behind Patroclus and slapped him smartly between the shoulders with his great hand. At this awful blow, the helmet-string broke and the helmet went tumbling, dabbling its proud plumes in the dust, and all the straps of the harnessing of the armor were sundered so that it fell at Patroclus's feet, leaving him naked. Even his spear shivered and splintered in his hand, and the shield dropped from the belt around his shoulders, plucked off by the angry god.

Then the Trojan jackals gathered around to worry Patroclus, and though many smote him, Hector killed him and Apollo gave him the armor as his prize.

Nothing daunted, the Achaeans raced over the Plain to where Patroclus lay, under the shadow of the very walls of Troy, and Menelaus was in the van. Long and valiantly they fought back and forth, over Patroclus's body, and in the end they brought it away, though the armor was lost.

But it took no spies to tell Troy about the hysterical excesses Achilles threw himself into when he had been given this fanciful tale. Like a woman, he tore his cheeks and pulled out handfuls of hair. He scooped up the dust and poured it over his head until he made himself filthy with it. From time to time he would rush to the corpse where it lay already on a bier awaiting the fire, and grab it by the shoulders, crying, 'Patroclus! Patroclus!' as if he would shake the life back into it.

And then he went running to Agamemnon who shrank back in fear and surreptitiously laid his hand on his sword. But Odysseus had done well in his story; Achilles only grasped the King's hands and brought them to his eyes from which the tears flowed freely.

'Why did we quarrel so, over a worthless girl?' he sobbed. 'If we had not, I would have been out there instead of Patroclus, and then the tale would have had a different ending! The Trojans have had their way long enough because of our disagreement. Come! Let us patch it up. Give back the girl, and all will be forgotten!'

And behind him, Odysseus could not hold back a smile that Achilles had not forgotten the cause of the quarrel even in his hysteria, and insisted upon Briseis's return before he went out to avenge his beloved Patroclus.

'Gladly,' said Agamemnon, for he had no other choice. But he made others of his champions give up some of their spoil, too. Tripods, nuggets of gold and other treasures grudgingly changed hands.

'Now!' cried Achilles, 'I will ride to war!'

'Patience, good Achilles,' said Odysseus soothingly. 'In your great grief and zeal you do not see that black night is all around us. We have seen that these Trojans are a wily lot; therefore, we must make sacrifices, and eat and drink in order to strengthen ourselves for the coming battle. With you before us once more, we are bound to prevail, and the Trojans will know it too and fight all the harder.'

'Yes, yes, you are right, Odysseus. You always had a longer head than mine, though you are nowhere my equal on the battlefield. I will let you lead me, for a while.' And then Achilles allowed Odysseus to put his arm around his shoulders and take him back to his hut, much to the relief of everyone else.

Now, anyone who ventured outside the walls was sure to fall prey to Achilles. The loss of his armor had been more of an insult than a handicap, as every warrior had more than one set. There was that which one wore in the practice yard, and that which one fought in with replacements in case a piece was lost or hewed beyond repair, and that which was his best, and was most richly ornamented. The armor which Glaucus had been forced to trade was of this last sort, which he had foolishly worn because of a broken strap on his everyday corselet. And though Sarpedon's fighting harness was gone, his beautiful armor which bore the royal emblem of Lycia had traveled back to Lycia with his body.

Now we got a look at Achilles's dress harness; and we made the uncomfortable discovery from where the story of his invulnerability had come. Where other men wore hardened leather breast-pieces inlaid with bronze and leather helmets similarly strengthened with horns set in pairs to deflect a blow, Achilles now strutted in what seemed to be solid bronze. Some consummate craftsman had wrought this for him, for even his helmet looked to be made of a single piece of metal. Arrows, and throwing-spears too for that matter, would bounce off like tossed flowers, and a man might hew away for a long time without finding a vulnerable spot in all that bronze.

'I hope he stumbles beneath the weight and can't get up again,' ran the mutters through the City. And, 'Let him broil in his bronze box. Only a fool would fight in it, when leather's so much cooler under this sun!'

There were not a few who were tempted beyond bearing to go out and try a man who was burdened like this; and of these, fewer still returned. For the first time, we saw the Achaeans take captives, leading them away with cords around their throats though heretofore they had unhesitatingly killed all who could not escape even when the Trojans had thrown down their weapons and appealed for mercy.

And then, the smoke of a pyre came billowing up from the Achaeans' camp, and the unbelievable story came whispering behind it, leaving men white-faced and stunned in its wake.

With the patience of a madman, Achilles had gathered captives, by preference sons of Priam, until he had a dozen of them. Polydorus, the youngest surviving son of Hecabe, made the thirteenth. He had been forbidden to fight, but had slipped out anyway and Achilles took him. Then and only then had he set the torch to Patroclus's funeral pyre, and had slit the throats of the Trojan captives for an offering to his beloved as the flames mounted. Even the Achaeans must have been revolted by this terrible outrage, but they had been afraid to lift their hands against him.

When he heard it, Æneas clenched his teeth grimly. 'Now we'll show the world what the Dardanians can do!' he muttered, and went away with a dangerously soft-footed step.

Presently, he and his men, every one hand-picked, could be seen speeding across the Plain. Half his troop peeled off near the ford of the Scamander, and his tactic began to become plain to the watchers behind.

Back they came to the ford, closely pursued by Achilles and a band of his own, so hot in the chase that they would not notice the ambush laid for them. Even so, Achilles would have had the best of it, for nothing could touch him in his bronze; but inexplicably, he turned away from combat with Æneas himself and waded out into the river.

Æneas told us about it later, shaking his head in bewilderment.

'We were going at it properly,' he said, 'and I thought that I might be able to get beneath all that bronze after all. The Achaeans and the Dardanians had had their fights, and now were drawn back, a group on either side of us, to watch the outcome. Achilles turned his foot on a stone and went down, one knee in the water, where a few bodies were floating. And then it seemed as if he forgot all about me, and went floundering out into the stream. Then he began slashing away at the water, if you please, screaming that the river itself had risen up to fight him.

' "I'll beat even the Trojan River!" he shrieked. "How dare you come against me and complain that I dump dead Trojans into your putrid stream! You'll think that's a mild punishment before I get through with you!" '

'What then?' asked Priam.

'Well, we stood dumbfounded for a minute, watching him go at it. And his Myrmidons just looked at my Dardanians, and we looked back. Their spears drooped in their hands. There didn't seem to be much that we could do after that, so we turned around and came home. I suppose the Myrmidons waited around until the madman had worn himself out trying to kill the river, and then they took him home, too.'

'God above preserve us from such a foe!' breathed my mother.

But behind her, Hector stood silent, his brows drawn together, and I could tell that deep thoughts were racing behind his still, dark face.

It was poor enough that we had to offer the god on his day. A few lambs, too small to make a warrior's meal, a handful of grain, one old bullock overlooked in the relentless search for food in the beleaguered City – these were the sort of things we had to lay before Apollo. I thought with a sigh of the days in the past, when we had given him the bright-skinned horses he loved, and had made no stint of them, either.

Helenus stood looking at our pitiful little heap of god-gifts as sourly as I. 'What does it matter, after all?' he said bitterly. 'All the gods hate us. I wish the Achaeans would hurry and put an end to it, for I am weary of waiting for the final blow to fall.'

'Every day brings fresh reports that the Achaeans are losing heart. They hoped to have the City in rubble long before Midsummer Day, and it still stands.'

'Yes, but what of the people inside? Just look at you! For a while it seemed that you were going to put some flesh on your bones, like Helen, and now you're back looking like a rag-tag bundle of sticks again. No wonder they call you Storm-crow.'

'People can live a long time on beans, and barley, and oil.'

'And when that is gone, what? We can't look for many more allies, if any at all this late in the summer, and though you tell me the Achaeans talk of leaving, they are still here.'

'Please don't quarrel with me, Helenus. It makes my head ache, and there is enough to worry about as to how we will make our proper sacrifice with that monster Achilles snuffling around outside our walls.'

'Then I'll leave it to you, as that was always more your concern than mine. For myself, I believe that we are lost already.'

And then shrill shouts from the walls made me leave the preparations where they stood and run to the Great Tower. There, by the Scaian Gate, Andromache sagged in the arms of her maids and she was wild-eyed and distraught beyond anything I had seen in her so far.

'I tried to persuade him!' she wept. 'I begged him. I have no father, no mother, no brothers, I told him. You are everything I have in one. I even brought little Scamander, to try to make him see reason! But no, he would go anyway!'

In his nurse's arms, Hector's son, whom the people affectionately nicknamed Astyanax, stared at his mother round-eyed. 'Red top scare me and I cry,' he lisped to his nurse. 'Scare Mamma too? Mamma cry?'

'Yes, yes, my darling,' the nurse murmured soothingly. And then Andromache took the little boy into her own arms, holding him fast as though she thought even Hector was lost to her now except in this child of their bodies.

'I cannot go up there,' she said faintly. 'I would if I could, but I have already made an embarrassing show before the people.

Dear Cassandra, go in my stead, and bring me any news that you see there.'

I had no idea of what had been going on, but I could guess. Hector had evidently gone outside the walls on some errand of his own, and his wife had tried to restrain him with every feminine weapon at her disposal.

'It is too bad that you are too little a woman, and Hector too much a man,' I said coldly. 'Yes, I will go up on the Tower for you, and I will call the encouragement to my brother that should come from his wife. Tears and sniveling! Could you give him no better farewell?'

And then I turned on my heel and began to climb up to the top of the Tower, propelled by my own curiosity as to what could have prompted Hector to interrupt the holy day as much as by the promise given to the weeping woman below.

But perhaps I am too hard on Andromache. Hector was, after all, the only person in the world she had left, outside of their son; and there was no doubt that she had always loved him to distraction and never had an eye for any other. She had been gently reared, and had never known a day of harshness or a moment's ill-wishing from anyone. She was, in a manner of speaking, like that tenderest morsel that lies near the bone when one goes to cut the joint; by contrast, I was a tough string of gristle, apt to be spat out and discarded. Only once had I ever softened, and now never again.

Even as I reached the Tower's top, I realized that I had been among the last to hear of this departure from ceremony, for Priam and Hecabe sat in their places, and all the surviving nobles of Troy now came gathering. And everywhere there were faces full of questions and wondering. Priam sat with his head bowed, though Hecabe sat forward in her chair, straining to see.

I rushed to the parapet, where I was accustomed to stand. Below me, on the scarp where he had joyfully awaited a champion the day he fought his mighty duel with Great Ajax, stood Hector; but this was a far different man from the bantering warrior who had strode impatiently back and forth while the vacillating Achaeans made up their minds.

Now he was as still as if he had been cut out of stone and put there to frighten any who approached the City. In one hand he held a sturdy spear, and the other braced the shield from where it hung around his neck. Tall and grim he was, made taller still by the blood-red plumes that crested his helmet. Now I knew the reason for his son's fright, for it was enough to daunt a sturdy warrior, Hector's appearance.

He wore his dress armor, and it was all black and silver. From black bulls the leather had come, and was stained again in the tanning, and it was always polished with lamp soot mixed in the oil. All the bronze plates were washed in silver, and silver studs edged his kilt below. There was no color anywhere on him except for the blood-colored plumes and the rich neck strap that he had won from Ajax. Even his spear was black, and ringed with silver. And he stood, feet planted firmly apart, as if he waited.

'Hector, dear brother!' I called. 'Why have you interrupted the preparations for Apollo's day, and left Andromache weeping behind?'

He turned slowly, and then I saw that it was my brother after all and not some image of the god of war who stood below me. He smiled, and for all his grim appearance, his tone seemed light and carefree when he answered me.

'Why, I have had an augury of my own, Cassandra,' he said. 'It seemed good to me that I should stand here in the morning's sun of Midsummer Day.'

'But it seems to me that your standing is for a purpose.'

'A storm-crow's eyes see far,' he answered with a smile. 'Even now, our herald is carrying my challenge to Achilles in the Achaean camp.'

'Achilles! If you wanted to fight him man to man, why did you pick today of all days?'

'Because today of all days, the outcome might be the best for Troy. I am sorry I have spoiled your holy planning, Cassandra, but there will still be plenty of time for those who will make their offerings and send up their prayers. And perhaps when I am through, Achilles will not be prowling around to ruin your ceremonies in a far worse way from what I have done.'

'Then I will not scold you, since you seem to be acting on an impulse that may very well have come from Apollo, on his day. I will send my faith and courage along with you instead, for you had little enough of it at the gate.'

Though he still smiled gravely, his eyes were shadowed. 'Andromache's tears are as pleasing to me in their way as your staunchness. They are both a measure of your love.'

And then others among us began to call down their own affection, and admiration, and encouragement to him. But he was already finished with dealing with those of us on top of the wall. Now he stood again with eyes searching the Plain, waiting for the approach of his enemy Achilles.

Magnificent in his self-confidence, Achilles came riding across the Plain. His shield was slung over his back and a long spear jutted from the weapon slot of the chariot that he drove, acting his own driver this day. No one but Achilles would have brought it to the fight where custom had always dictated otherwise, in a duel's weapons.

Carelessly he dismounted and looped the reins around a stone. I think he would have even presumed to have used the fig tree as a hitching post, except that even he did not care to bring his car so close to the walls.

'Your lickspittle came along to say that someone here wished to gossip for a while,' he announced. 'Achilles is no man to come at another's beck, but I have grown weary of chasing down Trojans at random as I find them outside your dung heap. Where is the champion, this great warrior who is audacious enough to summon me from my ease for a war of words, which is the only kind of fighting where Trojans excel?'

'He stands before you, Achilles,' answered my brother in his calm, heavy, measured voice.

Achilles's helmet plume nodded as he looked Hector up and down. 'You?' he scoffed. 'What, is there no better? This was hardly worth the trip.' He unlashed the long spear from the chariot with an air that clearly conveyed his bored indifference to something that would be quickly settled. 'Well, then, let us get it done. I left a certain matter half-finished at my hut, and I am a man who likes to complete what he has started.'

'You will have to come to me, Achilles, for here I stand,' said Hector, and it was plain that the other's insults had washed past him without touching.

Achilles's shield was already on his arm, and he stopped, looking keenly upward to where Hector towered inexorably. A new mood seemed to come over him and he grew wary and sly.

'What, and have your famous Trojan archers shoot me full of arrows in my arms and legs from the safety of the walls? It would be easy enough to have me down then, so that you could unlace my helmet and take my life with the little knife a woman uses to pare her nails!'

'This is between you and me only, Achilles. If you do not care to come to me to fight, then climb into your car again and drive away with the coward's mark on your back for all to see.'

'Coward, is it!' the Achaean shouted on a rising note, and his voice cracked. 'We'll see who is the coward when I am finished!'

He came up the scarp to the plateau in a bull-like rush, his head down, and dust sprang up from his hurrying feet. And Hector, who had been like one chiseled of adamant, moved to meet him. He turned aside the oncoming long spear with his own far shorter black-shafted thrower and for good measure rapped Achilles on the helmet with the blade, making it ring aloud.

Achilles stopped, for his ears must have been singing from the blow. Then he began a more cautious advance, and Hector led him around circling, until they were both where he wanted them to be.

'I said that you would have to come to me, Achilles,' he said now, and his tone was as light and indifferent as it had been when he had spoken to me. 'Let us see if you can match the pace I set!'

And then he turned and began to run, glancing once over his shoulder to see if Achilles was following. For a moment, the Achaean stood gaping, and then with a frustrated shout he started in pursuit.

Atop the wall there was an indrawn gasp, of dismay and consternation mixed. 'Is our mighty Hector a coward himself, that he runs from the Achaean?' ran the whispers among the shocked onlookers.

'No,' said the older warriors sternly, but they were at almost as great a loss to explain Hector's bewildering behavior.

'Perhaps he hopes to tire the madman in his bronze suit!' sang a clear voice that I recognized as Glaucus's, and the cry was immediately taken up in relief. No coward at all, but a clever strategist was incomparable Hector! Already men were pounding along the walls, trying to keep up with the chase, and others went swarming to the several towers. 'Of course,' smiled men to each other as they ran. 'If Hector wished to avoid meeting Achilles now that he is here, he would only have to approach a gate, and it would open instantly for him!' And indeed, some who were more respectful of Achilles's towering strength of arms were already calling out this prudent advice to Hector from along the course of the walls.

But this was not Hector's aim, and I knew it as surely as I knew the awful, forbidding chill that was beginning to coil along my belly. It was not decorum that kept me from racing along with the others to keep in sight of the runners, but the paralyzing certainty that what there was to see would happen on the plateau beneath the Tower on which I stood.

When they had completed the first circuit and started on the second, any doubts that I may have had were gone. I lifted my head and found that I had begun to weep.

'Your warning has come too late,' I thought, searching the empty sky for a sign of the gods who must surely be watching. 'But would I have stopped him, even if I could? Surely this noble thing that my brother is doing is beyond any earthly advice or consideration. No, it is no warning that I feel, only the knowledge before the rest begin to realize that Hector is the sacrifice this Midsummer Day.'

He had been dressed for death, and I would have known it if I had only opened my eyes to it. No wonder the child had been frightened. The black of his armor, the silver which is the Goddess's own, the red of his plumes which was the color of her immortality that comes only with death – he was giving himself up as an offering for the salvation of his city, and the sacrifice had been properly and becomingly ornamented.

No wonder there had been that air of impersonality about him as he spoke with me so cryptically about the ceremonies to come. I looked at Priam, and realized that he had known it all along, for he sat gray-faced, unable to look. Beside him, Hecabe had guessed, or perhaps he had told her, for she tore her garment and hid her head to weep.

'How amazing!' exclaimed a bright voice beside me, and I found Helen peering over the parapet. 'Who would ever have thought that Hector would turn and run away!'

'Be quiet, you slut!' I said viciously, 'or I'll push you over the side and see how nimbly you can run with them! You are meddling in something that is far beyond you, and if you are wise you'll go and leave the Trojans to their own concerns.'

She gave me a hurt look, but I ignored her, returning to the heartbreak below, and when I looked again, she was gone. I could have torn out her beautiful eyes with my fingers for having distracted me for even a moment when Hector was beginning the third prescribed circuit of the walls of the City, along the road that every sacrifice must go.

Here and there, realization was beginning to come at last to the Trojans, and each man told his neighbor so that Trojans and allies alike ceased their futile shouts for Hector to come inside this gate or that. Now, there was only the sound of their hurrying feet as they came back to the Great Tower white-faced and shaking, for everyone knew that it was on the very plateau where Hector had stood waiting that the sacrifices were given.

Here he turned, and waited for Achilles. Both men needed a moment to blow before further exertions; Achilles was panting hard from the strenuous labor under his burden of bronze. Hector's face was calm, and I knew that he had given himself long before he had gone out of the Scaian Gate, and now waited only for the taking.

'Be good to your servant,' I whispered. 'Dear Lady of Troy, let him not feel his death stroke, but take him gently into your Paradise. Let me bear his hurt instead, through the terrible prophetic chill that envelops me. And let all the gods witness that this day Troy has given up the greatest sacrifice it can make, so that we may be spared.'

Even as I prayed, Achilles began reviling Hector. 'You cur,' he snarled. 'Is this the way Trojans fight? Are you ready to stand now, or is it to be another foot race?'

'Come ahead, Achaean,' said Hector gently, 'for I am ready.'

Hector was a consummate warrior, and the habits learned from a lifetime in practice yard and field do not drop away in a moment. When he saw the long spear coming, clumsy in its flight because it was not meant for casting, he ducked aside and his own black-shafted thrower left his hand in a reflex he could not call back. His sword was already out by the time the spear-head clattered against Achilles's shield. And then he held out his own shield on one side and his sword on the other, looking from one to the other with amusement. What need, his attitude said clearly, did he have now for these heavy and cumbersome things? He dropped the one and shrugged the strap of the other off his shoulder with a laugh. He was still laughing when Achilles rushed at him and buried the edge of his sword in his neck.

For me, it was as if Hector's deathblow had been my own. A blackness came over my eyes and the breath left me. I remember a dim thought that there were two victims that day where the gods had expected only one, and was faintly pleased as I fell.

I was surprised, not too happily, to wake again in my own room, among my own familiar things. Bastos was nestled beside me, anxiously speaking now and then, while Orthia gave me broth to drink. Her face was very still and her eyes dry while she told me of Achilles's actions afterward.

'It was as if he knew nothing of the solemnity of the rite he had been induced to perform,' she said. 'Or if he knew, he cared nothing for it. He stripped off all of Hector's gear, all the black and the silver, and threw it into the car. And not content with that, he took the sword belt which Hector had won from Ajax and looped it around his poor, dead feet and tied it to the back of his chariot. And he dragged Hector, naked and helpless in his death, all the way back to the camp. We watched, unable to believe, while Hector's proud head trailed in the dust until all that was left were the stains of his blood on the ground.'

'Did no one try to stop him?' I asked, aghast.

'Who is there left who can stand against Achilles? But the King, overcome by his grief, would have gone straightaway to the Dardanian Gate where his cars and animals are kept in his stable, and followed with a spear in his feeble hand, except that the nobles kept him back.'

At this news, a random, nagging feeling of something being amiss began to steal over me, but it was lost in a sudden remembrance. I sat upright, nearly upsetting the cup in Orthia's hands. 'Andromache!' I exclaimed, stung by my awareness of failure in a solemn duty. 'I promised to take the news to her, and here I lie instead, as weak as any other woman!'

'She has been told,' Orthia said, pushing me back and offering the broth again. 'When she heard the wailing from the Tower, her hand trembled in the embroidery she had set herself to do while Hector was away. She reached the Tower in time to see Achilles dragging Hector away, insulting and despoiling him in the dust. In front of everyone she spoke a lament for him and for little Astyanax that moved even the rough soldiers to tears. Then, full nobly, she went back to her masterless house to do her own weeping in private.'

Still, for my own sake, I must go to her. The customs of her home did not demand scratching her cheeks, and her face was very white. She sat dry-eyed and proud, holding Hector's son on her lap. When I tried to offer my excuses for not doing as I had pledged, she cut in on what I was saying in a way that showed me she had been paying no attention.

'It pleased him to see me weep for him when he went out onto the field, did you know that, Cassandra?' she asked. And before I could answer, she went on. 'But no, I suppose not. You know only god-business, and that poorly. But weep I did, and not just the show that some women put on, either. Now I will never stop, though I do it where no one else can see. Will there be a ransom, do you suppose? It will have to be a very large one. I bear you no ill will, Cassandra, because you fainted. Your wits are deranged.'

As are yours, I thought. But your distraction will pass, though now you speak of this thing and that with no break between them as you sit so proudly, holding Hector's heir as your shield against your grief.

How sadly I had misjudged her, by my own harsh standards. Though I thought her to have shown herself weak before, when she still had Hector to lean upon, there was strength there beneath the surface. Truly, she deserved better than she had gotten.

She had spoken of a ransom for Hector's body; there was bound to be one asked, and I found the City buzzing with speculation about it. But day after day passed, and no word came from the Achaean camp, though we watched anxiously for a herald coming from that direction.

Instead, weird rumors came to me, concerning Achilles's recurring ill-treatment of the corpse. By now, he had come to realize – or perhaps clever Odysseus had enlightened him – that he had been duped into being the instrument of sacrifice that might well be the saving of the city that the Achaeans had labored so long to destroy.

'Three times around!' he would howl in a fury of vindictiveness at the ease with which he had been tricked. The unrelieved mourning for his beloved Patroclus rankled at his heart; and so each morning he would grab the strap that still bound Hector's ankles and drag him around the darkened spot where Patroclus's funeral pyre had burned, crying, 'I'll give you three times around, you filthy abomination on this earth!'

But these things I kept to myself, hoping that they would not leak past me to the warriors. Already it was becoming obvious that someone from Troy was going to have to go and bargain for my brother's body with this madman, and feeling was running high enough as it was without this added to the fire. Something of the sort must have been surmised, however, for word began to spread quickly that Priam himself planned to make that perilous visit to the Achaean camp. No one of lesser rank could hope to do so and live.

I pushed my way into the crowded council chamber to find my father, looking so old it was frightening, sitting strengthlessly in his chair facing well-meaning advisers who were harrowing him, trying to dissuade him from his chosen course.

'But why you, my lord Priam?' demanded Antenor. 'Is there no one else here in Troy, a younger man and stronger, who would not willingly bear this burden for you?'

'I am the King, and I am Hector's father,' Priam replied stubbornly, with the weariness of repetition. It was plain that he had stood this wall of words between himself and all opposition. 'There is no one else who might reach Achilles's heart. And if he kills me as well, then it was my fate and I will not turn away from it.' It seemed as if he would say more, but he clamped his aging lips over his teeth and bit it back, and I felt the uneasiness creep along my backbone again.

But there was no time to unravel the riddle. My father needed support, and instinctively I felt that he was right in his stand. I shouldered past warriors and women, seeing out of the corner of my eye beautiful, careless Helen smiling at some man who was not her husband and Laodice close beside her, aping every gesture. On the other side of Priam's chair stood Hecabe, tall and straight, but with her grief carved into her face for all to see. Togther we supported the King, but if she could not speak, I would.

'Leave him alone!' I said sharply. 'You who call me Storm-crow, listen now to my cawing. A warrior going into the Achaean camp would stand no chance at all of living past their sagging gateway; but who would harm an old man, gentle and kind, grown aged in the care of his people? And if you do not care to let your King venture out alone, then send him under the sacred herald's wand. Even Achilles must respect that.'

But in the crowd I saw elegant Idaios turn pale, and he hung his head and stared down at his shoes.

'What, Idaios? Have you no stomach for danger? I have seen you brisk enough on the field, and you even dared come between Hector and Great Ajax himself when they fought their celebrated duel until sunset.'

'That is one thing, my lady,' he said shamefacedly. 'But it is quite another to go boldly into the Achaeans's camp without a number of good soldiers at my back to see that the law is kept. It is certain that Achilles will remember me, from when I sent him Hector's challenge. My heart fails at the thought.'

'I will ask no one to do unwillingly that which I have set myself,' said Priam mildly, who had railed in a fine rage at far less in earlier times. 'You are excused, good herald, and no shame goes with you.'

'I have acted as Hector's spokesman on the field more than once,' said Glaucus in his high, clear voice that brought a look of admiration from Helen's direction. 'I will go with the King.'

There was a murmur of assent that would have swelled into a shout, except that Anchises, who now looked almost as old as my father, held up his hand. 'All of us here have been guilty of turning deaf ears toward Cassandra, and call her Storm-crow in derision. But today, at least, it seems that her wits are about her. So let us listen, until the same old tale of fire and death begins to creep into her speech, when we will know that she has wandered away again.

'Noble Glaucus, even wrapped in a herald's mantle, and bearing a herald's wand, could never be mistaken for anything but what he is: a bold and able warrior, who has brought down many an Achaean on the field. He would provoke revenge and retaliation where we hope for a safeguard for Priam. Who then among us is fit to go with the King?'

A long moment of silence came, when warriors looked at each other with the knowledge of the truth of Anchises' words. It seemed that there was no one who would not be more danger than help and that Priam would have to go alone to treat with the murderous Achilles. And then, a slender little figure slipped through the crowd and came and stood in front of Priam.

'I will go with my father, the King,' she said so softly that only a few heard her. And then she slipped her little hand into his.

It was Polyxena, the youngest of Hecabe's daughters and now Priam's youngest child since the death of Troilus. She was delicate in all her limbs and her hair hung like a silken brown ribbon down her back. Through her sun-touched skin one could clearly trace the blue lines of veins, not only at the wrist, but along her arms and legs and across her fragile shoulders and exquisite temples as well. The bitterness of the war had been kept from her as far as possible, for it was feared that she would not have been strong enough to bear it. Men smiled and nodded to each other when they sometimes caught a glimpse of her practicing dance steps in the corridors of the Palace.

Now an indrawn gasp cut through the silence, a protest that this frail child would willingly offer herself up to the peril that had been proposed. It was against the soldiers' instincts, but old Anchises nodded thoughtfully and gravely as he considered the possibilities newly opened.

'The very young and the very old alike are most secure when the war god walks through the world, insofar as anybody is safe. When warriors are still capable of thought and the killing lust has not blinded them to everything but spreading death around them in an ever-widening pool, these are the ones most tenderly preserved.' He placed his hand over hers where it was still clasped by Priam's wrinkled one. 'A god must have inspired you, daughter of Priam.'

But now Hecabe had found her voice and began to wail aloud. 'My husband!' she cried. 'Where have your wits flown? Once you were famous for your good sense through all the world, but now you propose a fool's journey to a madman, and would take along a little girl to shield you from the Achaeans' spears! Have you not heard that Achilles is a very cannibal, devouring a mouthful of your son's mortifying flesh each morning? How can you expect mercy, or sympathy, or even a shred of reason from such a man?'

'The more reason that I should go and ransom his body, if that be true,' replied Priam placidly. 'The time for revenge is not yet, if it lies with us. But the body of one who gave his life so that ours might be spared is worth a little sacrifice, and I will not grudge it. Cease your outcry, my good wife, lest you bring a bad omen upon me, because my course was decided long before I came to listen to any of you. Busy yourself instead with opening the storage-chests and treasuries. Bring out robes and tunics, rugs and finely woven sheets, such as Troy is famous for. Search the treasuries for such gold as has not already been paid out to our allies. Be generous, but do not beggar me, for we will need new allies and gold with which to pay them. Do not stint on caldrons and goblets and the like, and perhaps Achilles will not notice.'

'Add one more thing to your list, my father,' I advised, 'if you wish to please Achilles. Give him back the armor which Hector took from Patroclus.'

Priam's snowy brows drew together. 'It was Hector's last war prize,' he said heavily. 'But even that I will forfeit, to have my son's body returned for proper burial.'

'And one thing further.' Around me, I heard sighs and knew that they thought I was going to begin speaking of fire and death again. 'Let a Gorgon sign be painted on the sides of the wagon, and mark the same on your forehead and the forehead of my sister, to preserve you from any who would stop you before you reach the hut of Achilles.'

Relieved, the warriors nodded to themselves. The Gorgon sign, that of an open mouth with tongue protruding, was a talisman warning against interference from any who did not understand what was being undertaken. Bakers often chalked this mark on their ovens, so that unknowing folk who were attracted by the good smells of baking would not spoil the bread by opening the doors before the proper time. And I had seen Coronus put the same mark on jars of drugs that he could use skillfully but which might be fatal in the hands of the unlearned.

'Let it be so,' said the old King wearily. 'And let us purify ourselves and commend ourselves to Zeus who is king over all the gods, for I intend to go out of the Dardanian Gate this very evening.'

We sorrowed, all of us, even those who believed that Priam was god-inspired and Polyxena no less so, when we saw the mule-driven cart pass through the once-mighty gate and across the plaza where rich merchants had once come and gone. The crudely painted Gorgon sign was still damp in places, and here and there the paint had run down in streaks, though the pile of ransom goods it guarded was noble enough. Priam and Polyxena, dressed in plain, rough garments, sat together on the seat and Polyxena drove the mules though her fragile hands were unused to such a task. Their foreheads were marked with the same warning sign drawn in ashes, and the herald's wand lay across Polyxena's lap. Someone had remembered to grease the wheels of the cart well so that they would not screech a proclamation of their passing, though the clip-clop of the mules' hoofs and the occasional clink of the metal goods were enough to alert a sentry.

However, if any Achaean watchmen marked their passage, the Gorgon mark was enough to put them off and they passed without challenge across the Plain to the central gate of the Achaean camp. There, men opened the gates for them, piously averting their eyes though they had to wonder at the spectacle of such a Trojan deputation arriving at such a time.

Straight into Achilles's hut Priam went, leaving Polyxena with the wagon and mules in the stream of light from the open doorway. Two Achaeans were with him, but they too looked away at the sight of the Gorgon's mark on the King's forehead and left hurriedly by a back door.

With the humility that only a king can afford, Priam went to Achilles where he sat astonished, having just finished eating, for he was wiping his hands and face on a perfumed towel. A supplicant, Priam clasped Achilles's knees. Then he kissed his hands, those same terrible and murderous hands that had sent so many of his sons along the Road of Death, while Achilles sat dumfounded and amazed.

'As you see me, noble Achilles, remember your own father who must be heavy with years,' said the Trojan King. 'Once I could boast of more sons than you could tell on your fingers five times over, but no more. But there was one among them that outshone all the rest, as a tall oak towers above the scrub. That was Hector, who now lies dead by this very hand that I kiss in supplication. And in the face of your wrath, I have come without arms or armor, with a rich ransom to buy back his body, though you have not made the first move according to the custom that has existed time out of mind. I am your sworn enemy, and you are mine; but I ask you to remember your father as you look at me, and to think about the grief he would feel if you had fallen to Hector, and he had had to come begging for his son's corpse. And confident in your lordly mercy, I dare raise my hand to your chin in appeal and touch the lips of the man who slew my son.'

Achilles stared long and hard at old Priam where he knelt, and the King's fate trembled upon the whim of a madman. But as a god had inspired Priam to go to Achilles's hut, so a god had put the words into his mouth that would reach through to the stony heart of the Achaean champion. He stretched out his hands to Priam, accepting him into his protection as a supplicant, and raised him to his feet in full courtesy.

'You astonish me, King Priam,' he said now, and his tone was calm and rational, so much so that it was not easy to believe what he was. 'How can you bear to come to this place, and look at the face of the man who has killed so many of your noble sons? In the face of such meekness from my enemy, how can I fail to offer him the strength of my arm while he is in the jaws of the lion?'

Then Achilles led him to a skin-covered settle, and drew up his own chair nearby. 'You ask me to remember my own father, sir. I cannot care for him, except when I look at you. He had but one son to your many, and put me out of his house early when he saw that I was not going to be as other men. I have long known that my life was destined to be a short-spun thread.'

'I cannot mourn that, though you have given me your protection. Say only that you will accept the ransom, so that I may depart from the jaws of the lion.'

Achilles's face darkened, and for a moment it seemed that Priam had been too blunt in his speech.

'I do believe that a god has led you to me. Otherwise, you must have been filled full of Achaean arrows before you could reach the gate. Even so, do not provoke me further, or I will reach out now and strike you down where you sit, regardless of supplicant law, or god law; for when I am in my anger, only Achilles's law carries any weight.'

And then while my father sat silent and afraid, Achilles jumped up, calling the two who had fled through the back door. 'Automedon! Alcimos! Let us see what the Trojan has brought us in return for the body of Hector!'

They brought Polyxena into the hut and gave her a footstool to sit on, evidently thinking her a young lad, as her body was unformed. And then they began to unpack the ransom and bring it in, piling it in the middle where the firelight could hit it. The sheets and mantles and other woven goods they put into one heap, the vessels into another, and the gold into a third. Last of all they brought in the armor, and left again, seemingly unwilling to stay in the presence of such strange guests as these.

Achilles's eyes lit up when he saw the armor, and the reasonable calm with which he had greeted Priam seemed to burn away. With a satisfied exclamation he picked it up. 'It was this harness that last embraced Patroclus living,' he said ecstatically, hugging it to himself. 'It will hold the place of honor in my house as long as I live.' But then his eye went past the armor to the gold. There were ten nuggets, as the measure went in those days, and would have been a fortune in any man's hand. But the cupidity of the madman was beginning to dance in Achilles's face.

'Is this all that you could spare, Priam?' he asked. 'Surely you have not spent it all in luring fools to Troy to be spitted on Achaean spears?'

As a matter of fact, the gold had come from Priam's own treasury. The public coffers still held more than any man could ever spend though much had been pledged; and there were shrine-vessels and women's jewels and decorative studs on walls and furniture besides. In fact, gold was what we had more of than anything else, and it was beginning to become all the more irksome because it could not be eaten or metamorphosed into living, fighting men like that warrior made all of the precious stuff which had oozed from Medusa's body when Perseus cut her head off.

Polyxena's pride was stung. 'If you want more, then here it is, Achaean!' she cried, and stripping off her bracelets, she stalked across the hut and contemptuously dropped them clattering on the pile of goods.

Achilles's eyes opened wide. 'Who is this young mule driver, who comes wearing bracelets of gold?' he said.

'No mule driver, but Polyxena, Princess of Troy, and Priam's youngest daughter,' she answered proudly.

'I thought you were a lad,' Achilles replied. 'But even if you're not, you're as pretty as one.' He stared at her admiringly, and the memory of his strange sexual habits hung like a palpable thing in the air. 'Priam, I will make a bargain with you!' he exclaimed. 'Give me your daughter Polyxena, and I will return your ransom goods and Hector's body besides, excepting only the armor!'

Now for the first time, a flicker of fear stole over Polyxena's face, where she had been so stalwart before, even to the point of forgetting her timid nature. She looked back at her father, afraid of what he might say to this surprising, generous counter-offer from Achilles.

'I could agree to that only if you would persuade your fellow Achaeans to quit our shores forever and leave us in peace. That is the price of my daughter, and one that I think even she would be willing to pay.'

'What do you say, maiden? I confess that your boyish beauty has quite enchanted me as I never thought a woman could.'

'I say,' said Polyxena proudly, 'that I will do as my father commands.'

Achilles sighed deeply, narrowed his eyes, glanced at the ransom goods and back again at Polyxena. 'It is tempting,' he said at last. 'Very tempting. But I do not know if I can do what you ask. All I can promise you is that I will try. And in the meantime, I will accept your ransom for Hector's body so that no one in our camp will suspect anything. Odysseus would be quick to see through any uncharacteristic generosity on my part, but to show my good faith, I will return one of your well-woven mantles to be Hector's winding sheet.'

Priam nodded his assent, glad that Achilles's greed for the thing in hand had outweighed his impetuous offer. And yet, Priam realized, with a spark of his old bargaining skill, the door remained ajar for further negotiations. All in all, things might yet turn a profit for Troy.

Achilles went to call some of the camp women to the task of washing Hector's battered body and making it as comely as possible. As an added precaution, he gave orders that the mantle should be tied with many knots in deerhide cords, so that it might not fall open and show the corpse in its lamentable condition. Perhaps he feared Priam's anger and his own answering wrath; perhaps he wished to safeguard the extraordinary negotiations he had undertaken with the King. Who knows the mind of a madman? For when Hector's body had been loaded into the mule cart and Polyxena turned it around for its sad journey back to Troy, they caught a parting glimpse of Achilles through the opening in the hut that served him as a doorway. He was clutching his precious armor in one hand and singing softly to himself as he crouched down and caressed the gold with the other, turning it over and over in the firelight.

It was only a few of us who heard this: Deiphobus, Paris, Polites, Helenus, Hecabe, myself. The other daughters, even Polyxena who had played such a vital part in it, were sent away to their husbands, or in Polyxena's case, to bed. Helen, of course, never even glanced our way in curiosity when Priam gathered the closest of his intimate family after the mule wagon had been brought safely back into Troy and given over to the sorrowing inhabitants. Perhaps she fidgeted at Paris's absence from her couch for an hour's business; let her spend a little while with her poor, neglected and ignored son instead, was my thought.

Around me, my kinsmen's faces reflected sorrow and astonishment, resentment and awe, disgust and disbelief as the story unfolded. And when Priam was finished, he clasped his hands in his lap and waited for our reactions.

Hecabe was first. 'Can you mean, my lord husband,' she exclaimed, 'that you would even consider giving another of our children into the hands of this murderer after he has done us so much great hurt? I, for one, am bitterly opposed to it! Do you not remember little Troilus? I do, even if you might not. And Polydorus, who went to make Achilles's bed-partner's pyre more magnificent. No, I say! Hector may have given himself as a willing sacrifice to save the City, but I will not give my daughter to save a few more lives. It is as if you think Hector's death was in vain!'

'No, Mother,' said Deiphobus, who as next eldest had inherited Hector's position as Guardian of the City. 'I think there is more in it than that. A love-offering to bind the Achaeans's greatest champion to us might be worth nearly as much as Hector's noble gift.'

'Why should we think that Polyxena would meet the same fate as our brothers?' added Polites. 'It seems to me that Achilles may have shown more sheer humanity this night than he had known in far too many years.'

'But she is so young!' lamented Hecabe.

'I've had girls who were little older,' said Paris. 'I think that I agree with Polites and Deiphobus.'

'I think,' interrupted Helenus, 'that we should consider the matter of Hector's funeral. The rest is pointless conjecture as it stands now. Who can say if Achilles's scrambled wits will even remember this conversation with our lord father by tomorrow?'

'How many days of mourning should we observe?' asked Deiphobus. 'The fallen Guardian deserves our lamentations regardless of the sacrifice.'

'None,' replied Priam. 'Our days of mourning were accomplished while Hector's body lay in the Achaeans's camp, being worried by Achilles. I know that he had the body well wrapped and bound so that I would not see the cuts and scrapes, and the disintegrating flesh, but the wrapping could not keep back the smell of decay. Mortification has advanced rather farther than it should, due to the abuse that it has received. Let us build a pyre with the first morning's light, and burn him quickly and cleanly so that he will not have to suffer any more.'

Agreement was on every face, and Paris got up to leave, no doubt anxious to go to Helen's arms, but Priam turned to me.

'And you, my daughter, who were so wise in sending Achilles his armor and in advising the Gorgon signs that made the Acheans turn piously away from us in our errand. What is your reaction?'

'I think,' I said slowly, 'that I spoke truly last year – how long ago that seems! – when I said that you had learned strange bargaining tricks from the Achaeans. To send a daughter in love to a man who killed so many of your sons in hate strikes me as a bizarre maneuver. But no more so than many that have taken place recently. What does mad Cassandra Storm-crow know about war and love? Do as you think best. Anything that will end this useless and horrible killing may be worth the price.'

'So it seemed to me at the time. But perhaps it will be as Helenus said, and Achilles will not remember anything but the gold and goods I paid him. I think that I would not be unhappy at this. Now, let us all find our beds, for it is only a little while until dawn, and a royal funeral awaits us.'

For me, even that little while was too long, for my awful dream came to me with my first sleep, prompted perhaps by the foreseen vision of the flames of Hector's pyre. And so I was the first one stirring, directing the laying of the first tier of logs.

Our pyres were now built in the area behind the East Gate and the barricaded low town, where we were sheltered from the eyes of the Achaeans. In other times, the spacious Plain provided many a solemn site from which the souls of our dead ascended the column of smoke; but now we were crowded by necessity into this cramped little space. Whenever the hunters went out for the game that grew ever scarcer with the heavy demands that had been laid upon the supply, they always brought back wood to season for the melancholy task that ever awaited. Now, as I watched the pyre grow, there was more green than dry in it. 'It will make a smoke to suffocate us all,' I thought. But we could do no better.

There was not even wine enough to quench the flames when they had burnt his body to clean ashes; but the maids drew large jars of water from the nearby Water Tower and I poured a little wine into each one, so that his shade should have at least a weak last taste of it. Though it was customary to burn a man uncovered, I made the men lay Hector's body atop the pyre still shrouded. And even so, the stench of putrefaction came wafting down, as Priam had said.

And then, behind me, the King and his nobles, and my brothers and sisters with all the warriors who could be spared from the walls, came out of the East Gate and I went and took my place with them. I thought I saw a look of gratitude on my father's face through his mask of grief, for I had already accomplished the tedious part of it and made it more bearable for him.

Three of the royal women would take turns in giving the lament. Hecabe and Andromache, of course; but everyone was surprised when Helen stepped forward. She hailed him as her true friend and the most beloved among all her brothers-in-law. I wondered what cynical impulse on her part prompted this, because if anything she was continually irked at Hector for dragging Paris away from her and out onto the battlefield. Certainly there was no sign of mourning about her, apart from a dark veil thrown over her rich hair. She was still decked and bedizened and smelled so of perfume that it masked the odor of decay.

For the rest of them, my brothers and sisters grieved long and bitterly – not at Hector's death, for that would have been to deny the glory of his sacrifice, but at the treatment he had received afterward. Even Laodice was subdued and seemed uninterested in copying Helen's every gesture. Modestly hidden in the crowd I spotted Creusa. From time to time a wince of pain crossed her face, and I knew that her labor must be near. But she had risked the gathering to be with her brother's body at the last.

And then Priam himself put the torch to the bundle of twigs and faggots. Here and there, men threw precious oil onto the wood to encourage it to burn and presently the flames began to roar, making us all step backward from the heat. I had built a very large pyre, so that the great column of smoke from its burning would show the Achaeans how dearly we treasured the remains of Hector, who had suffered such brutal treatment at the hands of their champion.

Before it was all burnt down, Creusa uttered a stifled moan and leaned weakly against Æneas. Between us, we got her back into the City and I went to fetch her women and notify Coronus in case his help was needed. And so I missed seeing the quenching of the flames, and the reverent gathering of Hector's ashes and bones. They placed them in the splendid funeral jar that had been prepared against Priam's own death, and buried it far back into the hills in a hidden spot lest the Achaeans come and work a further outrage. The men said they had not been able to resist marking the place with a cairn of stones, and Glaucus promised he would show it to me, but I never saw it.

And that was the funeral of Hector.

15

STRANGE ALLIES

A few more allies came to us, though it was well past Midsummer Day – a trickle here, a dribble there, and of them only two were anybody of note. The first of these was a strange creature who made me jump and catch my breath as if I had seen a ghost.

She was dressed in barbarian fashion, as were her whole troop of women. They wore neither man's nor woman's dress, but peculiar leggings of brightly dyed leather from waist to ankles and topped with a kind of shift that ended at the hips. These were fringed and studded, and seemed to be made of the same kind of doeskin that went into women's buskins, but made supple and yielding from cunning tanner's work. We had occasionally seen backlands Scythians at the Fairs clad in garments of similar style, but dull and roughly made. They were scarcely civilized and very shy, coming to the Plain but seldom because they usually traded with others of their tribes who were possessed of a thicker veneer of cultivation; these generally did the bargaining for all. Always the sight of these backlanders was the occasion for much pointing and whispering behind hands, and so was a further inducement for the others, who seemed wary as wild animals, to stay away. Nobody did any pointing or whispering now, though, as the leader of this extraordinary band of warriors came up the ramp with a bold and purposeful stride to where Priam waited.

'A favor for a favor, King Priam,' the young woman announced, when the courtesies of greeting were past. 'Your need for fighters has come to me, even as far away as we live. Indeed, it would have been a much shorter journey to Colchis to accomplish what I seek. But I have always been one to repay in kind. I stand in need of purification, for I have been the accidental cause of my sister Glauce's death. We were out hunting, and a rustle in the bushes prompted me to send an arrow into them, thinking to bring down a deer. But it was Glauce instead, and she died in my arms. I am Penthesilea, daughter of Otrere and sired by Ares. You folk would call me the queen, but among my people I am thought of as a king. And so king to king, I ask for purification from your hands. In return, my band of warriors is at your command, for we are the Spearmaidens of Artemis.'

Priam seemed favorably impressed with her clear, direct manner. He took her hands in his and said, 'Welcome, Spearmaiden. We had not thought to receive aid from the Amazons, but do not think that you will be despised because of your sex. It shall be as you request and gladly, because everyone knows that there are few more formidable in a fight than such as you.'

Then Penthesilea turned to me. 'By your silver, I see that you are priestess of the Maiden here in Troy. Let us go to her shrine, for we are all virgins in my troop.'

'Indeed?' said Priam. 'Then you are very brave to come into a city with few women and many warriors.'

'Virgins make the best fighters. If one of us falls, she is taken directly into Artemis's keeping, and so when a woman begins to breed young Spearmaidens, she retires from the field. There will be no trouble between your warriors and mine.'

And truth to tell, there were few if any lascivious glances from the curious soldiers who had gathered to watch the Amazons come into Troy. Perhaps it was because of their strange manner of dress. In a way, it made them seem almost sexless, an effect heightened by the leanness of their bodies and the paucity of swelling bosoms.

As I led them to the Palladium, I found myself looking more and more closely at their leader. Was it a trick of the light, a mannerism, a way of carrying herself, or did she really resemble Sarpedon so closely it was as if they had come from the same womb? She was tall and straight, as he had been, with the same flawless forehead and easy movement. Wide of shoulder, narrow of hip, with long and well-formed limbs, if they had stood together in similar garb, it might have been difficult to tell them apart. Only the hair was different, Penthesilea's being darker, though they wore it nearly alike, clubbing it back neatly in hunting style. His had been held with wires of gold, and hers was bound with silver.

'Why do you look at me so, Trojan priestess?' she demanded now. I had forgotten her direct way, as I had forgotten my own manners.

'If I offended you, I am sorry,' I replied. 'It is just that you remind me strongly of someone – someone I once knew.'

'Another Amazon?'

'No. A man, a warrior.' A downward flutter of her hand expressed her distaste for such a situation, and her surprise that a priestess of the Maiden would so indulge herself. 'He is dead now. But you are so like him that he might have been your brother.'

Now she laughed, a short soldier's bark. 'Brother! You know little of the Amazons, lady. We kill the boy babies as soon as they see the light, although I have heard that some tribes have begun the soft and decadent practice of sending them back to the villages of the men who come and company with them. I could have had no brother, not from my mother's womb, and Ares was my father. But perhaps he bred your dead – friend?'

'Friend was all he was, and you need fear no contamination from a priestess who has broken her vows. But it is useless to dwell on the matter. Dead's dead, and perhaps it is just an accident that makes me see him in your face.'

'I could try to console you for his loss, if you wished,' she said kindly, and reached out to stroke my cheek with her firm, hard palm.

Only a strict inner discipline kept me from drawing back at this unexpected touch. I was aware, of course, that girls like these were often quite haughty in their preference for lovers of their own sex rather than submit to the usual congress between men and women. But there is only the one way to increase; so when they began to lose their swiftness in the field and were forced to turn to breeding young Spearmaidens, they endured it will or nill, though many of them were all impatience to return to the pleasures of their younger days. Customs varied from tribe to tribe; some Amazons were as lusty with male captives as any Achaean when they went to rape a village, but usually they were girls for girls and that was the end of it.

'I thank you, Spearmaiden King, but for now I prefer to remain virgin to every touch of love,' I replied now, with all the courtesy I had been taught. She shrugged, evidently thinking I was a fool, but was too civil to say so out loud.

We had reached the doorway to the shrine of the Palladium. 'Here I will leave you,' I said, unwilling to excuse myself to go and fetch Bastos. They would surely have found it even stranger that I would need my little servant of Artemis in order to participate in a rite to the Maiden. 'Behold the Palladium, which we believe embodies not only the Virgin Goddess, but the

Nymph and Crone as well, so that all the women may approach. Worship as you will, without my presence if you don't mind, for I fear it might inhibit you. Then we will find you quarters here in the City. It will not be difficult, now that so many have fallen. And be assured of a place in the King's Hall at meat tonight, or such other food as we may find to set before you.'

There were twenty-eight of them all told, and they were craning their necks and murmuring with pleasure at the prospect of coming into the presence of such a famous and exalted relic.

'You are wise, priestess,' said Penthesilea. 'You realize that our number is the same as the number of days from one full moon to the next, and that if you stayed within, one of us would have had to stand outside. We are well pleased at such courtesy. We will fight well for one who can breed a maiden of such discernment, even if he is only a man.'

I smiled and left, content to have it so, and as I went back toward my room I heard a hymn begin to rise in their strange Scythian tongue.

The other arrival of note could not have been more different from the troop of Spearmaidens if Zeus had sat up all night with his fellow gods around him, debating which to choose. Priam had early sent word to the King of the Hittites, with whom he had some ties either by blood or marriage, or as one trader to another, the kinship not being made clear. The latter suggests itself most strongly to me, for the inducement he offered was not only gold, but favorable trade considerations and – here my father put in a touch designed to appeal directly to the king – a shoot of the so-called Golden Vine. This was a species of grape grown exclusively for the Trojan King and yielded a wine of surpassing excellence that was of a clear, amber color. Only Priam's immediate family were allowed to drink it, and I could have counted the number of times I had tasted it on my fingers.

The king, Artaxerxes, had living in his court at that time a prince of the Æthiopians, sent in exchange for another son of good blood, in the manner that commonly bound one kingdom to another. His barbarian name has long been forgotten, and he was now called Memnon. He had been reared in the luxury of the Hittite court and had come almost to think of Artaxerxes as his father.

The land of the Hittites is very far away, as distant from Lycia as Lycia is from Troy. However, a fleet of warships could have easily made the journey by sea in half the time it would have taken overland, and this was what Priam had requested. He thought to catch the Acheans between the Trojans on the land and the flanking Hittites on the water, and crush them between the two forces. It was a good plan, and might well have worked, except that the sea force had run afoul of pirates at Rhodes. Luckily, the Hittite expedition had been split in two, and the second of these made it overland to Troy.

It was Artaxerxes's foster son, Memnon, who led them. The boy's imagination had been fired by the thought of warfare on such a scale, and his main worry in the impatient march had been that the war would be over before he arrived. It seemed a relief and glad news, if such a thing could be, when Priam dryly informed him that there was still enough fighting to be had for everyone.

He and his Hittites cut an even stranger figure in the avenues of Troy than had the Amazons. We were accustomed to seeing the black-bearded Hittite traders, of course, in their plain white tunics, sometimes relieved with a little embroidery around the neck if the wearer were somebody a cut above the ordinary merchant. But Memnon put the dusky-skinned Hittites to shame, making them seem pale and sallow with his exotic skin that was as black and shiny as polished ebony. And with it, he wore the royal raiment of Artaxerxes's court.

There was a skirt, reaching to his ankles, that seemed made of cloth cut into rows of stiff petals; or maybe it was the closely overlapped feathers on the wings of their man-headed bull this was supposed to recall. A heavy gold representation of one of these queer creatures hung from a massive chain around his neck, resting on a kind of wrapped over-tunic that came only to his waist and left his right shoulder bare. Æthiopians have not much beard and their hair tends to kinkiness; so he had elected to keep his cheeks shaven, and clipped his hair so that it fitted his well-shaped skull like a tight cap. Over this he wore the odd, conical hat that was a badge of Hittite nobility.

He came with a band of Companions, each more dazzlingly arrayed than the next, and most of them had skin only a little lighter than his own. They carried his arms and armor, all gold-washed, and it seemed that they were made like Achilles's fearsome harness, of solid metal. But it was not the armor that drew the glances of the crowd. The Æthiopian's Companions, those who would dress and undress him, bathe him, bring his food to him, entertain and amuse him, were all young and nubile girls.

Even as he was met and returned the greeting of my father,

he would reach out and caress one or another of them. If the thought had crossed my father's mind that the Æthiopian's clean, smooth cheeks might hint of a gelding in his youth, this notion soon vanished; but whatever he thought or felt, he kept his own counsel. But even Paris, who had never been known to turn shy when a pretty girl was near, made a sour mouth at the sight.

'Let us hope he is a better fighter than appearances would indicate,' he said in Helen's direction without turning his head. But she had already left in disgust. The Amazons she had been able to tolerate, for they were without gender and would take no attention and adulation away from her; Laodice's antics only amused her. But these half-Æthiopian girls were clearly playing at war and their bright glances around at the warriors nearby left no doubt that their loyalty was by no means with Memnon's couch alone.

'Competition, Helen!' I could not resist flinging at her back, and had the satisfaction of seeing her head go up a notch and her hurrying pace increase.

'For me,' Deiphobus said bluntly, 'I would not care if his girls drew his car and made a cushion for his feet with their bodies. Different peoples have different ways, as we above all should know, having been the gathering place for the world for so long. He looks stout and eager enough, and we cannot afford to despise an ally just because he chooses to bring a few girls along for his amusement.'

'You are right, as usual, Deiphobus,' admitted Paris cheerfully. 'You wear Hector's mantle well, though you often worry under the burden. And to show that I care nothing for customs we might think outrageous among ourselves, I'll go with Memnon as his companion next time there is fighting.'

And then someone else made a bawdy joke playing on 'Companions' and 'companion', so that there was a scuffle that made my father turn a stern eye on the offenders. But Memnon seemed to take it in good part; perhaps he had not even noticed, because he had turned to take his spear from one of the girls to lay at Priam's feet in the traditional gesture, and had become engrossed in the delicate curve of her breast.

The Memnonides, as they came to be called, were skilled dancers as well as being trained in other arts. That night and many thereafter, they entertained us with their swirling, swooping dances, as if they were imitating birds. And when Memnon had taken a half dozen or so with him to warm his bed, the rest came stealing out to find such diversions as they might.

A soldier that I treated for a spear cut told me that Memnon had learned his licentious ways in Artaxerxes's court. 'The girls say he is a good master for all that, because he has never indulged himself in the cruelty that is part and parcel of a woman's life there. At least not since he has been out of the King's palace. And he's a good man in the field, too; let the gossips be still about him. We've a foe in front of us whose indulgences make Memnon's girls look like virgin priestesses, begging your pardon.'

And so, the talk died down quickly enough, the more so when it was discovered that the Memnonides thought nothing of visiting several men in love during a night. There were few enough women in Troy for men who had long been hungering for a woman's warmth, and except for Laodice the few servants and slaves we kept were too tired at the day's end to make good bed companions.

More out of curiosity than anything else, I suspect, one of the Amazons took a dusky girl into her house and kept her till morning. It must not have been a success, because the experiment was not repeated.

16

THE DEATH OF ACHILLES

Memnon in his bed and Memnon in his chariot were two different people. He used one of Hittite workmanship, of course, and it looked odd among the light two-horse cars of the Trojans. His was heavy and four-wheeled, driven by a steady-looking warrior who looked to have his hands full with the lines guiding four onagers. Front and side, it bore the sign of the Hittite man-bull, and the brightly armored warrior who leaped eagerly into it bore no resemblance to the sensualist who lived for the pleasures his girls brought to his body. Black and gold he was, dazzling in the sunlight, and fearsome even though his conical helmet bore no towering plume.

Nearby the Spearmaidens gathered, and they were as colorful as bright birds of prey. They wore no body armor, preferring speed and lightness of foot to the protection of heavy, stiffened leather and bronze. Their leggings and shirts made a splash of color strange to see. Saffron and indigo, madder and leaf green, berry orange and bark brown were their colors; and for the Spearmaiden who termed herself king, it was sea-purple and crimson. There would be no trouble in picking them out of a fight. They bore silver-handled axes with greenstone heads, and slim swords rode their boyish hips from embroidered shoulder straps. Each Spearmaiden carried a shield shaped like a crescent moon; and when they had tucked their axes into their belts and had taken a couple of sharp throwers, they were ready for battle. They scorned even the leather helmets they were offered. When they had clubbed back their hair, they put on felt Phrygian caps, laughing at the men who went, as they put it, blinkered and blinded into a fight.

Penthesilea, purified by my father with precious, hoarded water from Ida that had stood three nights under the moon's light, tossed an insolent and gay salute to the men warriors. Then, with the shrill, laughing scream that is the war cry among all the Amazons, she led her women out through the gate, eager to be the first on the field. And the men, chagrined at being forced to follow a woman, were not far behind.

Twice they went out this way, quickly armed and quicker outside the walls, and the Spearmaidens proved themselves able and competent fighters. No man need be ashamed of following them onto the field, because not one of them failed to bring back a bloodied ax or a sword that needed re-whetting. They cared nothing for the armor of those they killed, for the only spoil of battle they cherished was the first; and then they took the scalp of the man – or woman – they killed.

Part of their strength lay in the surprise an enemy would feel, coming against a swift woman whose mirthless laughter ringing in his ears was enough to freeze the blood. Others of the Achaeans, who lay closer than they thought to the old times when the Queen was paramount, and any woman's body held the mystery of the Goddess, paused for a fatal instant. And this moment of hesitation was all that was necessary for a slim blade to come through the crescent shield, or for a brightly clad arm to swing a greenstone ax in a sharp, vicious arc.

Memnon was no less distinguished in his sallies. He killed a number of minor leaders, and by far his most important victim was a son of old Nestor.

In a way it was not a fair fight, because when Antilochus caught sight of Memnon, he dropped his arms and stared in dismay.

'Alas!' he cried. 'I was warned to beware of an Æthiopian, and never thought to see one on the Plain of Troy! Now my death is upon me!'

'Perhaps not, if you will fight for your life,' said Memnon. It went against his grain to strike a man who would not fight back, but when Antilochus began crying, wailing because his guardian had failed him, he put his spear through him to spare himself the sight of the man's blubbering.

But for both these courageous allies, the course they had to run was destined to be a short one. And though the Achaeans were losing men as well, steadily bringing reinforcements from Samothrace as their ranks thinned, it was our own losses that must weigh the more heavily upon us. The world had not seen such a bloodletting, here on the wind-swept Plain of Troy, since Zeus had destroyed the first race of men in the beginning of the world.

Penthesilea was the first to fall. Though she had been warned against approaching Achilles, her pride was such that she must seek him out regardless. And he, though he had seemed to avoid her on her previous excursions onto the field, waited for her this time.

But this was no common soldier to halt open-mouthed as a beautiful, stern-faced young woman rushed at him screeching her laughing challenge. He held his ground, while the Amazon's laughter turned joyful at the prospect of a good fight at last.

'My throwers against yours, Achaean,' she called, 'and then we'll fall to with swords! Have you an ax about you as well? I will fight only on equal terms!'

'I need no bludgeon, nor sword either,' Achilles shouted. He waited until she was poised to throw, at the moment when her shield had to fall away with the movement, and sent his spear into her chest, all unprotected without the breastplate she had scorned.

She fell with her weapons clattering about her, and he approached warily to stand looking down at her. She lived still, for he had not touched her heart, though her purple shirt was dyed a richer crimson than her other trappings and a red-tinted froth stained her mouth.

'Rejoice, Achilles,' she gasped, 'for you have brought down the King of the Spearmaidens. But know also that I die without fear because the Virgin I worship will take me into her company as she does all virgins who fall in battle for her sake.'

'Indeed?' said Achilles calmly. 'Then I will have another trophy from you for your boast besides this trash you carry. What good is a shield with a notch cut out and a little sliver of a sword useful only for picking my teeth? Felt caps and dyed leather! You deserve my revenge for denying me my proper battlefield spoil!'

Her eyes widened in dismay and disbelief as he knelt beside her. For a moment, the snug leather leggings baffled him; but a slash or two with his dagger liberated enough of her flesh for his purpose. Then she closed her eyes and turned her head in the bitter depth of her defeat. By the time he had finished he was embracing a corpse.

One of his companions of that day, an ugly fellow by the name of Thersites, came up to the dead Amazon as Achilles was gathering up the despised crescent shield and the greenstone ax. With one of Penthesilea's own spears he gouged out her eyes and cut off her nose. He had just begun to slice off her ears when Achilles turned and caught him at what he was doing.

'I was not afraid of her alive,' he shouted angrily, 'and I have no reason to fear her ghost! Let this teach you not to meddle!' And with that, he gave the man such a buffet on the side of the head that it broke his temple and he fell down dead.

It was well known, of course, that the Achaeans – and many Trojans as well, if the truth is told – considered the Spearmaidens to be witches steeped in both earth and sky magic. Otherwise, how could they go out day after day into battle wearing nothing but soft, thin leather and come back with weapons full-fed with the blood they had tasted? And, as such, they would surely not follow the rule that makes a man free of the torment from the ghost of the warrior he has faced and killed in open combat on the field. And so Thersites, thinking to do Achilles a favor, had begun to render the witch's ghost impotent to do him harm. Eyeless, she could not see him; without a nose, she could not smell him out. Deprived of ears, she would not have been able to find him by tracing his voice or his footsteps. And if he had not been interrupted, Thersites would have also cut out her tongue so that she could not have voiced her complaints to other sympathetic ghosts who might have been persuaded to render her assistance, now that Achilles had condemned her to their company rather than the train of Artemis which she had so ardently desired.

I cannot vouch for the truth or authenticity of this story, but only relate it as it came back to me. I never saw her body, for the Achaeans threw it into the Scamander close by their camp, where a lucky current caught it and carried it into the swift-flowing Hellespont. From there, nobody knows where the restless waters took it before finally depositing it in some uneasy deep-lying tomb. Personally, I never doubted a word of it, knowing from experience the sort of excesses which came so naturally to Achilles when his inhuman temper had been provoked.

That this same monster could have been so civil in his treatment of my father when he went alone to Achilles's hut seems all the more remarkable. Some pathos, some sympathy for the lonely old man who had suffered so terribly at his hands must have reached in and temporarily shored up the crumbling remains of manhood in Achilles's breast. And so, once again, with Bastos in my arms, I humbly gave thanks to my Goddess and whoever else had shielded him in his hazardous venture that had placed him only an arm's length away from Death in bronze armor.

Memnon had learned of Hector's plan of burning the Achaeans' ships, and he declared that nothing would please him better than the opportunity to complete that noble undertaking.

Though the fine edge had long gone off the Trojans, there were plenty who seemed pleased to have a try at it, and even the remaining Amazons willingly put themselves under the leadership of a man. They picked a day when the omens looked favorable for Troy, and set out over the much-traveled paths that had been beaten back and forth over the Plain.

But this time, the Achaeans were determined that the Trojans would not command their wall, as they had done when Hector had had his way. They met a goodly distance beyond the moat, and there the battle had to be joined.

Despite his appetite for pleasure, Memnon always slept alone the night before he fought. He was clear-eyed and fresh, and under the exotic garments of the Hittites that he wore, the Æthiopian warrior descended from a race of warriors shone through. Strong, loose-limbed as a leopard, with all the decadent Hittite airs fallen away from him, it was no wonder that men sought his company on the battlefield who shunned him in the City when he was surrounded by his fluttering girl Companions.

He caught sight of Achilles, and loosing a savage Æthiopian war whoop, made straight for him. He, who wore similar all-metal trappings, would best know how to get past them. But Great Ajax came out and cut him off from his objective.

'First me,' Ajax stated bluntly. 'And then, if you live, Achilles may have what is left of you!'

Memnon's ebony face split into a startling white grin. Audaciously, he made a Gorgon face at Ajax, waggling a pink tongue that looked somehow out of place in such a black countenance. 'If you're that eager to die, I'll be glad to oblige you,' he said, and hefted a thrower in his right hand.

'I fight this day with my sword,' said Ajax.

Memnon shrugged, dropping his throwing-spears on the ground. 'One way to die is as good as another,' he said indifferently. 'Let us begin.'

In an informal duel of this kind, other warriors customarily kept away, either watching the combatants or engaged in fights of their own. And so nobody noticed Achilles until he had come around behind Memnon, and with a sweep of his heavy long spear, nearly severed the Æthiopian prince's head from his shoulders.

'That is how to kill a man who dares ape the kind of armor that only I wear!' he boasted, as Ajax rushed to stand by him for the inevitable fight over the body.

Frantic it was, too, for Memnon had provoked a new spark of vigor in the exhaustion of the war. The Achaeans managed to strip the body by sheer weight of numbers. They had to leave the corpse, however, for the Trojans had no desire for a repeat of Achilles's outrageous behavior when they had been forced to leave Hector to his uncertain ministrations. The Achaeans only managed to finish cutting off the head, bearing it back behind their walls as a curiosity.

For me, the day brought sadness of a more personal sort. For in the fighting over Memnon's body, Great Ajax had managed to cut down Glaucus even as he ringingly shouted for aid in the fight. Poor Glaucus, whom I cherished for his brother's sake. I remembered how heartily Sarpedon had laughed when Diomedes the Argive had cheated Glaucus out of his best dress harness; today he lost the rest, for they stripped him as he lay.

We burned him on the same pyre with the headless body of Memnon, to honor our double loss, and the Memnonides sorrowfully danced their fluttering, whirling dance around the flames. When the funeral was over and the fire had burned down, Priam very courteously offered them an escort of such Hittite soldiers as wished to quit the battlefield if they wanted to return to the court of Artaxerxes.

Whatever their lineage, they had been brought up around kings, and they answered with equal grace. 'No, thank you, King Priam,' one of them said. 'We wish to remain near the ashes of our Prince, as we were with him in life.'

'And besides,' another spoke up, a spritely little gleam in her eye past the ritual tears, 'we find the beds of your soldiers comfortable, and their manners agreeable. Why should we want to return where we were not treated nearly so well?'

In spite of the solemnity of the occasion, several men in the crowd smiled broadly. Even my father could not repress a softening around his mouth at the girl's sauciness, for she was well known to have been one of the favorites among the soldiers. 'You are welcome to stay,' he replied. 'Enjoy yourselves, for it brings no harm. Indeed, enjoy yourselves, while you may.'

Without Memnon, there seemed no further chance of breaking through the Achaeans and burning their ships. The attack had deflated as abruptly as a punctured pig's bladder when he had gone down under Achilles's spear, and the Trojans had had no will to do anything but salvage his and Glaucus's bodies and retreat behind their own walls. For myself, I felt that the time for burning the ships had long passed. Let them keep them, I thought, and climb into them as quickly as they are able and go away. But of course, they would not do that.

My sister Creusa's faintness on the day of Hector's funeral had proved to be false labor, as often happens when a woman is bearing her first child. Now, however, she seemed to be in earnest and I was occupied with her when Deiphobus and Paris put their heads together and hatched their deadly plot. It was risky, and dangerous, and daring – the very sort of bold proposal which brings automatic opposition from those who are older and count themselves wiser because of it. I was not consulted, of course, and I wonder now if I would have spoken against it, not that they would have listened to me in any case.

Still, I would have liked to have had a hand in it, though they did well enough by themselves. I had, you see, slowly been beginning to command some respect among the dwindling nobles of Troy, what with Laocoön being so long absent at the Thymbraean Shrine and with my good advice to Priam concerning the Gorgon signs that had made the Achaean sentries avert their gaze. And even the dullest could not deny that I had spoken of fire and death long before death had begun to strike so frighteningly all across the Trojan Plain, and the fire blazed with terrible regularity at the burning-place behind the East Gate. I knew that there was other fire yet to come, but in this I was still ignored. So, it was my brothers' scheme start to finish, and they carried it off while I found myself unexpectedly serving as midwife to Creusa since no other could be found and she refused to have Coronus see her.

Using my idea of the Gorgon sign, my brothers put the mark on the forehead of one of the servants and sent him trembling to Achilles with a sealed wax tablet. In it, they promised to deliver Polyxena in trust to the agreement between him and Priam, provided he come alone, barefoot and unarmed, to the neutral ground of the Pastoral Shrine. There, he would be expected to sacrifice to Apollo, and with Polyxena as his willing bride, begin his work of persuading the Achaeans to end this ruinous war that was proving equally destructive to either side. And they, well-armed except for the telltale helmets, set out secretly together to wait in ambush in the sanctuary until he should come.

I think that in their hearts they expected Achilles to smell out a trap and refuse the bait. Any sane man would have rejected the proposal out of hand; but then Achilles could hardly have been considered in his right mind. And sure enough, just as dusk was falling, he came riding across the Plain.

He was dressed in a spotless white tunic, and there was a garland of laurel on his head in token of his subjugation to Apollo. He had gold bracelets on his bared upper arms and wrist, contrasting richly with the superb musculature thus exposed, and a necklace bearing the royal sign of the Phthians hung around his neck. And, obedient to the stipulation in the tablet, when he dismounted from his car, it was seen that he was barefoot.

A single brazier lighted the gloom of the central chamber in the sweet-smelling Pastoral Shrine, made all of fragrant cedarwood. On either side, just out of the shadows, stood Paris and Deiphobus. Both had throwing-spears, Paris carried his bow and a full quiver and Deiphobus loosened his great sword in its sheath. The other occupants of the shrine, Laocoön and his illicit family, were nowhere to be seen, either having been warned by my brothers to stay away or prudently remaining hidden of their own accord.

Achilles mounted the low flight of steps that surrounded the shrine on all four sides, drawn by the single light, and as he entered the dimly lit room and looked from one to the other, awareness came into his face. Deiphobus took a step forward, gripping the handle of his sword, and Paris nervously touched his bowstring.

But there was no anger flooding into the eyes of the Achaean champion, no rage at having been tricked into an ambush. Rather it seemed that there was a kind of relief on the face that was raised in the firelight, and he almost smiled.

'It is time, then?' he asked.

Paris was at a loss, but Deiphobus dared to answer him. 'Yes,' he said cautiously. 'It is time.'

'I felt it,' Achilles said tranquilly, 'when Hector cozened me into performing his kingly sacrifice. I knew then that my own death could not be far behind. I, too, am the son of a king, descended from many kings, and we know such things. What kind of death awaits me?'

'What kind of death do you desire?' asked Deiphobus quietly.

Achilles turned to him with a look of wonderment. 'You would let me choose?' he said with gratitude. 'It is more than I ever hoped or expected. Well, then, know that in the old days, the good days, when it came time for the kings of my House to die, they came dressed simply to a holy place and were pricked in the sacred left heel with an arrow dipped in poison while a friend embraced them. That is how I, too, would die, as a sacred king of my House.'

Deiphobus nodded to Paris, who left quickly. 'That is how it will be, then, Achilles, for you are the greatest son that your House has produced. And I will be your friend and hold you tenderly in my arms and shield your eyes against the sight of the approaching arrow.'

'It is good.' Achilles seemed exalted, calm, nearly in a state of rapture. 'It will be a relief, you know,' he added in a curiously conversational manner, as if he and Deiphobus really were friends who might have played together in their youth. 'The burdens I have borne have nearly been too much for me.'

'They will soon be over,' Deiphobus replied gravely, 'and you will find peace.'

Paris returned, carrying a jar. He had found it in the healing-woman's cubby, where it had been left the last time we had ransacked it for herbs and drugs. It contained venom milked from the slender brown serpents that were so plentiful around Troy, and was marked with a snake on the lid and a Gorgon sign to warn the unwary. Having no use for its content of death when life was our goal, we had left it there.

Gingerly, Paris opened the jar, and taking an arrow from his quiver, dipped it deeply into the thickened, murky liquid. Then he carefully laid the arrow aside, closed the jar and returned it to its shelf. When he came back, Deiphobus moved from his place behind the brazier toward Achilles where he stood in the center of the room.

'The time is now,' he said kindly, holding out his arms.

But as Achilles suffered himself to be enclosed in Deiphobus's embrace, he pulled back, looking around with a puzzled frown. 'Where is the Queen?' he asked plaintively. 'Where is Polyxena? The Queen must observe, or it will all be spoiled.'

'She will be here presently,' Deiphobus said soothingly. 'Come now, and let me be your support and bulwark against the coming night.'

'Yes, yes,' Achilles agreed. 'She is tender, and could not bear to watch the arrow touch me. It is enough that she sees me while I die.'

And then, while Deiphobus wrapped his arms around the pitifully quiet madman and compassionately shielded his eyes by pressing Achilles's face into his neck, Paris took the poisoned arrow and drove it deeply into Achilles's exposed left heel. Achilles gave a great convulsive spasm when the arrow went in, but then relaxed in Deiphobus's firm grip.

He raised a peacefully smiling face, and moved by something he did not understand, Deiphobus kissed him gently on the forehead.

'My thanks go with you,' said Achilles, 'for your great kindness.'

He buckled at the knees, for the venom was a swift poison. Paris and Deiphobus lowered him onto the polished floor near the brazier. Now they were anxious to leave, because they knew that Achilles's departure could not have gone unnoticed in the Achaean camp, but Achilles took hold of Deiphobus's arm. His eyes were already wandering.

'The Queen . . . ' he whispered hoarsely. Behind Deiphobus, Laocoön's woman peered into the room from another doorway, her eyes wide and her knuckles pressed against her mouth. As Deiphobus turned, she fled the way she had come. Neither of them knew how long she had been standing there.

'She is with you,' Deiphobus reassured him, willing to use her presence in their need. They could delay no longer, so they went swiftly through a side door of the shrine, where they had hidden their car. As they whipped the horses furiously along the darkened road they fancied they could already hear the rumble of wheels and the sound of hoofs behind them, coming from the direction of the camp.

17

QUARREL IN TROY

Shaken as they were by the enormity of their deed and the mysterious circumstances surrounding it, they lost no time in telling of it. And the City burst into a delirium of rejoicing. Even Æneas left the side of Creusa and their newly born son to join in the celebration. I could not help but be glad with the rest because Achilles was dead at last; but I found much to ponder in the strange docility with which he had allowed himself to be put to death. The deceitful device by which Paris and Deiphobus lured Achilles to his doom weighed on me less heavily than it might have in other times. When a lion is ravaging the flocks, does the hunter courteously point out the twig that springs the trap?

In the camp of the Achaeans there was uproar as well, but of a different sort. I could well imagine their mixed feelings, for there were nearly as many among them who feared and hated Achilles as there were with us. And certainly by now the wax tablet had informed them of Achilles's traitorous leanings. Still, they gave him a magnificent funeral, and when it was over they put his ashes into the same jar that held those of his beloved Patroclus, whom he had never ceased to mourn.

A nameless foot soldier, scarred and grizzled, put it best for me: 'He's dead at last, and no one cares enough to cry for him. He got better than he deserved at the end by far, but dead's dead and that's a blessing, to both sides like as not!'

A quarrel sprang up in the Achaean camp over who should get Achilles's mighty armor. Odysseus and Great Ajax both claimed it, as they had been the ones to find the body and bring it back. They laid their case before Agamemnon, who begged to be allowed to sleep on his decision, for he was sure to offend one of the two. But in the morning, Ajax was found with the hilt of the silver-knobbed sword he had won from Hector protruding from under his right armpit. Odysseus quickly circulated the story that Ajax, being fearful of the decision going against him, had gone mad and killed himself. But the position of the sword was surely an awkward one for a right-handed man to manage, and Ajax had been discovered lying peacefully in his accustomed place. Odysseus claimed the armor and no more was said about it.

With Achilles gone, Agamemnon now brought the last of his reinforcements from Samothrace. They were led by Philoctetes the archer, who claimed that he carried the bow of Heracles. His arrows were poison-tipped, treated with a mess brewed and steeped by a secret formula in his homeland, and were so deadly that the lightest scratch meant death. Philoctetes himself was immune, having been given dilute broth to drink from his earliest childhood in the manner of certain snake-cult priestesses. The poison that saturated his system gave his sweat and other bodily excretions a foul and offensive odor so that he was greatly avoided by all save his own men, who had grown accustomed to the stench. But he sowed death in the ranks of the Trojans whenever they met, and with an unlucky shot became the one to bring down Paris.

Paris, thinking that his own bow had a longer range than that of Philoctetes, made for him on the field. But Philoctetes, too, carried a bow of the Scythian mode, as Paris should have known from the boast about its being Heracles's own, and his shot grazed Paris on the hand. Menelaus, eager to finish off his wife's lover, came hurrying up; but the Trojans managed to beat him back and carry Paris into the city.

We took him to the bedchamber he had shared with Helen, though by the expression on her face I am certain that she would have greatly preferred that he be laid in the House of Aphrodite. She fussed and fretted about the coverlet, laying towels under the wounded hand that oozed its stinking, poisonous serum. He was never fully conscious before he died. I had seen enough men start down the Road of Death in this condition to know that they most often called for their mothers, and sometimes their wives' names followed if there were time. But oddly enough, Paris spoke only of Oenone and that just once before his breathing grew labored and ceased.

'Oenone?' said Helen, puzzled. 'That is strange. He never called me that in play or earnest. "Wine-queen." Very odd.' Her eyes were dry, as if it had not occurred to her to mourn.

'It was not you he meant,' I said shortly. 'But you can't reproach him for it now, Helen. He is dead. Haven't you even the decency to weep?'

And then, belatedly, she managed a tear or two from her lovely eyes and loosened her hair so that it would fall over her face and hide the light scratches on her cheeks that brought no drop of blood. I remembered how she had cast insultingly small hair trimmings onto Hector's pyre, and wondered if she would even do as much for Paris.

Another funeral, I thought tiredly. Another son of Priam stretched out lifeless in his youth. Well, at least it would free me from the odious presence of Helen, who had professed to love my brother so urgently that she committed the most celebrated adultery known in history, and yet had cared so little at his death that she forgot to weep.

But if I thought that Helen's presence in Troy was now a thing apart from the lives of Priam and his sons, I was mistaken. When the funeral fire had burnt itself out and the sad chores accompanying it had been accomplished, we all gathered as usual in Priam's Hall for the cheerless evening meal, as had become our custom. And there I learned how deeply Helen had become intertwined in the fabric of Troy.

When we had all eaten, all of us in the silence of our own broodings, and the tables had been cleared away so that what passed for wine these days in Troy could be brought in for such cheer as we could find in it, Helen rose from her place near the hearth to address my father. Her hair was rearranged flawlessly, and her face bright and clear with no marks on her cheeks or reddened eyes to mar her carefully tended beauty. For once she was modestly covered from chin to heels, though the dress, which was a delicate rose cotton, was in no way suitable for a widow fresh from her husband's burning. Her scent was subdued too, so that one did not reel from it in the wake of her passing.

'Dear King Priam, whom I have come to love as a daughter loves her father,' she said now, standing with unaccustomed dignity before us. Even her hands were composed and clasped before her instead of busy fingering her bodice and fidgeting with her skirt as had always been her habit before.

'Yes, Helen?' said my father courteously.

'I have a thing to ask of you.' She took a deep breath and lowered her eyes as if in humility. 'Now that my beloved Paris is dead, I wish to be allowed to return to Menelaus whose side I left for Paris's sake. Perhaps then this terrible, long war will end.'

The sound of indrawn gasps around the room, quickly stifled, brought an upward twitch to one corner of her mouth. Dismay or approval, I do not think that Helen cared. She had sought an effect, to rivet all eyes and attention upon herself, and she had succeeded. But I watched Priam. He had been sitting heavily, his cup of water flavored with a few drops of wine a burden in his hand, and his snowy brows were drawn together sharply. For the space of a heartbeat I thought that he might grant her request, for she had made it gracefully and reasonably and the gods knew we would be well off without her. And had he not done as much for the girls of Memnon? But then a chill finger traced its way through my belly and I knew that Helen had finally started something she could not finish.

My father drew himself up in his chair and something in his movement made every eye swing to him and away from the brilliant figure in the firelight. 'I am sorry, my child,' he said now, kindly but firmly. 'That is impossible.'

She nearly winced, but caught herself. Clearly, she had never dreamed that she would be denied. Nor, for that matter, had nearly everyone else. 'But why, my father?' she asked, still hoping to charm him to her side with sweet and agreeable words. 'It was for my sake, wretch that I am, that this terrible war has come to you. Would you deny me the chance to end it by offering myself to my former husband's mercy?'

Heads began to nod in agreement here and there. But Priam sat more erect than ever and stared down any who would oppose him. His face was white where it had been gray with fatigue and sorrow before, and two spots of color came into his cheeks. 'It was not for your sake,' he replied coldly. 'Do not deceive yourself. Though I own that is very easy for you to do, since you seldom look beyond your mirror. A war of this magnitude could never be fought for the recovery of one errant wife, no matter how great her beauty.'

She reeled backward a step, shocked by his words. I suppose that no one had ever spoken to her like this in her life. And now an air of tension caught and spread through the Hall, as the men and women there leaned forward to listen. It was like the moment when everything goes still before a gush of wind and rain begins a sudden storm, and they looked expectantly from Helen to Priam and back again.

The storm was not long in breaking. Helen would have begun it for the advantage, but Priam silenced her with an imperious wave of his hand before she could get a word out. Within myself, I applauded silently, rejoicing that the blindness had finally fallen away from the King of Troy, and that he had found his voice at last. Worthy father of worthy sons! He must have been very like Hector in his youth, I thought, and my own blood tingled along my veins knowing that it had come from him.

'Trade,' he said, making it a word of disgust. 'There's the answer, not some pretty face with nothing behind it. They wanted what we had. But the fools do not realize that they have wrecked the economy of the whole world in their mad scramble to get it. Where will they find a merchant stupid enough to bring his goods to a place where the twittering of ghosts would drown out any bargaining? How many Eastern cities and towns have been laid waste? How many fields burnt and ruined? How many good and simple farmers lie dead, never to bring in a crop again? And how many Western houses have been bled manless in the ceaseless outpourings that came to be slaughtered? Who are left to defend their homes against an invasion against them? Old men, if they haven't died already, and children barely old enough to run!'

His voice grew in power until it thundered through the Hall, echoing and reverberating back against the woman who cowered under the full force of it.

'And think of this, Helen! What makes you imagine that you would be welcomed into the Achaean camp? You revel in the looks of desire you receive as you walk in the City, but have you seen the faces of the men when the moment of flesh-hunger has passed? You, who think yourself loved by all, are despised in Troy!'

'No . . . ' Helen whimpered, crushed by this most telling blow of all. But my father would not be stopped.

'Do you think your lot would be better among the Achaeans? I think not. There are enough of them that believe, or have come to believe, the fiction that you seem to find so flattering, and you would not live past a day. There in the open camp, there are no doors to lock and no strong rooms in which to hide. And the leaders would not lift a finger to protect you. Why should they? You are too convenient a scapegoat. If the anger of those who hate you, believing you to be the cause of the deaths of their friends and kinsmen, were set at the right doorstep, Agamemnon and his gallant champions would suffer from it. No, lovely Helen. Though you deserve it, I cannot bring myself to let you go to the Achaeans, there to perish under the righteous anger of my enemies. It is a fine irony that you are safer here in Troy. But you need a guardian – a new husband. And I do not know where one might be found for you.'

'I will marry Helen,' said Deiphobus heavily, rising from his place.

'No! I will!' cried Helenus, jumping up in his turn.

Now all the indrawn breaths were let out suddenly and a murmur of surprise tinged with the undercurrent of scornful laughter ran through the room.

Helen, flushed and angry, sought to recover some of her self-possession. I'll give her this; she was game, and she still tried to come out winner. 'I will not be handed along from son to son, not even yours, King Priam!' she announced with a toss of her head. 'If I must have a new husband, I will find him myself!'

'The choice is no longer yours, Helen,' he said so sternly that she cowered again. 'Consider yourself exceedingly fortunate that two of my sons are ready to quarrel over you, where I thought to have some trouble finding even a common foot soldier to burden himself with your care. May I ask why you two seem so eager for this foolishness?'

'You mentioned desire, my father,' said Deiphobus with a half-smile. 'I have wanted to lie with her since the moment Paris brought her through the Dardanian Gate.'

'And I also,' said Helenus.

'And beyond that, Helen has taken the trouble on occasion to amuse herself with me by holding out her charms like a radish under a mule's nose. Let her finish what she has begun, though I would not touch her while my brother lived. But now I think I might fill her bed very well, though I would have to lock the door when I left her and take the key with me.'

'Helen has never bothered to glance my way,' said Helenus with a thin edge to his voice. 'But I have seen her when she let her dress slip from her shoulder, or when she let the wind blow her skirt open past her thigh.' He paused, swallowing, and his face reddened. 'If you would bring her down, give her to me. I am young, and strong, and it will take both to make Helen happy.'

Deiphobus shrugged. 'I have never lacked for strength, though I have seen a few more years than my little brother. I think that I could entertain Helen until she wearied of it and begged for sleep. And to further advance my claim, if it is needed, be reminded that I am now the Guardian of the City, and by reason of rank alone I should be considered first. Unless, that is, humiliation is indeed my father's aim, which I do not believe. Moreover, it was I who slew Achilles with the help of Paris. For my valor on the battlefield, let others speak. I have no need of it.'

'You only held Achilles while Paris stuck the arrow in him! A nasty, treacherous business for a valiant warrior!' cried Helenus. His voice cracked in desperation, and to my surprise I saw that he was very near tears. His face had now gone white. 'It was I who drew first blood from Achilles in fair and open combat out on the field!'

'Stop!' commanded my father. 'I will not have wrangling in my Hall unless it be for a more worthy cause than this. Helen must go to Deiphobus. He is by far the better of you two. It is Helen's safety, not her shaming, which is the question here, and I will not lower myself to debasing a woman. You are still bound to Apollo, Helenus, and presently excluded from marriage though you may have forgotten it.'

'I have forgotten nothing!' he shouted. 'Always I have been passed over, ignored, shunted aside! What about *my* humiliation? Just because Cassandra is weak-headed and wants to live in a shrine doesn't mean that I have to! But was I ever consulted, even once? No! And now this! I cannot even have Paris's leavings! Well, then, we shall see if I cannot find somewhere to go where I can be appreciated. It is certain that I will never find it here!'

Bitter and raging, he ran out of the Hall. I ran after him with the cold boiling through me at his outburst and caught him by the sleeve. He jerked it away angrily. 'Scorpion!' he hissed, so vehemently that I drew back half-afraid. 'Witch! Adder-tongue! If it weren't for you, I'd be the equal of any of them in there! But no, you're mean, and hard, and so wrapped up with your precious Apollo you can't see out, and crazy, too! And it's rubbed off on me! Well, I never wanted to have anything to do with it. It's all your fault, everything is your fault, and I hate you!'

He ran away again and I made no move to stop him, standing gasping in the outgush. How long, I wondered numbly, had my twin harbored this stinging hatred of me, blaming me for his every failure? I turned back slowly toward the Hall, stiff and chilled through, dreading this warning that seemed to have Helenus at its core.

But the folk within appeared to have treated Helenus's outburst as the tantrum of a balked child. They were much more interested in seeing Helen, her face positively mutinous, being led away to her new bridal chamber, and in following, tossing bits of ribald – and totally unnecessary – advice even while Deiphobus closed the door behind him with his long-awaited prize.

I was betrothed again. His name was Eurypylus, and he came with a band of stout Mysians at his back. And he greeted me with such courtesy in Priam's courtyard and lavished such attention upon me when he was in the City that if I had not known about the slip of Golden Vine and other such gifts and bribes, I might have thought he cared about me.

I suppose he could have been considered a prince. And it is certain that my father owed the Mysians something, for they had felt the first blow against Troy. It was at Mysia that the Achaeans first made contact with the Eastern mainland, and Achilles could not resist raiding the place. Telephus, Eurypylus's father, was still crippled as a result of a blow from Achilles's spear. And so it had taken no little persuasion to convince my new betrothed's mother that her son should go and fight at Troy.

'I hope, Eurypylus,' I said dryly, when we had been allowed to walk sedately along the Third Terrace avenue to 'become acquainted' in the growing dusk, 'that you do not suffer the fate of others who have declared for my hand.'

'Oh?' he replied politely. 'And what might that be?'

'They died.'

To my surprise, he laughed carelessly. 'Is that all!' he exclaimed. 'I thought that you meant that you changed your mind and refused them after all. Now there is a fate to be dreaded!'

I remember that I smiled. Poor fool, he was so transparent. And yet, he was charming, too, and far above the first man to whom my father had promised me. But he could never hope to measure alongside of the man to whom I had promised myself. Perhaps he sensed my lack of response, for he set himself to wooing me industriously; and with a wisdom beyond him, he approached me through my beloved Bastos, discoursing learnedly on his origins and traits.

'A very handsome cat he is,' Eurypylus said, running the backs of his fingers along Bastos's chin. And he, heartless traitor that he was, stretched and purred, rubbing this stranger's hand with shameless pleasure. 'He is descended from Ægyptian hunting-cats, trained to swim out through the marshes and retrieve their master's game. It is said that the best of them could bring back a bird so cleverly that no feather was disturbed, except from the arrow. Many of this close-furred breed still like the water. Does this one?'

'Yes,' I admitted, pleased in spite of myself at the trouble he was taking in my wooing. 'Sometimes he jumps into my bath before Orthia or I can catch him, apparently enjoying a swim. Other ladies of the court used to think it just another symptom of my oddness that I harbor an unnatural creature like Bastos.'

There was a sudden movement, and an answering shadow overhead. An owl had spotted a mouse, though it was early for owls to be out hunting. It missed its stoop, but a stray cat from the City didn't. The cat trotted off, head high, with its prize clenched proudly in its mouth.

'No more unnatural than that,' he said, 'or that your pet was too well fed to bother challenging an owl for its prey. We all have our dislikes and our differences. Who's to say that the unfortunate mouse would not have passed up grain for cheese, when it was still up and about?'

He won a laugh from me for his lighthearted foolishness. I daresay I might have grown more and more accustomed to him, given time, and might even have come to concede to him some of the qualities I thought were Sarpedon's alone.

That was the evening of our first meeting; by morning, I had decided to submit to the formal ceremony I had shunned with my former suitor whose very name I had forgotten. And there had not been the chance with Sarpedon. But in war, events move quickly or not at all, and we needed the support of the Mysians far too greatly to risk giving offense.

As Orthia put it, 'He's not as fine as your lover was, but then who is? But he's decent, and kind, and you could do far worse. Take him, and be glad for it.'

The formal betrothal would come at nightfall; in the afternoon, Eurypylus took the field in high spirits, and to show off for me a little, I think. He was certainly brave enough, and showed his wry sense of humor there, too, for he was given sole credit for killing Machaon. He was the Achaeans's surgeon, the one who fought when he felt like it and retired behind his calling when the struggle began to go against him.

'Men who carry weapons and who stand against me are likely to be killed,' he said cheerfully, 'even when they begin jouncing the standard of Asclepius up and down and howling that they are doctors and not warriors. He looked like a warrior to me, and stripped like one. I've got his corselet to prove it!'

Well content, the City was willing to give us a lavish show, as great as they could manage as warworn as they were. Would that I had refused Eurypylus, even at the risk of losing his warriors; for during the merrymaking, we discovered how things had fared with Helenus after he had run headlong out of my father's Hall, with hatred for me and everything Trojan in his heart.

Calling upon the gods to witness, in front of my father and the nobles of Troy, I promised that I would marry Eurypylus immediately after I had been released and purified from my virgin's vows in the service of Artemis. And in token of the coming marriage, we were led with torchlight and much gaiety around all three avenues so that everyone in the City could get a look at the prospective bridal couple. Helen was conspicuously absent, and I wondered if she watched from a window, and listened in galled fury to the contrast between this and her latest wedding.

As we descended among the warriors, I began to be embarrassed when the jokes got progressively more rustic. Eurypylus, unruffled, grinned and gave back as good as we got, so that I would know that I was not getting a slow-tongued weakling for a husband.

But the merrymakers were suddenly hushed and we all looked at each other in dismay and fear, the torches guttering and flower wreaths drooping, when we returned to the Palace and discovered that the Palladium had been stolen during the revelry. In its place now stood a rough-hewed wooden column, blatantly and insultingly phallic in its form. And men, who had been jesting coarsely a moment before, now rushed forward in shocked silence to hurry the abomination away.

'Helenus!' I said.

'No!' protested my mother.

But a quick consultation with the guards at the East Gate proved my intuitive guess to be correct. Unsuspecting, they had allowed my brother and two companions garbed as rustics into the City, thinking he had come to share in the celebration. And this was the result. He knew every crevice and crack of the City, and it would have been an easy matter to climb unnoticed to the Palace shrine and remove the great thunder-stone. And they were further aided in their theft by Helenus's relieving the guards to go and join in the revelry. Of course it had been Helenus. Who else would know what alarm and panic would result from such an injury? This, then, was the revenge he had taken for the loss of Helen! Such a great retaliation, I thought, for such a shabby cause.

Once more my dwindling number of spies set to work, and before another day had passed I had found out the depth of Helenus's treachery.

The rumor had been that he had gone off down the road in the direction of Mount Ida. Perhaps he had wanted to cool his hot head for a while at the Stronghold; nobody thought much about it, for the feeling was that when he had recovered from his pique he would return the same as always. But instead, he had doubled back and contrived to send word from the Pastoral Shrine that he was now willing to go over to the side of the Achaeans. And he had even had a plausible excuse ready at hand. He had called Achilles's killing a treacherous ambush; and he used that in turn for treason for his own.

Odysseus came and fetched him under heavy guard, for they were doubly alert after the way Achilles had met his end. But Helenus had seemed honest enough in his new allegiance, and to prove it had given three auguries which, he said, would surely result in Troy's downfall. The first of these was already at hand, that being the carved ivory shoulder harness of Pelops, that dreadful sign of a blood-drenched House. The second was that the Palladium be stolen from Troy. And the third was that if there was a son of Achilles's body, he should now come and fight in his father's place.

At this, I smiled sourly, wondering if any son of Achilles would ever be found, knowing his peculiarities.

It seemed that there was one. Years before, he had been sent to live at the court of King Lycomedes, on Scyros. Even at that young age, his tendencies were well marked. Thinking to turn it to a jest, Lycomedes had dressed Achilles as a girl, calling him 'Pyrrha', and had put him with his daughter and her women. They liked men, too, he said, and so they should all get on well together.

Much to his surprise and chagrin, the daughter, Deidameia, confessed herself to be pregnant some months afterward, and said that Achilles was responsible. When questioned, young Achilles replied innocently that he was merely attempting to do as the women did among themselves, but his doing had taken a totally unexpected turn. And so Deidemeia was presently brought to bed with a son. Lycomedes put the best face he could upon the matter for it was clearly his own fault; he named the boy Pyrrhus, and brought him up as his own son.

They sent a swift ship to Scyros to fetch the boy, who was about seventeen or eighteen years of age by now. And that he was a true son of his father was immediately apparent the first time he appeared on the battlefield; the set of his shoulders, the wild, mad gleam of his eyes, the way he brandished his father's armor was enough to brand him Achilles's get, even to a stranger. They renamed him Neoptolemus, 'new war', because he was supposed to be the magic touchstone to bring victory out of the old war that had sickened everyone on either side; and the first time he went out to fight he killed Eurypylus.

Though I scratched my cheeks and gave the lament, the real tears did not come until after his funeral and I was alone in my room with Bastos and Orthia for comfort. And then I think that I wept more for myself than for him.

'Is it to be my fate to bring death upon any man who looks at me?' I demanded. 'Is my touch poisonous like that Achaean bowman's, the very air I breathe contaminated so that when a man comes close he falls down dying?'

'There, there,' soothed Orthia, stroking my hair. 'You do not know what you are saying.'

'I know only too well. Orthia, do you remember when I was a little girl, how you would tell me my name meant "entangler of men"? And how I used to have tantrums because I was not pretty enough for a little boy to look upon with pleasure? And how later I came to hate the whole lot of them?'

'Yes, and I wondered at the time. You have never told me why.'

'Nor will I tell you now, for it would do no good to rake it over again. But when I met Sarpedon, everything changed for me. And even with poor Eurypylus, I thought that I could manage to find a kind of peace and be a wife like any other woman. But now I wonder if my man-hate had not a sound basis after all if my smile only brings death.'

'Be silent, Cassandra. You are overwrought. Sleep if you can, and I will hold you close if the dream comes again. It is war, after all, that takes men, and not any fault of yours. You will know this better in the morning.'

But I lay long awake, staring at the dim rectangle that was the window and brooding upon my own dark thoughts. Orthia had spoken common sense, and anyone would recognize it. But – and now I hugged sleepy Bastos tighter against my empty chest – I had spoken truth, though no one might ever recognize it but me.

18

THE SERPENT OF POSEIDON

Summer was rapidly drawing to a close, and when the City did not fall immediately upon the fulfillment of Helenus's three predictions Achaean morale plummeted to its lowest ebb. They turned upon Helenus, as if it had all been his fault. Because it is forbidden to spill the blood of a prophet as it is with various other sacred persons, they killed him by pelting him with lumps of clay which soon piled up around him where they had him tied and made a tomb wherein he still lived briefly. But when they had finished stamping down the clay and packing it tight he was dead.

Priam considered sending Antenor to Agamemnon to begin negotiations for a peace; but before he could make up his mind to it, the Achaeans departed. As quickly as they had arrived, they were gone. When the sun had set, they pushed their ships, those that were still seaworthy, into the Hellespont and vanished before the morning's light.

We could hardly believe our eyes. We rubbed them again and again, and still all that we could see on the shore of the Hellespont between the two rivers were a burnt-out hull or two, some deserted huts, and a few torn and dilapidated tents flapping dismally in the freshening autumn breeze. The gates of their sagging wall were open, creaking back and forth, and nowhere was there a sign of our enemies.

As if from a single throat a paean of thanksgiving went up from the City and the low town alike. Our own gates were likewise thrown open and we streamed out, men, women, servants, slaves, all equal in our joy at running free on our own Plain that had been so long denied to us. Some of the more daring ventured into the stockade enclosure, as if fearing that Achaeans were still in hiding somewhere. But they had vanished and nothing was to stop the jubilant Trojans from pushing over the huts, hacking down the tents, shoving over a few more logs in the wall, and generally completing the destruction of the hated camp.

Now, from closely guarded hiding places came small jars of wine, sacks of grain, a few cruets of oil threatening to go bad. A number of hunters laughingly went into the hills, and to our surprise brought back two stags and a number of wild pigs. Though we still faced an empty winter after the devastation of the war-filled summer, we would have a feast now, with bread and meat and wine to drink, in thanksgiving of our deliverance.

One of the pigs we burnt whole, and offered it in gratitude to the gods who had spared us. The rest we attacked greedily, and even I ate with a better appetite than I had had in months. At last, it seemed, the shadow had left us and we were free again.

We set up our tables outside, glad to be able to set our feet on our beloved Plain without fear. Walls could not have held us. Priam and his family and nobles were on the scarp beneath the Great Tower, and the rest of the soldierly population of Troy found such places as pleased them beyond.

But nothing pleased them quite so greatly as when Priam got up to speak while the grease still made our chins shine in the torchlight.

'My most honored friends, guests, and well-beloved allies!' he said, and a cheer answered him. 'Know that I am well satisfied and pleased with the service that you have given me so unstintingly. In return, I offer in addition to the gold and other considerations promised you, the privilege of citizenship in Troy for which you have fought so valiantly. Or, if you prefer, you are now free to return to your homelands and my love and gratitude will go with you.'

An even greater cheer went up. Mighty Priam! Citizenship in Troy! This was not a boon given lightly. I could hear excited speculations running here and there among the more highly born of them. With Priam's gold, and a stake in the market place of the Troad, they could wash away the blood in a season's time! Maybe two, at the outside. It was a shrewdly given opportunity to repair the old king's fortunes and make their own at the same time! Heaven's blessing on good and generous King Priam, who still had not lost the touch of the born trader!

But there were enough who wanted nothing more than to go home. The Mysians were latest come and soonest gone from Troy, for they had not had the time to grow into the war that had occupied the rest of us for so long. And others were not far behind. But many, who had far to go, were in no hurry to begin their long journeys. The Amazons were among these last, and the Lycians and the remnants of the Hittites.

Priam called Æneas into his council chamber on the day following the great feast, while the City was busy with its emptying of departing warriors. 'I want you to take your brave Dardanians, and go with Antenor and Anchises to the Stronghold. It is time to bring back the people there. And perhaps they will have been able to put together some stores of food to sustain us through the coming winter.'

Æneas frowned. 'I would rather take my Dardanians in pursuit of the Palladium. That theft still rankles.'

'Do not concern yourself, my son,' said Priam with a smile. 'The Palladium knows where it belongs. I am confident that it will return.'

'I am not, but I will do as you request. Let me only say goodbye to Creusa, for she is still not well, and I will depart this day.'

Poor Creusa had not recovered from the birth of their son and was still in bed. The last few days, even her milk had begun to dry away, and she complained of feeling feverish. I happened to be with her, trying to cajole her into taking a drug said to be good for fevers, but she pushed it away.

'It smells foul,' she complained, 'and tastes worse.'

'But if it will help you – ' I coaxed, but then Æneas came through the door and Creusa forgot all about me.

Her wan face lit up when she heard Æneas's mission. 'It will be good to have the City back as it once was,' she said. 'Almost – '

'Do not think of that. Think only that the war is over at last!' said Æneas, holding her two thin hands in his.

'Take the boy,' Creusa said suddenly, an urgency in her voice.

'What?'

'Our son! Take him with you. There is sure to be someone in the Stronghold who can nurse him. I . . . I cannot,' she said shamefacedly, and Æneas's face changed as if he realized for the first time how things stood with his wife.

'I will not leave you.'

'You must. I will be as I am, whether you stay or go. But our son will surely die if we do not find someone to feed him!' She managed a tired smile. 'There has been a great scarcity of wetnurses in Troy lately.'

He clasped her hands for a moment longer, a sharp frown on his face. Then he nodded, kissed her, and left. At a weak gesture from Creusa, a slave went to bundle the baby up for the journey.

'I will be dead before he returns, Cassandra,' she said quietly, still smiling. 'Did you know that? You know about such things, or are supposed to. But did you know about my death?'

'I know of no such thing, my sister,' I replied as stoutly as I was able. But I had seen that same look, heard that same calm foreknowledge from too many, and my voice broke on my lie. 'I think that you will live.'

'What nonsense you do speak sometimes. Æneas will come to me again before he leaves. Please, take your useless medicine away.'

Without protest, I gathered up the rejected fever cure and left. She was quite right, of course, and the only thing I could do for her now was to let them say their goodbyes in peace.

While I watched the receding figures as they marched along the various roads that led from Troy, a gloomy foreboding came and settled over me. Was the contamination spreading then, to women as well as men? Perhaps I should have stayed away from Creusa, for it had begun to seem that anyone I came near was automatically sentenced to death.

No, I told myself sternly, remembering Orthia's sensible words and trying to shake off the shadow with them. I had seen enough of death that I should not allow one more to upset me so, even though it was my sister. At least her passing would be a natural thing. Childbirth was always a hazard, as everyone knew, and more than one had failed to get up from it.

But still my uneasiness would not pass.

That it was caused by something more than Creusa's dying came clear that very night. The watchmen on the walls, grown careless in less than two days, found themselves startled out of their doze by a shriek coming out of the darkness.

They quickly kindled torches, lighting the plaza before the Dardanian Gate, and then cried out themselves in superstitious fear.

The woman in the flickering light might have been one of Night's Daughters. She was wild of eye and her hair was torn and tangled. Her dress looked as if frantic hands had ripped it into tatters. So a Maenad, in the grip of the wine god, might appear as she wandered her dangerous path under the god's urgings. And she crouched and moaned in the torchlight.

'Who is she?' asked the watchmen into the crowd that was quickly gathering, attracted by the screams. 'Is she a woman, or some foul demon?'

Polites shouldered his way through the people. 'Why, it is Antiope,' he said in slow recognition, 'the woman Laocoön took. He put her in the Pastoral Shrine, and she has been there for years. Antiope!' he called to the shivering woman below. 'Be calm, Antiope. No one will harm you.'

She looked up sharply, and her head began to weave back and forth. 'Antiope?' she croaked. 'That is not my name! I am the Serpent of Poseidon, and no one *can* harm me! Beware the wrath of the god!'

'And what might that be?' he asked, to humor her, since it was plain that she had lost her senses.

She straightened scornfully and leveled her bony finger at the watchers on the wall. Frightened by the power that came out of her, they shrank back in alarm.

'Do not mock me, Priam's son!' she said loudly. 'The Serpent of Poseidon has struck once already this night!'

'I meant no offense. What is your message, Serpent of Poseidon?'

'Beware!' she repeated. 'You have a warning, from the charity of the god. Take it, or his curse on all of you!' And then she turned, and ran crouching and howling past the circle of light and into the darkness. No one ever saw her again.

Polites bit his lip for a while and then went to fetch Deiphobus from Helen's reluctant arms. Together, with men to light the way, they took the well-worn road to the Pastoral Shrine to find out for themselves what, if anything, had happened.

It had not needed the jar of serpent venom lying overturned on the floor where she had dropped it after dipping the dagger in. Laocoön and the two boys he had bred from the demented woman whose shrieks had aroused Troy lay dead with gaping wounds in throat, chest and belly. From the looks of things, she had killed the priest first, and then the sleeping boys, one after the other. Then she had turned again to Laocoön's body and had dragged it from the couch, overturning lamps and furniture and trailing bloody linen. She had stabbed him again and again, going back for more snake venom, for the drops were plain as a trail on the floor. And as an added macabre touch, she had tenderly marked the boys' names on their foreheads in their own blood. Antiphus and Melanthus they had been called. But their bodies bore none of the savagery of the assault that had been made upon Laocoön. They had just the single death wound, and their faces looked like sleep.

'It was like a charnel house,' Deiphobus declared to Priam, who had been roused from his sleep to hear of it.

'What does it mean, Cassandra?' asked my father. As usual, I was awake and about the palace, for my dream would not let me rest.

'Why ask me, father?' I said with a short laugh. 'All I know is fire and death, death and fire. And this is one of the two.' I suppose that I was near to my own breaking point or I would have never spoken that way to my father who had finally turned to me for assistance.

'But I am asking you,' he said so gently that I was ashamed of myself.

I took a deep breath. My eyes felt full of sand. I had not slept more than one hour running since the Achaeans had departed, and my very bones felt ready to collapse from weariness. 'It is not over yet,' I said now, no longer caring who knew about the hideous dream I had carried in secrecy ever since I could remember. 'When I close my eyes I can see Troy in flames.'

'But how, daughter? The Achaeans are gone; there is no one left who wishes us ill.'

'Poor Antiope called down the curse of Poseidon upon us.'

'Her mind snapped. No one sane could have done what she did.'

'Yet there it is. Death, and the fire I have seen all my life in my dreams.'

'When we have passed through the winter and have begun to rebuild our economy once more, I will send you on a long and curative journey, my daughter. Would you like to go to Cyprus? Or even Ægypt? You need to get away, with time to yourself, so that you can clear your mind of these terrible things that trouble you.'

'A journey?' I said, and I remember that I smiled dryly. 'Why should I want to leave Troy? It is my home, and everything that I have said or done has been for its ultimate good and your own, my father.'

'Yes, a voyage,' he repeated, caught up with his idea. 'You will return refreshed and ready to take your place among the new people who will come to live here and wipe out the memory of this enormous war we have lately endured.'

'If ever I leave Troy,' I said somberly, 'I will never return.'

And then I turned on my heel and made my way back to my room. It was still dark. If I was lucky, I might get another hour's sleep before the dream sent me back shivering and sweating into a wakefulness that was only a little less tormenting than the sleep had been.

The birds vanished. As abruptly as the Achaeans had left, between one sunset and another sunrise, they were gone. Hera's crane, Aphrodite's dove, Artemis's owl, they all left. Even the small birds, the hoopoes, the larks, the nightingales, and all the other myriad nameless chirpers and twitters, deserted their trees and nests and left us with a silent dawn.

More alarming, the cats were gone. Even the dogs seemed cowed, and slunk along the streets with their tails between their legs, shivering in the doorways. And over it all hung the thick, lowering silence, still and ominous, so that it seemed nearly impossible to breathe. It was a 'breeder', said the Amazons, wise in such things. But a breeder of what?

My head ached abominably. And when I called Bastos for his breakfast, he was nowhere to be found. Even he, obeying some instinct more powerful than his fondness for me, had disappeared with the rest. I went out into the courtyard, hoping to catch sight of him. The air was so heavy, it seemed incredible that I could see through it from one end of the courtyard to the other. I snapped my fingers in irritation. The Father of Storms must be on its way. Good enough for him if he gets soaked, I thought. And then, with my finger snap I felt the first faint jar as the earth shifted beneath my feet.

It could have been the result of little food and less sleep; I had sometimes felt faint in the mornings before now. But then the second shock came, hard enough to rattle pots on shelves and raise dust.

'The curse of Poseidon!' I cried aloud. 'This was what the poor, insane woman meant! She could feel it coming!'

And then, with a deep-throated rumble that seemed to come from far below, spreading until it was everywhere at once, the earth beneath me lifted, heaved, and shook with a violence I would not have dreamed possible only a moment before. Up, down, sideways, I do not know how the City was tossed; I was knocked down in the courtyard and rolled about helplessly without anything to cling to. I could hear things overturning and breaking somewhere and cries of dismay and fear beginning to go up.

Above all the rest, I now heard an unearthly shriek and groan that seemed to come from the very stones of the City itself. Silent they were when they were quarried; without outcry they allowed themselves to be mauled and dressed into fair building blocks. But now, when their very fabric was rent in the tumultuous upheaval, they found voices and shouted and screamed their agony of destruction, almost obliterated in the shattering crash of their downfall. But I heard, I heard!

Before me, as I cowered and groped for any chance handhold, a rent opened and dropped away along the middle of the courtyard. I only just escaped being sucked down into it before it abruptly closed again, the edges oddly uneven where it had been level before. And then it was quiet, except for the shocked and stunned outcries of those who had, like me, lived through the terrible ruination of my city.

I pulled myself to my knees, and unsteadily got up again. The ground was still uneasy beneath me and I could feel minor shocks coming through the soles of my feet. I forgot my family, the Palace, the errand that had brought me outside where I must have been safer than those within. One glance assured me that the Palace still stood shivering, and now my one thought was to get down to the First Terrace where poor, dying Creusa lay. I don't know why she was my only concern in those first minutes; suppose it was because she had been my latest patient, and had seemed to be the one most recently touched by the destruction that I felt was destined to walk along in my footsteps.

A shrine, smashed as easily as if it had been a child's toy broken in a fit of pique, caught my eye as I left the courtyard. A little foot in a Western sandal and a scrap of filmy dress-hem all blood-streaked showed in the wreckage. Helen! But no, Helen would be in Deiphobus's chamber in the Palace and must even now be battering futilely at the sturdy doors in panic. He had not turned out Andromache from the Guardian's house on the First Terrace so as to put Helen in her place. It could only have been Laodice, and I wondered at the god who could pause in his great work to administer this richly deserved punishment to a Trojan who would mock her marriage vows.

But then, I thought as I hurried down the ramp, it probably had not put him out to do it.

Everywhere around me fires were beginning to blossom, and a thin line of smoke was even coming from the Palace itself. It would be from braziers, of course, and lamps thrown out of their holders. Cooking-fires for breakfast must have been lit, and then scattered when the City was tossed on the back of the god. The steadiest of those few who still remained in Troy were already hurrying to the Water Tower or grabbing heavy cloaks and rugs to try to beat out the flames. And then, as I neared Æneas's house, mercifully still standing, I saw the awful thing that the earthquake had done.

The Dardanian Gate and the walls to either side of it were intact, though many portions of the mud-brick ramparts were now lying in dust. Its tower was standing, though a crack had appeared, separating lines of stonework. But to the north of the Great Tower facing the Plain, the wall had been thrown down entirely and the great stones scattered as if they had been pebbles. The Tower itself was deeply rent and creaking, shivering with each new motion of the unsteady ground on which it stood. I noticed that the thin portion of the wall, the one the Lelegian had refused to touch or alter, stood as firm as it had after that other earthquake, when the fellow who called himself Heracles had come and killed King Laomedon and put my father on the throne. I could have laughed at this, and once begun never stopped.

Creusa was dead. But her face was calm, through the rubble of plaster and dust that lay on her bed, and I knew that she had died during the night and been spared terror in her last moments. At least her end had been peaceful, and not like Laodice's, whose dead eyes must still carry the sight of the wall collapsing upon her. The one maid who had remained with Creusa was dead also, her skull crushed by a heavy pot that had fallen from the shelf. The whole house, rocking on its sturdy stone foundation, threatened to come down upon me, and so I left. There was nothing there that I could do.

One thing we were spared in the catastrophe that had overtaken us. A gigantic earthquake such as this had been, was always accompanied by the phenomenon of the sea draining away and then rushing back. It was as if Poseidon always pushed forward a huge wave to set his mark the more firmly upon what he had done. But here, the sucking away of the waters was confused and frustrated by the heavy current through the Hellespont. There was a churning and a clash in the watery maelstrom that sent geysers of water hundreds of feet in the air when the opposing fluid armies came crashing together. But thwarted by the natural current as it was, the following wave still managed to surge with such force up onto the Trojan Plain that it came near the Pastoral Shrine. And when it retreated, we were awestruck to see that it had carried away nearly every vestige of the Achaean camp. Only the great ditch remained, and it was clogged and filled with water and mud and debris, in which a few unhappy sea creatures had been trapped. But everything else, the burnt-out ships, the logs that had made up the stockade wall, the wreckage of the tents and huts, was washed away as cleanly as if it had never been.

And then a single voice from a sharp-eyed soldier who had

climbed atop the Dardanian Gate to see cried out the alarm. 'Sails!' he yelled. 'And there, to the north, along the line of hills! Moving figures! It is the Achaeans! It was a trick, a trick! They did not leave but hid themselves so that they could fall upon us when we were hardest hit!'

Men paused in beating out fires to look at one another, and dismay was on every face. This second blow, coming on the very heels of the first, was more than we could bear. And then Deiphobus was among us, stern, unshakable, already armed.

'Poseidon has knocked Troy down around our ears,' he shouted grimly, 'and the Achaeans come scavenging in his wake! But I'll not stand meekly by and let them have what we have defended all summer, if I have to stand alone! Who among you will back me?'

'Shouts of 'I!' and 'I!' again, as the faltering few soldiers left of the many who had been in Troy only a day or so before reached out to find new firmness in the strength that surrounded my brother. A burst of shrieking laughter came from one of the Amazons. 'It will be a fight to remember!' she yelled jubilantly.

'Get any women you find and take them back to the Palace, Cassandra,' my brother instructed me. 'This is no place for you. And hurry.'

I nodded my head in obedience. 'Die well, Deiphobus, Guardian of Troy,' I said. But he was already gone.

They poured through the enormous, gaping rent in the wall like water from a jar. Nothing could keep them outside; the breach was too large, and the Trojans too few. We watched it all from the height of the courtyard, and fresh tears ran from nearly every eye whenever we saw another Trojan fall.

I had lived with this moment so intimately for so long that I forgot to weep, forgot to even be afraid. The repetition had finally dulled the sting of it when it became real, and I could only feel a curious kind of relief now that it was happening at last. All that was lacking to complete my release was the Achaeans's rekindling the fires the earthquake had begun, after stripping the houses of rich furniture and ornaments. And that, too, was inevitable.

Patiently, relentlessly, they forced the swiftly dwindling Trojans past the First Terrace. Now they ranged through the ruined women's quarters on the second level. A quick glimpse near the ramp showed young Polites fighting desperately with an Achaean who seemed but little older. Another look told us that this was Neoptolemus, for he was wearing the armor of Achilles.

Priam turned to Hecabe, a sudden wave of resolution washing over him, making his features stern. 'I will go to him,' he said. 'He needs me, for he is overmatched.'

'No, my husband!' cried Hecabe, taking his arm as if to stop him. But he gently removed her grasping fingers, holding both her hands in his as courteously and gravely as if they were young lovers again.

'You have been a good wife, sweet heart,' he said lovingly, and he smiled a little. 'Know that, in the days to come. And I have tried to be a good husband, and father, and king. But I failed at the last, and now I must go and pay for my error. It is the only way I will ever find rest.'

He paused only to take a spear from the tumbled weapons-racks in the courtyard and marched out firmly without breast-plate, helmet or shield to face Achilles's son. Even as he came near, Neoptolemus delivered the death stroke, and looked up to find himself confronting the Trojan king.

With a last burst of strength, old Priam heaved the spear at the astonished young man. Neoptolemus ducked by instinct, and then in the next moment the aged father and the young son lay side by side in the companionship of death, and their blood mingled on the same weapon.

There, I thought calmly. That is what troubled me about Hector's sacrifice. It must be the king, no other. There is a word newly formed, in these days when men try to explain and understand what has happened to them. *Harmatia,* they say, meaning the 'tragic flaw' that pushes a man toward unintentional sin; and this was what had overtaken my father. What words had Hector used, to persuade Priam to allow him to take his death for him? An old man, facing an outlaw killer, the Guardian who was now king in all but name, the shame a young and vigorous man would feel to see his white-haired father go out to die while he stood safely back and watched – I could almost hear my brother marshaling his arguments. Well, he had won, for all the good it did him or Troy. And now the sacrifice had come too late.

I turned to go back into the Palace.

'Cassandra!' cried my mother sharply. 'Where are you going?'

'To pray I suppose, Mother,' I replied. 'It is the only thing left to do now.'

I think she would have rebuked me for leaving the King dead to go about other business; but I knew that the time was upon us when all the people cowering in the courtyard would seek shelter in the Palace. Shrieking and wailing, they would flee through the corridors in the ultimate flight from the triumphant Achaeans, seeking another moment, another breath of freedom. And I wanted a few minutes of quiet to myself before that happened.

I went to my own room before I turned toward the desecrated house-shrine that had held the Palladium. I think I half-hoped to find Bastos, returned after the appalling upheaval of the earthquake had sent the animals and birds into instinctive hiding for their own safety. Instead, it was Orthia that I discovered, dead by her own hand, her face as calm and stern in death as it had been in life.

Strong, upright Orthia! She had seen how things were, from my window. Only a fool would have continued to hope that the Trojans would prevail when the Achaeans began to come through the wall. And so, she had chosen to die when she would, in dignity, in the place she loved, knowing that she would not be spared when it came time to select the women who would be added with the other spoil. She was too old, too plain, and so by her own indomitable will she had deprived the conquerors of taking another Trojan's life.

I do not know now what kept me from following her example. But at the time, it simply did not occur to me that I could ease myself of what was sure to come. The cool and placid calm that had descended upon me and closed me within when the earthquake had set in motion the inexorable fall and destruction of Troy, with which I had lived all my nights, had also made it seem that I was exempt in some strange way from the consequences. Had I not suffered it all beforehand? Why should I suffer it again?

I looked around impersonally, as if it were another's bedchamber that I gazed upon. The wolfskin on the floor beside my bed, the embroidered coverlet, the dyed leather curtains, new just a year or so before – what a stench they would make in burning! I touched my jewel box with its meager contents. The greenstone chain with its peach-colored pendant and the carved cup, the barbaric earring from under the sleeping soil of Troy, were all that remained. They, too, seemed to belong to another person in another time, and I left them there.

I went unhurried to the house-shrine where the empty plinth stood. I began to pray mechanically, to whom I do not know, for the easement of my father's soul. It had been a terrible decision laid before him, after all, when Hector came seeking the deliverance of his city and his countrymen by royal sacrifice. Who among us might have chosen differently?

I heard cries of terror and hurrying feet outside. The Achaeans must have already gained the Palace. And still I knelt, quiet and serene in the peace that had been so long in coming to me. I was smiling when the door crashed open thunderously and harsh footsteps scarred the polished floor.

'A prize!' a man's voice exclaimed hoarsely, and a moment later I was jarred from my enveloping indifferent serenity when strong and lusty hands hauled me up and swept me into an unwelcome embrace. The smell of him, the ruttish war-smell of his triumphant sweat, filled my nostrils thickly. One of his brawny hands dug into my buttocks while the other fumbled impatiently with his short kilt and my long, hampering skirt. I felt the insistent man-gristle urgent against my belly and knew what was about to happen.

'When they ask, say it is Ajax who claims you,' he grunted harshly. But it was not the face of Ajax that I was seeing, short-statured Ajax who had fought in his taller namesake's shadow. Another set of features swam before me, of a priestly set, and I was seeing again Laocoön's dark and suffused countenance on that awful day long ago in the schoolroom.

'No!' I cried, and it rose to a drawn-out trembling scream. My blood began to hammer in my head and I twisted and squirmed in his hateful grasp, brought back to the terrible realities of what was happening around me and, inevitably, to me as well.

Sharp, bony elbows jabbing at his eyes. A knee, made thin by fasting, seeking its target. Fingernails breaking on his unyielding flesh. Teeth sinking into the underside of his arm and the taste of blood in my mouth. Knowing that my small strength could not outlast his, but hoping to anger him sufficiently that his sword would do the work I had neglected in my blind complacency. Fingers tangling in my hair, forcing me to give up my teeth-grip.

An unexpected reprieve. A man in fine armor, shining with gold, wading in and plucking Ajax away with as little effort as the hunter beats off the hounds when the stag is down.

'Find another prize,' the newcomer said unsmiling. 'This is Cassandra, and I have promised myself that she would be mine.'

'Your pardon, Agamemnon!' cried Ajax. His eyes were suddenly glassy with fear, and he scuttled off without a backward glance.

No reprieve at all! 'Agamemnon?' I panted. 'Agamemnon!' Of course! It had all been in my dream, and there he stood before

me! 'Murderer!' I shrieked. 'Killer of Troy!'
'You may call me that,' he replied indifferently.
'Then kill me too, for I am Troy!'
'No. You will live, though Troy dies.'
'It will be far better if you kill me.'
He allowed himself a small smile. 'I think that you will not find life with me unpleasant, once you are accustomed to it.'
Like a hunted animal at bay I made a sudden, desperate dash for the door. There was still the fire to come, I knew, and I longed to lose myself in its welcome burning.
He caught me easily. 'You may be small, but your spirit is fierce,' he said. 'Well, then, if you will not go easily, you will go keeping your pride.' He motioned to a couple of his warriors outside the shrine and they came and bound me firmly with deer-hide ropes. 'Put her with the cart I have set aside for my personal takings,' he instructed, 'and see to it that another like Ajax does not try to violate her, for I will kill him with my own hand.'
It was go with them, tethered and helpless, or be dragged – or even worse, be carried, and I could not have tolerated being touched by them. And so I walked, choosing to make the ropes on my arms the single dignity that a captive may possess, for they were the symbols of an unconquered spirit.
As busily as ants in an ant heap, they were already stripping houses of anything worth having; and when they had finished ransacking, they applied the torch. It goes quickly, for valuables are easy to spot and easier to remove. Most of the houses on the First Terrace were in flames, and here and there a tongue of fire showed itself on the Second Terrace. I averted my eyes from the sight of my father and brother lying lifeless outside the courtyard, but a gust of smoke brought the tears that I had been unwilling to shed. I swallowed them back as quickly as I could, turning it into a fit of coughing, lest the Achaeans jeer at my weeping.
At the Second Terrace, I stopped in spite of myself, caught by a glimpse of a small, familiar form emerging cautiously from a snug refuge in a house's foundation.
'Bastos!' I exclaimed involuntarily. He heard me, and knew my voice, for one of his ears laid flat against his head twitched. But he was wild and frightened. His object seemed to be to dash from hiding place to hiding place until he could escape from the deranged tumult in the City to the safety outside.
Beyond reason, I hoped that he would be able to find me so that I would have his soft, comforting presence in the uncertain

days ahead. It was even on my tongue to ask my warders, begging if necessary, to find a bag or a basket so that I could put him into it now, wild as he was. But as he gathered himself for his next desperate scurrying dash to an unknown shelter, I heard a wager offered and quickly accepted by a group of Achaean soldiers behind me. Laughing, the man nocked an arrow to his string and let fly before I could speak.

It bowled him off his feet as neatly as if he had been a running rabbit. He came to rest close by the steps of a house that was beginning to burn. Shortly, part of the roof would come down and cover him.

I nodded absently, feeling with surprise the coolness of tears on my cheeks. Well, let them come. I no longer cared what the Achaeans might think, for my pride was now gone from me. They could even have taken off the cords binding me and I would have meekly followed them to my fate.

Here and there, I could begin to distinguish other women fettered as I was, through the thickening smoke of the burning. Memnonides, laughing and flirting with their captors, not caring whose beds they were in; comely slaves unmoved by this change in masters; a few Amazons, bleeding and sullen. And then, with a lurch of my battered heart, I saw Polyxena, so small and fragile she looked like a doll in the grip of the Achaean who carried her. Only Hecabe, Polyxena, and I were left of the family of Priam, and I could not see my mother anywhere.

Helen I saw, however, liberated from her Palace prison. She was already sitting in a cart outside the Dardanian Gate with a glowering Menelaus standing near. Behind her, the former queen Æthra held Helen's poor, neglected little son, and the other royal slave whose name I could not remember sat by numbly. She seemed to be recalling within herself how it had been when she had been taken. But Helen sat laughing, dangling her foot gaily and rummaging through the contents of what I recognized as my mother's jewel box. From time to time, a champion would come by and drop another handful of trinkets into her lap, though the common soldiers gave her nothing but black looks.

This, then, had been her stake. Jewels and ornaments, pretty things to hang on her precious body. And also, I thought sourly, a summer's diversion with a younger and more ardent lover than heavy, lumbering Menelaus. As I watched, she reached out and patted him blithely on the cheek, her face cheerful and without care of any kind.

But Menelaus had something else eating at him, and it had had all summer in which to gnaw. Something in the tilt of his head made me know that he found his wife altogether too sleek and debonaire, as if she had enjoyed overmuch the captivity in which she had found herself. And with that, the hatred she had gathered, as Priam had accurately foretold, must have washed against him as well. Yes, I thought. There would be words between husband and wife. Menelaus might do well to adopt Deiphobus's device of the locked door to contain Helen from now on.

They tied me to the rail of the cart, and a scream startled me. It was my own, for I had seen the first licking of fire high on the Third Terrace. I had thought myself drained long since, but now I stood and screamed, wailing the dead, bruising myself with my grief. My throat tore and the blood came gushing up, mercifully silencing me. And then the blackness, like clouds of buzzing hornets, mingled with the smoke and the cinders. I knew that if I looked up I would see it forming itself into a ghostly foot, an unearthly Murderer's foot, and with a great sigh of relief I yielded myself up to it as it came down and blotted me away forever into the dust and burning and ashes of Troy.

BOOK THREE

MYCENAE

19

CAPTIVE

It is such a small thing, the pleasure of a king. Later, when I had realized the triviality of it, I wondered why I had fought.

But fight him I had, as desperately as I had struggled against Lesser Ajax. This one, however, was not a man taken out of himself by the triumphal lust that decrees rape for everything female, when the scowling grin on the man's face is somehow more horrible than the act itself. No; this Achaean king, this Murderer, this man whom I must learn to think of as my master, had set himself the task of bedding the Trojan king's daughter. And he went about it as efficiently and competently as if forcing terrified girls was a thing he did every day of his life.

There was no longer any semblance of a camp for the Achaeans on Trojan soil; the shelter in the fold of the hills toward Canakkale had been that only, a bivouac from which they might descend upon Troy when the earthquake had done its work. But the ships, which had fallen back behind Samothrace for hiding and for protection from the crazed gush of water to follow, were already in position for loading. It was to be Imbros for us, the nearest of the attendant islands close upon the Hellespont, which had known uninterrupted Achaean occupancy from the first day of the war.

Even against the deepening night I could see the column of red-tinged smoke that was the burning badge of Troy. I wondered about my mother, hoping her mercifully dead in the tumult; wondered too about Andromache, sure to be spared for her beauty, and the little boy who was now King of Troy. Would she have wit enough to try to pass him off as a servant's brat, though his noble blood was plainly stamped upon him?

There were bales and bundles of plundered goods piled along the route to the Hellespont's shores; time enough to collect them in the days that lay ahead, for Agamemnon would not be content with merely burning the City. His avowed purpose was to level Troy, stone by stone, and it would be a most ambitious undertaking, in view of the sturdy building that had gone into it. But for now, the living spoils were the main concern of the conquerors.

They put me into the King's hut, barring the doors and guarding the windows against my escape. I rummaged frantically through the sparse furnishings for a weapon, a pot to smash for a sharp edge, anything with which to remedy my tardiness in following my nurse's example. I could not even rip up my already tattered gown to make a rope and hang myself from a rafter, for the delicacy of the fabric would not have held my weight, slight as it was. And they had taken away the deer-skin cords.

My mouth was bitter; they had revived me with wine from my faint, and had allowed me a good drink before they took it away. But the taste of blood was still with me, and my throat was hurt and sore from the useless screaming. At last I gave up my fruitless search for death, and I think I must have fallen asleep from exhaustion, for when I opened my eyes the Murderer, my new lord and King Agamemnon, stood before me.

I tried to scream again, but only a hoarse croak came out of my torn throat. And when he came toward me, I gathered myself for the grim combat, determined that he would not have me easily.

But where Lesser Ajax had parried and dodged my kicking and elbow-stabbing, Agamemnon seemed to take no notice whatsoever. Calmly, without haste, he pinioned one and then the other of my poor, thin hands outstretched on the couch. I was crushed and breathless under the weight of him, and he patiently maneuvered until he had unclamped my stubborn legs. I could breathe again, but found that he now pinned my thighs cruelly with his hard knees. This was so painful that I scarcely noticed as he transferred both captive arms to one fist, and shoved one bruised thigh higher so that the joint cracked with the strain. A quick, poised thrust, an instant of sharper pain nearly smothered in the other clamorings of my mauled flesh, and the thing was done.

Before dawn, he awoke and approached me again. This time, however, I lay quiet and passive. It seemed to puzzle him.

'You fought before,' he said. 'Why not now?'

'What I fought for is gone,' I replied indifferently. 'Would another struggle bring it back?'

He grinned in the dim darkness. 'A prudent observation, Cassandra,' he said. 'I told you it only needed getting used to me.'

As if it had been something happening to another, I watched him at his pleasure. A few thrusts and heaves, ridiculous in posture and graceless in execution, and he fell back panting. I have been more stirred watching a partridge's mating-dance.

'I find you very pleasing, Cassandra,' he said now. It seemed he would talk, after his latest performance, his tongue loosened as well as his limbs. 'I think that I like you better than that girl Astynome, or Chryseis, or whatever she chose to call herself. It was always touch me here, and stroke me there, with her. And always complaining that I had not done my part. I finally gave her to my nobles. Among them, maybe they could pat, and pinch, and tweak enough to suit her. Keep me in good humor, and you may find yourself better off than the usual concubine, for all that you are a Trojan.' And then he fell asleep and began to snore heavily.

Beside him, I stared at the ceiling, thinking. Without realizing it, he had given me the key to himself, and had even told me that I need not pretend any passion for him, a thing which I could never have done.

He had not kissed me, not murmured any affectionate prattle into my ear; indeed, he had scarcely touched me except to put me on my back and mount. He ignored all but the receptacle, and his own crisis was so quick in coming that I wondered if it was pleasure he sought so much as relief of just another bodily urge. Whether it was lack of tutoring or simple disregard for any desires of his partner, I did not know.

A priestess, even a virgin, cannot help but learn much about the intimate life between a man and a woman. I had often seen servants give each other knowing glances and then stay out of the way of the mistress who rose heavy-eyed and with nerves on edge from an unrewarding night's love-making. Even I had suffered somewhat during the time when there had been a man I loved but dared not touch.

At least I would be spared that. There are old stories, about reluctant maidens and their ravagers, and how hatred often brought a more primitive thrill than love to their congress together so that they were bound to each other more surely than any tender beginning might have done.

I, on the other hand, was as unmoved after my ravisher embraced me as before. The simple act of entering a woman, I discovered, was no act of love by itself. I would have hated to have been pawed at, and fumbled over, by a man seeking a response. But unwilling as I would always be, I could endure to lie quiet for the passive rape that seemed to please my captor so much.

I could have followed Chryseis's example, I suppose, and made him tire of me as well; but the prospect of being passed along to this one and that one was even more distasteful than the graceless invasions of Agamemnon. He had pulled Little Ajax off me, after all, and I suppose I felt I owed him something for that. If lying on my back like a lump of cold clay would pay the debt, then it was little enough to do.

He gave me three women, for though I was now a slave, I was the King's slave, and so, higher than they.

'Feed her,' he said brusquely. 'I bruised myself on her bones.'

And I touched the sore places on my thighs where great black marks were already beginning to show, and smiled ironically. Bruises indeed. But I could find no fault with his complaint. I was thin, and to remain so would be a reproach he could not endure. And since it appeared that I had no other choice, I would have to act the part of the slave that I was.

'If I have pleased you,' I asked now, so submissively that one of the women stared, 'may I also have Polyxena in my care? She is still just a child, and is certain to be terrified by what has happened.'

Agamemnon looked at me expressionlessly, his eyes nearly colorless in the morning's light. 'She's the one who was promised to Achilles, in return for the treachery he had no chance to perform, is she not? Well; no one would touch her, for that reason alone, so she is yours if you want her. Only keep her out of my sight.'

'I thank you,' I said, and added, though my tongue nearly stumbled over the words, 'my lord King Agamemnon.'

In comforting poor, trembling little Polyxena and in organizing my new household into some sort of order, I found some measure of solace for myself in being busy. For my servants, Agamemnon had given me one of the Æthiopian girls, an Amazon, and a serving woman to one of Troy's noblewomen. In other days, she had followed her mistress's example and scorned me more or less openly as a deranged fool; now I felt a certain tired amusement that she fawned upon me gladly, thinking herself saved from being left for the pleasure of the common soldiers.

Before the day was out, the Amazon, being more resourceful than I, had managed to find a way to die. And yet it was simple enough; she merely ran from the camp while nearly everybody else was busy with the midday meal, and scaling a cliff with the agility of a deer, cast herself headfirst onto the rocks below. I assured Agamemnon that two women were quite enough for me, so she was not replaced.

As for me, the mood as well as the time for death had passed, since I had received Polyxena into my care. Nysa, the noblewoman's former servant, was willing to do two women's work, and Shahba, the little Æthiopian, was openly admiring and a little envious of me, because I was now the property of the great Achaean king. In addition, she proved herself to be a clever hairdresser and talented with cosmetics. She could also prepare strange and delicious Hittite dishes that lured even my indifferent appetite; and so, if it had not been for the circumstances, I was in some ways better off than I had been in Troy.

Gossip of all kinds travels with the winds, the more so in a crowded camp like this. That it was quickly relieved of two of its more illustrious inhabitants was one of the first pieces of news to reach me.

It was late summer, dangerously late for sailing, but Menelaus dared not linger through a winter with his careless Helen. Even Agamemnon seemed relieved to see her go. He was not, however, prepared for two petitioners close on Menelaus's heels.

'We are sons of Theseus of Athens,' said Demophon, the spokesman of the two because Acamas was apt to stutter. 'The Lady Æthra is our grandmother, and the Lady Thesadië was the sister of our father's greatest friend. Therefore, if we have rendered you any service in this long and weary war, give us these two noble ladies, that they may be restored to the honorable positions they deserve.'

Agamemnon frowned, for though he now detested Helen as heartily as any common soldier, he still feared to anger her, and through her, his brother Menelaus. For the first time, scarcely aware of what he was doing, he turned to me.

'The former Queen Æthra had my protection in Troy, though she was too proud to use it,' I said now, calmly so that he might not think that I was instructing him. But I wanted that beautiful and dignified woman out of the humiliating service of Helen. 'I do know, however, that my brother's wife would sometimes put her foot on Æthra's head and pull her hair, if she were displeased about some trifle.'

I had hit the right note. By reminding Agamemnon of Helen's shameless enjoyment of the situation that, according to the tale that was now almost universally believed, had caused the hateful war by itself, I had relieved him of any sense of duty or obligation to her.

'Take her then, by all means,' he said darkly. 'And the other one with her. But,' he added, and I saw a glimpse of the king who had attempted to bargain with Achilles, to his own loss, 'you must forfeit your shares of the Trojan spoil, taking only what you brought with you.'

The Cretan's dark face went pale; he had not expected this. But he was a gentleman, and took it well. 'It is a small price to pay,' he said with a nod of his head, and then he left.

They took their kinswomen to Crete; Menelaus took Helen, suffering from a fit of the sulks because of her fancied insult in being deprived of her highborn body servants, to Ægypt. The only one hurt by the transaction was little Pleisthenes, the neglected Spartan prince. The boy had grown to love Æthra and cried when she was taken away from him. I'm sure that Æthra felt sorry for the child, but that could not help but be overshadowed at her joy in being released from servitude and reunited with her own grandsons.

Andromache, as Hector's widow, went to Neoptolemus, the son of her husband's killer. She did not have to endure the nightly loveless passion that I did, for the boy was his father's son in more ways than one. She was now a figure of sorrow, and she awed even the Achaeans because of the great dignity of her conduct when the City had fallen.

There had been no time to hide Hector's son among the servants even if the thought had occurred to her. The Guardian's house, situated as it was on the First Terrace hard by the Dardanian Gate, was one of the first entered. They came upon her as she knelt, sheltering the little boy in her arms.

'Your name, lady!' one of them demanded. 'And the boy's!'

She rose to her feet, holding the child's hand firmly, and she stared at them so proudly and haughtily that they stopped where they stood, though others crowded behind them. 'I am Andromache,' she replied, sending a challenge into every helmeted face. 'And this is Scamander, Hector's son, and the heir to Troy.'

The men grew quiet, and some of them began to take off their helmets in respect.

'I regret, my lady,' said one of them at last, 'the thing that we must now do.'

'I recognize you, Diomedes of Argos,' replied Andromache, 'for I have often watched you from the walls. And I know well what you mean. But can you find someone low enough, debased enough, to do it?'

By the sheer force of her own will, she had made them into men again from conquering, ravening animals. It was unthinkable that the Achaeans would allow the Trojan heir to live; a few minutes before, and any one of them would have tossed him onto the waiting spears and thought nothing of it. But now, men once more with their honor pricked by the proud woman before them, they shrank from the task.

'It is not a question of debasement,' said another warrior heavily. Now he too doffed his helmet, revealing a seamed and hardened face. He came toward her, a man subtly ill-proportioned from one leg being shorter than its mate; but his rolling, limping gait was easy for he had lived long with his deformity. 'It is a question of whether the line and seed of Priam dies, according to our overlord's command, or whether we allow such a potentially dangerous enemy to survive, and bring down Agamemnon's wrath upon us all.'

Andromache's eyes went bleak. 'I could have prevailed, except for you, Odysseus, and kept the boy alive and ignorant of his heritage. I know how your clever tongue can twist anything the way you want it. But I think that you must do it yourself.'

And around him, the warriors would not meet his gaze. Even his friend Diomedes looked the other way.

The little boy had been staring wide-eyed at the grim, armored men filling the room, not understanding all the talk. He had grown accustomed to such sights through the summer, but there was something different now that disturbed him. He tugged at his mother's hand. 'Mamma?'

She knelt quickly. 'What is it, my darling?'

'Don't like.'

'I know, I know. They'll be gone soon. But listen, darling! I have a surprise for you!'

'Surprise?'

'Yes. You are going to get to go and meet your pappa!'

'Meet Pappa?' the child cried, delighted.

'Yes, isn't that wonderful? And this is the man who will take you to him.'

He looked up at the grim Achaean dubiously. A shadow of a frown crossed his young forehead. 'Mamma come too?' he asked.

'Not right away, darling,' she replied. She smiled, and her eyes were very bright. 'But soon. Just as soon as I can. I promise.'

The boy nodded, satisfied. Then he toddled confidently to Odysseus and held up his small hand for the Achaean to take. 'Meet Pappa!' he told the warriors who drew aside so that they would not touch Odysseus as he passed. 'You go 'way. Meet Pappa!'

There were tears on more faces than Andromache's alone, but Odysseus's face seemed carved from wood, grim and set. And then, when they were gone, she allowed herself to be taken and led away.

Like a man under a compulsion to do more than he was required, Odysseus carried his small charge through the street until he came to the place he sought. Cracked and ruined, groaning under its own weight and threatening to tumble into rubble at any moment, the Great Tower still stood, that had been the vantage point of Trojan nobility throughout the war. Now he began to climb to the precarious summit. He lifted the little boy high above his head and as the child shrieked his terrible, dawning awareness of his fate, cast him down onto the scarp where Hector had died.

'I have shed no blood,' he announced to anyone who would hear, 'and my hands are clean.'

With his usual cunning, he had managed to come out ahead, for a time at least. Children's blood makes for as persistent ghosts as that of witches, seers, poets, and the like. He would not come near Andromache, however, though she seemed to take as little notice of him as any other Achaean. It was as if she had wrapped herself in a winding sheet of her own sorrowful making, and it surprised no one when she failed to survive the winter.

Grim as this was, the tale concerning the Queen of Troy, Hecabe my mother, was even more unhappy. It seemed that she had been spared after all, in spite of her years, out of consideration for her station. Was it mere chance that she was assigned by the lottery to this same Odysseus? She was fearless, having nothing left to lose nor anything to dread from being bedded since she was beyond stirring anyone's desire. Calling on her Thracian heritage, she sat huddled over a fire daily, casting in herbs that gave off a bitter, acrid smell, muttering curses and calling up such dire invective that she put dread into anyone who would come near. Every time Odysseus dared enter his own hut, she rose screeching, making Gorgon faces and magical signs with her fingers.

At last, when she had contrived to steal some of his hair as he slept, he knew that his very life was in danger from her ill-wishing, for this would give her that power over him. He had found it hard enough to keep a good face on it under her never-ending cursing, for she never allowed anyone to forget that he had been responsible for her grandson's death. Now he dared endure it no longer.

As it had been with Helenus, and then with Astyanax, so it was now with Hecabe. And true to his policy of skirting along a tangled problem, he would see to it that no blood was shed. Nobody doubted that Hecabe was a witch now, and because of her curses laid indiscriminately upon any and all, Odysseus found plenty of helpers to put her under the ground with lumps of clay as they had Helenus.

I had not thought of my mother in this way up until now; but I had been – and still was – commonly considered a witch myself, and it was from her body that I had come. I had not thought her to have so much power in her.

Though I run ahead of myself, it became common knowledge in later years that she had indeed called up the dark forces of earth magic to follow the Achaeans in general and Odysseus in particular. Who has not heard of how he was blown this way and that for ten long years, and every time he tried to go home the smiling and favorable breeze would turn into a contrary gale so that he was swept still further away? And then, when he did finally manage to get back to his wretched little island, he found his wife living in riotous adultery with a whole company of young men who had come under the guise of suitors for his empty throne. It was said that she enjoyed them all in turn, night after night, and had spawned a ruttish, goat-footed monster as a result.

The empty-headed suitors, exhausted and drained from the excesses that only made his wife gay and frolicsome, took to their heels when Odysseus came home. A handful tried to bluster their way out of it, but he dispatched them easily. However, the Queen's person was sacred, and her he could not touch even with his skill at murders that shed no blood. To save his own pride, he was forced to give the lie to the whole shabby episode; and so sternly and rigidly has he enforced this new telling that the very name of Penelope has come to mean a faithful wife by definition. There are a few, perhaps, who smile quietly; but the young and ignorant have swallowed it whole. The fools.

Once, perhaps twice, I allowed myself to wonder what it would have been like if it had been Sarpedon beside me on the couch. But this only upset me so that I had trouble maintaining my detachment. I could not afford to show revulsion, nor even feel it, for cool containment was what kept me sane these days. When I thought of Sarpedon, the thought of what my life was now rushed up into the back of my throat with all the bitterness of wormwood. Sternly, I put away all memories of my only love; they were luxuries that I could not afford.

But though I might lie distant and unmoved during Agamemnon's quick, loveless passions, this did not keep me from its natural and ultimate result. When he learned that I was with child, he openly and for the first time spoke of his pride and admiration for me for his warriors to hear. And though I was ill and wretched, fighting nausea while he forced me to sit beside him, I did not miss the quick looks here and there, from one to another. Now, I thought, I was surely doomed by this heedless boasting. Clytemnestra might have tolerated me as a concubine, even a greatly favored one, but she would never allow another to be placed in the royal seat at Mycenae; and this was clearly what was in Agamemnon's mind. That the impossibility of this course would become apparent to him the moment he crossed the threshold of the Mycenaean palace was not at issue; now others knew how he felt, and would be eager to go tale-telling before him.

At least this would be put off for a while. We would be this winter on Imbros, and perhaps the next one as well because a single summer could not suffice for the ambitious plans Agamemnon had for the further ruination and humiliation of proud Troy. I thought of Æneas and his little son, of old Anchises and Antenor. They were now all that was left of Trojan manhood. How fortunate that my father had sent him to the Stronghold! With his quick wits, he was sure to have known from the gigantic earthquake that Troy must have fallen with it; he among others equally as distrustful was unwilling to believe that the Achaeans had left it as it had appeared, letting the war dribble off into irresolution. He had more respect for Agamemnon's generalship than that.

A strange man, complex, secretive, and often baffling, was my lord Agamemnon. It pleased him to see me in yellow, though it was a color I had not much fondness for, thinking it made me sallow. I greatly preferred green, or indigo, or the bluish mauve one gets from crushed hyacinths. But yellow was Agamemnon's choice, even when I was ill and nauseated, dragged down by the growing child, and the mere thought of saffron was enough to start my head spinning and my stomach churning.

For my own sake I desired to make as good an appearance as I could; let these Achaeans know that there were Trojans of sufficient grace available so that it had not been strictly necessary to go and steal a light woman from Sparta. There were few enough cosmetics with which Shahba might work her magic, for the plunderers cared nothing about such things. She was remarkably clever at making do with what she had, however, concocting pomatums from sheeps' fat, and color for lips and cheeks from crushed berries. Young Polyxena scarcely needed a touch of anything, for she was perfect in the firm, healthy, high-colored skin that is sometimes the gift to slim and delicate girls. Would that I had had her looks, for she was allowed to stay in the shadows while I must be revealed in the light. Beauty was something I had done without and not missed these past several years, and now it was a hardship to manufacture with nothing with which to work.

An unexpected windfall occurred when someone found a casket that had been left behind by Helen and gave it to me, thinking to ingratiate himself with Agamemnon through his new favorite. To Shahba's delight, it contained a few cosmetics, mainly powder which she had no way to concoct, and a jar of perfume which I could not abide with its overpowering, ripe smell. The slightest whiff brought back a picture of Helen sweeping along, her skirt coming apart with every step and her bodice spilling open.

I gave it to Shahba, with strict instructions to use it only when she was on her way to the bed of one of her admirers. One would have thought I had presented her with a handful of rubies, from her delighted capering. Æthiopian girls love perfume, the muskier the better, and Helen's scent was designed to stir every sense.

I do not think that Agamemnon either knew or cared about the difficulties we underwent, trying to keep Trojan dignity intact.

There was Cretan blood in him; Menelaus and he were born of a princess from the House of the Ax, whom their father Atreus had stolen in years past. The mixture with the rotten blood in the House of Pelops, about which shocking stories circulated only in whispers, had produced an odd pair. Menelaus, dark with the Cretan coloring, was nonetheless large and shambling like the early Hellenes, though he was now going to fat. Agamemnon, on the other hand, had the tawny coloring of most of these Hellenes-turned-Achaeans, but was slighter of build, more wiry and compact. There was little fat on him though he was in his middle years, and he recalled paintings of the Cretans one often saw on better-quality jars.

Often I thought about the women who had fled to the Stronghold; there had been some grumbling among the Achaeans about the scarcity of new and lithe young females to fill their beds. But Agamemnon retorted that there were women enough, what with those who had been taken previously. If change and variety was what they wanted, let them trade among themselves. He knew, if others under his command did not, that the wise ruler would send the women away.

At first, I was greatly alarmed lest he send part of his army along the road to the south to go against the Stronghold. But though he knew that such a place must surely exist, he didn't know the exact location. It might be costly to blunder along deeply into hostile territory, against a fortress of unknown strength, the very whereabouts of which was uncertain. And besides, winter was drawing on fast, with chilling and icy winds more blustery than usual as if to make up for the gentle season the year before. I hoped with all my heart that Æneas would use this opportunity to make his escape from this end of the world. And I prayed that Apollo would guide him safely in his journeying, wherever it might lead him. Let him send the women who had lived on the Second Terrace back to their own homes, for they would only delay him. Let him take his Dardanians and such other remnants of soldiers as he could find and go swiftly. He carried with him the last living male descendant of the line of Priam. Perhaps he would yet return to Troy, when he was grown to manhood, and build again. But now he must live!

Nysa was a gossip; over the cooking fires or at the brook with laundry her tongue was never still, and she brought everything back to me. Shahba, of course, went lightly and happily into any of a large number of welcoming beds when I had dismissed her for the evening. And so, from these two to start, and some several thereafter, I fell once again into my habit of learning everything there was to know. In this way, I got many of the stories and incidents which have been put into their proper places in the long, sad tale of the war; and in this way also, I got a good idea of the state of affairs on the Western mainland that had prompted such an expedition.

It did not please me, with the child in me, to be hearing constantly of death, of the madness of the Pelopid clan, of the warring and petty struggles that were the very breath of everyday life in the West. I thought of finding a singer, if there was one in the camp, and having him fill my ears with good songs, the sweet songs of love and honor and peace. I hoped that I might filter some of this to the child, and perhaps offset some of his uncertain Pelopid heritage.

There was a singer, a highborn youth who amused himself in this fashion, having some talent for it. But the song he was most fond of, his latest, composed since we had removed to Imbros, was the only one he would sing these days. It was on every Achaean's lips as well, and they bawled out the chorus along with him every evening when he sang.

The brave and clever Achaeans, so the song went, seeing that the walls of Troy were not to be breached by any ordinary means, bethought themselves of a magnificent stratagem. Hermes Herald told it to them, but Athene Spearmaiden had been the inspiration.

They built a gigantic horse, all made of wood, mounted on great wheels, for the horse was sacred to the Goddess who inspired it. The horse's belly was hollow, and capacious enough to hold thirty shiploads of men, which gave some indication of its enormous size.

Contriving to bring this monstrosity unnoticed to the Trojan walls, the Achaeans then departed in all haste, abandoning their camp and putting out to sea far enough so that they were hidden from Trojan eyes. But one man they left, Sinon 'the plunderer', to explain its presence. This Sinon claimed to have been the Achaeans's scapegoat, left behind to bear the Trojans' retribution as a blood-offering for favorable winds.

Furthermore, said Sinon, the magnificent wooden horse, which the Trojans just now noticed, had been made as a placatory offering to Athene. That goddess had been offended by the theft of the Palladium. And, continued Sinon, it had been made very large and unwieldy so that the Trojans could not on any account bring it into their city, lest Athene smile upon them rather than the Achaeans who had made it for her. With Athene's aid, the Trojans could even invade the West and conquer Mycenae!

With this sort of tempting bait held out, all the Trojans immediately began to clamor for the thing to be pulled inside, whatever the cost. Only two voices dissented; the redheaded witch Cassandra, whom everybody thought to be mad, and

Laocoön, the dissolute priest of Apollo. Nobody had ever paid any attention to Cassandra before, and they certainly weren't going to begin now. But with Laocoön, it was a different story, and they began to doubt among themselves.

When the priest dared cast a spear at the wooden horse, Poseidon intervened. From the peculiar noise the spear made hitting the image, making it give back a hollow, metallic boom, it was clear that there was more to it than showed on the surface. To forestall any closer inspection, Poseidon sent two great, poisonous sea serpents slithering up out of the water. They made for Laocoön where he stood with his two illegally begotten sons and wrapped their slimy coils around all three of them, alternately crushing and stinging them to death. Apollo allowed it, because Laocoön had dishonored his vows of celibacy.

Sure that this had been a sign warning against interfering with the designs of the Immortals, and thinking that Laocoön had been punished for throwing his spear at the image, the Trojans began immediately to drag the great wooden horse into Troy.

It was far too large to go through any gate; and so the foolish Trojans actually began to tear great pieces out of their walls! Houses, too, had to be razed, for nothing would satisfy them but that the gigantic image must rest in the courtyard of the Palace, high on the Third Terrace for all to see.

And there it finally stood, after the Trojans had stupidly demolished half their city in getting it there. But they didn't seem to mind; instead, they had a great feast of celebration, and everyone got themselves drunk to the point of staggering and singing through the rubble in the streets. Only Helen had the presence of mind to remain sober. She amused herself, and Deiphobus who was with her, by strolling around the horse there in the courtyard, patting its flanks and calling out to the men inside, imitating the voice of each one's wife in turn.

At length, when all the Trojans lay in swinish, drunken slumber, Sinon crept to the highest tower of Troy and lighted a signal torch. Then he rapped out a prearranged signal on the horse. Silently, the Achaeans crept out. Before the Trojans could come out of their sodden, wine-soaked dream, it was all over and most of them died without striking a single blow in return.

And thus had the proud and arrogant city of Troy fallen.

Odysseus tried to lay claim to the authorship of this tale; it was exactly the sort of specious, satirical mockery he enjoyed most.

But he was now known by all as a man who had lost all of his luck and nobody paid him any notice.

The first time I heard it, I could feel myself grow pale with anger, and my fists clenched tighter in the fold of my dress each time they came to the derisive chorus. Up until now I had tried to accept my lot as equably as it was in my nature to do so; even the unwanted invasion of my body with Agamemnon's child I tried to treat as something more mine than his. But this piece of shabby ridicule, directed not at some half-tame, ignorant nomadic tribe, but at cousins connected by blood and marriage ties as well, seemed for a moment more than I could bear. A dozen criticisms rose to my lips, each one sharper and more acid than the last.

An image capable of holding thirty shiploads of men? Make it only thirty men, and it would still be beyond the Achaeans' skill to construct! They had no artists, no builders among them. Witness the stockade wall! It had fallen when Hector only touched it with his hand!

Bring this monstrosity unnoticed up to the Trojan walls? A pretty feat, when even the silent owl did not go unmarked by Trojan sentries.

So the Achaeans now openly boasted that their Maiden Goddess had conquered our Maiden Goddess, and then tried to pretend that they were the same thing, after all. It would seem that to an Achaean a Maiden is a Maiden, and there's the end to it. Trade an imaginary wooden horse, belly full of armed men, for a sacred thunder-stone that had stood in Troy since the first great city rose on the site – aye, there's a typical Achaean bargain!

I was not flattered that I had been included in the song; but I was curious about the way the singer had incorporated Laocoön's shocking ending into his song, and about where he had heard it. This was nearly forgotten, however, in my deep and stifling rage at the way the Achaeans guffawed at the way the singer depicted the Trojans, as witless fools knocking down their own walls, in order to bring the nonexistent wooden horse into their city.

Either he had not known the plan of Troy or he had not cared in his desire to mock an honorable opponent who deserved respect instead. Why, one *would* have had to pull down half the city and make a ramp of the rubble in order to drag something that large to the steep summit! And how dare he make the preposterous claim that the Trojans had committed the folly of breaching their own walls, and that it was accomplished in the time it takes to tell of it! Let Poseidon, who struck down the city in punishment for the manner in which he had been expelled from Troy in earlier times, likewise reward the man who would make light of this awful deed.

I remembered the bitter fighting with the 'drunken' Trojans, sorely diminished in number because of Priam's generosity in dismissing the allies so quickly – too quickly, as it turned out. When I thought of how dearly each one had sold his life, my mouth turned sour. But it was words that I would vomit now. And then, for the first time since Troy had fallen, I felt a line of chilliness creep through my belly. I shut my mouth, already opened to spew out my hotheaded challenge, regardless of consequences. I saw, reflected in the firelight around me, a gleaming eye here, a shrewd glance there. And then, all the heat in me went cold and I was in command of myself again, although I could not help trembling at the abyss I had been on the verge of rushing into, all unheeding.

Agamemnon's queen was not the only Achaean who was not pleased at the prospect of a Trojan princess, nominally a captive and a slave, who sat by her doting master's side, able to influence and sometimes advise. No matter that she kept herself calm and unscreaming only by the greatest effort of will. She might yet come to enjoy her position and come to love her owner; such things had happened before. Agamemnon had once sworn that there was not room enough in this world for any of Priam's blood to live along with him. And now he was breeding more Trojan brats from Priam's daughter. There could not be any luck in this. No wonder that they had caused the insulting song to be performed in my presence! Agamemnon evidently saw nothing out of the way in this; it would never occur to him to imagine our roles reversed, with himself being forced to endure mockery that made his kinsmen appear to be fools.

If I had begun my denunciation of the song, I would have been swept along by my own rage into reviling its composer. From there, it would have been but a step easily taken to prod me into the same sort of cursing that had brought my mother to her death. Not that I looked forward to anything else, but I would far rather take my chances with Clytemnestra. And without me, what would become of Polyxena?

They were waiting expectantly for my reactions to the song. Even insensitive Agamemnon turned to me indulgently, a question in his upraised brows. So I bit back the bilious outflow the conspirators expected, and let Apollo's cool good judgment guide my words.

'A lively melody, fairly sung,' I said now, 'though it wanders into extravagance in the story toward the end.'

There was a sigh of disappointment from some of them, but Agamemnon laughed with delight. 'Exactly!' he exclaimed. 'It was a mistake to make the giant image Athene's symbol, rather than Poseidon's, for everyone knows it was the Horsefather who brought our victory! But let it stand, let it stand. It will amuse the people when we return home, and they will need diversion when they learn how hard-bought our victory was from those Trojans of yours, my dear.'

I had escaped, by a hair. But escaped into what?

In the end, it was Polyxena who helped me most. Where I had thought to shelter her and keep her safe and protected to the best of my ability from our hostile surroundings, now it was she who shielded me. In her clear, childlike voice she sang to me, and told the old stories one would not have thought she had had time to learn. But then I thought of the delicate maiden dancing by herself in the corridors of the ruined palace and knew that she came to it as one born for music, and the gay, innocent pleasures of the song.

I tried to keep her away when I felt the first clutch of the birth pangs. I did not think it would be good for her to be present and watch the primitive, stark process that was the same for every woman, princess, slave or peasant. But she sat with me during the whole grueling time, sponging my face with cool water and letting me grip her fragile hands when instinct forced me to pull against something, anything.

I do not remember much about it, for the painful surge, washing higher each time it came, soon carried me out of myself. I have heard that peasants often did their birthing clearheaded and unafraid, squatting by a roadside or the field they were working, rising unburdened and continuing in much the same manner as before this minor interruption. But I was greatly fearful, and most unwilling, so that my body worked against itself and caused me such anguish that I was certain that I would not live through it.

If I had not gone out of my head early in my labor, I daresay I would have perished. The only clear recollection I have after this was when the women coaxed me up and placed me crouching onto the roughly constructed birthing-stool. I could hear the soothing murmur of Polyxena's voice as she must have been speaking to me all the time I could not hear; and now, it seemed that I had come out on a level that just skimmed the top of the pain. There was work that my body must do whether I wished it or not. My reluctant loins parted for the final surge, and Nysa caught Agamemnon's son as I fell back exhausted. I remember smiling with such triumph as I could summon; but it was not for the infant whose departure had eased my heavy, burdened body. For that I felt nothing, nor would for days to come. Rather, it was because I had come through it after all, and the thing was finally done.

Agamemnon named the boy Teledamus, 'far tamer'. By this, he said, he thought to make the first move in healing the breach between East and West. Thinking to turn his pleasure with me into my own advantage, I begged him to leave the broken and empty city of Troy as it was.

'It will be safe to sail in a few weeks,' I said. 'Let well enough alone, and release your men to return to their homes.'

His brow darkened. 'I have work to do in Troy yet,' he replied coldly. 'That proud Citadel tormented me far too long to leave it half standing, so that anyone may come along and claim it. And I am in no great hurry to return to my tender and loving queen.'

Though I might coax him on almost any other subject, I could not budge him on this one. And so I was forced to spend an entire summer on the island, virtually in sight of my poor city, while Agamemnon and his warriors tramped through the ruins, pulling down the few houses that had escaped destruction, sifting through ashes for bits of gold, poking futilely at the great walls that had defied all but a god's strength. Finally, they were reduced to demolishing the low town. That was easy enough, for it was the mud-plaster on stone foundations common all through the area. They could scatter these stones easily enough, and threw most of them into a common heap a little way beyond the Water Tower. But as for the walled city itself, after they had burnt everything that would catch, they faced frustration. It was too strongly made, and the Achaeans had only flimsy prying bars and pickaxes with which to work. They could not damage the fabric of this workmanship, and it made me smile, though secretly and to myself, because now the ruins would endure for all time to come.

20

IMBROS

It had not occurred to me until Agamemnon's departure for the Trojan Plain that I was now in a far better state of health, both physical and mental, than I had been in for years. Motherhood, though it had threatened to tear my body apart, had ripened it a little. I was becoming fond of the baby, who seemed all the more mine now that his sire was absent. And best of all, the degrading, tormenting dream had ceased to trouble me. Not once since Troy fell had it visited me, and I could now sleep through the night undisturbed.

I had confided my secret concerning the dream to Polyxena early in the first days of our captivity. All the others who had known of it, in whole or in part, had taken it with them when they died. Now, when I told Polyxena of its absence, she smiled.

'Of course it is gone,' she said. 'When you saw it happen, and it was all made real before you, there was no longer any need for it. You should have spoken of your dream long before.'

'I do not think that would have stopped its happening,' I replied. 'Do you not remember how I was always ignored? "Fire and death, death and fire," they would chant. But Troy knew both before it was through. And in any event, something kept telling me to be silent.'

'It is a mystery,' she sighed. And then she added, in a voice strangely fierce, 'I am glad that they cannot make any progress in tearing the City apart. Troy has suffered enough.'

'And the Trojans,' I said.

Someone else – how long ago? – had told me much the same thing as Polyxena had. It was a mystery truly, if I had been put here just to see Troy in flames before its burning, and yet bidden to be quiet about it. Could there be something else waiting for me, that I had been saved alive and set on the road to Mycenae? If so, I had no foreknowledge. It had all dried away in the heat of the City's flames and all that remained to me was the occasional icy touch of the god in my belly.

The baby, creeping about, had pulled Agamemnon's dolphin ivory shoulder harness down upon himself. I hurried to rescue it, and him, lest one or the other be harmed and Agamemnon become angry for my negligence.

Agamemnon and his work crews would stay on the Trojan Plain for several days at a time, and then return to Imbros. It was obvious that they were becoming impatient, and were openly chafing at the whim of a king who would keep them at a task for which they were ill-equipped and found impossible to accomplish. After all, the war was over. Why linger, dabbling in the ruins? The Trojans were all dead, except for a handful of women. A few of the worst malcontents among them slipped away surreptitiously, unwilling to let the sailing season go by without them. But the most part of them, Agamemnon kept working at a task that even he began to admit was beyond him.

'Sometimes,' he confided to me one evening when he had returned to Imbros, 'I get a strange and uneasy feeling when I am going among the men. They seem to feel it, too, for they tap so listlessly at the stones that they would do better to try to throw them down with kisses.' He shook his head. 'They say that the ghosts of men who died in battle rarely come back to haunt. But here there were so many, Trojan, Achaean, Lycian, Thracian, all meeting in a struggle to rival the gods' battle with the Giants, that I fear the Plain will never be free of them. Do you know why I wanted Troy leveled?'

He was lying on the couch where he had thrown himself in exhaustion. I sat close by, as he expected, with Teledamus on my lap. The child had learned to reach out and grasp, and he had a tangle of my yellow dress clutched in his fist. Surprised by the question, I paused to loosen the baby's fingers before I answered. 'I suppose it was for vengeance, my lord,' I said.

'Yes, that, and something more as well. I had grander schemes than mere vengeance, Cassandra. I had hoped to rebuild a citadel, a proper Achaean city that would bear no resemblance to the stylish Eastern mode of your precious Troy. I would have made it into a Western trading place, with the Achaean mark clearly set upon it so that the merchants would hold no memories of the old times. But I find now that I cannot.'

'Oh?' I said carefully, still busy with the baby who had begun to wriggle and fret. Shahba came and took him away for his nap.

'It would seem that Troy has triumphed after all,' he continued when the Æthiopian was out of hearing. 'All this summer I have battered against the walls in growing futility. After the low town was destroyed, and the ashes picked through for anything we had missed, our work was done, though I have not admitted it to anyone but you. But with the ghosts twittering after us and the walls standing impervious to our best efforts, it is clear that in its downfall Troy has destroyed us with it. There will have to be a new place found for barter, if trade ever rises again.'

I remembered my father's words, almost identical, that night when he put Helen to rout for all her wiles and dimpled charm. In that moment, I came as near to Agamemnon the man as I ever would. I could respect one who admitted his folly and acknowledged that he had trampled down far more than a single stubborn city. If things had been different in another time long ago, King Priam and King Agamemnon might have had much to say to one another, for all that one was a mild and generous ruler beloved by all, and the other a product of the blood-soaked and unstable House of Pelops.

Yes, respect I could give him now; affection, never. We stared at each other across too many shadowy ghosts for that. But with this new side of him revealed, my life would be easier to bear.

'The thing that made me realize that I had been defeated by Troy's ashes was the Great Tower, did you know that? It creaked and groaned in every wind, but we could not pull it down to our satisfaction. And then, in the night, we were all awakened by a mighty crash that brought us out of our sleep. The Tower had fallen by itself, as if to tell me that Troy belonged only to itself now, and all my scratchings against its stones were vain. The owls have made Troy their own where we have not. They nest in every crevice, and you dare not turn over a rock for fear one of your accursed brown vipers sting you for your trouble.'

'The owl was Artemis's bird,' I said, scarcely aware that I had spoken.

'It has always belonged to Athene. The men say that Athene has taken possession of the ruins. They have even begun to add that title of your Maiden to her name. Pallas Athene they call her now. I would set up the Palladium in her honor when I return to Mycenae, but I do not think that Odysseus would give it up. He claimed it, after he and Diomedes stole it and he clings to it now for fear of the cursing he got from Hecabe. If it were not for the open revolt it would cause, I would have it taken back to Troy and left there.'

'I would have clung to the Palladium, if it had been in its shrine.'

He frowned, remembering. 'Yes. Ajax. There has been no

punishment for the insult he offered you. Well, I promise you that you will be paid for that, although I do not know what I will do yet.'

'Hasn't there been enough of revenge? Must you make it go on and on?'

'Some things call for it. And that is one of them.'

'Even if I do not wish it?'

'Even so.' He smiled then, and reached for me. 'You were mine, even then, with your white skin and fire-red hair and big eyes that see clean through to the heart of a man. Tell me, Cassandra, what do you see now?'

I knew what would follow, what was expected of me. The meaningless words came to my lips perhaps a little more easily, but inside me there was still the same dead indifference I would always feel in his embrace.

'I see you, my lord,' I said dutifully. 'Only you.'

If it had not been for the presence of Teledamus, it might have been the previous winter being relived. Once again Agamemnon's seed had rooted in me. Once again the days must be lived through, cold and uncomfortable, with Polyxena close beside me. I wondered how long I might be able to keep her safe, for she was flowering swiftly into a desirable woman. Surely it would not be long before some warrior, homesick for his wife and couch, would take her, by stealth if necessary, for the promise to Achilles was as dead as he was. If I were lucky, I might yet arrange an honorable marriage for her, and avoid the humiliation I had learned to endure.

As the winter dragged along its weary way to its end, there came a fresh spirit among the men still encamped with Agamemnon. This time, when the warm weather came back, they were going home!

Home! The taste of the word was a joy in the mouth. But for me, my home was across the Hellespont and I was going to a strange new land, with strange and inhospitable people. And what would become of me then?

I calculated that my second child would be born at about the same time of year as Teledamus had been, which meant that I would be recovered reasonably well for the journey. Though I knew what to expect this time, it proved nearly as difficult as the first, for my spirit continued to rebel at my captivity. With a sigh, I regarded this new son of Agamemnon's. I had hoped, since I had to have a child, that it would be a girl. Somehow, I felt that I would be closer in spirit to a girl. Teledamus was already very much his father's son and had as little to do with me as he could.

'I will name this one Pelops, for the founder of my House!' he exclaimed. 'More and more I am pleased with you, Cassandra! Clytemnestra bore me only one boy, and he is weak-headed with the family illness that comes sometimes. I have three daughters from her; Chrysothemis the eldest, who is also a little foolish, Laodice, and Iphigeneia. Laodice is my favorite. She is my image, flesh, blood, and bones! Ah, if she had been a boy. I nicknamed her Electra, 'amber', for the color of her hair. You and she are about of an age; you should get on well together.'

One of the early stories circulated in the war stirred a memory in me. 'And Iphigeneia?' I asked, not wanting to.

'They made her the Chosen One and gave her to the Goddess for a fair wind to Troy,' he answered, 'though it was against the custom.'

A shudder ran along my spine. 'Then she is dead?'

He frowned. 'Do not inquire too closely, Cassandra. I said that she had been given to the Goddess, but whether she died or serves in an obscure shrine somewhere is no concern of yours.'

I was more than willing to drop the subject, and in the bustle of packing and loading the ships as the days grew warmer, I nearly forgot it altogether. My mind was fixed on Mycenae, and the uncertainty of my welcome there. And Polyxena, always Polyxena. She was handier than I was with the children by far. I grieved that she would have to go to a rough-handed Achaean rather than the refined Trojan prince as should have been her due.

And then, when the time came when we should be departing from Imbros and Troy would be left behind forever, the winds failed. Either they were from the wrong quarter, or they refused to blow entirely.

The ships were ready, and bales of goods and treasure replaced many of the men who had filled them on the outward journey. The fine Tros-bred horses waited to be driven on board, the last act before plunging out across the waters that separated us from Achaea. And still the winds failed.

The men began to look at one another and mutter among themselves. And sometimes, they would look in the direction of Odysseus. It was becoming increasingly plainer as each day went by that they would not need much encouragement to blame him. He had lost his luck anyway, and so he would make an admirable scapegoat.

But though his luck might be gone, his cunning was still with him. For one night, as they sat gloomily around a fire, he proposed a sacrifice to bring the winds that caught every man's fancy with the form of it, as one side of a scale balances another. A royal virgin had died to bring them winds to Troy; now a royal virgin should die to bring them winds away from Troy. It must now be Polyxena's privilege to be slain so that her people's conquerors should have safe passage home again.

21

THE FLOTILLA

For a long time I sat silent in the little chair Agamemnon had allowed me to use, a gift from his store of Trojan spoil. Now I ran my fingers over familiar carvings on the arms, my head turned toward the walls as I stared with bitter, dull blankness at nothing.

I longed to scream, to shout, to take some strong piece of woven goods and rip it to shreds. I wanted to fly at Agamemnon and beat him with my fists. I felt near to bursting with the suppressed passions seething within me.

Just this one thing, I shrieked silently. Just this one small favor, an innocent girl's life! Was there nothing to be left from the ruins of Troy? Gods above, have you abandoned me entirely? Nothing was my own, not the clothes I wore, nor the chair I had graciously been allotted from what had once been mine – no, not even my violated and invaded body which now belonged to an ever increasingly strange captor. But Polyxena, at least, had been free. She had been the part of me that Agamemnon had been unable to touch.

A soft hand on my arm brought me back to myself, and I found that I had been unconsciously pounding the carved hand rest with my clenched fist hard enough to bruise my flesh. I suppose that I had been imagining it to be Agamemnon's hated face. I turned my head, and found Polyxena kneeling beside me.

'Do not grieve, dear sister,' she said, and her face was clear and untroubled beyond her concern for me. 'Do not accuse yourself, for you could not have stopped my fate.'

'Could I not?' I echoed bleakly.

'Don't you see, Cassandra? They think to send me to Achilles, and untie the west winds in the doing, but I know that it is not Achilles who waits for me on the other side of life.' Her eyes filled and sparkled, and she actually began to smile, so that I knew hers were tears of joy. 'The ghosts of our family and friends stand waiting for me there, Sister! I have often heard them whistling faintly on the evening breeze!'

'I have heard nothing but the nightjar, and the rustling of leaves.'

'That is because you are not yet called, perhaps. Think of it, Sister! I will return to them as I left them, unchanged, except that I have grown a little older.' A light laugh, as at a secret joke between us, trembled on her lips. 'They believe that they will send me to the arms of Achilles, but I will escape them after all! Oh, how lucky I am!'

I could only stare, amazed, at this delicate sister who should have been cowering in a corner, her head veiled to hide her pale face and trembling body. Who would have thought she could have found the strength Hector had, to face her coming sacrifice with happiness and a light heart?

Then her face changed abruptly, and she put her arms around me. 'Oh, Cassandra, I am sorry!' she murmured contritely. 'How selfish and unthinking of me to rejoice when it's you who will be left behind in the shame of captivity!'

I dared do nothing but allow her to comfort me as she would, biting my tongue so that I would not begin to shout that I would be alive, alive, while her freedom lay only on the far side of the Road of Death. How strange it was that it should be this fragile child who would come to offer me her solace and sympathy while I sat crushed beneath this latest Achaean betrayal, and wondering what words I might say to her so that she would not think hardly of me for failing to protect her.

And then I clung to her in earnest, my head cradled on her firm young bosom. Had it not been ever thus, in the months of our captivity? I had thought myself so tough, so strong, beyond caring, entirely self-sufficient. But it had been Polyxena's strength upon which I had drawn, even while I had thought of myself as her protector and guardian.

With this humbling knowledge, I wept for the last time in my life.

It was Odysseus who did it, roughly flinging the frail maiden upon the mound that marked Achilles's grave and quickly slicing through her tender throat to hide her frightening compliance that would have sent her to the sacrificial spot with a firm step and steady smile. He would have left her where she lay, but others who had marked the change in the timid girl thought that Achilles would be displeased if his beloved were left to molder into corruption, and her bones be scattered by predators.

Piously, some of the common soldiers hastened to bury her nearby, and awed whispers ran through the army when it was seen that her face was pure and happy, unmarred by pain or irresolution, and that her eyes had set in the look of someone who glimpses loved ones from afar.

The Achaeans were not inclined to question the strange way that a Trojan princess had gone to be a willing sacrifice on the tomb of Troy's worst enemy; they took only the favorable omen that the consenting gave. And in a day or so the winds swung around, blowing westerly and fair, neither too swiftly so as to drive a ship beneath the waves from which it would never emerge, nor so listlessly that the rowers must work overtime.

Past Lemnos the groaning, heavy-laden ships went, and the peak of Samothrace sank beneath the lapping sea, the last familiar landmark of my home. I stood tight-lipped and dry-eyed, wrapped in a woolen mantle against the chill of the salt spray, straining to catch my last glimpse. It was gone, and still I stared backward, when a heavy hand on my shoulder pulled me around.

'Face forward, not back, Cassandra,' Agamemnon said harshly. His face was cold and unsmiling, and there were heavy lines from nose to chin. His eyes, sunk in dark, unhealthy-looking flesh, had a strange look in them. 'You must look ahead now. We will be in Mycenae soon. Aye, Mycenae.' And his lips curved in a mirthless smile.

Here, I thought, my heart sinking, is the ruler who came against Troy. He is not the man I thought I had come to know on Imbros, the man who could admit that his victory had turned to ashes in his hand. And I did not know this new man at all. Then his gaze held and deepened and he moved closer to me in a way that I had come to know only too well.

'Would you couple with me in the view of all here, my lord?' I murmured, and lowered my eyes modestly. But my heart was beating rapidly with dread that he would, indeed, want it although there is no privacy aboard an Achaean warship even for making water or the other thing. 'If you wish it, I would not deny you,' I added carefully so that he could not be displeased with me. I dared not let that happen.

'No,' he said abruptly. 'There is time enough later on.' He shrugged indifferently and turned away.

Grateful that I had been spared his attentions and would probably be able to avoid them for the duration of the journey at least, I hurried back to where a little shelter had been set up for

Nysa, Shahba, and the children. Only Shahba chafed at the restrictions shipboard life put upon intimacy and she managed to slip away and join the men who departed from the convoy at Thessaly. I was sorry to see her go, but not overmuch; and hoped that she would be happy in the life she had chosen for herself.

Down the coast we went, leaving Euboeans and Boeotians as we went, so that Agamemnon's flotilla steadily numbered fewer and fewer. Now all that were left were those survivors from the companies whose homes were in the wild Peloponnesian lands, south and west of the great Isthmus. The Athenian forces departed early, unwilling to chance the Sounion Cape just to get to the Piraeus, the harbor of Athens. When we got there, I saw that their choice had been a prudent one.

It is a beautiful place, but in the same way that a fierce wild boar is beautiful; for it is filled with danger so that even a sailor who suckled a steering-oar in his infancy approaches with caution.

Here one current in the sea flows to meet another, so that the waters fight against themselves and breed storms in which no ship may survive. Even in the fairest weather, a vessel may suddenly turn broadside to a gush of water angered by its own clashing, swamp, and sink before one can fill his lungs to shout a warning.

There is, I am told, a shrine to Poseidon high atop the tumbling cliff that marks the division of the waters that rush to their battlefield here. Strong currents were nothing to me, who had lived in sight of the swift Hellespont, but I had never seen what could happen when two such floods met in enmity. Small wonder the Achaeans seek to placate Poseidon of the Blue Hair, but it would seem that the god visits his sanctuary infrequently.

Even with a sacrifice duly given, a sudden wind came upon us as we crept carefully along, steersmen gripping their rudders tightly and every man at his oar. In a twinkling the waiting waters began to rear great horse-headed waves and the choking outcries of men rose as ships were greedily sucked under. The Spartans were the heaviest hit, those who had stayed with Agamemnon after Menelaus had fled with his faithless Helen to Crete for safety; only five of their ships cleared the cape unharmed.

But other chieftains felt the weight of Poseidon's hand as well. Even Agamemnon's own vessel, that was nearly through the worst of it before the squall struck, was tossed and buffeted until I thought we were all surely lost, and had to cling hard to the mast to keep from being swept overboard. Beside me, Nysa cowered and sniveled, filling the air with her lamentations, and I took little Pelops from her so that she might put one arm around the mast beside me and hold Teledamus with the other. The little boy set up a howl, wishing to go and stand by his father. But I glimpsed Agamemnon's face, and it was black and stern. In its grim set, his men might read bravery and determination; but I knew that in his eyes there lived madness, and with it, fear. One of his hands was laid on the ship's railing, and the knuckles were white. If Teledamus had gone to him, he might have been perfectly capable of hurling the child into the waters, thinking that by such a sacrifice he might save himself.

Greatly shaken by this disaster so close to home, the survivors pulled hard for the Piraeus, so that they might regroup themselves for the rest of the journey homeward. Though the several contingents customarily kept to themselves, the way around Sounion had mixed the ships helter-skelter and we would not know the extent of our losses until they had sorted themselves out again. Each leader hoisted his emblem to the top of his mast as a rallying point when we were in the harbor; and here and there ships moved aimlessly, the men having lost their leader without knowing it.

I counted; and counted again. Yes, Little Ajax was gone! Good riddance, although in another time Agamemnon might have been pleased at how the gods had punished his transgression against me. But he forgot this, in his dismay at losing so many loyal leaders.

With disgust I saw the emblem of Odysseus. Why couldn't he have perished, instead of some other chief or kinglet who might well have been the better man? But then, as order began to be established once more, my heart lightened. The Ithacans, and then others of the nearly demolished flotilla, began to search frantically. There was no use in looking above the waters, for the ship that had carried the Palladium must have foundered and sunk with the rest.

Could anyone be sure that the Goddess had not reached out and carried her Palladium back to Troy, where it belonged? Could it not have been that she had waited until now to punish the unholy conquerors who had stolen it? How else could it be explained, when Poseidon had been appeased with a large and unstinting sacrifice before the Cape had been attempted?

For myself, I hid my head in my mantle and smiled. Whether

the Palladium had been whisked back to Troy, or lay deep beneath the uneasy waters, it was all one. It would never be set up in Agamemnon's unclean shrine, nor go on to Ithaca if Agamemnon had been unable to dupe Odysseus into leaving it with him.

We bypassed Tiryns and the strong citadel there, for Agamemnon had gotten it into his head that the first Achaean citadel I should enter must be Mycenae. If it could not be that way, he said, then he should not go home at all, but must wander aimlessly the rest of his days. It seemed that he must think I would become enamored of the first Achaean citadel I saw, and that I would stay there.

He had, in fact, promised that I should visit the wonders of Athens and the palace that Theseus had once lived in, high on the scarp overlooking the low town. But I saw no more than the wharves and quays of the Piraeus and then he was reluctant to have me set foot on land. A strange man, my lord Agamemnon, and daily growing more and more odd as the distance shortened between himself and the Lion City. I think it was the rotten blood of his Pelopid inheritance springing up strongly in him again as it smelled its familiar homeland once more.

Still, he could not forbid my looking at Tiryns as we passed. My impression of the huge, rough-worked fortress, so different from the neat stonemason's craft of the Trojan walls, was that shaggy goat-gods from the forest's depths must have come in the night and piled it up. These walls were patterned as well, in a crude mockery of Troy's that revulsed me. I could only glimpse the roofs of the warren of palace rooms inside. There may have been beauty hidden behind the stern and forbidding walls that faced the sea, but what I saw was only the look of strength that Tiryns turned toward all who came near.

I could not repress a shudder. In Troy, the fortifications had spoken of the pleasant and civil dwellers within; but the face these Achaeans chose to put forward was as untrusting, as suspicious, as wary as the worst of them. And I was beginning to believe that the worst of them had not been Achilles after all, but was in truth Agamemnon. Moody, morose, his temper uncertain and unpredictable, given to fingering sword or dagger nervously, he was impatience itself as slaves unloaded his ships in the nameless town that served the port situated where the sea lapped its inmost way toward the Plain of Argos.

Only when it came time for me to be tied to the rail of his

chariot, in the manner of all nobly born captives, did he come back to himself a little.

'No,' he said, frowning. 'She shall not walk in the dust and be humiliated. Perdition take the customs. She had been in Agamemnon's bed, and has borne me sons. She shall go in better dignity because of it.'

And so, despite those who would have protested if they had dared, I was put into a cart wherein also rode Nysa and the children. I do not know if I was grateful or not. It didn't seem to matter. I only knew that if it would have prolonged the journey, pushed back the moment when I would come under Mycenae's shadow, then I would have gone the whole way on my knees.

The Plain of Argos is a lovely thing in that arid and rocky land where the soil is scarce and sometimes sour. But the Argive Plain is deep, and rich, and so fertile that it might produce of itself without invoking the Goddess to make it fruitful. It narrows as it sweeps up from the sea, and finally one climbs above it and can see it spread out at one's feet. It looks like a lapful of jewels or flowers.

Even before I saw it, resting securely on a twin-peaked mountain, I could sense Mycenae's presence. The very air grew dull and it was an effort to draw it into my lungs. The back of my neck prickled and tingled, and I began to rub it fretfully. Beside me, Nysa sat stolidly, gazing off into the hills, and I envied her in that moment. She cared nothing about one palace or another. Servitude was servitude to her. Why should she care where she went, or which city she lived in?

The road was well marked, though it showed signs of having been let go into disrepair in several places. I could see Agamemnon glance from side to side, and there was displeasure in his face. He looked now toward the Lion Gate, so well-known that even Troy might envy its fame, and his face darkened.

The road plunged into a narrow passageway along the huge, rough-stoned walls after making a sharp turn toward the city. Then it ran straight through the citadel, through a kind of tunnel where the walls reached out to embrace the road. It was a closely fitting trap that few warriors, no matter how rash and foolhardy, would care to attempt. The great wooden doors, many layers thick, swung back to welcome us and the afternoon sun glinted on the bronze-washed heads of the famous lions over Mycenae's gate.

They were cut out of pale stone and rested their front paws

with perfect ease upon a tall plinth. The plinth supported a tapering column of Cretan design that was set between the lions, and atop the column was an image.

This must be the Achaean notion of the Maiden, I realized. To my silent wonder and bewilderment, I saw that she had been allowed to grow shabby. Her wooden cheeks were dull from lack of paint, and her garments were sadly tattered and weather-worn. I could not take my eyes off her, and as we clattered over the rutted threshold, I could see that only the holes were left now where earrings had once hung from her carved ears.

This ill-dressed and impoverished Goddess stirred up the uneasy feelings the city had already evoked. For a panicky moment, I thought that I would disgrace myself by vomiting over the side of the cart; but I knew that Agamemnon would never forgive my ruining his homecoming with so inauspicious an omen.

Never mind that the dilapidated Athene above the gate had been ill omen enough for anybody. I told myself grimly, clenching my teeth against the bitterness welling up in my throat. This was why he wanted the Palladium, without a doubt. He knew that the Achaean Maiden would have short shrift from the women back at home, as they turned for comfort to the older Goddess.

I fought down the nausea by sheer willpower alone, and felt a little better. But then, with a sinking heart, I realized that we were passing the strange walled circle that held graves of ancient Mycenaeans, and were turning up the ramp that led to the palace.

As we had come through the gates, we had seen three figures standing stiffly on the portico above the strangely designed propylon, the entrance-porch to the palace. Now, as the ramp cut the palace off from our sight for the moment, they were free to hurry down so that they would be at hand to greet their lord when he should set foot upon his own threshold.

It had not been the arrival at the city, nor the disturbing sight of the neglected Goddess atop the gateway, that had put dread into me, after all. My fear was for the moment when I would have to come face to face with Agamemnon's wife and queen, Clytemnestra. But what I had been totally unprepared for was the rank, choking smell of centuries-old evil that seemed to be breathed out at me from the very stones themselves. This place was a canker on the face of the earth; and like such a pustule, I could feel it quivering beneath me, aching to discharge its purulence so that it could be at rest again for a while, before rising up to spew again. Black sparks began to swim before my eyes.

'My lady, you are pale,' said Nysa, giving up her neck-craning to glance at me. But she seemed disinclined to put little Pelops aside to aid me.

'It is nothing . . . the heat . . . it will pass,' I managed to say. I would have swooned entirely, but a little breeze began to blow past me, and I drank its clean breath gratefully.

Agamemnon was already in the propylon. He had embraced his wife formally, and had allowed his two daughters to give him their greetings. One merely touched his hands to her forehead and then ran out into the plaza to pet the horses and cast bright, empty eyes at the soldiers; but the other threw her arms around his neck with a warmth that nearly made him lose his balance. This one had bright eyes, too, I could see, as he led his wife and daughter back out of the shadows so that his men could see them. This must be Laodice, whom Agamemnon had nicknamed Electra, the amber one. He had said that she was entirely his own, and he had been correct. She had his lionlike mane of coarse yellow hair, and her features were far more his than her mother's. But most of all the eyes were Agamemnon's; both girls had his trick of looking about sharply so as to miss nothing, but with Chrysothemis, the elder, it was mere pretense, an empty echoing. Not so Electra, whose close clinging to Agamemnon only emphasized their likeness to one another.

But is was Clytemnestra at whom I gazed fearfully. I do not know what I expected. Some fat and aging frumpy female tyrant, I suppose, or a woman so dried up and hollow that a man would shrivel from her arid touch.

She acknowledged my presence with nothing more than a calm look. No raised eyebrow, no twitch of the mouth betrayed anything but the gracious receiving of a noble spear-captive of her husband's. Her hair was immaculately combed and groomed, and it lay earth-dark upon her head. Her fingertips were exquisitely dyed with henna, and she held her hands lightly and gracefully clasped before her. Her feet were bare, rouged and hennaed, and were adorned with jewels. Her face, a trifle narrow for real beauty, was serene and untroubled.

It was as hard to believe that she and Helen were sisters as it was to imagine Agamemnon and Menelaus as true-born brothers. Not that she repelled where Helen conscientiously attracted; but hers was the sort of femaleness that sends a quieter challenge to a man. Helen's hot-bloodedness gave open notice that she would gladly couple with whomever struck her fancy at high noon in the market place if the notion appealed to her. Clytemnestra, on the other hand, would choose her lovers with care and in privacy. And she would demand repayment in kind, a thing that Agamemnon detested, as I already knew. No wonder he had been reluctant to return to the trials of her bed, where he could only fail time after time.

Through my musing – I suppose that I had gone a little light-headed – I became aware that Agamemnon was repeating his order to me to get down from the cart, and his voice had turned harsh.

I had been cold with a chill that no clothing could warm when we had landed, and I still wore the woolen mantle. Now, however, the sun had begun to beat strongly down upon my head. The black sparks were whirring again, and everything seemed to go red before me.

'You have blood upon your face, my lord,' I heard myself saying faintly.

'Get down, Cassandra!' he shouted impatiently. 'You are keeping everybody standing here with your stupidity. She always used to talk about blood and death, nothing but death and blood,' he complained to Clytemnestra. 'I thought I had cured her of that, but I suppose today has brought it back again.'

'Then you will surely cure her again, my husband,' said the Queen in a cool and amused voice.

'Blood indeed!' exclaimed Electra with a short laugh through her nose. 'She must smell it. The gods know there have been rivers let flow here. Come, Cassandra,' she said, striding briskly toward me where I sat staring down into the dust, unwilling to touch my feet to it, unwilling to let it soil me. 'I'll give you a hand over the blood, you poor, crazed thing.'

I looked up, grateful for her rough courtesy, and stared full into her bright, disturbing eyes. She pushed the mantle off me that I had been too confused to remove, and Nysa too lazy or uncaring, or both. 'Now you'll feel better,' she said, and grasped my hand. Immediately I began to shiver, for a different cold touched my belly when she took hold of me. I looked from her to Agamemnon, and back again at Electra, so much alike in everything.

Here, I knew with the certainty that had never failed me when the chill gripped my vitals, was my enemy in Mycenae. It was not Clytemnestra, and perhaps had never been. My true foe was this girl of my own age who now held my hand and pulled me inexorably into the murderous household that dwelt in Mycenae.

Electra, I realized with a sharp and panicky flash of insight, was as brilliantly mad as any child the House of Pelops had ever spawned.

I took a step, then another, on legs that seemed not to belong to me. And then the black sparks and the red washed over me and I fell oblivious into the deadly dust of Mycenae.

22

MYCENAE

The alternating chills and fever which I suffered made it quite clear to everyone that I was ill; and so, in truth, I was, with a sickness no less of soul and spirit than of body. For nearly a week I coughed and choked, tossing about restlessly with an ague that rendered every joint painful, wishing that I might die. But then one day I woke cool and tired, conscious that I was better in spite of the weakness that sapped the strength from every limb. I asked for barley soup; it was the first time since entering Mycenae that I had requested food. This was taken as a favorable sign for my recovery, and so it was quickly brought to me. It tasted surprisingly good. I had almost come to think that every mouthful I consumed in this terrible place would be like ashes on my tongue.

Unwilling to display myself in the megaron, I prolonged my taking of all my meals in privacy until it became an established fact long past the time when I was quite able to go to the Hall. If Agamemnon himself did not invite me, a command actually, I would not go down in the evening to the feasting in the megaron.

My apartment was in the royal wing, close enough to the King's chamber for convenience, but far enough away for decency's sake. In other times, my rooms had been those of the absent Prince of Mycenae. There were weapon hooks on the walls, and the furnishings were of the simple and sturdy type that befitted a young man. It was, in fact, a trifle too masculine, as if someone had wanted to bolster a faltering youth's confidence in his inevitable manhood. The walls were all painted with hunting scenes in stark and harsh colors, pictures of deer being slaughtered, with their entrails falling from slit bellies while the wild hunters continued to stab at the fallen animals, and other pictures not so agreeable.

One looked in vain for a harp, or any trace of relieving tenderness in the things that had been provided for the prince. How fearful they must have been for him, I thought, remembering the easy way my brothers had lived with music and luxurious fittings, unafraid of being turned soft by them.

Agamemnon would have changed it all in Orestes's absence, but I would not have it. The children grew accustomed to the hideous walls and soon stopped being frightened by them. The bed, so narrow and hard that I could have bruised myself upon it, was a welcome cruelty. I would not have this barbaric chamber altered, lest I begin to forget in comfort where I was. Also, I would not have the prince think that I had turned him out of his own house when he should decide to come back to it and to his pitifully male bedchamber.

I told the King that the rooms pleased me well enough, as in truth they did insofar as anything in this accursed place could please me, and that the smell of fresh paint and the annoyance of the craftsmen underfoot would likely bring my illness back upon me. With the brusque impatience that was characteristic of him these days, he was content to have it so, and said nothing further about it.

In spite of the harshness of their decorations and furnishings, the rooms were airy, and comfortable enough in that way. I used them seldom, by my lord Agamemnon's desire, and so there was plenty of room for Nysa and the children to stay with me. She slept with them in a small side chamber, into which new beds had hastily been put, and from which they could be as quickly taken away. I wanted no trace of permanence, no lingering touch of my own in the living quarters to which I was assigned in Mycenae.

I never saw Clytemnestra except across the dim and smoky Hall on my rare visits there in the evenings. I sought an obscure corner, the privilege of the captive which even Agamemnon could not dispute, and she was always in her place near the dais, remote and queenly. There was never any cause for our speaking to each other, and I always avoided any possibility of such an opportunity.

I often caught sight of her two daughters, however, the simple one and the mad, bright one, for they roamed where they would. They were remarkably similar in appearance; but the younger had a watchful vitality that the blank-eyed one lacked.

Much to my discomfort, on those few occasions when I must dine in the presence if not the company of my lord Agamemnon, Electra would sometimes come and sit by me in my corner, forcing tidbits that I did not want onto my platter and urging me to eat. I had not lost my first instinctive feeling that she was my bitter enemy, though to all appearances she was friendly, kind, and even solicitous. But there was something disquieting in her attitude as she sought to tempt my nonexistent appetite, a kind of grim inner amusement in her brilliant eyes. She played with me, much as poor Bastos would sometimes play with a mouse he did not intend to eat until I would be forced to rescue the battered little creature and dispatch it to a merciful end.

By preference, I stayed in the upper story of the palace in the lurid rooms of Prince Orestes, out of the way of everybody, leaving them only when I was summoned to Agamemnon's bedroom. It was Nysa who began to tell me in her gossipy way of the intimate doings of the great ones in Mycenae.

She had grown plump and complacent, well pleased to be so highly placed in an alien land. As the servant of King Agamemnon's royal concubine and the nursemaid to his children by her, she gave herself airs and queened it over the other palace women. She awarded herself the position of leadership, and her notions of her own superiority inevitably attracted a certain following among them.

Nothing, or very little, is hidden from palace servants; the least doings of the lowest-placed inhabitant are common knowledge, and no threats of punishment for betrayal of secrets will prevent discussion among themselves. And Nysa, being what she was, must prattle and parade her knowingness to me while she dressed my hair, or arrayed me in the thin yellow garments which my lord Agamemnon demanded.

It seemed that during Agamemnon's absence, Queen Clytemnestra had brought back the old customs. The people demanded it, fearing that the Mother was preparing to bring total destruction down upon them by taking away all the warriors on a half-understood errand clear across the world. For their own protection, therefore, they turned again to the ways they had known long before the king came to be the ruler, rather than the queen, and Clytemnestra acquiesced to her people's preferences for her own pleasures and inclinations as much as for the soothing of their unease.

She had chosen for her consort Agamemnon's cousin Ægisthus. This Ægisthus, the son of Agamemnon's disfavored uncle, had been long absent from Mycenae due to the long-standing strife between Atreus and Thyestes in the days before Agamemnon had come to rule. He was in no wise a warrior, being portly of body and thin of shank and inclined to spend long hours with stylus and wax tablet. If he had been of common blood he would have been well-suited for the life of a scribe, or even a teacher; and in many ways, mostly unpleasant, he remined me of Laocoön.

But though the notion of Ægisthus with spear and armor was enough to set one to laughing behind one's hand, in the royal bedchamber it was another matter. Even though the servants were carefully shut out when the couple retired behind the great carved door, Clytemnestra's slow inward smiles and the lazy languor with which she greeted her maids in the mornings told well enough of how skillfully Ægisthus managed those weapons every man is born with. He, in turn, took to sleeping through the afternoons and his meals were heavy with those foods that were known to strengthen sexual vigor.

Agamemnon's return did not disturb this comfortable situation. In fact, he grew calmer after his return, as if what he had dreaded was far worse than the reality that greeted him. He was willing to accept Clytemnestra's so-called sacrifice for the good of the people since he knew that the fate of the surrogate-king was to die at the end of the year. Clytemnestra had also shown the good taste not to embarrass her husband by allowing her conceptions to mature. She took the medicine when it was required, and buried the disgorged fetuses in the Mother's precincts. The Queen had been fertile so that the grain had grown plentifully; and her graceful avoidance of bearing any sons not from the true king's loins could only be appreciated by Agamemnon. The kingdom was secure, more so in fact than it had been before he had left it; and so far from Agamemnon's being harmed by Clytemnestra's irregular activities in his absence, he now felt himself to be in a more advantageous position than ever before.

Not only had he come home laden with riches to a land that had prospered in his absence, but he now stood to be presently rid of a person who might be a danger at some other time. Ægisthus, it might be argued, had as strong a claim to the throne of Mycenae as himself; and so the revival of the custom of the sacrifice of the substitute-king was all to his advantage. Ægisthus, so far from feeling Agamemnon's displeasure, was given the title of War Leader and was moved from the palace itself to the sumptuous columned house that lay against the wall of the citadel, a short distance away from the palace.

Though others might be convulsed with secret laughter at the thought of Ægisthus being War Leader for a cowshed much less the mighty citadel of Mycenae, there was one who did not smile. This was Eurymedon, who had held the important post of King's Charioteer throughout the war, and who had expected to become War Leader himself as a matter of course since the former one had fallen in the fighting. But Agamemnon laughed at him and had joked that being War Leader was not as secure a position now as it might be a short while hence. Eurymedon ceased his grumbling, but he continued to cast black looks at Ægisthus whenever they met.

The whole precarious situation seemed settled enough to satisfy even Agamemnon's uncertain temper. He was well-occupied with me as his preferred bed-mate; and so it was no concern of his if Clytemnestra discreetly continued her pleasurable activities with his doomed cousin. He would embrace her as the law demanded, of course, and he had me at the other times, and all was well.

I did not feel so secure as I learned the twisted ways of life in Mycenae. I shared none of Agamemnon's careless confidence as to the ultimate outcome of all this intrigue. I already had one foe here, watching and waiting for what opportunity to strike me down I did not know. A dozen times a day I found myself wondering what would happen when Ægisthus had gone under the ax and had been plowed into the cornfields. Would Clytemnestra still be the contented and complacent queen when her lover was gone from her? Or would she put herself against me as well in an unequal contest I had no way of winning?

I had a respite, no more, from the terrible fate I had felt awaiting me from the first moment Agamemnon had laid his hand upon me to claim me for himself.

I do not remember now the errand that took me into Agamemnon's chamber. I know that I would not have gone there of myself, and so I think that I was searching for a lost toy of Teledamus's, some trifle that the obstinate child must have and which he was threatening to scream himself into a black-faced fit if it were not speedily found. He ran in and out of the King's rooms freely, allowed to do so by his indulgent father, and so I must have gone there to search for it since it could not be located in my own apartment.

I remember that I was down behind the bed, threatened by a cramp, groping under it and thinking sourly that the dust was heavier than it should have been if the maids had been more observant concerning their work and less eager to gossip. I heard the door open, and then the heavy tread of Agamemnon's footsteps as he went to his jewel box and began to rummage about in it. I crouched lower, to conceal myself from him. He would surely have taken my presence in his bedroom as a sign that I had come hoping for love-making, and no protests I could make would have dissuaded him. I held my breath against the dust, fearful of a sneeze that would betray my presence, thinking that he would be gone in a moment and I would escape his embrace for a little while.

And then a small creak as the door was swung shut and quick, light footsteps told me that someone else had come seeking the King, where I had not.

'Oh, it's you,' said Agamemnon.

'Yes,' a young voice replied. I knew that vibrant tone well, from the evenings when Electra had burdened me with her false tenderness in the Hall.

A warning cold finger traced along my belly and I hugged myself flat to the floor. Under the hanging edges of the coverlet, I could just see the tops of Agamemnon's sandals and Electra's skirt hem. I put my hand over my nose, more fearful than ever of my presence being discovered.

'I must go back down immediately,' said the King, a fretful edge to his voice. 'If you must speak to me, can't it wait until another time?'

'I think that you will be glad I came to you when you hear what I have to tell you,' Electra replied, and there was a current of barely suppressed excitement in her voice. 'Let the ambassador cool his heels for a while. Why should he not wait upon the King of Mycenae, instead of the other way around? He will not need your seal at the bottom of his tablet for the time it takes to draw ten breaths.'

'Very well, then, but do not prattle. Get to the point quickly.' Resignedly, he sat down in his great chair and Electra knelt before him so closely that she was almost between his knees.

'The point is quickly made,' she declared, her voice shaking with strong and urgent emotion. 'It is not Ægisthus who is to be the year's-end sacrifice, but you.'

Agamemnon drew in his breath sharply and straightened in the chair. 'I!' he exclaimed. 'How do you know this?'

'The ambassador is waiting,' she teased, and I knew that she was taking a curious and demented sort of pleasure in the moment.

'To perdition with the ambassador. Tell me what you know,

and how you come to know it.'

'It is the Queen's secret, and Ægisthus's. When they hid themselves behind the Queen's door, they could speak freely with no fear of being overheard as they whispered together beneath the covers. But there is not the same kind of privacy in the columned house and I suppose that they have grown careless. It was no trouble to be nearby and hidden from their sight as they walked together in darkness. In fact, they have now become bold, for they think there is nothing more left standing in their way. You were gone a long time, and while you were away the land prospered. Why should they not think that the people would be glad to have you gone for good, with Ægisthus, the king who is of a placid and peaceful nature, in your place? The people make much of peace these days.'

'Ai!' I sensed him putting his head in his hands, leaning forward close to her flushed and upturned face.

'Does my father think that I would bring him such evil news without also bringing him a way out of the trap that has been so cunningly laid for him?'

'Then tell it to me quickly,' he groaned, 'and do not torment me further, for I cannot think of one now.'

Why, it is simple! You must move before they do, that is all. Sacrifice Ægisthus now. Say that you do it in thanksgiving to the Mother who brought you safely through the war, if you need an excuse. Clytemnestra also must die, for you cannot let her live to plan your death again. Let her be given poison, a painless one if you are tenderhearted, to avoid the people's wrath which would be aroused if you executed her openly as she deserves. According to law, I would then be queen, for I am now the youngest daughter of the ruling House with Iphigeneia dead. My husband would become king through me. And that would be you.'

Rapidly, panting with excitement, she spilled it out. For a long, long moment there was only the sound of her quick breathing to fill the heavy silence in which he must have stared at her in blank disbelief.

I found myself clenching my fist, almost pounding the tiled floor. This vile, monstrous proposal must surely make him recoil with horror and loathing. How could she dare? I waited for his denunciation, the shout that would loose the flood and put an end to this unnatural creature.

'You, Electra? You, my daughter?' he croaked at last, his voice harsh and abrasive with strain.

'Yes, I, Electra, your daughter! *She* would take your throne from you and your life with it, but not I! *She* is a treacherous whore, but with me as your queen you would have all my devotion and loyalty and you would be king forever!' Her voice strengthened and soared with confidence. 'Why do you even question it, my father? Did not the old ones of the House of Pelops marry whom they would, and breed from the women they themselves had bred? Who else is fit to mate with a Pelopid? I will give you fine sons, strong and lusty, children of the old line – not like the weak-headed one you got from Clytemnestra, nor Cassandra's puling brats!'

'You have always been the closest of my children, mine more than any other,' he said. His voice was low, as if he would prolong the time before he must call the soldiers to come for her.

'Have you not always said it? I am yours now.'

'When I first saw you in your cradle I thought that Clytemnestra must have welcomed my embrace when I begot you, for you were so very much like me.'

'And so it has always been. You are in me, and I am in you.'

'Even when you were little, you said that you would marry me some day. I passed it off as a childish fancy, for high-spirited little girls often say such things even as boys often declare that they will marry their mothers when they are grown.'

'It was no child's dream, nor is it now.' Then her voice grew hard, mocking, goading the man she faced to leave his wavering on the edge of decision and commit himself irrevocably one way or another. 'How unbecoming is this hesitation, my father! You, a son of Pelops! Or are you afraid of what the people might say? Has the line of Pelops come to be so thin-blooded in so short a time that all boldness has departed from it?'

'I am not afraid,' Agamemnon said slowly. 'Nor am I weak, nor thin of blood.' He was still leaning forward in his chair and his face must have been very close to hers as she knelt between his knees. There was a rustle as her hands moved purposefully on his thighs. 'I am as bold as any man of the House of Pelops. And even if it were not for that, what you offer is enough to set any man's blood to stirring.' As he spoke, his voice thickened in the way I knew. 'You are mine, and we have always known it. Let the rest of the world know it as well. I will kill Ægisthus, and Clytemnestra with him soon, very soon, and you will be my queen.'

He stood up, bringing her with him. For a horrible moment I thought they were going to consummate their awful bargain then and there, for the bed that was my uncertain hiding place was only a step away. But Electra was far too clever for that. She would take no chances before Clytemnestra was safely removed. I suppose she knew as well as anyone that Agamemnon was fully capable of keeping the Queen alive and having his pleasures from both of them.

'The prize is yours for the taking,' she said, moving back quickly, 'but not until it is won – my lord Agamemnon.'

And then she was gone with a laugh of triumph over the man who was now to be addressed as 'my lord father' no more.

The revulsion against incest is one that has lived with every people who thought themselves above the common beasts. When I had heard the stories about the Pelopid clan, I had thrust them away with a shudder, certain that they were the malicious inventions of blood enemies. But they were true, as true as the unspeakable thing I had heard her propose, and him accept.

Were they less than the beasts, or in some twisted way had the Pelopidae tried to show themselves beyond even the laws of men? No wonder Mycenae had a putrid taint!

I scarcely heard her when she slipped out of the door, hardly cared about any danger if Agamemnon should discover me while he stood in the middle of the room breathing hard, striving to regain his composure before taking up the prosaic, inconsequential business that had been interrupted. My thoughts were for myself, not for either of the less-than-beasts.

I had been Agamemnon's property, after all, and I found that I felt a wistful regret that he had not called his soldiers. His failure to do so soiled me.

How contemptuously she had demanded and received the promise of her own mother's death, casually labeling her 'whore' in the doing. It was certain that her other rival would be brushed aside as well, even more callously. But whereas Clytemnestra's ending must be quiet and without a ripple, nothing would keep her from giving me to the torments she would have dealt her mother if she could.

The mad, smiling girl who had helped me across the threshold of Mycenae would send me to the darkest, most painful death her depraved imagination could devise; and her smile would only deepen with my screams as she thought about the man who would now be hers alone, forever.

23

CLYTEMNESTRA

Anyone who works with linen, or with wool, whether in the weaving of it into cloth or the embroidery of it with needles and bright colors, knows how sometimes the most carefully folded skein will fall of itself into a matted snarl. Then you must let your work sit cooling while you patiently pick at the knot, mindful not to spoil the thread. Sometimes, if you are very lucky, you can tug on a single strand and the whole tangle will fall open and lie so straight that you can scarcely believe the mess it was in only a moment before.

That was how it was with me. I had been a fly, an ant, a thing, trapped by a cruel child armed with a brooch-pin. I had nearly beaten myself senseless against the walls of my prison not knowing when, or from what direction, the impaling stab would come.

But now I was free of the maze, and my road lay clear before me. I knew what I must do, to prevent this obscene and unholy thing from happening. That it would bring my own end with it I accepted without complaint; wherever I looked, death stared back. At least I could go to it open-eyed, and show these Achaeans how a Trojan could die. It was the indignities I might suffer that would rob me of my pride, being denied the decent approach to life's ending that should be given to anyone, that had terrified me. I would not be butchered like a beast because I stood in the way of a lecherous princess's abominable passion.

I could even smile grimly at the thought that it might not be as she imagined if she got all her desire.

Cautiously, I slipped back to my apartment, making certain that I was not seen. I must wash myself, making myself neat and tidy, calling up my breeding and manners for the interview that lay before me. I sent Nysa away, taking little Pelops and the bawling Teledamus with her. I wanted privacy for a while.

I stripped off the hateful yellow, and rummaged around in a clothespress until I found a dark blue chiton. It must have belonged to Orestes, and I had to gird it up around my waist to keep from tangling my feet in the hem. The fabric was harsh, and grated on my skin. Even in this, I remember thinking, the Mycenaean prince must be reminded of his manhood.

A captive is forbidden ornaments or trinkets, although Agamemnon sometimes hung them on me for the amusement of taking them off again in the privacy of his room. But I wanted none. Even if I had not been what I was, I was going as suppliant and should not be decked with jewels. A humble appearance was what I must seek.

I combed my hair, intending to let it lie loose down my back; but on second thought twisted it into a hank and pinned it around my head. That humble I would not be, for it must be remembered also that I had once been a princess. I left my face clean and unpainted, not wanting to hide the pale cheeks and the dark shadows like bruises under the eyes.

With an assurance I had not felt since before the Achaeans came to Troy, I made my way to the great storehouse where the bulk of the Trojan treasure lay.

'I have come to select a gift for one so high that you are not fit to tread on her shadow,' I told the guard, staring at him so steadily that he backed away with his clenched fist to his forehead.

Another time I might have wept to see the Trojan goods piled up carelessly in a conqueror's treasury. But now, dry-eyed, I searched patiently through the jumble until I found a beautiful dress-length of fine cloth, dyed purple, and ornamented with a delicate embroidery, like cobwebs. It might have come from my mother's own loom, and been stitched by her women, it was so well-made, but it could just as easily have been some of the better work of the weavers' guild. It seemed suitable for my purpose, neither trifling nor of ostentatious value.

I left the guard worrying whether he would be punished for letting me into the storeroom, and with the same firm step found my way into that part of the palace I had never entered until now.

I found Clytemnestra in the midst of her women being beautified for the banquet honoring the unknown ambassador that evening. Her dark hair, freshly washed, was braided into a thick rope on her neck, and her lips were being touched with carmine. Her eyelids were smooth and glossy under the blue paste, and her fingers and toes were newly hennaed. A maid had just opened a small jar, and held a brush poised ready to gild the

Queen's breasts while another stroked rouge into the natural folds of her body. Her eyebrows rose a little when she saw me, but she gave no sign of any great surprise as she beckoned me forward carefully so as not to smear her damp fingers.

'Cassandra!' she said courteously. 'What brings you here, little Trojan?'

'I thought that there should be no enmity between us, my Queen,' I said, 'and so I have come bringing you a gift. Perhaps you might wear it tonight, and think of me.'

She waved her hands gracefully to dry them before taking up the rich purple cloth. A corner of her mouth twitched with amusement as she fingered a fold of it.

'A Trojan's gift from a Trojan,' she said lightly. 'You show a certain audacity in giving me from what is my own. Nevertheless, I will wear it because it is a fair gift and I thank you for it. But I do not think it is any unease between us that has prompted you to come to me now, in all the time that you have been here.'

'Your perception is excelled only by your beauty. It is only audacity that could send me to you now, and only my own poverty that forces me to give you what was once mine.'

'Then both shall be rewarded, and we will speak for a while in privacy. Leave me with the Trojan princess, and I will call you again when we are through.'

The women rose obediently, pausing only to replace the lids on the cosmetic jars. The Queen sat easily, her eyes never leaving my face. I found myself wondering what the outcome might have been if, long ago, pliant Helen had been married to Agamemnon, and Clytemnestra's strength had gone to bolster up Menelaus.

'Now,' she said kindly when they had shut the door behind them. 'You may speak freely, for I believe that is your wish.'

I dropped to my knees before her. 'My wish is for the safety and well-being of your gracious self, my Queen, and I desire you to know that I seek your friendship in whatever measure you care to give it. I was never your enemy, even when the King your husband lay by my side. I have never wished to take your place though there are some who would have it so, and I hope with all my heart that my truth against their lies will turn your heart from its present set against me. Far better had I been left to perish with the rest of Troy!'

Clytemnestra smiled and gestured toward a footstool. 'Sit down, Cassandra. One daughter of a king should never have to kneel to another. It is true that I heard the rumors you mention, and half-believed them at the time. But I soon found that you were far from being the ambitious schemer the stories made you out to be. You have wanted nothing but solitude, and this I have been glad to give you. You may live here always in peace, if you have feared me.'

I swallowed hard, gathering my boldness for the next step. 'Even after Agamemnon is dead, my Queen?'

'Surely the King will live forever.'

'A king will always live in Mycenae,' I agreed, 'but he may not be Agamemnon.'

Clytemnestra shrugged and smiled as if the conversation had begun to bore her. She reached for a little hammer to strike a small cymbal to summon her women.

'Please!' I cried. 'Let us speak frankly!'

'Have we not?'

I had to find some way of reaching this self-possessed woman who could carry on an elegant courtier's conversation, going so closely to the danger line, and never once committing herself. 'Not frankly enough,' I said, and my own urgency made my voice harsh in my ears. 'I know that Agamemnon is going to die.'

'As do we all, someday,' she replied, her face blank and smooth. But then her eyes swept over me again, noting every detail of my dress, of my strained, taut face, the coronet of hair I had wound around my head. Her eyes changed and she laid the hammer down again softly. 'How do you know this?'

I nearly swayed with relief at this first crack in her composure. I could now spill out my terrible secret. 'I heard it when the Princess Electra told it to my lord Agamemnon.'

Her face set as grimly as my own, and her eyes narrowed. She leaned forward with her hands clasped before her. 'The rest of it, Trojan. Now.'

Without fear, because I knew that her cold anger was not for me, I told her what I had heard in the King's bedchamber, and I did not mince words. She interrupted me from time to time, asking how I had come to be there, requesting that I repeat the exact words as I remembered them. And then she had me tell her again, from the beginning, without interrupting me at all.

Then she rose from her chair and walked to a window, staring out so long that I almost began to believe that she had forgotten me. Only the single unanswered question of my own fate kept me where I was, waiting. Sympathy, even a queen's sympathy, can be set aside if conditions demand.

At last she turned, and her face was light and clear. 'I had thought at first that Cassandra must die with Agamemnon,' she said as pleasantly and inconsequentially as another might remark upon a beautiful day. 'I had changed my mind, when I found that she was Agamemnon's victim no less than I. But now it seems that Cassandra must die after all.'

I bowed my head. 'As you will, my Queen.'

She went on as if she had not heard me. 'It must be sooner than we had planned, Ægisthus and I, and there is sure to be a scandal. But what else can we do? We cannot wait until the year's end, for Agamemnon will not. And so we must save ourselves speedily before he falls upon us and makes an end to us.' She roamed aimlessly through the room as she talked, and then she stopped, as if she had just now noticed me waiting where she had left me before she went into the dark inner world of her own scheming. 'It is growing late, child. There is much to arrange before the banquet. You must do exactly as I tell you now, and you must ask no questions, for you already hold more knowledge than is good for you. Leave the palace. Leave the city, if you can. Find a place to hide, far enough away for safety, but not so far that you will become lost. Do not return to the palace before morning under any circumstances, no matter what you may see, or what you may hear. Believe me, you have my gratitude, and in return I will give you what help I can, but you must trust me by obedience in every detail. Now, go, go!'

There is a love of life in us all great enough to laugh at proud pretensions to a noble death, for it is instinct and the other just a veneer. I turned without a word and fled from the queen who had decreed my death in one breath and promised her aid in the next. Whether she, too, was mad, or some chink had opened in the fabric of her schemings, made no difference. The instinct for life in me took command and I forgot everything under its prodding.

Leave the city, she had said. The Lion Gate would never open for me but the cunning of the fleeing animal I had become knew of another.

I coaxed the guard at the postern, pleading the excuse of the banquet that night. I wheedled and charmed, as winsomely as I was able. I was allowed no ornaments, I told him. Please let me out, just to pick a few wild flowers to weave a chaplet for my hair?

Perhaps the old soldier had a daughter of his own who must go in flowers because he could not afford to give her gold. He stared at me from under bushy brows, and then nodded his head.

My own head felt light and dizzy, and my heart beat wildly when the gate opened, so that I had to force myself to keep from running through the lengthening shadows as I began to put distance between myself and the rough, cruel walls of Mycenae.

Every instinct in me cried 'Run!' in a thousand clamoring voices. Where? Any direction at all, just away from Mycenae. Beneath the smothering rush of panic reason strove to make itself heard, and failed. I had been cool enough until I got outside the gate; and then I became as cowardly as a coney, running from the hunter.

Once out of sight of the walls a paralyzing indecision took hold of me. The road? Oh, no, *no*! It was too straight, too level, too open. The wooded hills? *No!* Wild beasts must surely be waiting there in the tangle to take me in their heavy claws and tear me to pieces with their bloody, reeking teeth. It did not occur to me that what I had left behind in Mycenae was surely worse than anything I might meet outside.

I was a feather blown in the wind. Wavering first one way, then the other, I let the precious hours slip away while I huddled cold and miserable in the doorway of one of their barbaric tombs. There was a precinct of them set into a fold of the hills; and the whistling squeaks of the ghosts mingled with the inner tumult bombarding me. Once I thought that I heard other outcries, faint, dim, terrible, borne to me on the wind, but they were lost in those that my feverish imagination was conjuring up.

The first flash of the dawning sun banished the ghosts and cleared my head a little. A pang of hunger, sharp and real, brought me out of indecision at last. Now panic was replaced by the kind of hard fear that hones one's wits to a keen edge.

I filled my belly with clean, cold water from a half-hidden fountain on the hillside. I washed my arms and bathed my face in its refreshing pool, and cursed myself for an idiot. Until now I had gone without a misstep through quagmires that would have bogged a mouse; but when freedom lay just within my grasp I had been unable to move.

Keeping the morning sun at my back, I struck out through the edge of the wooded places. I stayed hidden as much as I could, and still keep the road within sight so that I would not lose my bearings. I stopped to rest only when I could go no further, for I was weakened by exhaustion and lack of food. Once I came upon a crude, rustic shrine of some sort. Someone had left a cake of bread on the rough altar, and I stole it without a second thought and devoured it on the spot. It was only coarse peasants' bread, and so stale I could scarcely gnaw it. But I will swear that I, who had always had the most delicate of victuals, have never tasted anything so delectable, and so strengthening.

I apologized hastily to whatever god or goddess whose offerings I had violated, and took up my flight again. The going got rougher as the day wore on and I covered less ground than I had in the morning, before the mountains had begun to grow before me. The road twisted and turned like an agonized serpent, seeking its own way through them; and soon it had dwindled into little more than a cart track. I made up my mind to risk the open path, for the brambles were growing thicker and tangled upon themselves, and had begun to catch me with every step. And then I heard the clatter of hoofs and the creaking of wheels.

One last flight, heedless of the thorns, and it was all over for me. The Mycenaean soldiers, fresh and strong and smelling of sweaty leather, put me into one of the swift, light hunting cars, handling me with a deference I had not expected. Then they turned back on the road in the direction from which we had come.

It was absurd, the little distance I had gone with such trouble. It seemed hardly any time at all before I could see the walls of the city, and the palace rearing ominously over all.

There is only one road for wheeled vehicles into Mycenae. When I saw the Lion Gate again I grew weak and sagged against the side of the car. The shabby wooden Athene was gone. Had even she fled the city? It did not seem possible to me that the hands of men could have taken her down, but her absence appeared as a terrible portent instead.

'Apollo!' It came out in an involuntary choked whisper.

A hollow humming began in my ears, rising in its rich and melodious strain like a single, unending note from a harp played by divine fingers. It swelled around me until I wondered that the soldiers did not notice it. But when I looked at them, certain that they must hear it also, they seemed strangely far away. It was as if I peered dimly through a long, hollow reed and what I saw was remote and isolated. I moved untouched and untouchable in the web of a private hymn.

At most, I had expected the icy tracing through my belly that had always come with the god's truth. But now, I was wrapped in the ecstasy of swelling, protective music filling my ears and blotting out everything else with its sweet drug. Was this what had sustained Hector? And Polyxena? And the countless others, known and nameless, who had finally come face to face with their Ananke, the share they had been allotted by the gods? Surely, I thought, my fate had reached out and caught me by the foot during the night when I had tarried in the precinct of tombs. For a little while I had shaken it off; but no one can outrun it for long.

I saw Queen Clytemnestra and Ægisthus waiting casually near the grave circle, meaningless and impossibly remote little figures in the small circle of light in which it was given to me to see the things of this life. Did it please them to make it appear that they had gone for a stroll for their own refreshment and now desired me to walk for a while with them? Let it be so, then, for it did no harm.

It seemed that the Queen greeted me with a gentle, almost affectionate chiding in her voice. I did not answer, for she was a fool and I had no time to listen to anything but the music. They began to chatter to each other, filling their own empty silence, laughing together at the ludicrous memory of the ambassador running away into the night when the spears began to flash. I remember that I was annoyed at their silly prattle. Why could they not be silent, and let me alone?

I set my foot upon the steps of the palace and the harp notes soared, rising louder and ever more sweetly as I climbed. The moment was nearly upon me, I realized, and I went faster, nearly leaving these nameless people behind me, forgotten. I was drawn along irresistibly by the rapturous music, reverberating in my head, letting it lead me to where the dead king waited for me. I rushed forward and the glad singing swelled to its deafening, ecstatic peak. Now, *now*!

The harp string snapped.

Darkness closed in, unearthly silent. Everything was stilled and hushed, breath forgotten, blood stopped in its pulsing. As quietly as it had left, flecks of light broke scintillating through the black and I could see as I had before the music began.

They lay straight and neat, composed and washed clean of the marks of their violent ending. The clay funeral masks were already in place, waiting until the smith could make gold ones for some of them. The clay was smoothly and conventionally molded, hiding the death-rictus so that even the delicate-stomached might look upon them in comfort. He was dressed richly and fittingly, with the dolphin ivory shoulder harness of the Pelopidae to mark his rank. She was clad in yellow, and her pale, unadorned hands were clasped over her breasts. Her thick lion's mane of hair flowed out from under the edge of the mask, and it was still damp and curling from the henna they had sponged into it.

I hadn't the slightest doubt that I had died with the smashing of the harp. Ghost-time is a strange thing, I thought, for it seemed but an eye-wink ago, and yet while I had been groping my way back to this place, they had washed me and dressed me and covered my face, and had laid me beside the king.

There were others with them, there in the antechamber of the Hall, all laid upon hastily-gathered beds of fresh rushes. The cool, green smell filled the room. It would do no harm to go and look at them, too.

I had scarcely a glance for the charioteer and those other companions who had shown themselves loyal to Agamemnon in the final count. But beyond them, there were three others I had not expected to see. The large, fleshy one could not be given any dignity, even now; but the two small ones were light and easy on the rushes, as if they only slept.

I went swiftly to them and even as I flung myself down on my knees an anguished, keening wail came up from the depths of my soul. My hands went of their own volition, lacerating my cheeks and tangling in my hair. I tore it out and didn't feel it, for the dead was mourning the dead.

I had known grief beyond tears before, and so it did not seem unnatural that I did not cry. Ghosts have not that ability. But they must feel much as living men, for sheer pain choked off the wordless lament. I rocked back and forth, open-mouthed and mute.

Even in war, children were tenderly spared and protected in Troy. Why hadn't I guessed that they could not have been expected to escape in this foul dung heap? I bitterly hated and despised myself for abandoning the poor little mites to the mercies of Mycenae. I hated the selfish way I had run, thinking only of my own precious skin. And most of all I hated myself for not loving them while they were alive.

With an instinct as strong as grief itself, I cast the fistfuls of hair onto their bodies, and raising my hands above my head, brought them down hard and flat and began to beat upon the ground.

With powerful blows, lifting high and bending low with each great effort in a primitive and awful rhythm, I sent my appeal straight through the rushes, the polished tiling, past the foundations of the palace, and deep into the earth beneath. In a moment, I would find my voice, and cursing would begin. Already I could feel the venomous power flowing up through my arms, as the dark magic below heard, and answered.

'How do you like it, little Trojan?' Electra stood in the doorway to the Hall, looking straight at me. She blinked her eyes, and then giggled through the paint on her face.

I hung foolishly, hands upraised, staring at her, and what I had built flittered away and drained out of me as the truth slowly dawned. I was no ghost. It was not my body beside the dead king. And it was not even Electra who had spoken to me, but only the silly, biddable, simple one.

'We worked most of the night through, my lady mother and I,' she simpered. 'We fixed the masks with our own hands. I think that we did it very well, don't you?'

'Yes.' Futile, empty, a hollow ache. 'It is all quite perfect, Chrysothemis.'

'Oh, I am not Chrysothemis any more.' She whirled around, sending her skirts flying and making the gold ornaments flash and jingle. 'Isn't my dress pretty? It was Laodice's. Electra was only her nickname, you know, and it is mine now. I will have all her clothes, and all her jewels too. They are much finer than mine. *He*' – she gestured airily at the dead king – 'was ever more openhanded with her. I think he liked Laodice better than me. I like being Electra.' She preened happily, swishing her skirts with her hands.

'Take her away, Ægisthus,' said Clytemnestra coldly. 'She needs coaching in the art of silence. I would have spared you this, little Trojan, but you rushed ahead as if you did not hear me.'

She took me unresisting to her chamber. Tired and hollow-eyed as she seemed, and showing her age for the first time since I had known her, she was still buoyant with her triumph; and I was only weary and sick.

She closed the door firmly, to keep out inquisitive servants. 'I will say that Chrysothemis has gone away to be married. No one knows where Orestes is, but I think that he will be no trouble to me if he should return. There is only one thing left to finish in this night's work, and that is what is to be done with you.'

'Done with me? I had thought you intended to kill me with Agamemnon. What else is there?'

The Queen smilingly put me into a softly cushioned chair. On a nearby table there was a platter of food, fresh bread still warm from baking, and a flagon of wine to refresh the fugitive. She filled a dish for me and poured a cup with her own hands.

'Poor little Trojan. What a fearful time you have had. Let me tell you a story about myself, while you eat a little and regain some strength. Perhaps in the telling you will come to understand me a little better.

'You see, when I was a young girl, I had a husband – oh, yes, there was one before Agamemnon – and him I loved with all my heart. But Agamemnon was unwilling for Sparta to go to Menelaus alone with his marriage to Helen. He feared the strength it would bring to Menelaus, thinking it would make his brother too bold for his own safety. So my beloved Tantalus had to die for Agamemnon's ambition, and my infant son with him. I was his prize of war as surely as you were, little Trojan, except that he married me and made me his queen so that my father would have no cause to make war upon him. He bred his children from my unwilling body and went his own way as he would. Everyone knows this old tale, though from fear of Agamemnon most have chosen to forget it. I thought surely that you knew of it yourself.

'No, little Trojan, I do not hate you, and never did. So far from that, I have pitied you. And my sympathy was most strongly aroused when you came bearing your pathetic gift and the terrible story that would save me. How small you looked, how alone, with your sad little crown of hair, quaking beneath your boldness. If you had known that I was your sister in captivity to Agamemnon, you would not have forgotten my promise to help you. Cassandra is dead, as I said she would be. But you are alive.'

I almost laughed. No one, not even the soldiers who had been sent after me, had called me by name. According to Mycenaean notions, Achaean notions, I had none. Cassandra was dead.

'We must find you a new name, my child,' the Queen continued serenely. 'It would not do to discover Cassandra alive when she is supposed to be lying dead beside her lover. What was your brother's name, the one who was duped into carrying Helen away to Troy so that Agamemnon might have his excuse to make war upon you?'

I was curious to see what else was in the mind of this smiling, cool queen who had managed her affairs so competently and so cleverly. 'Paris,' I said finally.

'Oh, no, not that childish and undignified nickname.'

'Alexandros?'

'Yes, that's it. It has seemed to me that he was cruelly used.

Let us call you Alexandra now in his memory, so that his ghost might rest a little easier, and not trouble me for Agamemnon's sake.'

Well, then, that was surely reasonable. There were ghosts enough that she had set loose to plague her. I shrugged. 'If I am not Cassandra, then I may as well be Alexandra, or any other name you choose to call me. My life has been bought at a dearer price than it was worth to me, so what does a name matter?'

But she brushed that aside. 'That is easily settled. Now tell me. Shall we find you a decent husband so that you may have more children to comfort you? Do you want to live here, with Ægisthus and me? We would gladly call you our sister and our niece, and you would be much honored and respected. Or is there something else that you would like to do? I owe you much, and I am not one to forget a debt.'

Was it really true? Did Clytemnestra actually have no idea of what she was proposing to me? I could not believe she did not understand the depth of the insult she had given me, that even now lay on the rushes below. Slaying the lecherous princess, putting an end to her unnatural lust, was only just, and even pious. And I could surely understand her killing Agamemnon for all his manifold crimes. Let her hang it on some obscure point of religious dogma, it was all one.

But to call this abomination by my name, and redden her hair and prink her up to be me, and then think to smooth it all away with a few pretty baubles, lightly given? Oh, no.

She had even stolen my death from me. But she was not the only cunning witch here. Perhaps I could contrive to steal it back.

I took a deep breath, and felt the earth magic stir in me again. I was as fearless as Hecabe had been when she had beaten the earth and called up its curse upon Odysseus. The same power had answered me a little while ago, and it was with me now.

'You have favored me with your story, Queen Clytemnestra, and so I cannot be less courteous,' I said, and the Queen smiled. Were we not Royal Kin, speaking to one another?

'When I was a child, I was dedicated to Apollo. Circumstances denied me his holy company, and so I went to his Maiden sister and lived that life without a blemish until Agamemnon put an end to it.'

She nodded, so understanding.

'Consider. I want no marriage. I will not lie under another Agamemnon and bear more children. My children are dead, and you killed them, Queen Clytemnestra.'

Her face grew still.

'Consider. I want no kinship with you. I detest Mycenae and all Mycenaeans. They reek of death. You reek of death, Queen Clytemnestra.'

Her face set in its stillness.

'Consider. You killed Cassandra, but I am alive. You have not stopped my wagging tongue as you did that of the nursemaid, Queen Clytemnestra.'

Her eyes glittered snakelike, but she was able to answer me, though her voice was low and shaking. 'You are exhausted, or you would not say such things. So am I. I am sorry about your children, but surely you can see that Agamemnon's seed had to die with him.'

'I can see that they make excellent trappings for the lie you have made of my death. I pity Orestes, if he should be foolish enough to return to Mycenae, Queen Clytemnestra.'

The endless repetition of her name and title seemed to gall her beyond bearing. She stood up and began to pace, trembling angrily, clasping and unclasping her hands.

'Oh, I see through you, you sour witch! You are trying to provoke me into killing you, too, and have the embarrassment of two dead Cassandras to explain away! Oh, how you would love that.'

'I would, Queen Clytemnestra.'

'Be quiet, you piece of Trojan trash!' she shrieked, as common as any fishwife. 'It was stupid of me to expect any simple, decent gratitude from someone like you. You're too crazy to feel it.'

'I feel more than you will ever know, Queen Clytemnestra.'

She turned her snake's eyes on me, and I knew that she could call upon earth magic, too. 'I do know this, sister witch. You are still my chattel, my thing, and I can dispose of you as I will, though the time for killing you has passed. I have never killed anyone yet without a reason, whether state, political, or religious, and for you I have not the excuse at my hand now. I have never killed to satisfy my own anger, nor to evade a debt I no longer wished to pay, and I owe you much, both good and bad. You want death from me, but I will give you life, as much to irk and annoy you as to please myself.

'You were a priestess; return to your shrines. Babble as much as you like about Mycenae, and see who will listen to your ravings! I cannot decide where will be the worst place for you, but there is one who will know. She owes me a favor, and so she cannot refuse me.' She began to smile, a terrible, snaky smile. 'Oh, a nice touch, this! A delicate touch, and a fine irony. You were a fool to match wits with me, but then you were always weak in the head. I am charmed with my own cleverness, for I am going to send you to Delphi.'

An armed company of the most trusted of Clytemnestra's soldiers took me to the remote shrine, hidden away in the craggy mountains beyond the great Isthmus. It was done secretly, and I was hurried out of the citadel before the funerals could begin. I went veiled and hooded, hidden from the stares of the curious behind a fence of Mycenaean spears. Except for the soldiers, I might have been any noble lady going on a pilgrimage to fulfill some vow.

The leader gave me a sealed tablet, and the royal mark on it brought me into the presence of Pythia herself. She lived in a little cubicle, indifferently furnished, close by the cleft in the earth. Deep below stood the three-legged bronze stool situated over a fissure that led directly to the Underworld itself. Here rose the sulphurous fumes that inspired her most prophetic utterances, and close by the holy earth-serpent lived in his little house.

While she broke the seal and laboriously studied the contents of the tablet, I took my opportunity to look at her closely. I tried in vain to read her face as she scanned what the Queen had said about me and which I did not know, and I was curious about this great and powerful priestess as well. She was old, very old, for all the Pythias are, and her face told me nothing as she read. Her hair was white and somewhat carelessly braided into a single plait, and her garments were of plain and severe gray weave, for no vanity was permitted here. Her eyes were heavily-lidded and her features of a common mold; and yet she carried a regality in her person that I had not seen since Hecabe was alive.

'Well, then,' she said when she had finished with the tablet. 'It says here, most emphatically, that you are Alexandra of Troy and none other, and you are a captive and a stranger in our land. Your master is lately dead and you are now homeless and without protection. Queen Clytemnestra has taken pity upon you and sent you to us, thinking that we might find a place somewhere for you.'

From her tone, I sensed that she doubted some of it and accepted the rest. And like any good priestess, she would try to sift from me the truth from the falsehoods. But I did not know what else was in the tablet, and so I must be cautious.

'I have been sent here. It is for you to say now.' The old manner of priestess's speech, wherein one may say nothing, or just a little, began to come back to me. It was only a little more subtle than courtier's speech after all.

'You were once a shrine servant, and you wore the silver of the Maiden. Have you ever known love, or the embraces of love?'

'I have known both, but not from the same man.'

'Tell me.'

'When I served the Maiden, I fell in love with the noblest of men. He would not touch my virginity, for he was pious and reverent. The one who took me cared nothing for such trifles. He forced me; and so I became the concubine of a man I detested, whose embraces I must endure, and whose sons I bore.'

'Our rules are hard, and the restrictions of our numbers exacting,' Pythia said. 'Many secrets come to us, and we must hold them among ourselves. To betray them is to die.'

I nodded agreement. 'So it was always in Troy.' What was she getting at?

'We live chastely, priestess and common shrine servants alike. If one of us has congress with a male pilgrim, she dies and her lover with her, for chastity is our most precious possession.'

My heart grew still within me. On the way, it had been no trouble to learn that Delphi was unique in the world; for though it was dedicated to Apollo, it was peopled by women. And for a little while, I had begun to hope that I might stay here after all. Now I knew that it was just another cruel joke of Clytemnestra's, for I had incautiously confided my longing for the god to her. I had not known how very much I wanted to lose myself in the life of Delphi until I heard the Pythia's words placidly cutting the shaky footing out from under me.

'Tell me of your master,' she said. 'Did you ever, in all the time that you were in his company, desire his embraces? Did you perfume your body, thinking of him? Did you come to enjoy your manner of servitude, and endure his couch with secret pleasure? Such things are not unknown. Before you answer, remember that you stand in the precinct of Truth-bringing Apollo.'

I lifted my head high. 'I have not forgotten it. Never! Never, to all your questions. Why do you even ask? If maidenhood is your requirement, I have none. I have confessed it already.'

But she persisted inexorably, determined to drag out all of the facts that concerned her. 'And the man you loved. Did you lie with him in some hidden place, closed away from the eye of man or god?'

'Never!' I repeated. Desolate pride was all that I had left while I stood before her, and little enough of that. 'Never, though I desired it ardently. A few kisses passed between us, nothing more. I came here willingly, hoping for a scrap of kindness in Achaean lands. Give me a place among the lowest servants, if that can be allowed, and I will never trouble you.'

'Most of what we have spoken about was here beforehand,' Pythia said, indicating the tablet, 'and more that was not as flattering besides. But scratching in wax sent by a lady who might want nothing more than to have you safely gone from her presence are without weight beside spoken words that must be true, here of all places in the world.'

I barely listened to her, anxious to escape with my rapidly crumbling pride. What else could she say to me? If only the chaste and virginal could serve here, she did not need to give me a formal denial. I could go of my own accord.

'Innocence does not reside in the possession of a maidenhead,' she continued serenely, 'for it is a thing both of body and of spirit. To know love without passion, or passion without love, does not violate it. A long, long time ago, when I was young and comely, a noble's son found me filling water jars to carry back to the peasant hut where I lived with my family. He overcame me and gave me another burden to carry. My family could not understand the disgrace I felt, for a child more or less was nothing to them. But the manner of the thing had wounded me; and when the child was weaned, I slipped away in the night. I risked a great deal to come and stand where you are standing, asking another Pythia only for the easement of my sore spirit. I had not even thought to ask for shelter here, because like you, I felt that I would be rejected.'

My face must have shown my astonishment.

'I must ask your pardon for prying into your tender memory, but I had to be certain that you had not yielded yourself to your lover. Likewise, I had to know the straight of the matters that were set down about you by the Queen of Mycenae. She must have been very agitated when she wrote this, for she has contradicted herself in every sentence, asking first one thing and then another.

'She knew nothing about the man you loved, for nothing is

mentioned here. If you had lain with him, I would have sent you to a sanctuary of Hera the Nymph which is open to those who have known joyful embraces. It is a dignified refuge for women whose husbands or lovers have died, and who cannot open their hearts to another man.'

'I do not desire the company of any man.'

'I believe that. I also believe that you did not come to love your captor's couch, though the tablet instructs me otherwise. If that had been the case, a place would have been found for you in the House of Aphrodite, but not the mean and degrading brothel such as the good Queen has recommended. We are stern here, but we are also merciful and generous to those who have been ill-used by life. Tell me: what dower-gift do you bring to the shrine that will receive you?'

'Dower-gift?' I looked down at the rough blue chiton and the servant's castoff cloak I wore. 'I have nothing. Even the clothes in which I stand are borrowed. I can't even offer a clean and undefiled body.'

'Haven't you been listening? I do not think there is a whole maidenhead among us. But never mind, the dowry will come in its own time. Poor child, I believe that you have not guessed that I will not allow this holy place to be used as an instrument of revenge against one slight girl, even to discharge my obligation to the Queen of Mycenae. She will not know the difference, for I will send her a message worded so that she may interpret it as she chooses. You will be safe, and well-valued and cherished. Only one who has known the things that you have known can presume to offer aid to other souls in trouble.' Her eyes crinkled, and she smiled. Her voice was warm and kind. 'You will become a priestess of Apollo in the shrine of Delphi.'

She held out her arms to me in welcome. And as simply and naturally as if I had been coming home to Hecabe's greeting, I walked into them.

24

DELPHI

It is a life within a life here. The great and the humble, the rich and the poor, the noble and the peasant, the young impatient ones hungering for a taste of the future and the old ones beaten down by the fate they eagerly sought – all come, sooner or later, to Delphi.

The shrine is difficult to reach, nearly impossible for some of the infirm and elderly who attempt it. It is perched precariously between crags of a mountain whose slopes are well-nigh a straight drop. One can look down upon black thunderstorms that stalk their way through the narrow valleys on thin and deadly shanks of lightning. Summers are pleasant enough, and bring the bulk of the supplicants with them; but the winters send snow and gnawing winds that threaten to tear the shrine from its moorings. I always welcomed the winters, for the wind reminded me of Troy, even though the cold was sure to carry off some of the weaker and more aged priestesses. It was said that their souls descended into the sulphurous fissure, for that was the most convenient of the many terminal places of the Road of Death.

Such is the nature of man, Delphi is the more treasured for its inaccessibility, for only the most pious and reverent dare undertake the journey, or live to complete it. Some little distance away, there is a honeycomb of cliffs in the mountainside; until recently, they housed the pilgrims. But, as is ever the case, men who hope to make money from other peoples' sufferings have come even here. There is a little town composed solely of inns and taverns that now caters for the well-to-do and better class of supplicants. A pestilence upon them, I say. There has even been a rumor that Delphi itself will become a town, so that the wealthy pilgrims will not have so far to walk to go to their purifications. But I do not think that this will ever happen.

Given my nature, I was curious as to how the shrine had come to be the religious oddity it was. And, as its history was one of the first things a novice learned, I was not long in finding out.

Many, many years ago – so far in the past that by my reckoning the first Scamander had not yet come to the Troad from drowning Atlantis – Delphi was the heart of the old religion. Here, the Goddess was known and revered as the ultimate Mother, Gaea, the earth itself. The symbol of the Earth Mother has always been the serpent; and there was a rough shrine wherein Python himself communicated with Gaea, and brought her messages to the waiting priestesses.

When the first yellow-haired men came down from the lands beyond the North Wind, Delphi was conquered by the god-worshipers. The priestesses were forewarned by Gaea, and with the warning came the instructions as to how they were to treat the newcomers. Rather than struggle uselessly with the strong and well-armed warriors, they were told to go to meet them with open hands. By cooperation with the invaders, they could keep the sacred precinct intact, and not have it utterly destroyed and trampled out of existence. Priestesses in other places ignored or misinterpreted similar messages, and suffered badly as a result.

The Pythia of that time made a shrewd bargain with the men, wherein the Goddess would continue to live peacefully side by side with the most noble of their gods, Apollo. One of them, who styled himself Apollo's priest, was given a serpent to kill, so that the story might be told that Apollo himself had been victorious over the Python. The real Python, of course, remained safe and secure in his little house deep in the sacred cleft, but the simple-minded men did not know that.

The god-men claimed nearly all of the outer portion of the shrine; but the most important part, the *Oömphalos*, which everyone knew was the navel of the world, remained in the Goddess's keeping. From this central point, the god's holdings was divided into four parts. The navel stone and the little space around it were situated at the inmost corners. If a thread were stretched from the inner boundaries north and south, and another east and west, they would cross at the stone itself.

'The middle, the circle, is the woman's,' Pythia told me. 'The Goddess has always been known by this sign. Consider her tokens; the apple, the pomegranate, the shape of each individual grain of corn and of barley. Consider the roundness of the belly when it is heavy with life. And even when the belly is flat once more, consider how each of us, even a man, carries the touch of her finger in the middle of our bodies to remind us that we are all her children.

'But the four parts of the shrine around the navel stone, those are the man's. Three belongs to the Goddess, in the three faces she has made known to us, and the three faces of each face therein. Five is also hers, for it is the Goddess and her children, the man and the woman. It is the imprint of her hand upon each leaf of the sacred oak which she allowed the invaders to take away from her and give to Zeus. Four is the unnatural thing that lies between. That is why one of the gravest punishments administered to a lawbreaker, short of demanding his life or his manhood, is that he must suffer the loss of one of his fingers. His mutilated, four-fingered hand is the mark for all to see that his was the kind of sin so grave that it will never entirely wash away.

'The men do not know this, for it is a woman's mystery. And so, thinking to spite us, they have taken the obscene four to themselves, clamoring that it is just and proper because a man has two arms and two legs. They forget the head, which controls all, and even that other member which sometimes overrides the head. They think that they have brought order into their lives, pointing to the four walls of a house for proof. But that is just a simple trick of building, and means nothing. And so we have allowed them to block off the precincts as neatly as any competent stone-mason, just as they wished. But even so, the Goddess triumphs!'

Pythia's eyes sparkled with a sudden youthful mischief. I knew that she was preparing to tell me another closely-held secret of the shrine.

'Name for me the precincts of Apollo,' she demanded.

'Why, they are Apollo Truth-Bringer, Apollo the Healer, Apollo the Singer, also called Pythian Apollo, and . . . and – ' I stopped, for I did not know to whom belonged the last one.

'It is the precinct of Dionysus,' Pythia said. 'In him, god and goddess come together and mingle part for part. In the old days, Dionysus was the consort of the Lady of Delphi, and he came riding on a dolphin, crowned with ivy and bearing clusters of grapes in either hand. He died with the year's end, and was reborn into a new Wine-King. Now, the men think he is only a mystical bridge between Apollo and the Goddess, and they leave us alone during the four months of the year that the earlier Pythia demanded and got from the ignorant warriors who took the shrine. Every year a new Wine-King, a new Dionysus, comes to us, and we send him to the Goddess when his time is finished.'

'That is something new to me, and I am steeped in many

mysteries and cults of the East!' I exclaimed. 'How does it happen?'

'He comes of his own accord, for the Goddess beckons to him and he must go to her. A few things have changed, with the coming of the men. We used to devour his tender flesh, but the men put a stop to that custom. Now all of him goes under Gaea's mantle to be digested just as thoroughly. Nor do we choose, as we used to in the days when the candidates were numerous and eager. But I have been Pythia for many, many years, and there is always a Wine-King for us when the season approaches.'

Almost by force of habit, I was drawn into the precinct of Healing Apollo. I was not particularly suited to it, for the bulk of my experience had been that of working with hurt warriors. The frailties of the flesh and ailments of ordinary people were, I found, beyond me. But, as I had learned from the healing-woman in the cubby at the Pastoral Shrine, common sense often does the work of skill.

I even made a small, and I felt undeserved, reputation for myself. There had been a plague that appeared among the rustics, and no priestly cleansing or scraped-together sacrifices would cure it. Long ago, in Troy, we had faced an outbreak of fingers and toes going black and dropping off, leaving foul, ugly wounds. The priests advised lustral washings; the old woman examined some of their sour grain and found it as black as the disease. Obviously, she said, someone had offended Mother Grain-Grower. The Goddess had blasted the fields, and the poison carried on into the bread. They shunned the grain thereafter, and the plague ceased though its sufferers were marked for life.

This affliction was so similar that I gave the same advice, and got the same results. The peasants counted it a very miracle, and began to call me 'Daughter of Asclepius'. The name caught and held, and I must own that I liked it far better myself than the one Clytemnestra had tried to hang on me in Mycenae, on the day that Cassandra had died. I have never been called anything else since.

My position was secure, though as I have said, I had really done little to earn it. With the others in the Precinct of Healing Apollo, I worked to ease the myriad complaints to which men fall heir. Scrofula, goiter, infestations of boils, lung sickness, thick fevers; these and all the rest paraded through Delphi. And if anyone noticed that I held back watching from most of these, although quick enough with an infected cut or a joint out of socket, they were kind and did not mention it.

For some of the patients, there was little we could do but make them as comfortable as we could until the god claimed them. That was a sad time, for it reminded us that no matter how much we might have learned, there was much, much more hidden from us.

There are few secrets among the priestesses at Delphi, although they hold them close within their number. As the seasons wore on, I came to hear of intimate doings of people whose names had become as familiar to me as my own in the days when the Achaeans had camped on the Plain of Troy, and then later when I had been an unwilling resident of Mycenae.

When I had been at Delphi ten winters, through the reign and demise of ten Wine-Kings, a new supplicant was found in the shrine one morning, clinging to the *Oömphalos* itself. It was Orestes, wild-eyed and haggard with the burden of guilt he carried. And with him, a part of his oppression, he brought the news of Clytemnestra's ending.

For nearly eight years he had prudently stayed away from Mycenae; but one day a message came to him to return, and he did not ignore it. He crept back into the city by night, and learned of how Agamemnon had been murdered, rather than offered up as a pious sacrifice, so that Clytemnestra could continue to enjoy her lover, Ægisthus. It was Electra who told him, the Electra who had once been Chrysothemis.

She had tired of the rigid discipline that had been forced on her so that her mother's secret might be kept. Clytemnestra had cared as little for her as for her other children; the rich husband, the idleness, leisure, and pleasures she saw every day had not come to her. It had finally penetrated her weak brain that the other Electra had not been put out of the way for her sole benefit, and Orestes helped to guess the rest. It was not as much fun being Electra as she had thought it would be. Secondhand dresses and jewels did not measure up to having a man in her bed, for this had been denied her; and she found herself to be as concupiscent as her sister.

And so, taking her sister's example, she had helped Orestes put his sword into the lovers; and they also slew the second Helen whom Clytemnestra had borne to Ægisthus. They plotted to kill the other Helen as well, for Menelaus had finally brought her back to Sparta. They willingly took upon themselves the divine task of administering punishment to her for the great suffering she had brought upon the world.

Then, they thought, they would rule Mycenae as king and queen. Orestes's friend Pylades, the one to whom Chrysothemis had supposedly been married when her absence from the city must be explained, had reluctantly joined the plan. It was understood that he was to be War Leader, and that Chrysothemis-Electra would reward him the same way that Clytemnestra had repaid Ægisthus.

Their scheme worked admirably, Ægisthus, little Helen and Clytemnestra fell without a struggle, for they took them by surprise. Now they had only to wait until Menelaus came back to Mycenae. To make certain that he would, they circulated the story of Agamemnon's death. Custom would then demand that Menelaus seek vengeance against his brother's killers; and he had no way of knowing that Orestes had already accomplished it for him. He completed his bloody tasks by murdering Helen when she came primping and preening, cutting off insultingly small snippets of hair to lay on her sister's tomb.

Menelaus, who was not far behind, now looked up startled to see Orestes and Pylades standing together against him. He turned without a word and fled for his life. He certainly had no more business in Mycenae. Perhaps it even seemed a fair trade – a brother of uncertain temperament for the burden of Helen, whose infidelities had made him the butt of too many jokes.

Menelaus never returned to Sparta. Rumor has it that he sank relieved into obscurity and became a farmer. It is said that he took another wife – a quieter sort, it is to be hoped – and lives in peace to this day.

Not so Orestes. This last murder loosened his remaining hold on reason. He recalled the story about Helen that had caught the fancy of the people, and began to tremble with belated pangs of conscience.

In Eastern lands, the Goddess in her most implacable, man-hating mood is known as the Dancer upon Skulls. Here in the West, she bears many names, according to the area and the different peoples. She is known variously as Erinnya, Nemesis, Brimo, and other names both obscure and seldom-mentioned.

The tale that swept loose Orestes's sanity had it that Father Zeus caught sight of this grim goddess one day and a perverse urge to possess her overcame him. She fled, changing her shape as she went, and he followed, matching he-goat to nanny, boar to sow, ram to ewe, buck to doe, and steadily gaining on her all the while. At last, spying a flock at a river's edge, she turned herself into a goose and hid among them. But Zeus immediately became a swan, found her straightaway in the flock, and covered her then and there. Furious, the Goddess knew that her womb had become fertile from this monstrous and unwanted mating. She was presently delivered of an egg, and nestled within the egg was Helen.

Helen, it was said, inherited the worst parts of both her parents. She took the desire for rape from Zeus and the answering urge for the destruction of her ravisher afterward from the Dark-Faced Goddess. Now her name became a synonym for lasciviousness. She was a coupler upon dung heaps, a dog howling in the moonlight.

By now, the part of the story that holds the Grim Goddess up to ridicule has been suppressed, of course. It is Leda, Helen's earthly mother, who suffers the indignity of Zeus's rape in the form of a swan. But this had not happened in Orestes's time.

With rising panic, he realized that he had killed the daughter of the most fearsome of all goddesses. To compound his sin, he had killed her namesake as well, and had put to death her sister, who also happened to be his mother. As if that were not enough, he was now sharing his own sister's bed, and a man whose hands were scarcely less bloody than his own slipped under the coverlet when he left.

He fled shrieking from Mycenae, closely followed by Electra and Pylades, and only a step or two ahead of the citizens of the kingdom. With these last several murders, the people had finally risen up full of righteous anger at the terrible way the House of Pelops perverted and destroyed everything it touched. The people wanted to have done with the Pelopidae for all time, and were prepared to live kingless if necessary to do it. But a new king came speedily to the city, a grandson of Perseus the Mighty, whose memory shone all the brighter in contrast to the ugliness festering in all members of the House of Pelops.

Eurystheus is his name, and I wish him well in his present difficulties. They are not of his making, and so perhaps the canker that dwelt in the bones of Mycenae has finally flushed itself clean in the actions of Orestes.

Orestes never stopped running. And no matter how fast he went, his terrible memories flew along beside him. Extravagant tales have sprung up around his memory, for the whole world was intrigued with the novel crime of a mother's murder by her own son. It furnished a topic of debate for years thereafter, and the issue is not settled yet. The old peoples, whose loyalties lay with the Goddess, were horrified at the sacrilege. The newer folk argued that the father is the true parent, and the mother only provides the receptacle for his seed. Why not, they say, honor the field above the sower, if the mother be the greater? He was only acting piously, avenging his father's murder by a perfidious and adulterous bitch. And so it goes.

Every place must have a share in Orestes. The cities and towns that claim the honor of his death and burial would fill a large tablet. It is said that he sought relief from persecution by living on the deltas of various great rivers in turn, even seeking out the Scamander. That, of course, is a silly lie, but there are those who believe it, just as they believe that a delta is safe from ghosts because it is 'created' land.

There was, however, a time of restless and unknown wandering before Orestes came to Delphi. Electra and Pylades were not with him, and their fates can only be guessed. But from the way he never left off looking behind him with eyes made flat and shiny from fear, I can easily imagine that their ghosts had joined those others that dogged his every footstep.

'Erinnyes, Erinnyes!' he would burst out even in the midst of some solemn rite, sending chills up every back. 'Leave off, it is enough!'

'They have all become Erinnya,' a priestess whispered to me. 'The mother, the daughter, the receptive nymph. He has got it all mixed up in his mind with half-understood parts of the old religion. Poor man, he is hopeless. I do not think that Apollo can heal him, even if he should happen to want to.'

We all did what we could for him at Delphi, for that is our duty regardless of private feelings. Pythia submitted herself to the subterranean fumes for his sake. According to her instructions, we administered the most extreme purifications we knew to give him.

He sacrificed a pig, letting the blood flow into a bowl for the ghosts to drink. Then, he went quickly to wash in running water while they were still at the blood, and shaved off all his hair. With luck, he could throw the ghosts off the scent, and go into a welcome exile untroubled.

To remove the curse of shedding his mother's blood, however, sterner measures were ordered. He must undergo the mutilation of which I had learned, and he must accomplish it himself. He hesitated, wavering back and forth, but when it was explained to him that it was that or suffer gelding in its stead, he bit off the finger as required and cast it into the bowl of pig's blood.

We were glad enough to see him go, for he disturbed everyone and took no peace with him when he left. We heard that he went on to Athens, and later Phocis for more purification, still plagued by the pursuing 'Erinnyes'. He never got free of them, and they troubled him without ceasing until he finally died, perhaps gratefully, at Cerynea. And that is the truth.

Another came who earned Pythia's immersion in the sulphurous fumes from the cleft in the earth, and this was Neoptolemus, Achilles's son.

He had left the great convoy early, escaping the storm off Sounion that took such a great toll of the Achaeans. One would have thought he would be content to find a kingdom of his own in the northern wilderness, but not the son of Achilles. He wandered unsatisfied until he came to the Peloponnesian lands, whereupon he sought out Menelaus's and Helen's daughter Hermione, whom the Spartans had allowed to live in sad isolation there. He claimed falsely that Menelaus had betrothed her to him at Troy, ignoring the fact that she had been promised to Orestes all her life. But Orestes was certainly in no condition to press his claim and so the marriage was allowed. Hermoine, fortunately for all, proved barren; Neoptolemus dragged the poor girl to Delphi, seeking to correct her fault.

Once here, he tuned his harp to a different mode and demanded reparation for the death of Achilles. His father had died by treachery in a sanctuary of Apollo, he announced arrogantly, and so Delphi and any other of the god's sacred places must pay him for his loss.

Pythia ignored him. She was willing, she said, to undertake the cure of Hermione's childlessness, but there was no satisfaction to be had for him here in regard to this ridiculous and unwarranted claim.

No one ever refused Achilles for fear of his wrath; and Neoptolemus was his father's son. He went into a blind, killing rage, and while it was upon him we gathered such things as we could lay hands upon and fled for our lives to the shallow safety of the caves.

He knocked down what he could and set fire to whatever would catch. And when the fit had passed, he stood meekly and allowed the eunuchs to take him. To his credit, he seemed shocked at the blackened, smoking ruins of the shrine when he was calm and rational again.

Then Pythia went into the cleft and sat breathing the fumes, for this kind of sin was unprecedented.

'For the first time in untold years, it has been given to a Pythia to choose the Dionysus,' she said. 'You will be this year's Wine-King. All your wealth is forfeit. And instead of the usual disposition of your body into the vineyards, you will be buried under the threshold of our new sanctuary to guard us against another attack of this nature.'

I half expected him to rage anew and burst the cords that bound him, but he bowed his head and accepted his fate without a murmur. Hermione, a gaunt and melancholy wraith, left her jewels behind and departed, without a backward glance, for one of Hera's shelters.

I helped kill him when the time came, forgetting that my business was preserving life. We put him living into a pit and then covered him up. With a barbaric intensity that should have shocked me, I regretted that I was not allowed to use my teeth on him. However, I threw my handful of earth in the face of my father's killer and ground my heel rather harder than was necessary in it.

Later, Pythia came to my little cell, bearing a bundle in her hands.

'Your dower-gift has been paid at last,' she announced cheerfully, 'and it is only fair that you should share in it.'

I unfolded a woolen mantle, lined with warm fur. It was a welcome gift, for even my bones had come to creak in the winter's chill; I tried to return it to Pythia, but she assured me that there was plenty for all.

The new place that we built with Neoptolemus's treasure was far more glorious than the old. To tell the truth, it had grown somewhat shabby and stained with the years. And so, all told, we were far better off than we had been before he came, for all the destruction that he brought with him.

There is only one more tale of a supplicant at Delphi that I wish to tell, for I have grown weary of the telling. But this one concerned me, for I had a hand in it.

The West was shattered as surely as the East had been in the senseless war before Troy; and it lay helpless and open to another great invasion, such as it had suffered in times past.

Dorians, they called themselves, and their roughness and wildness knew no bounds. They made the rude outlanders of the East look like cultivated courtiers by comparison. Man and woman, they wore leather leggings with the hairy side turned outward, not even bothering to tan the hides properly. They lived in crude tents when they were not on their cobby little ponies that were no better groomed than they. Wherever they went, they destroyed and did not rebuild. But fortunately for us, they were superstitious. The sacred places they avoided when they could, and so Delphi escaped.

They occupied most of the great cities – Tiryns, Mycenae, Argos, Sparta, Corinth. They kept the kings alive, for it was easier for them to keep the people quiet that way. Plunder was what they wanted, not crowns. Eurystheus, the proud inheritor of Perseus's city, became their underling. And his kinsmen came to Delphi seeking holy assistance and blessings for their difficult task of going to aid him.

They were Thebans by their dress. One was a handsome and personable young man of himself, but the other made him look frail and girlish. In him, Perseus himself must have been reborn. The elder of the two was Iphicles, and the giant's name was Alcaeus. It came as no surprise to me that he was already beginning to be referred to here and there as the true Heracles, come at last to deliver his people from the Dorians.

Pythia sat coughing in the smoke, but no message came from any god or goddess. And so, as was her habit when she was balked in divine communion, she came to one and another of the lesser priestesses. She sometimes found in the mind of another the answer that had eluded her down in the fissure.

'I believe that Alcaeus has some of the instincts of the born mystic,' she told me. 'He has never cut his hair, even to the dedication of his first beard, and has never lain with a woman. And yet, when I asked him the reason, he could not give me one.'

'Why come to me? All my prophetic powers, such as they were, dried up in me long before I came to Delphi.'

She laughed a little. 'You know as well as I do, Daughter of Asclepius, that most of the oracles that come out of Delphi are nothing but good, common sense done up in puzzling trappings. The people would pay no attention otherwise. But set a mystery before a man and he will worry it until he unravels it. Then he will proclaim Pythia wise and himself no less so for discovering what could be told him in a few blunt words.'

I laughed with her, for what she said was true.

'I have come to you because you must know many of the tales peculiar to the East about their strong men, and I would like to hear them.'

Well then, I could certainly do that, and gladly. I told her about the one who had killed the sea monster Taimut. I told her about Ægyptian Horus, the Avenger. But she listened closest of all to the story of the strong man of the Hiribu, Samson.

I cannot imagine what she got out of these tales, but she went away satisfied and kept her own counsel. When she finally did speak with them, it was in secret. But later, she blessed them publicly at the gate of the shrine. As she did so, she gave a little alabaster bottle only a finger's length from base to stem to Alcaeus, telling him that it held three precious drops of milk from Hera's own breast. Whatever was in it now, I knew that it had once contained Hermione's perfume, and we had had no use for such pretty trash here. But with the frugality of the peasant she had been born, Pythia had kept it, hoping for a use. Now the giant hung it around his neck, apparently deeply impressed by the greatness of the gift, and cradled it lovingly in his great paw. He could not leave off looking at it.

They looked cleansed and pure as the newborn when they left.

I have grown old in the service of Apollo. My hair has gone from red to dirty pink, to white. I laid aside my mirror long ago, and such frivolities as combs with it. Now I smooth and braid my hair with my fingers, just as Hecabe used to do, so many years ago.

Even my eyes, which were once my sole beauty, have faded. The color has dimmed to milky blue, and they have grown watery and shortsighted. There is no trace of the proud Trojan princess who screamed futilely of blood and death in the sedate and elderly priestess that I have become.

Pythia – my Pythia – died from old age and a chill. I mourned her passing for she had been a second mother to me, but I kept my dignity for she would have had it so. Another Pythia, tall and grave and spare, replaced her and the thread of life at Delphi continued unbroken. And new initiates, young and wet-eyed with their sorrows, have come to us and I have watched them, too, grow solemn and matronly.

It has come to me that I have spoken much of the stories of others in the years since I have been here and only a little of myself. Well, then, that is only reasonable; the tumultuousness of my life ended when I had stumbled my awkward way along the stony path to Apollo. I was always his; and from my first breath he used my body for his own mysterious purposes. And now, he has given it back.

Perhaps Cassandra really did die at Mycenae.

Will I ever become Pythia? I do not think so. I am not yet the eldest, and Pythia must be older than all the rest. In any case, she must be fifty years of age and of unblemished reputation. I know that the unsettled temperament I suffered for so long has left an inner mark upon me. I do not believe that I was truly mad, for I have seen too much of it not to know the difference. But I was not entirely sane, either. I wandered in some thin gray boundary dividing the two worlds, even as I am half-way between the living and the dead now.

I have spoken much of the icy chilling in my bowels that came when Apollo spoke through me. Lately it has turned to pain; sometimes it grips me so hard that I lose consciousness for a while. Most of the time, after a seizure of this sort, I am eased by a flux of dark blood and then I feel better for a day or so.

Even the infusion of mint which used to soothe me as a child is not easily tolerated by my uncertain digestion. A bite of curds, a little milk, some plain bread; that is what sustains me these days. The other priestesses try to control their faces when we meet. But I have learned to read any countenance whether its owner will or nill, and I see in their faces the pity that one has upon beholding the walking dead. The odor of death is with me, too, although I cannot smell it. I see it in the faint wrinkling of their nostrils, the grave control with which they try not to show it. And I, who have always kept myself scrupulously clean, crush the unwanted mint into my garments and against my dry, wrinkled old body so that I may give as little offense as possible.

When it became clear to me that Apollo was finished with me, I left the precinct of the Healer. It would have been most unfitting to try to continue, almost indecent. And so I keep much to myself these days, waiting.

Therefore, I am certain that I will never be Pythia. I never really had that ambition, to tell the truth.

For a while, I was unhappy, knowing that the god had gently set me from him, and lonely, too. But then I remembered the words of the singer when he put his hand upon the child Cassandra in the Hall of Troy. I can hear him as clearly today as I heard him then, and I found comfort thereby.

'It is a hard life, to be a god's beloved,' he had said, 'but one that brings satisfaction at the end of it, even though happiness might not be your lot.'

He had spoken truly. And I do not believe that I even have much longer to wait; for you see, I have begun to be visited by ghosts.

The first time I saw Pythia, she was going about her business in such a natural and matter-of-fact manner that I quite forgot that she was dead. She nodded to me briskly, and then between one eyewink and another, she vanished.

I have seen her often since then, and the glimpses of her compact, sturdy figure are not in the least frightening but are deeply comforting instead. She walks along the paths of the various precincts, careful to avoid any contact with the living. Once, when her attention seemed distracted elsewhere and I was too bemused to think of getting out of her way, she walked through me as if I had been empty air. That was when I was sure that I belonged more with her kind than with those around me.

There must be the terrifying sort of apparitions such as those that hounded poor Orestes. But the ones that I see take away all fear of the Road of Death. Ask any healer; it sometimes happens this way when someone is due to die and is peaceful and clear-headed. They come for him, and he goes gladly. That is why I refuse to take poppy leaves. I would not spoil this sweet joy for any amount of pain.

Pythia is not my only ghost. Once I thought I saw Orthia, and she was holding Bastos. Anyway, there was a tall, straight woman with a brown, close-furred cat in her arms in the midst of a group of pilgrims; when they came closer, she was not among them.

And yesterday, I saw Hecabe, my mother. She was as proud and beautiful as she had ever been in the best days of Troy. I would have run to her despite creaking and twinging knees, but she smiled and shook her head. She laid her finger on her lips, as if she had a secret she was unready to tell me, and then she faded slowly and gracefully out of my sight.

I think that I know her message, and have guessed her secret. I think that soon, very soon, I will look up and see a strong, laughing warrior in Lycian armor. He will hold out his arms to me, and the young woman flushed and breathless with her first and only love that still exists somewhere in me will leave this wornout and empty husk without a second thought, and go flying joyfully to meet him.

Peace is mine, even as I wait impatiently. It is enough. I am content.